THE WAY TO
PARADISE

THE WAY TO
PARADISE

MARIO VARGAS LLOSA

TRANSLATED BY NATASHA WIMMER

FARRAR, STRAUS AND GIROUX

NEW YORK

Farrar, Straus and Giroux
19 Union Square West, New York 10003

Distributed in Canada by Douglas & McIntyre Ltd.
Printed in the United States of America
Originally published in 2003 by Alfaguara, Spain, as *El paraíso en la otra esquina*
Published in the United States by Farrar, Straus and Giroux
First American edition, 2003

Library of Congress Cataloging-in-Publication Data
Vargas Llosa, Mario, 1936–
    [Paraíso en la otra esquina. English.]
    The way to paradise / Mario Vargas Llosa ; translated by Natasha Wimmer.
        p.   cm.
    ISBN 0-374-22803-5 (alk. paper)
    1. Tristan, Flora, 1803–1844—Fiction.   2. Gauguin, Paul, 1848–1903—Fiction.
I. Wimmer, Natasha.   II. Title.

PQ8498.32.A65P3713 2003
863'.64—dc21

                                                                        2003056379

Designed by Jonathan D. Lippincott

www.fsgbooks.com

1   3   5   7   9   10   8   6   4   2

To my lifelong friend Carmen Balcells

What would become of us without the help of what doesn't exist?

Paul Valéry, "Petite Lettre sur les mythes"

THE WAY TO
PARADISE

FLORA IN AUXERRE

APRIL 1844

S he opened her eyes at four in the morning and thought, Today you begin to change the world, Florita. Undaunted by the prospect of setting in motion the machinery that in a matter of years would transform humanity and eliminate injustice, she felt calm, strong enough to face the obstacles ahead of her. It was the same way she had felt on that afternoon in Saint-Germain ten years ago, at her first meeting of Saint-Simonians, when she listened to Prosper Enfantin describe the messianic couple who would save the world and vowed to herself, You'll be that Woman-Messiah. Poor Saint-Simonians, with their elaborate hierarchies, their fanatical love of science, their belief that progress could be made simply by putting industrialists in government and running society like a business! You had left them far behind, Andalusa.

Unhurriedly, she got up, washed, and dressed. The night before, after the painter Jules Laure visited to wish her luck on her tour, she had finished packing her bags and, with the help of Marie-Madeleine, the maid, and the water-seller Noël Taphanel, moved them to the foot of the stairs. She herself had carried the freshly printed copies of *The Workers' Union*, stopping every few steps to catch her breath because the sack was so heavy. When the carriage arrived at the house on the rue du Bac to take her to the wharf, Flora had been up for hours.

It was still the dead of night. The gas lamps on the corners had been extinguished, and the coachman, buried in a cloak so that only his eyes were visible, urged the horses on with a whistle of his whip. As she listened to the tolling of the bells of Saint-Sulpice, the streets, dark and lonely, seemed ghostly to her. But on the banks of the Seine, the wharf swarmed with passengers, sailors, and porters preparing for departure. She heard orders and shouts. When the ship set sail, trailing a foamy wake in the brown waters of the river, the sun was shining in a spring sky and Flora sat drinking hot tea in her cabin. Wasting no time, she noted the date in her diary: April 12, 1844. And at once she began to study her travel companions. You would reach Auxerre by dusk, so you had twelve hours in this floating specimen case to expand your knowledge of rich and poor, Florita.

Few of the travelers were bourgeois. Many were sailors off the boats that carried the agricultural produce of Joigny and Auxerre to Paris, and were now on their way home. They were gathered around their master, a hairy, gruff, redheaded man in his fifties, with whom Flora had a friendly exchange. Sitting on deck surrounded by his men, at nine in the morning the master gave each man as much bread as he could eat, seven or eight radishes, a pinch of salt, two hard-boiled eggs, and, in a tin cup passed from hand to hand, a swallow of wine. These freight sailors earned a franc and a half for a day of labor; over the long winters, they barely scraped by. Their work in the open air was hard when the weather was rainy. But in the relationship of the men with their master, Flora saw none of the servility of the English sailors, who hardly dared meet the eyes of their superiors. At three in the afternoon, the master served them their last meal of the day: slices of ham, cheese, and bread, which they ate in silence, sitting in a circle.

In the port at Auxerre, it took an infernally long time for the baggage to be unloaded. The locksmith Pierre Moreau had made a reservation for her at an old inn in the center of town, and she arrived there early in the morning. Day was dawning as she unpacked. She got into bed knowing she wouldn't sleep a wink. But for the first time in a long while, during the few hours that she lay watching the light grow through the cretonne curtains, she didn't daydream about her mission, the suffering of humanity, or the workers she would recruit for the Workers' Union. She thought instead about the house where she was born, in Vaugirard, on the outskirts of Paris, a neighborhood of the bourgeoisie whom she now detested. Were you remembering the house itself—spacious, comfortable, with its manicured gardens and busy maids—or the descriptions of it your mother gave when you were no longer rich but poor, the flattering memories in which the unhappy woman took refuge from the leaks, disarray, clutter, and ugliness of those two little rooms on the rue du Fouarre? You and your mother were forced to move there after the authorities seized the Vaugirard house, claiming that your parents' marriage, performed in Bilbao by a French expatriate priest, wasn't valid, and that Mariano Tristán, Spanish citizen from Peru, belonged to a country with which France was at war.

Most likely, Florita, your memory preserved only what your mother had told you of those early years. You were too little to remember the gardeners, the maids, the furniture upholstered in silk and velvet, the heavy draperies, the silver, gold, crystal, and painted china that adorned the salon and the dining room. Madame Tristán fled into the splendid past of Vaugirard so as not to see the poverty and misery of the foul-smelling place Maubert, crowded with beggars, vagabonds, and lowlifes, or the rue du Fouarre, full of taverns, where you spent several years of your childhood—*those* years you remembered well. Carrying basins of water up and down, carrying sacks of rubbish up and down. Afraid of meeting, on the worn, creaky steps of the steep little staircase, that old drunkard with the purple face and swollen nose, Uncle Giuseppe, a man with wandering hands who sullied you with his gaze and sometimes pinched you. Years of scarcity, fear, hunger, sadness, especially when your mother fell into stunned silence, unable to accept such misfortune after having lived like a queen with her husband—her legitimate husband before God, no matter what anyone said—Don Mariano Tristán y Moscoso, a colonel of the Armies of the King of Spain who died prematurely of apoplexy on June 4, 1807, when you were barely four years and two months old.

It was just as unlikely that you would remember your father. The full face, the heavy eyebrows, the curly mustache, the faintly rosy skin, the ringed fingers, the long gray sideburns of Mariano Tristán that came to your memory weren't those of the flesh-and-blood father who carried you in his arms to watch the butterflies flutter among the flowers of the gardens of Vaugirard, and sometimes offered to give you your bottle; the man who spent hours in his study reading chronicles of French travelers in Peru; the Don Mariano who was visited by the young Simón Bolívar, future Liberator of Venezuela, Colombia, Ecuador, Bolivia, and Peru. It was the Mariano Tristán of the portrait your mother kept on her night table in the tiny apartment on the rue du Fouarre; the Don Mariano of the oil paintings hanging in the Tristán family house on Calle Santo Domingo in Arequipa, paintings that you spent hours studying until you were convinced that that handsome, elegant, prosperous-looking gentleman was your father.

The first morning noises began to rise from the streets of Auxerre, and Flora knew sleep had fled for good. Her appointments began at nine. She had arranged several, thanks to Moreau, the locksmith, and the good Agricol Perdiguier's letters of introduction, addressed to his friends at the workers' mutual aid societies of the region. But you had time. A few moments longer in bed would give you strength to rise to the circumstances, Andalusa.

What if Colonel Mariano Tristán had lived many years more? You'd never have known poverty, Florita. Thanks to a good dowry, you'd be married to a bourgeois, and maybe you'd be living in a beautiful Vaugirard mansion, surrounded by gardens. You'd have no idea what it was like to go to bed with your insides twisted by hunger; you wouldn't know the meaning of such concepts as discrimination and exploitation. Injustice would be an abstract term. But perhaps your parents would have given you an education—schooling, teachers, a tutor. Though they might not have: a girl from a good family was educated only in order to win a husband and learn to be a good mother and housewife. You'd have no knowledge of any of the things necessity had forced you to learn. True, you wouldn't make the spelling mistakes that had embarrassed you all your life, and doubtless you'd have read more books. You would spend the years occupying yourself with your wardrobe, caring for your hands, your eyes, your hair, your figure, living a worldly life of soirees, dances, plays, teas, excursions, flirtations. You'd be a lovely parasite burrowed deep into your good marriage. Never would you seek to discover what the world was like beyond your sheltered existence in the shadow of your father, your mother, your husband, your children. A machine for giving birth, a contented slave, you'd go to church on Sundays, to confession on the first Friday of every month, and now, at forty-one, you'd be a plump matron with an irresistible passion for chocolate and novenas. You would never have traveled to Peru, or seen England, or discovered pleasure in the arms of Olympia, or written the books that you've written despite your poor spelling. And, of course, you would never have become conscious of the slavery of women, nor would it have occurred to you that in order for women to be liberated it was necessary for them to unite with other exploited peoples and wage a peaceful revolution—as crucial for the future of humanity as the emergence of Christianity 1,844 years ago. "It was better you died, *mon cher papa*," she said, laughing, as she leaped out of bed. She wasn't tired. For twenty-four hours she had felt no pains in her back or womb, nor had she noticed the cold presence in her chest. You were in great spirits, Florita.

The first meeting, at nine in the morning, took place in a workshop. The locksmith, Moreau, who was supposed to accompany her, had had to leave Auxerre urgently because of a death in the family. You were on your own, Andalusa. As planned, the gathering drew some thirty members of one of the associations into which the mutual aid societies of Auxerre had split, a group with the lovely name of Duty to Be Free. These members, almost all shoemakers, greeted her with wary, uncomfortable glances, one or two mocking, when they realized their visitor was a woman. She had become accustomed to receptions like this ever since, months ago, she had begun to present her ideas about the Workers' Union to small groups in Paris and Bordeaux. When she spoke she kept her voice steady, feigning more confidence than she possessed. The distrust of her listeners gradually evaporated as she explained how, by uniting, workers could get what they yearned for—the right to work, education, health, decent living conditions—while so long as they were scattered they would always be mistreated by the rich and those in power. All murmured their assent when, in support of her ideas, she made reference to *What Is Property?*, Pierre-Joseph Proudhon's controversial book, which had prompted so much talk in Paris since its appearance four years before, with its emphatic assertion that property is theft. Two of those present, who seemed to be followers of Charles Fourier, had come ready to attack her, with arguments Flora had heard before from Agricol Perdiguier. If workers had to subtract a few francs from their miserable salaries to contribute to the Workers' Union, how would they feed their children? She responded patiently to all their objections. At least as far as contributions were concerned, she thought they allowed themselves to be convinced. But their resistance was stubborn on the question of marriage.

"You attack the family and want it to disappear. That isn't Christian, madame."

"Indeed it is," she replied, on the verge of losing her temper. But she softened her voice. "What isn't Christian is when a man buys himself a woman, turns her into a child-bearing machine and beast of burden, and on top of it all beats her senseless each time he has too much to drink—all in the name of the sanctity of the family."

When she realized that they were staring at her wide-eyed, in dismay, she suggested that they change the subject and instead imagine together the advantages that the Workers' Union would bring peasants, craftsmen, and workers like themselves. For example, the Workers' Palaces—modern, clean, airy buildings where their children would be educated and their families treated by good doctors and nurses when they were in need of care or had been injured at work. When their strength failed, or they were too old for the workshop, they would retire to these welcoming homes to rest. The dull and tired eyes gazing at her grew livelier, began to shine. Wasn't it worthwhile to sacrifice a small part of their wages in exchange for such gains? Some listeners nodded.

How ignorant, how foolish, how egotistical so many of them were. She realized this when, after answering their questions, she began to interrogate them. They knew nothing, they were completely lacking in curiosity, and they were content with their animal lives. It was an uphill battle to get them to devote any of their time or energy to fighting for their sisters and brothers. Exploitation and poverty had made them stupid. Sometimes it was tempting to believe that Saint-Simon was right, Florita: the people were incapable of saving themselves; only an elite could manage it. They had even been infected with bourgeois prejudices: it was hard for them to accept that it should be a woman—a woman!—who was urging them to take action. The cleverest and most outspoken of them were unbearably arrogant—they put on aristocratic airs—and Flora had to make an effort not to explode. She had sworn to herself that for the year her tour of France lasted, she would give no cause, not ever, to deserve the nickname Madame-la-Colère, which she was sometimes called by Jules Laure and other friends because of her outbursts. In the end, the thirty shoemakers promised to join the Workers' Union and tell the carpenters, locksmiths, and stonecutters in the Duty to Be Free society what they had heard that morning.

As she was returning to the inn along the winding cobbled streets of Auxerre, she saw in a little square where four poplars were growing, their leaves very new and white, a group of girls playing, making and unmaking patterns as they ran about. She stopped to watch them. They were playing the game called Paradise, which, according to your mother, you used to play in the gardens of Vaugirard with other little girls from the neighborhood, under the smiling gaze of Mariano Tristán. Did you remember, Florita? "Is this the way to Paradise?" "No, miss, try the next corner." And as the girl ran from corner to corner seeking the elusive Paradise, the others amused themselves by changing places behind her back. She remembered the surprise she felt one day in Arequipa in 1833, near the church of La Merced, when all of a sudden she came upon a group of boys and girls running around the courtyard of a big house. "Is this the way to Paradise?" "Try the next corner, sir." The game you thought was French turned out to be Peruvian too. And why not? Didn't everyone dream of reaching Paradise? She had taught the game to her two children, Aline and Ernest.

For each town and city, she had set herself a strict schedule: meetings with workers, the newspapers, the most influential landowners and industrialists, and, of course, church authorities. She would explain to her bourgeois listeners that, contrary to what was said, her project heralded not civil war but rather a bloodless revolution,

Christian at its roots, inspired by love and brotherhood. And that the Workers' Union, in bringing liberty and justice to the poor and to women, would in fact prevent violent outbursts, inevitable in France if things continued as they had gone on so far. How long would a handful of the privileged keep growing fat at the expense of the poor? How long would slavery, abolished for men, persist for women? She knew how to be persuasive; her arguments would convince many bourgeois and priests.

But in Auxerre she couldn't visit a newspaper, because there weren't any. A city of twelve thousand, and no newspaper. The crass ignorance of the local bourgeoisie was remarkable.

At the cathedral, she had a conversation that ended in a fight with the parish priest, Father Fortin, a fat, balding little man with fearful eyes, foul breath, and a greasy cassock, whose narrowmindedness managed to infuriate her. ("Temper, Florita.")

She went to see Father Fortin at his house, next door to the cathedral, and noted how big it was and how well furnished. The maid, an old woman in a cap and apron, limped ahead of her to the priest's office. He kept her waiting for a quarter of an hour before receiving her. When he appeared, his dumpy body, shifty eyes, and slovenliness made her dislike him instantly. Father Fortin listened to her in silence. Trying to be pleasant, Flora explained her reasons for coming to Auxerre. Her Workers' Union project meant the alliance of the entire working class, first in France, then in Europe, and finally all over the world, for the purpose of forging a truly Christian society, infused with brotherly love. He listened with an incredulity that turned gradually into suspicion and finally horror when Flora said that once the Workers' Union was established, the delegates would go to the authorities—including King Louis Philippe himself—to present their demands for social reform, beginning with absolute equal rights for men and women.

"But that would be revolution," the priest sputtered, letting fall a fine rain of saliva.

"On the contrary," Flora corrected him. "The Workers' Union is conceived to avoid revolution, so that justice may triumph without the least bit of bloodshed."

Otherwise, there might be more deaths than in 1789. Didn't the priest, from hearing confession, know the sufferings of the poor? Didn't he realize that hundreds of thousands, millions of human beings, worked fifteen, eighteen hours a day, like animals, yet didn't earn enough even to feed their children? Wasn't he, who saw women and spoke with them every day at church, aware of how they were humiliated, mistreated, exploited, by their parents, their husbands, their children? Their fate was even worse than that of the workers. If nothing changed, there would be an explosion of hatred in society. The Workers' Union was created to prevent this. The Catholic Church should help it in its crusade. Didn't Catholics want peace, compassion, social harmony? In this the Church and the Workers' Union thoroughly concurred.

"I may not be a Catholic, but Christian philosophy and morality guide my actions, Father," she assured him.

When he heard her say that she wasn't Catholic, although she was Christian, Father Fortin's round face grew pale. Giving a little jump, he wanted to know whether this meant the lady was Protestant. Flora explained that she wasn't: she believed in Jesus but not in the Church, because in her judgment Catholicism's hierarchical structure suppressed human freedom. And its dogmatic beliefs stifled intellectual life, free will, and scientific endeavors. Also, its teaching that chastity was a sign of spiritual purity strengthened the prejudices that had made women little more than slaves.

The priest passed from pallor to near apoplexy. He blinked rapidly, flustered and alarmed. Flora fell silent when she saw him brace himself against his worktable, shuddering. He seemed ready to collapse.

"Do you realize what you are saying, madame?" he stammered. "For *these* ideas you've come to ask the help of the Church?"

Yes, precisely. Didn't the Catholic Church claim to be the church of the poor? Wasn't it opposed to injustice, the spirit of lucre, the exploitation of human beings, greed? If so, then the Church had the obligation to support a project that proposed to bring justice to this world in the name of love and brotherhood.

Flora tried a good while longer to make herself understood, but it was like talking to a wall, or a mule. Impossible. The priest wouldn't even argue with her. He gazed at her with fear and repugnance, not bothering to disguise his impatience. At last he muttered that he couldn't promise to help her, since that would depend on the bishop of the diocese. She should go to the bishop and explain her proposal—although, he warned her, it was unlikely that any bishop would sponsor a social initiative that was openly anti-Catholic. And if the bishop prohibited it, no churchgoer would help her, since the Catholic flock obeyed its shepherds.

And, thought Flora as she listened to him, according to the Saint-Simonians, the principle of authority must be reinforced in order for society to function properly. The same respect for authority that makes Catholics into automatons, like this wretch.

She tried to take her leave of Father Fortin in a friendly manner, offering him a copy of *The Workers' Union*.

"Read it at least, Father. You'll see that my project is full of Christian sentiments."

"I won't read it," said Father Fortin, shaking his head vigorously without taking the book. "It's clear from what you've told me that this book is unclean. That it was inspired, perhaps without your knowing it, by Beelzebub himself."

As she returned the little book to her pocket, Flora began to laugh. "You're one of those priests who would build bonfires in every square again to burn all the free and intelligent people in the world, Father," she said as she left.

In her room at the inn, after some hot soup, she took stock of her day in Auxerre. She wasn't discouraged. Chin up, Florita. Things hadn't gone well, but they hadn't gone badly either. Putting yourself at the service of humanity was hard work, Andalusa.

THE SPIRIT OF THE DEAD WATCHES

MATAIEA, APRIL 1892

He owed his nickname, Koké, to Teha'amana, who was his first wife on the island, since Titi Little-Tits, the New Zealander–Maori chatterbox he lived with for his first few months in Tahiti—in Papeete, then Paea, and finally Mataiea—wasn't his wife, properly speaking, just a lover. In the beginning, everyone called him Paul.

He had arrived in Papeete at dawn on June 9, 1891, after a journey of two and a half months from Marseille, with stops at Aden and Noumea, where he had to change ships. When he set foot in Tahiti at last, he had just turned forty-three. He had brought all his belongings with him, as if to show that he was finished forever with Europe and Paris: one hundred yards of canvas, paints, oils, and brushes, a hunting horn, two mandolins, a guitar, several Breton pipes, an old pistol, and a bundle of old clothes. He was a man who seemed strong—but your health was already secretly undermined, Paul—with prominent, darting blue eyes, a straight-lipped mouth generally curled in a disdainful sneer, and a broken nose like a hawk's beak. He had a short, curly beard and long brown hair, shading to red, that he cut shortly after coming to this city of barely three thousand souls (five hundred of them *popa'a*, or Europeans), because Lieutenant Jénot, of the French navy, one of his first friends in Papeete, told him that his long hair and little Buffalo Bill cowboy hat made the Maori think he was a *mahu*, or a man-woman.

He arrived full of expectation. Breathing the warm air of Papeete, dazzled by the brilliant light shining from the bluest of blue skies, and feeling all around him the presence of nature in the explosion of fruit trees that sprang up everywhere and filled the dusty little streets of the city with smells—orange, lemon, apple, coconut, mango, exuberant guava, nutritious breadfruit—he was seized by a desire to work that he hadn't felt in a long time. But he couldn't start immediately, because he had gotten off on the wrong foot in the land of his dreams. A few days after his arrival, the capital of French Polynesia buried the last Maori king, Pomare V, in an impressive ceremony that Paul observed with pencil in hand, filling a notebook with sketches and drawings. A few days later, he thought he was about to die too. At the beginning of August 1891, just as he was beginning to adapt to the heat and the penetrating fragrances of Papeete, he suffered a violent hemorrhage and a racing of the heart that made his chest rise and fall like a bellows and left him gasping for breath. The helpful Jénot took him to the Vaiami Hospital, named for the river flowing by on its way to the sea, a vast complex of buildings with coquettish wooden railings and windows screened against insects, its gardens riotous with mango trees, breadfruit trees, and royal palms with lofty topknots where songbirds clustered. The doctors prescribed a digitalis-based medicine for his weak heart, mustard plasters to treat the sores on his legs, and the application of cupping glasses to his chest. And they confirmed that this attack was yet another manifestation of the unspeakable illness with which he had been diagnosed months before in Paris. The Sisters of Saint Joseph of Cluny who ran the Vaiami Hospital scolded him, half in jest and half seriously, for swearing like a sailor ("That's what I was for many years, Sister"), for smoking his pipe ceaselessly despite his ill health, and for demanding with brusque gestures that his cups of coffee be dosed with splashes of brandy.

As soon as he left the hospital—the doctors wanted him to stay, but he refused, since the twelve francs a day that they charged wreaked havoc on his budget—he moved to one of the cheapest boardinghouses he could find in Papeete, in the Chinese quarter behind the Cathedral of the Immaculate Conception, an ugly stone building erected just a few feet from the sea. He could see the cathedral's reddish-shingled wooden steeple from the boardinghouse. Concentrated in the neighborhood, in wooden shacks ornamented with red lanterns and inscriptions in Mandarin, were many of the three hundred Chinese who had come to Tahiti as agricultural laborers but, because of the poor harvests and the ruin of some of the colonial estates, had migrated to Papeete, where they devoted themselves to running small businesses. Mayor François Cardella had authorized the opening of opium dens in the neighborhood; only the Chinese were allowed to visit, but shortly after moving in, Paul managed to sneak into one and smoke a pipe. The experience didn't seduce him; the pleasure of narcotics was too passive for him, possessed as he was by the demon of action.

He was able to live cheaply in the Chinatown boardinghouse, but the cramped quarters and pestilence—there were pigpens in the area, and the slaughterhouse, where all kinds of animals were killed, was nearby—diminished his desire to paint and forced him out onto the street. He would go and sit at one of the little portside bars and spend hours playing dominoes over a sugary absinthe. Lieutenant Jénot—slender, elegant, gracious, very well bred—let him know that living among the Chinese in Papeete would ruin his reputation among the colonists, which Paul was happy to hear. What better way of becoming the savage he had long dreamed of being than to be shunned by the *popa'a* of Tahiti?

He didn't meet Titi Little-Tits in any of Papeete's seven little port bars, where sailors passing through went to get drunk and look for women, but rather in the big Market Square, an open space around a railed-off square fountain from which issued a languid trickle of water. Bordered by the rue Bonard and the rue des Beaux Arts, and adjacent to the gardens of City Hall, Market Square was the central place for selling food, household goods, and cheap wares from dawn until midafternoon; at night, however, it became the Meat Market, as it was called by the Europeans of Papeete, whose terrifying visions of the place were associated with licentiousness and sex. Swarming with roving vendors of oranges, watermelon, coconuts, pineapples, chestnuts, syrupy sweets, flowers, and trinkets, it was the site of festivities and dances that ended in orgies in the pale glow of oil lamps, drumbeats echoing in the dark. It wasn't just the natives who took part; there were also some Europeans of dubious reputation: soldiers, sailors, traveling merchants, vagabonds, nervous adolescents. The freedom with which love was bargained for and practiced there, in scenes of true collective abandon, thrilled Paul. When it became known that the Parisian painter who lived among the Chinese in Papeete was also an assiduous visitor to the Meat Market, his reputation touched bottom among the families of colonial society. Never again was he invited to the Military Club, where he had been taken by Jénot shortly after he arrived, or to any ceremony presided over by Mayor Cardella or Governor Lacascade, who had received him cordially upon his arrival.

Titi Little-Tits was at the Meat Market that night, offering her services. She was a woman of mixed New Zealander and Maori blood, friendly and talkative, who must have been beautiful in a youth spent early in rough living. Paul agreed with her on a modest fee, and brought her back to his boardinghouse. But the night they spent together was so pleasant that Titi Little-Tits refused to take his money. Enamored of Paul, she moved in with him. Although she looked older than she was, she was a tireless lover and in those first months she helped him stave off his loneliness and adjust to his new life in Tahiti.

Soon after they began living together, she agreed to accompany him to the interior of the island, far from Papeete. Paul explained that he had come to Polynesia to live the life of the natives, not a European life, and that to do so it was necessary for him to leave the Westernized capital. They lived for a few weeks in Paea, where Paul never felt quite comfortable, and then in Mataiea, some sixty-five miles from Papeete. There, he rented a hut on the bay, from which he could bathe in the sea. Across the bay was a small island, and behind the hut rose a steep wall of sharp mountain peaks, dense with vegetation. As soon as they were established in Mataiea, he began to paint, with true creative fury. And in the hours spent smoking his pipe and sketching, or standing in front of his easel, he lost interest in Titi Little-Tits, whose incessant talk distracted him. After painting he would strum his guitar or sing popular tunes, accompanying himself on his mandolin, so that he wouldn't have to talk to her. When will she leave? he wondered, curiously observing Titi Little-Tits's evident boredom. It wasn't long before she did. When he had finished some thirty paintings and had been in Tahiti for exactly eight months, he woke up one morning and discovered a farewell note. It was a model of concision: "Goodbye and no hard feelings, dear Paul."

He didn't mourn her much; really, once he was painting seriously, she had become more of a nuisance than good company. She plagued him with her chatter; if she hadn't left, he would probably have had to throw her out. At last he could concentrate and work in peace. After illnesses, difficulties, and missteps, he began to feel that his coming to the South Seas in search of the primitive world hadn't been in vain. Not in vain at all, Paul. Since burying yourself in Mataiea, you had produced thirty paintings, and although none might be masterpieces, your painting was freer, bolder because of the wild world around you. But were you happy? No, you weren't.

A few weeks after the departure of Titi Little-Tits, he began to crave a woman. His Mataiea neighbors, almost all Maori, with whom he was friendly and whom he sometimes invited to his hut to drink rum, advised him to search for a companion in the villages on the east coast, where there were many girls eager to be married. In the end, it was easier than he had supposed. He went on a horseback expedition that he dubbed "in search of the Sabine," and in the tiny settlement of Faaone, at a shop by the side of the road where he stopped for a drink, the woman serving him asked what he was looking for there.

"A girl who'd like to live with me," he joked.

The woman, broad in the hips but still pretty, studied him for a moment before speaking again, scrutinizing him as if she were trying to read his soul.

"Maybe my daughter would suit you," she proposed at last, very serious. "Do you want to see her?"

Taken aback, Paul agreed. Moments later, the woman returned with Teha'amana. She said that the girl was only thirteen, despite her developed body, with its firm breasts and thighs, and fleshy lips that parted over a set of bright white teeth. Paul moved closer to her, somewhat flustered. Would she like to be his wife? The girl nodded, laughing.

"You aren't afraid of me, even though you don't know me?"

Teha'amana shook her head.

"Have you ever been sick?"

"No."

"Do you know how to cook?"

Half an hour later, he set out home for Mataiea, followed on foot by his brand-new acquisition, a local beauty who spoke charming French and was carrying all her belongings on her shoulder. He offered to sit her on the horse's rump, but the girl refused, as if he had proposed some sacrilege. From that day on, she called him Koké. The name spread rapidly, and soon all the residents of Mataiea—and later all Tahitians and even many Europeans—would call him that.

Many times he would recall those first months of conjugal life with Teha'amana in the hut in Mataiea in the middle of 1892 as the best he had known in Tahiti, and maybe the world. His little wife was an endless source of pleasure. Willingly, without reservations, she gave herself to him when he asked, and loved him freely, with gratifying delight. She was a hard worker, too—so different from Titi Little-Tits!—and she washed clothes, cleaned the hut, and cooked with as much enthusiasm as she made love. When she swam in the sea or the lagoon, her inky skin was dappled with reflections that moved him. On her left foot she had seven toes instead of five; two were fleshy growths that embarrassed the girl. But they amused Koké, and he liked to stroke them.

Only when he asked her to pose did they quarrel. It bored Teha'-amana to stay still in a single position for a long time, and sometimes she would simply walk away with a scowl of annoyance. If it hadn't been for his chronic problems with money, which never arrived in time and slipped through his fingers when it did arrive—the remittances sent by his friend Daniel de Monfreid from the sale of paintings in Europe—Koké would have said that in those months happiness was at last catching up with him. But when would you paint your masterpiece, Koké?

Later, with his habit of turning minor incidents into myths, he would tell himself that the *tupapaus* destroyed the sense he had in the early days with Teha'amana of nearly being able to touch Eden. But it was to those demons of the Maori pantheon that you owed your first Tahitian masterpiece, too: you couldn't complain, Koké. He had been on the island for almost a year, and still he knew nothing about the evil spirits that rise from corpses to poison the lives of the living. He learned of them from a book he was loaned by Auguste Goupil, the richest colonist on the island, and this—what a coincidence—at almost the same time that he had proof of their existence.

He had gone to Papeete, as he often did, to see if there was any money from Paris. These were journeys that he tried to avoid, because a round trip on the public coach cost nine francs, and there was the bone-jarring torment on the wretched road, too, especially if it was muddy. He had left at dawn in order to return by afternoon, but a downpour had washed out the road and the coach let him off in Mataiea after midnight. The hut was dark. That was odd. Teha'amana never slept without leaving a small lamp burning. His heart skipped a beat: might she have left him? Here, women changed husbands as easily as they changed clothes. In that respect at least, the efforts of missionaries and ministers to get the Maori to adopt the strict Christian model of the family were quite futile. In domestic matters the natives had not entirely lost the spirit of their ancestors. One day, a husband or wife would simply decide to move out, and no one would be surprised. Families were made and unmade with an ease unthinkable in Europe. If she had gone, you would miss her very much. Yes, Teha'-amana you would miss.

He entered the hut and, crossing the threshold, felt in his pockets for a box of matches. He lit one, and in the small bluish-yellow flame that flared between his fingers, he saw a sight he would never forget, and would try to rescue over the next days and weeks, painting in the feverish, trancelike state in which he had always done his best work. As time passed, the sight would persist in his memory as one of those privileged, visionary moments of his life in Tahiti, when he seemed to touch and live, though only for a few instants, what he had come in search of in the South Seas, the thing he would never find in Europe, where it had been extinguished by civilization. On the mattress on the ground, naked, facedown, with her round buttocks lifted and her back slightly arched, half turned toward him, Teha'amana stared at him with an expression of infinite horror, her eyes, mouth, and nose frozen in a mask of animal terror. He was frightened himself, and his palms grew wet, his heart beating wildly. He had to drop the match, which was burning the tips of his fingers. When he lit another, the girl was in the same position, with the same expression on her face, petrified with fear.

"It's me, it's me—Koké," he said soothingly, going to her. "Don't be afraid, Teha'amana."

She broke into tears, sobbing hysterically, and in her incoherent murmuring he caught several times the word *tupapau, tupapau*. It was the first time he had heard it, though he had read it before. As he held Teha'amana on his knees, cradled against his chest while she recovered, he was immediately reminded of the book he had borrowed from Goupil, *Travels to the Islands of the Pacific Ocean*, written in 1837 by a French consul to the islands, Jacques-Antoine Moerenhout, in which there appeared the strange word that Teha'amana was now repeating in a choked voice, scolding him for leaving her there with no oil in the lamp, knowing how afraid she was of the dark, because it was in the dark that the *tupapaus* came out. That was it, Koké: when you entered the dark room and lit the match, Teha'amana mistook you for a ghost.

So those spirits of the dead did exist, evil creatures with hooked claws and fangs, things that lived in holes, caves, hidden places in the brush, and hollow trunks, and came out at night to frighten the living and torment them. Moerenhout's book was meticulous in its descriptions of the disappeared gods and demons that existed before the Europeans came and eradicated the Maori beliefs and customs. And perhaps they even made an appearance in that novel by Loti, the novel Vincent liked so much and which first put the idea of Tahiti in your head. Not all was lost, after all. Something of that lovely past still beat beneath the Christian trappings the missionaries and pastors had forced on the islanders. It was never discussed, and every time Koké tried to get something out of the natives about their old beliefs, about the days when they were free as only savages can be free, they looked at him blankly and laughed—what was he talking about?—as if what their ancestors used to do and love and fear had disappeared from their lives. It wasn't true; at least one myth was still alive, proved by the fretting of the girl you held in your arms: *tupapau, tupapau.*

He felt his cock stiffen. He was trembling with excitement. Noticing, the girl stretched out on the mattress with that cadenced, slightly feline slowness of the native women that so seduced and intrigued him, waiting for him to undress. He lay down beside her, his body on fire, but instead of climbing on top of her, he made her turn over and lie facedown in the position in which he had surprised her. He was still seeing the indelible spectacle of those buttocks tightened and raised by fear. It was a struggle to penetrate her—she purred, protested, shrank, and finally screamed—and as soon as he felt his cock inside her, squeezed and painful, he ejaculated with a howl. For an instant, while sodomizing Teha'amana, he felt like a savage.

The next morning he began to work at first light. The day was dry and there were sparse clouds in the sky; soon a riot of colors would erupt around him. He went for a brief plunge under the waterfall, naked, remembering that shortly after he had arrived, an unpleasant gendarme called Claverie had seen him splashing in the river with no clothes on and fined him for "offending public morality." Your first encounter with a reality that contradicted your dreams, Koké. He went back to the hut and made a cup of tea, tripping over himself. He was seething with impatience. When Teha'amana woke up half an hour later, he was so absorbed in his sketches and notes, preparing for his painting, that he didn't even hear her say good morning.

For a week he was shut away, working constantly. He only left his studio at midday to eat some fruit in the shade of the leafy mango tree that grew beside the hut, or to open a can of food, and he persisted until the light faded. The second day, he called Teha'amana, undressed her, and made her lie on the mattress in the position in which he had discovered her when she mistook him for a *tupapau*. He realized immediately that it was absurd. The girl could never reproduce what he wanted to capture in the painting: that religious terror from the remotest past that made her see the demon, that fear so powerful it materialized a *tupapau*. Now she was laughing, or fighting to hold back laughter, trying to make herself look frightened again as he begged her to do. Her body lacked the right tension, too, the arch of the spine that had lifted her buttocks in the most arousing way Koké had ever seen. It was stupid to ask her to pose. The raw material was in his memory, the image he saw every time he closed his eyes, and the desire that drove him those days while he was painting and re-working *Manao tupapau* to possess his *vahine* every night, and sometimes during the day, too, in the studio. Painting her he felt, as he had only a few times before, how right he had been in Brittany at the Pension Gloanec when he assured the young men who listened ardently to him and called themselves his disciples, "To truly paint we must shake off our civilized selves and call forth the savage inside."

Yes, this was truly the painting of a savage. He regarded it with satisfaction when it seemed to him that it was finished. In him, as in the savage mind, the everyday and the fantastic were united in a single reality, somber, forbidding, infused with religiosity and desire, life and death. The lower half of the painting was objective, realist; the upper half subjective and unreal but no less authentic. The naked girl would be obscene without the fear in her eyes and the incipient downturn of her mouth. But fear didn't diminish her beauty. It augmented it, tightening her buttocks in such an insinuating way, making them an altar of human flesh on which to celebrate a barbaric ceremony, in homage to a cruel and pagan god. And in the upper part of the canvas was the ghost, which was really more yours than Tahitian, Koké. It bore no resemblance to those demons with claws and dragon teeth that Moerenhout described. It was an old woman in a hooded cloak, like the crones of Brittany forever fixed in your memory, timeless women who, when you lived in Pont-Aven or Le Pouldu, you would meet on the streets of Finistère. They seemed half dead already, ghosts in life. If a statistical analysis were deemed necessary, the items belonging to the objective world were these: the mattress, jet-black like the girl's hair; the yellow flowers; the greenish sheets of pounded bark; the pale green cushion; and the pink cushion, whose tint seemed to have been transferred to the girl's upper lip. This order of reality was counterbalanced by the painting's upper half: there the floating flowers were sparks, gleams, featherlight phosphorescent meteors aloft in a bluish mauve sky in which the colored brushstrokes suggested a cascade of pointed leaves.

The ghost, in profile and very quiet, leaned against a cylindrical post, a totem of delicately colored abstract forms, reddish and glassy blue in tone. This upper half was a mutable, shifting, elusive substance, seeming as if it might evaporate at any minute. From up close, the ghost had a straight nose, swollen lips, and the large fixed eye of a parrot. You had managed to give the whole a flawless harmony, Koké. Funereal music emanated from it, and light shone from the greenish-yellow of the sheet and the orange-tinted yellow of the flowers.

"What should I call it?" he asked Teha'amana, after considering many names and rejecting them all.

The girl thought, her expression serious. Then she nodded, pleased. "*Manao tupapau*." It was hard for him to tell from Teha'-amana's explanation whether the correct translation was "She is thinking of the spirit of the dead" or "The spirit of the dead is remembering her." He liked that ambiguity.

A week after he had finished his masterpiece he was still giving it the final touches, and he spent whole hours standing in front of the canvas, contemplating it. You had succeeded, hadn't you, Koké? The painting didn't look like the work of a civilized man, a Christian, a European. Rather, it seemed that of an ex-European, a formerly civilized man, an ex-Christian who, by force of will, adventure, and suffering, had expelled from himself the frivolous affectations of decadent Paris and returned to his roots, that splendid past in which religion and art and this life and the next were a single reality. In the weeks after finishing *Manao tupapau* Paul enjoyed a peace of mind he hadn't known for a long time. In the mysterious way they seemed to come and go, the sores that had appeared on his legs shortly after he left Europe a few years ago had disappeared. But as a precaution, he kept applying the mustard plasters and bandaging his shins, as Dr. Fernouil had prescribed in Paris, and as he had been advised by the doctors at the Vaiami Hospital. It had been a while since he'd hemorrhaged from the mouth as he had when he first came to Tahiti. He kept whittling small pieces of wood, inventing Polynesian gods based on the pagan gods in his collection of photographs, and sitting in the shade of the big mango tree, he sketched and started new paintings only to abandon them almost as soon as they were begun. How to paint anything after *Manao tupapau*? You were right, Koké, when you lectured in Le Pouldu, in Pont-Aven, at the Café Voltaire in Paris, or when you argued with the mad Dutchman in Arles, that painting wasn't a question of craft but of circumstance, not of skill but of fantasy and utter devotion: "Like becoming a Trappist monk, my friends, and living for God alone." The night of Teha'amana's fright, you told yourself, the veil of the everyday was torn and a deeper reality emerged, in which you were able to transport yourself to the dawn of humanity and mingle with ancestors who were taking their first steps in history, in a world that was still magical, where gods and demons walked alongside human beings.

Could the circumstances in which the bounds of time were transgressed, as they were the night of the *tupapau*, be artificially produced? In an attempt to find out, he planned the *tamara'a* on which he would spend, in one of those unthinking acts that punctuated his life, a good part of an important remittance (eight hundred francs) sent to him by Daniel de Monfreid, product of the sale of two of his Brittany paintings to a Rotterdam shipowner. As soon as he had the money in hand, he explained his plan to Teha'amana: they would invite many friends, and they would sing, eat, dance, and drink for a whole week.

They paid a visit to the grocer in Mataiea, a Chinese man named Aoni, to pay off the debt they had accumulated. Aoni, a fat Oriental with the drooping eyelids of a turtle, was fanning himself with a piece of card; he gazed in astonishment at the money he no longer expected to be paid. In a show of extravagance, Koké bought an impressive array of canned food, beef, cheeses, sugar, rice, beans, and drink: liters of bordeaux, bottles of absinthe, flasks of beer and rum made in the island's distilleries.

They invited a dozen native couples from around Mataiea, and some friends from Papeete, like Jénot, the Drollets, and the Suhas, functionaries in the colonial administration. The courteous and amiable Jénot arrived, as always, loaded down with foodstuffs and drink that he had bought at cost from the army commissary. The *tamara'a*—a dish of fish, potatoes, and vegetables wrapped in banana leaves and baked underground with hot stones—was delicious. When they finished eating it, night was falling, and the sun was a ball of fire sinking behind the blazing reefs. Jénot and the two French couples took their leave, since they wanted to return to Papeete that same day. Koké brought out his two guitars and his mandolin and entertained his guests with Breton songs, and others that were popular in Paris. Better to be left with the natives. The presence of Europeans was always an impediment, preventing the Tahitians from giving free rein to their instincts and truly enjoying themselves. He had discovered this in his first days in Tahiti, at the Friday dances in Market Square. The fun really began only when the sailors had to return to their ships and the soldiers to their barracks, and the crowd that was left behind was almost entirely free of *popa'a*. His Mataiea friends were drunk, men and women alike. They were drinking rum mixed with beer or fruit juice. Some danced and others sang aboriginal songs, in unison and to a steady beat. Koké helped light the bonfire not far from the big mango tree; through its tentacular branches, heavy with greenery, the stars twinkled in an indigo sky. He could understand quite a bit of Tahitian Maori now, but not when it was sung. Very near the fire, dancing with feet planted, hips undulating, and skin incandescent with the reflection of the flames, was Tutsitil, owner of the land where Koké had built his hut, and Tutsitil's wife, Maoriana, still young and slightly plump, her elastic thighs showing through her flowered pareu. She had the typical column-like Tahitian legs, ending in big flat feet that seemed to merge with the earth. Paul desired her. He brought the couple beer mixed with rum and drank and toasted, his arms around them, humming along with the song they were singing. The two islanders were drunk.

"Let's take off our clothes," said Koké. "Are there mosquitoes, do you think?"

He took off the pareu that covered the lower part of his body and stood naked, with his half-erect cock very visible in the watery light of the fire. No one imitated him. They looked at him with indifference or curiosity, but no sense of involvement. What were they afraid of, zombies? No one answered him. They kept dancing, singing, drinking as if he weren't there. He danced beside his neighbors, trying to imitate their movements—that impossible roll of the hips, the rhythmic little leap on both feet with the knees hitting each other—without succeeding, though he was filled with euphoria and optimism. He had wedged himself between Tutsitil and Maoriana, and now he was pressed against the woman. He held her around the waist and pushed her slowly with his body, moving her away from the circle illuminated by the fire. She offered no resistance, and the expression on her face was unchanged. She seemed not to notice Koké's presence, as if she were dancing with the air, or a shadow. Struggling a little, he made her slide to the ground, neither of them uttering a word. Maoriana let him kiss her but she didn't kiss him back; she sang softly to herself through her teeth as he opened her mouth with his. He made love to her with his senses roused by the chanting of the guests who were still on their feet, in a circle around the fire.

When he awoke a day or two later—impossible to be sure exactly—with the sun stabbing at his eyes, he was covered with insect bites, and suspected that he had somehow found his own way to his bed. Teha'amana, half her body uncovered by the sheet, was snoring. His breath was heavy and acrid from the mix of drinks, and he felt generally unwell. "Should I stay or go back to France?" he wondered. He had been in Tahiti for a year and had finished nearly sixty canvases, as well as innumerable sketches and drawings and a dozen wood carvings. And most important of all, a masterpiece, Koké. To return to Paris and exhibit the best of a year's work from Polynesia—wasn't it tempting? The Parisians would be flabbergasted by the explosion of light, of exotic landscapes; by the world of men and women in their natural state, proud of their bodies and their feelings. They would be overwhelmed by the bold shapes and daring color combinations, which made the impressionists' games seem like child's play. Would you do it, Koké?

When Teha'amana got up and went to make a cup of tea, he was lost in a waking dream, his eyes wide open, savoring his triumphs: the glowing reviews in newspapers and magazines; the gallery owners full of glee at seeing collectors fighting over the paintings, offering insane prices that not even Monet, Degas, Cézanne, the mad Dutchman, or Puvis de Chavannes had ever commanded. Paul would graciously enjoy the glory and fortune that France grants the famous, without letting it go to his head. He would refresh the memory of those colleagues who had doubted him: "I told you my method; don't you remember?" And he would help the young with recommendations and advice.

"I'm pregnant," said Teha'amana, when she came back with the steaming cups of tea. "Tutsitil and Maoriana came to ask whether, now that you have money, you'll return what they loaned you."

He paid them and some other neighbors what he owed them, but then he discovered that all he had left from Daniel de Monfreid's remittance was one hundred francs. How long could they eat on that? He was almost out of canvas and stretchers, his heavy paper had been used up, and he had only a few tubes of paint. Should you return to France, Paul? In the state you were in, and with the dismal future that awaited you here, was Tahiti still worthwhile? But if you wanted to return to Europe, it was necessary to act immediately. There wasn't the slightest chance you could pay for your own ticket. The only way out was to get yourself repatriated. You had the right, according to French law. But since it was one thing to say so and another to make it happen, it was urgent that Monfreid and Schuffenecker, in Paris, should start proceedings at the ministry. It would take six or eight months at least for them to act and for the official response to reach you. To work, then, without a moment's delay.

That same day, his body still aching from what he had drunk at the *tamara'a*, he wrote to his friends urging them to plead his cause at the ministry so that the minister of fine arts (was it still Monsieur Henri Roujon, who had given him letters of introduction when he came to Tahiti?) would agree to repatriate him. He also wrote a long letter to Roujon, justifying his request on grounds of ill health and total insolvency, and finally, a letter to his legitimate wife, Mette, in Copenhagen, telling her that he would see her in a few months because he had decided to return to France to show the results of his work in the South Seas. Without telling Teha'amana his plans, he got dressed and left for Papeete to mail his letters. The post office, on the capital's main street—rue de Rivoli, lined with tall fruit trees and the mansions of Papeete's leading citizens—was about to close. The oldest employee (was his name Foncheval or Fonteval?) told him that his letters would be sent off soon along the route to Australia; the *Kerrigan* was preparing to set sail. Although that way was longer, it was safer than the San Francisco route, because there weren't as many transfer points at which the mail could be lost.

He went to have a drink at a bar on the port. Barely a year after his arrival, he had decided to return to Paris. He wouldn't change his mind, but he didn't feel at ease with himself. Plainly speaking, it was an escape, forced by defeat. With the mad Dutchman in Arles; in Brittany; in Paris with Bernard, Morice, and good old Schuff—in all his conversations and dreams about the need to seek a still-virgin world that had not yet been captured in European art, a central consideration had also been escape from the cursed daily quest for money, the everyday struggle to survive. The urge to live in nature, off the land, like primitive man—the healthiest of peoples—had inspired his adventures in Panama and Martinique, and later had led him to investigate Madagascar and Tonkin before deciding on Tahiti. But despite your dreams, here you couldn't live "in nature" either, Koké. One couldn't subsist solely on coconuts, mangoes, and plantains, the only things graciously offered on tree branches. Then, too, the red plantains grew only in the mountains, and one had to scale steep slopes to gather them. You'd never learn to farm the land, because those who farmed dedicated the kind of time to their labor that you needed for painting. Which meant that here too, despite the landscape and the natives—a pale reflection of what was once the fertile Maori civilization—money ruled people's lives and deaths, and condemned artists to enslave themselves to Mammon. If you didn't want to die of hunger, you had to buy canned food from the Chinese merchants, and spend, spend a kind of money that you, misunderstood and rejected by the despicable snobs who dominated the art market, didn't have and never would have. But you had survived, Koké; you had painted; you had enriched your palette with the colors of the island; and living by your motto—"the right to dare anything"—you had risked all, like the great creators.

Only at the last minute would you confess to Teha'amana your plans to return to France. That was over, too. You should be grateful to the girl. Her young body, her languid ease, her alertness, had given you pleasure, rejuvenated you, at times made you feel like a true primitive. Her natural liveliness, her diligence, her docility, her companionship, made life bearable for you. But love had to be excluded from your existence; it was an insurmountable obstacle to your mission as an artist, since it made men bourgeois. Now, with that seed of yours inside her, the girl would begin to swell up, would become one of those monstrous lumbering natives toward whom you would feel repulsion instead of affection and desire. Better to terminate the relationship before it ended badly. And the son or daughter you would have? Well, it would be one more bastard in a world of bastards. Rationally, you were sure you were doing the right thing in returning to France. But something inside you didn't believe it, because for the next eight months, until you finally embarked in June 1893 for Noumea on the *Duchaffault*, the first stage of your return trip to Europe, you felt uneasy, upset, afraid you were making a serious mistake.

He did many things in those eight months, but one of the times he thought he might paint a second Tahitian masterpiece, he was mistaken. He had traveled from Mataiea to Papeete to see if he had received any letters or money, and in the city there was a commotion at the house of his friend Aristide Suhas, whose young son, a year and eight months old, was dying from an intestinal infection. Koké arrived just after the boy expired. Upon seeing the dead child, the sharp little face, the cerulean skin, he felt a tickle of excitement. Without hesitation, and feigning a sorrow he didn't feel, he embraced Aristide and Madame Suhas, and offered to paint a portrait of the dead child and give it to them as a gift. Husband and wife looked at each other with tears in their eyes and agreed: it would be another way of keeping their son by their side.

He made a few sketches immediately, and others during the wake. He then painted the portrait on one of his last canvases, with great caution and attention to detail. He carefully studied the face, which expressed the precise instant of the child's passing, its eyes closed and its hands clasping a rosary. But when he delivered the painting, instead of thanking him for the gift, Madame Suhas was furious. She would never allow the portrait into her house.

"But what's wrong with it?" asked Koké, not entirely displeased by her reaction.

"That isn't my child. That's a little Chinaman, one of those yellow people who're overrunning the island. What have we done to you to make you mock our pain by giving our angel the face of a Chinaman?"

Koké couldn't contain his laughter, and the Suhases threw him out of the house. On his way back to Mataiea, he looked at the portrait with new eyes. Yes, without realizing it you had orientalized him.

Then you rebaptized your newest creation with a mythical Maori name: *Portrait of Prince Atiti*.

Some time later, upon noticing that Teha'amana's belly wasn't growing, although four months had passed since she had announced that she was pregnant, he noted the fact.

"I bled and I lost it," she said, without interrupting her mending. "I forgot to tell you."

3

BASTARD AND FUGITIVE

DIJON, APRIL 1844

Instead of going directly from Auxerre to Dijon as planned, Flora made two stops, spending one day each in Avallon and Semur. She left copies of *The Workers' Union* and posters in the bookshops of both towns. And in both, since she had no letters of introduction or referrals, she went to seek out workers in the bars.

On the central square of Avallon near the church, whose gaudily painted saints and virgins reminded her of the Indian chapels of Peru, there were two taverns. She went into L'Étoile du Jour at nightfall. The fire in the hearth reddened the faces of the patrons and filled the cramped room with smoke. She was the only woman. Loud talk gave way to whispers and laughter. Through the white clouds of pipe smoke, she could make out winking eyes and leering faces. A hissing noise followed her as she made her way through the sweaty crowd, which parted to let her pass and closed behind her.

She felt perfectly at ease. When the owner of the establishment, a short man with an unctuous manner, came up to ask who she was looking for, she answered him brusquely: no one.

"Why do you ask?" she inquired in turn so that everyone could hear. "Aren't women allowed here?"

"Decent women are," exclaimed a drunken voice from the bar. "Harlots aren't."

He's the poet of the place, thought Florita. "I'm not a prostitute, gentlemen," she explained, without losing her temper, imposing silence. "I'm a friend of the workers. I've come to help you break the chains of exploitation."

Then, by their faces, she saw that they no longer took her for a harlot but a madwoman. Refusing to give up, she kept talking. They listened out of curiosity, as one listens to the song of a strange bird, without paying much attention to what she was saying, more aware of her skirts, her hands, her mouth, her waist, and her breasts than her words. They were tired men with defeated faces, men who wanted only to forget the life they led. After a while, their curiosity satisfied, some started up their conversations again, forgetting her. At the second nightspot of Avallon, La Joie, a small refuge with blackened walls and a fireplace in which a few last embers were dying, the six or seven patrons were too drunk for her to waste time talking to them.

She returned to the inn with the acid taste in her mouth that from time to time plagued her. Why, Florita? Was it because you had squandered time in this town of ignorant peasants? No. It was because your tavern visits had stirred up old memories and now you were smelling the winy exhalations of the dens full of drunks, gamblers, and lowlifes on the place Maubert and the surrounding streets, where you spent your childhood and adolescence—and your four years of marriage, Florita. How frightened you were of the drunks! They swarmed in the neighborhood around the rue du Fouarre, in the doorways of taverns and on corners, sprawled in entryways and alleys, belching, vomiting, snoring, uttering indecencies in their sleep. Her skin crawled as she remembered her walks home in the dark from André Chazal's engraving and lithography workshop, where her mother had managed to get her hired as an apprentice colorist shortly after she turned sixteen.

At least you were able to make use of your talent for drawing. In other circumstances you might been a painter, Andalusa. But she didn't regret having been a wage earner in her youth. At first it seemed wonderful to her, liberating, not to have to spend days shut up in the squalid hovel on the rue du Fouarre, to leave the house very early and work twelve hours at the workshop with the twenty women Master Chazal employed. The place offered a true university education in what it meant to be a working woman in France. Of the master, she was told by the girls in the shop that he had a famous brother, Antoine, a painter of flowers and animals in the Jardin des Plantes. But André Chazal liked to drink, gamble, and spend his time in taverns. When he had had a few drinks, and sometimes when he hadn't, he would take liberties with the girls. And so it was to be. The very day he interviewed you to see if he would accept you as an apprentice, he examined you from head to foot, brazenly resting his vulgar gaze on your breasts and hips.

André Chazal! What a poor devil you were sent by fate, or maybe God, to lose your virginity to, Florita. A tall, somewhat stooped man, with hair like straw, a very broad forehead, bold and roguish eyes, and a protuberant nose that constantly monitored the smells around him. You seduced him at first sight with your big deep eyes and curly black hair, Andalusa. (Was André Chazal the first to call you that?) He was twelve years older than you and his mouth must have watered as he dreamed of the forbidden fruit represented by such a child. Under the pretext of teaching you the trade, he would stand close to you, take your hand, put his arm around your waist. This is how you mix the acids, this is how you change the inks, careful putting your finger there or you'll burn yourself—and instantly he was all over you, rubbing your leg, your arm, your shoulders, your back. Your fellow workers joked, "You've won the boss's heart, Florita." Amandine, your best friend, predicted, "So long as you don't give in, so long as you resist, he'll marry you. Because you're driving him mad, I swear it."

Yes, you were driving him mad—André Chazal, engraver-lithographer, taverngoer, gambler, and drinker—so mad that one day, reeking of cheap wine and with his eyes starting out of his head, he went so far as to paw at your breasts with his big hands. Your slap knocked him backward. Pale-faced, he stared at you in astonishment. Later, instead of dismissing her, as Flora feared, he appeared, contrite, at the hovel on the rue du Fouarre with a little bunch of daisies in his hand, to present his excuses to Madame Tristán. "Madame, my intentions are honorable." This made Madame Aline so happy that she burst out laughing and embraced Flora. It was the only time you ever saw your mother so joyful and affectionate. "How lucky you are," she kept repeating, gazing at you tenderly. "Give thanks to God, my girl."

"Lucky because Monsieur Chazal wants to marry me?"

"Lucky because he's willing to marry you even though you're a bastard. Do you think there are many others who would? Give thanks on your knees, Florita."

The marriage was the beginning of the end of her relationship with her mother; from that moment on, Flora began to love her less. She had known that because her parents' marriage ceremony, performed by the French priest in Bilbao, wasn't valid under civil law, she was an illegitimate child, but only now did she become conscious that as a bastard she bore a guilt as terrible as original sin. That André Chazal, a man of means, practically bourgeois, was willing to give her his name was a blessing, a piece of luck for which she should have been thankful with all her heart. But instead of making you happy, Florita, the whole affair left you with the same disagreeable taste in your mouth that now you were trying to wash away by gargling with mint-water before bed in the inn at Avallon.

If what you felt for Monsieur Chazal was love, then love was a lie. It was nothing like love in novels, that delicate sentiment, that poetic exaltation, those burning desires. When, in his office at the shop after the other workers had left, André Chazal, not yet your husband and still your master, made love to you on the chaise longue with squeaky springs, it didn't seem romantic or beautiful or poignant. Rather, it was painful and repellant. The heavy body stinking of sweat, the viscous tongue tasting of tobacco and alcohol, the feeling that she was being mauled from thighs to belly, made her ill. And still, idiot Flora, foolish Andalusa, after that disgusting rape—which is what it was, wasn't it?—you wrote André Chazal the letter that the wretch would make public seventeen years later, in a Paris courtroom. A stupid, lying note, full of everything a girl is supposed to tell her lover after surrendering her virginity. And riddled with spelling and grammar mistakes! How ashamed you must have felt hearing it read, hearing the titters of the judges, the lawyers, the spectators. Why did you write it if you rose sick with disgust from that chaise longue? Because it was what the heroines of novels did when they were deflowered.

They were married a month later, on February 3, 1821, at the municipal hall of the eleventh arrondissement, and thereafter lived in a little apartment on the rue des Fossés in Saint-Germain-des-Prés. When, huddled in her bed at the inn in Avallon, she realized that her eyes were damp, Flora made an effort to put those unpleasant memories out of her head. The important thing was that, instead of destroying you, your setbacks and disappointments had made you stronger, Andalusa.

In Sêmur things went better than in Avallon. A few steps away from the famous towers of the Duke of Burgundy, for which she felt not the slightest admiration, there was a tavern where during the day people came to eat. A dozen farm laborers were celebrating someone's birthday, and some barrel makers were there too. It wasn't hard for her to strike up a conversation with the two groups. She explained why she was touring France, and they looked at her with respect and apprehension, although, Flora thought, without understanding much of what she was telling them.

"But we are farm laborers, not workers," said one of them, by way of excuse.

"Peasants are workers too," she explained. "And craftsmen and servants. Anyone who isn't a master is a worker; all those who are exploited by the bourgeoisie. And because you are the largest group and suffer the most, you will save humanity."

They exchanged glances, taken aback by this declaration. At last they worked up the courage to ask her questions. Two of them promised to buy *The Workers' Union* and join the organization when it was established. So as not to hurt their feelings, she had to have a few sips of wine before she left.

She arrived in Dijon at dawn on April 18, 1844, with strong pains in her uterus and bladder. The pain had begun en route, perhaps because of the jolting of the stagecoach and the irritation produced in her bowels by the dust she had swallowed. She spent her whole week in Dijon bothered by this discomfort in her lower abdomen, which made her horribly thirsty—she took frequent swallows of sugared water—but in good spirits because she was busy every minute in this clean, pretty, friendly city of thirty thousand. Dijon's three daily papers had announced her visit, and she had many meetings planned in advance thanks to her Saint-Simonian and Fourierist friends in Paris.

She was excited to meet Mademoiselle Antoinette Quarré, the Dijon dressmaker and poet whom Lamartine had called "a model for women" in one of his poems, praising her artistic talent, her ability to overcome obstacles, and her passion for justice. But after exchanging a few words with her at the offices of the *Journal de la Côte d'Or*, Flora realized that Mademoiselle Quarré was vain and stupid. Hunched and twisted front and back, she was also enormously fat and practically a dwarf. She had been born into a very humble family, and now her literary triumphs made her feel she was bourgeois.

"I don't think I can help you, madame," she said rudely, waving her little hand, after listening impatiently. "From what you've just said, your message is intended for the workers. I don't mix with the townspeople."

Of course not, you'd scare them to death, thought Madame-la-Colère. She made her farewells briskly, neglecting to give Mademoiselle Quarré the copy of *The Workers' Union* that she had intended as a gift.

The Saint-Simonians were well established in Dijon. They had their own meetinghouse. Alerted by Prosper Enfantin, they received her in a solemn session on the afternoon of her arrival. From the entrance to the building, next door to the museum, Flora saw them and took their measure in just a few seconds. These were the usual sort of bourgeois socialists and impractical dreamers—amiable and ceremonious Saint-Simonians who worshiped the elite and were convinced that by controlling the budget they would revolutionize society. Just like the Saint-Simonians in Paris, Bordeaux, or anywhere else, they were professionals and government officials, property owners and men of independent means, well educated and well dressed, believers in science and progress, critical of the bourgeoisie but bourgeois themselves and distrustful of working men.

Here too, as at the meetings in Paris, they had put an empty chair on the stage, symbolizing their wait for the arrival of the Mother, the Woman-Messiah, the superior female who would join in sacred intercourse with the Father (Prosper Enfantin, since the founder, Claude-

Henri de Rouvroy, Comte de Saint-Simon, had died in 1825) to form the Supreme Couple. Together, Mother and Father would precipitate the transformation of humanity, which would lead to the emancipation of women and workers from their current servitude, and to the dawning of an era of justice. What were you waiting for to go and sit in that empty chair, Florita, and surprise them by announcing, as dramatically as the actress Rachel, that their wait was over, that the Woman-Messiah was before their eyes? She had been tempted to do it in Paris. But she was restrained by the growing differences she had with the Saint-Simonians over their idolatry of a select minority, which they wanted to bring to power. Also, if they accepted her as Mother, she would have to mate with Father Enfantin. You weren't willing to do that, even if it was the price of freeing humanity from its chains, though Prosper Enfantin was said to be a handsome man and many women sighed over him.

Copulating, not making love but copulating, like pigs or horses: that was what men did with women. They lunged at them, spread their legs, stuck them with their spurting members, made them pregnant, and left them with their wombs damaged forever, as André Chazal did to you. You'd had those pains down below since your ill-fated marriage. "Making love," that tender, delicate ceremony in which the heart, feelings, desires, and instincts all played a role, and in which the two lovers both took pleasure, was an invention of poets and novelists, a fantasy not borne out in pedestrian reality. Not between women and men, anyway. You, at least, hadn't made love even once in those frightful four years with your husband in the little apartment on the rue des Fossés. You had copulated or, more accurately, had been made the object of copulation each night by that lascivious beast who, stinking of alcohol, crushed you with his weight and fondled you and slobbered all over you until he collapsed beside you like a sated animal. How you cried with disgust and shame, Florita, after those nocturnal violations to which you were subjected by the tyrant who robbed you of your freedom. Without ever bothering to find out whether you wanted to make love, without wondering at all whether you enjoyed his attentions—should those repugnant gasps, those tonguings and bites, be called that?—or whether he was hurting you, repelling you, making you sad or despondent. If it hadn't been for sweet Olympia, what a poor idea you'd have of physical love, Andalusa.

But even worse than being the object of copulation was being made pregnant by those nighttime attacks. Yes, worse. To feel that you were bloating, becoming deformed, that your body and your soul were ravaged; to feel thirst, dizziness, heaviness, the least movement requiring two or three times as much effort as usual. Were these the blessings of motherhood? Was this what women yearned for, the satisfaction of their deepest dreams? This? Swelling up, giving birth, becoming a slave to one's children as if it weren't enough to be a slave to one's husband?

The apartment on the rue des Fossés was small, though lighter and cleaner than the one on the rue du Fouarre. But Flora hated it even more, feeling herself a prisoner, a being stripped of what from then on she would learn to value more than anything else in the world: freedom. Your four years of matrimonial slavery opened your eyes to what was true and what was false in the relationship between men and women, to what you wanted and didn't want out of life. What you were—a receptacle for giving pleasure and children to André Chazal—you certainly didn't want to be.

To escape her husband's arms after the birth of her first son, Alexandre, in 1822, she began to invent excuses: sore throats, fevers, migraines, nausea, vapors, overpowering sleepiness. And when that wasn't enough, she would refuse to perform her conjugal duties, even when her lord and master flew into rages and cursed her. The first time he tried to strike you, you jumped out of bed, grabbing a pair of scissors from the bureau.

"If you touch me, I'll kill you. Now, tomorrow, the next day. I'll wait until you're asleep, or looking the other way. And I'll kill you. Neither you nor anyone else will ever lay a hand on me. Ever!"

Seeing her so resolute, so beside herself, André Chazal was frightened. Well, Florita, in the end you didn't kill him. In fact, the poor idiot practically killed you. And after continuing to force himself on you, making you pregnant, and causing you to have a second child (Ernest-Camille, in June of 1824), he made you pregnant yet again. But by the time Aline was born you had shed your chains.

The Saint-Simonians of Dijon listened to her intently. Afterward, they asked her questions, and one of them insinuated that her idea for the Workers' Palace owed much to the model conceived by the disciples of Saint-Simon. They weren't wrong, Florita. You had been a diligent student of Saint-Simon's teachings, and there was a time when his obsession with water—he believed that the currents of human knowledge, money, respect, and power should flow freely, like rivers and waterfalls, in order for progress to be achieved—had fascinated you, as had his personality, and the grand gestures that enlivened his biography: for example, he gave up being a count because, he said, "I consider it a title very inferior to that of citizen." But the Saint-Simonians had only gone halfway, since although they defended women, they didn't give workers fair treatment. They were polite and pleasant people, certainly. All those present promised to join the Workers' Union and read her book, although it was obvious that she hadn't converted them. They were skeptical of the idea that only the union of all workers would bring about emancipation and justice for women. They didn't believe in reforms undertaken from below, alongside the rabble. They viewed the workers from a lofty height, with the instinctive wariness of property owners, officials, and the independently wealthy. They were so naive they believed that a handful of bankers and industrialists could remedy all of society's ills by drawing up a budget with scientific expertise. But ultimately, at least, the liberation of women from all kinds of servitude and the reinstitution of the right to divorce figured most prominently in their doctrine. If only for that, you were grateful to them.

More interesting than the meeting with the Saint-Simonians were her sessions with the carpenters, shoemakers, and weavers of Dijon. She met with each group separately, since the mutual aid societies of the Compagnonnage were very jealous of their autonomy and reluctant to mix with workers in other trades, a prejudice that Flora tried to cure them of without much success. The best meeting was the one with the weavers, a dozen men crammed into a workshop on the outskirts of the city. She spent several hours with them, from late afternoon well into the night. Destitute, dressed in simple smocks of coarse woolen cloth and worn shoes—or no shoes at all—they listened to her with interest, often nodding their agreement, standing stock-still. Flora saw their tired faces light up when she said that once the Workers' Union had spread throughout France and then Europe it would have so much power that governments and parliaments would make the right to work into law, a law that would protect them from unemployment forever.

"But you want to give women this right, too," one of them reproached her when she turned the floor over to them for questions.

"Don't women eat? Don't they wear clothes? Don't they need to work to live too?" Flora rapped out as if giving a recitation.

It wasn't easy to convince them. They were afraid that if the right to work was extended to women, unemployment would spread, since there would never be enough work for so many people. Neither could she persuade them that children under ten should be prohibited from working in factories and workshops so that they could go to school to learn to read and write. This frightened and angered them: they said that under the pretext of educating children the meager income of families would be reduced. Flora understood their fears and mastered her impatience. They worked fifteen hours or more out of every twenty-four, seven days a week, and they were clearly malnourished, haggard, sickly, aged by their animal existence. What more could you ask of them, Florita? She left the workshop with the certainty that the exchange would bear fruit. And despite her fatigue, the next morning she did her duty and visited a few tourist spots.

The famous Black Virgin of Dijon, Our Lady of Good Hope, seemed to her an ugly toad, a sculpture unworthy of occupying its privileged spot on the cathedral's high altar. She said as much to the two girls from the Guild of the Virgin who were adorning the icon with bracelets and diadems, and tunics and veils of satin, gauze, and organdy.

"To worship the Virgin in the form of that totem is superstition. You remind me of the idolaters I saw in the churches of Peru. Do your priests permit it? If I lived in Dijon, I'd put an end to this display of pagan obscurantism in three months."

The girls crossed themselves. One of them stammered that the Duke of Burgundy had brought the figure back from his travels in the East. For hundreds of years the Black Virgin had been the region's most popular object of worship, and had granted the most miracles.

Flora had to leave in a hurry—regretfully, since she would have liked to continue her conversation with the two pious young women—so as not to be late for her appointment with four grand ladies, the organizers of charity drives and sponsors of homes for the elderly. The women were intrigued by their visitor. They scrutinized her thoroughly, curious to know what she was like, this outlandish Parisian who wrote books, this secular saint who declared without blushing her intent to redeem humanity. They had set a little table for her with tea, cold drinks, and pastries, which Flora didn't touch.

"I've come to ask for your help with a profoundly Christian undertaking, ladies."

"But what do you think we do, madame?" said the eldest, a little old woman with blue eyes and an energetic manner. "We devote our lives to charitable causes."

"No, you don't," Flora corrected her. "You give alms, which is very different."

Taking advantage of their surprise, she tried to make them understand. Alms served only to gird those who gave them with good conscience and righteousness; they didn't help the poor escape poverty. Instead of giving alms, they should use their money and influence to support the Workers' Union, to finance its newspaper, to open offices for it. The Workers' Union would bring justice to suffering humanity. One of the ladies, dumbfounded, fanned herself furiously, muttering that no one could give *her* lessons in charity—she, who neglected her family to dedicate four afternoons a week to charitable works—and certainly not some arrogant woman wearing muddy shoes full of holes. That she should permit herself to scorn them! Madame, you're mistaken: Flora believed in her good intentions and wished only to channel her efforts more efficiently. The tension eased, but she received no pledge of support. You left them, amused: those four ignoramuses would never forget you. You had opened their eyes a little, planted a seed of guilt.

Now you felt confident, Andalusa, capable of confronting all the bourgeois in the world with your excellent ideas. Because you had a very clear notion of good and bad, of victimizers and victims, and what the cure was for society's ills. How you had changed since that terrible moment when you discovered that André Chazal had impregnated you for the third time and you secretly decided to leave your husband, without warning even your mother. "Never again." And you had done it.

She was twenty-two years old, with two small children in tow and another quickening in her belly. She had no money, and no friends or family to support her. Despite this, she decided to commit what amounted to suicide for any woman who cared about security and her good name. But nothing mattered to you anymore if it meant continuing to live the life of a slave. All you wanted was to escape the barred cage called matrimony. Did you know what lay in store for you? No, certainly not. She never imagined the dramatic consequence of her flight, that bullet lodged in her chest, the cold metal that she felt suddenly in coughing fits, when things went wrong, and at moments of discouragement. You had no regrets. You would do it again, exactly the same way, because even now, twenty years later, you shuddered when you imagined what your life would be like if you were still Madame André Chazal.

A sad state of affairs made her departure easier: the chronic feebleness and constant illnesses of her oldest son, Alexandre, who would die in 1830 at the age of eight. The doctor insisted that it was necessary to take him to the country to breathe clean air, far from the miasmas of Paris. André Chazal gave his consent. He rented a little room near Versailles, in the house of the wet nurse who cared for Ernest-Camille, and he allowed Flora to go and live there until she gave birth. How free she felt the day André Chazal said goodbye to her at the stagecoach station. Aline was born two months later, on October 16, 1825, in the country, into the hands of a midwife who made Flora push and bellow for nearly three hours. And so your marriage ended. Many years would pass before you'd see your husband again.

After Flora insisted three times, and sent him a signed copy of *The Workers' Union*, His Excellency the Bishop of Dijon deigned to see her. He was a distinguished-looking and well-spoken old man, and Flora spent a most agreeable time sparring with him. He received her in the episcopal palace, with much kindness. He had read the little book, and before Flora could open her mouth, he showered her with compliments. My child! Her intentions were pure, noble. There was in her an obvious understanding of human suffering, and the fervent will to alleviate it. But . . . but . . . There was always some *but* in this imperfect life. In Flora's case, her not being Catholic. Was it really possible to undertake a great moral work, of spiritual import, outside of Catholicism? Her noble intentions would be distorted, and instead of producing the desired results, her venture would have harmful effects. Therefore—it deeply pained the bishop to tell her this—he wouldn't help her. In fact, it was his duty to warn her. If the Workers' Union was formed—and with Flora's energy and willpower it seemed likely that it would be—he would fight it. A non-Catholic organization of that magnitude could mean disaster for society. They argued for a long time. Flora soon realized that her reasoning would never sway Monsignor François-Victor Rivet. But she was charmed by the bishop's refinement; he spoke to her knowledgeably and discerningly of art, literature, music, and history. Whenever she heard someone like him talk, she couldn't help feeling a twinge of regret for everything she didn't know, for everything she hadn't read and never would read, since it was too late now to fill the gaps in her education. That was why George Sand looked down on you, Florita, and why you always felt a paralyzing inferiority in the company of that great lady of French letters. "You're worth more than she is, silly," Olympia would say to encourage her.

To be uneducated as well as poor was to be doubly poor, Florita. She said this to herself many times in the year she escaped André Chazal's yoke—1825—when, with her oldest son ill, the second living with a wet nurse in the country, and Aline a newborn, she confronted a circumstance that she hadn't foreseen, obsessed as she was with the sole idea of freeing herself from the burden of family. The children had to be fed. How could it be done, when you hadn't a cent? She went to see her mother, who was then living in a less squalid neighborhood, on the rue Neuve-de-Seine. Madame Tristán couldn't understand why you wouldn't go home to your husband, the father of your children. Flora! Flora! What madness was this? Abandon André Chazal? The poor man was justified in complaining that he received no word from you. He thought his little wife was in the country, caring for the children. In the last few weeks, André had been visited by financial disaster: creditors were besieging him, he had had to give up the apartment on the rue des Fossés, and his workshop had been seized by the courts. And precisely now, when your husband needed you most, you were abandoning him? Your mother's eyes filled with tears, and her mouth trembled.

"I've already done it," said Flora. "I'll never go back to him. I'll never give up my freedom again."

"A woman who abandons her home sinks lower than a prostitute," her mother, horrified, said in reproach. "The law forbids it; it's a crime. If André denounces you, the police will come looking for you and you'll go to jail like a common criminal. You can't do such a thing!"

You did it, Florita, despite the risks. True, the world turned hostile, and life became exceedingly difficult. To begin with, you had to convince the wet nurse in Arpajon to take in all three children while you looked for a job to pay her for her services and support your children. And what kind of job could you find, you who were incapable of writing a sentence correctly?

To keep herself out of André Chazal's clutches, she avoided the printing workshops, where she might have been hired. And she left Paris, hiding herself in the provinces, first in Rouen. She had to begin at the very bottom, selling needles, spools of thread, and embroidery supplies in a little shop, which she mopped, swept, and dusted after it closed. Her humiliatingly tiny wages were all sent to the wet nurse in Arpajon. Then she served as the nursemaid of the twin children of a colonel's wife who lived in the countryside near Versailles while her husband was at war or commanding a barracks. It wasn't a badly paid job—she spent nothing and had a decent room—and she would have stayed longer if her temper had permitted her to endure the twins, filthy beasts who, when they weren't deafening her with their screams, pissed and vomited on clothes she had just changed them into because they had soiled the ones they were wearing before. The colonel's wife threw her out the day she discovered Madame-la-Colère, beside herself at the twins' screaming, pinching them to see if that would make them stop.

Although ever since she was young, Flora had tried to compensate for the deficiencies of her education with all the means at her disposal, when she met someone like the Bishop of Dijon, who knew so much and spoke such elegant French, she was always oppressed by the feeling that she was uncultured and ignorant. And yet she wasn't discouraged when she left the episcopal palace. Instead, she was heartened. After hearing him, she couldn't stop thinking how pleasant life would be when, thanks to the great peaceful revolution she was setting in motion, the Workers' Palaces would give every child as careful an education as Monsignor Rivet himself must have received.

On the day before she left Dijon, after a meeting with a group of Fourierists, Flora traveled outside the city to visit Gabriel Gabety, an elderly philanthropist. He had been an active revolutionary—a Jacobin—during the Great Revolution, and now he was a rich widower who wrote books on the philosophy of justice and law. It was said that he sympathized with the ideas of Charles Fourier. But again, Flora was gravely disappointed. She obtained no promise of help for the Workers' Union, a project that the ex-follower of Robespierre dismissed as a "mad fantasy." And she had to endure a nearly hour-long monologue from the chilly octogenarian—besides a woolen robe and scarf, he wore a sleeping cap—about his researches into the relics of Roman life in the region. Not satisfied with law, ethics, philosophy, and politics, he was an amateur archaeologist in his spare time. While the old man droned on, Flora followed the comings and goings of Monsieur Gabety's little maid. Young, nimble, cheerful, she wasn't still for a second: she pushed her mop over the corridor's red tiles, dusted the china in the dining room with a feather duster, and brought in the lemonade that the humanist had ordered in a brief parenthesis to his dull lecture. That was you, Florita, years ago. Like her, you spent three years mopping, cleaning, sweeping, washing, ironing, and serving day and night. Until you found a better job. Maid, servant, hired help of the family whose fault it was that you contracted, as one contracts yellow fever or cholera, your boundless hatred for England. Nevertheless, if you hadn't spent those years in the service of the Spence family, you wouldn't be so certain now about what had to be done to make a worthy and human dwelling place of this vale of tears.

Upon returning to the inn after her useless trip to Gabriel Gabety's country house, Flora had a pleasant surprise. One of the maids, a timid adolescent, came knocking at the door of her room.

She had a franc in her hand, and she stammered, "Would this be enough to buy your book, miss?" She had been told about *The Workers' Union*, and she wanted to read it, because she knew how to read, and she liked to do it in her free time.

Flora embraced her, signed a copy for her, and refused to take her money.

4

MYSTERIOUS WATERS

MATAIEA, FEBRUARY 1893

&

In the eleven months it took him to make good his decision to return to France, from the *tamara'a* at which he ended up wallowing with Tutsitil's wife, Maoriana, until—thanks to the efforts of Monfreid and Schuffenecker in Paris—the French government agreed to repatriate him and he was able to set sail in the *Duchaffault* on June 4, 1893, Koké completed many paintings and made countless sketches and sculptures, though never with the certainty of having produced a masterpiece, as he had had when he painted *Manao tupapau*. The failure of the painting of the Suhases' dead child (Jénot eventually managed to reconcile Koké with the couple) discouraged him from trying to make a living painting portraits of the colonists of Tahiti, among whom, according to his few European friends, he was regarded as a socially unacceptable eccentric.

He hadn't said a word to Teha'amana about his attempts to be repatriated out of fear that if she knew he was soon going to abandon her, his *vahine* would leave him first. He had grown very fond of her. With Teha'amana he could talk about anything, because although she knew nothing about many matters of importance to him, like beauty, art, or ancient civilizations, she had a nimble mind and made up for her cultural lapses with her intelligence. She was always surprising him with some idea or joke. Did she love you, Koké? You could never be sure. When you wanted her, she was always willing; she was an enthusiastic lover, and as skilled as the most experienced courtesan. But sometimes she would disappear from Mataiea without the slightest explanation, returning two or three days later. When you insisted on knowing where she had been, she would lose her temper and simply repeat, "I was gone, I was gone, I told you." She had never shown any signs of jealousy. Koké remembered that on the night of the *tamara'a*, as he and Maoriana lay on the ground, he saw Teha'amana's face in the glow of the fire, as if in a dream, her big jet-black eyes gazing mockingly at him. Was her complete indifference to what her mate was doing the natural form of love in the Maori tradition, a sign of her freedom? Doubtless it was, but when he questioned his Mataiea neighbors about it, they refused to answer, giggling evasively. Nor did Teha'amana ever display the slightest hostility toward the women from the village or the nearby countryside whom Koké invited to pose for him, and sometimes she helped him convince them to pose naked, which they were generally reluctant to do.

How would your *vahine* have reacted to the story of Jotefa, Koké? You would never know, because you never dared tell it to her. Why not? Did the prejudices of moral, civilized Europe still flicker in you? Or was it simply because you were more in love with Teha'amana than you would admit, and you were afraid that if she found out what had occurred on that excursion she would be angry and leave you? Well, Koké! Weren't you planning to leave her yourself, without any scruples at all, as soon as you were granted your repatriation as a penniless artist? Yes, true. But until then, you wanted to keep living with your beautiful *vahine*—up to the very last day.

When hardships later beset him, he would remember life in those months as pleasant and, above all, productive. It would have been more so, of course, without the endless money worries. The infrequent remittances from Monfreid or good old Schuff were never enough to cover his expenses, and he was always in debt to Aoni, Mataiea's Chinese storekeeper.

He would rise early, with the light, take a dip in the nearby river, and after a frugal breakfast—the inevitable cup of tea and a slice of mango or pineapple—set to work with unfailing enthusiasm. The intense light, the bright and contrasting colors, the rising heat and noises—animal, vegetable, human, and the eternal murmur of the sea—were all pleasing to him. The day he met Jotefa, he was carving instead of painting. Small and based on quick sketches, the carvings were an attempt to capture in a few strokes the firm faces of the Tahitians of the region, with their flat noses, wide mouths, thick lips, and stocky bodies. There were also idols of his own invention, since to his disappointment no traces were left on the island of statues or totems of the ancient Maori gods.

The young man who cut trees around Koké's hut was less timid or more curious than Koké's Mataiea neighbors, who rarely took it upon themselves to visit if Koké didn't seek them out. He wasn't from nearby, but from a small village in the island's interior. Ax on his shoulder, face and body drenched in sweat by his efforts, one morning he came up to the cane awning under which Paul was polishing the torso of a girl and, with a childish curiosity in his gaze, crouched down to look at it. His presence disturbed you, and you were about to ask him to leave, but something stopped you. Perhaps his beauty, Paul? Yes, that too. And something else, something that you vaguely intuited, as, pausing briefly from time to time, you observed him out of the corner of your eye. He was a male, close to that hazy boundary at which Tahitians became *taata vahine*, or androgynes, hermaphrodites, that third, in-between sex, which the Maori, unlike prejudiced Europeans, still accepted among themselves with the naturalness of the great pagan civilizations, behind the backs of the missionaries and ministers. Many times Paul had tried to discuss them with Teha'-amana, but the existence of *mahus* seemed so obvious and natural to the girl that he wasn't able to get more than a few banalities or a shrug of the shoulders from her. Of course there were men-women—so?

The boy's muscles swelled beneath his dusky copper skin when he chopped down a tree or carried it over his shoulder to the path where the buyer's cart would come to take it away to Papeete or some other town. But when he crouched next to Koké to watch him sculpt—his smooth-cheeked face lengthening and his deep, dark eyes with their long eyelashes opening wide as if seeking, deeper and beyond what he was seeing, a secret reason for the task at which Paul labored—his posture, his expression, the pout that parted his lips and showed the whiteness of his teeth were softened and feminized. His name was Jotefa. He spoke enough French to keep up a conversation. When Paul took a break, they talked. The boy, with a small, tight cloth around his waist that barely covered his buttocks and sex, besieged Paul with questions about the little wooden statues of native figures and imaginary Tahitian gods and demons. What made you so attracted to Jotefa, Paul? Why did he have that familiar air about him, as if he were someone you remembered from a long time ago?

Jotefa stayed with him after work sometimes, talking, and Teha'-amana would prepare a cup of tea and something to eat for the woodcutter, too. One afternoon, after the boy had left, Koké remembered. He ran to the hut to open the chest where he kept his collection of photographs, color plates, and magazine clippings of classic temples, statues, paintings, and figures that had caught his fancy, a collection to which he returned time and again as others turn to family keepsakes. Rummaging through the jumbled mass, he came upon a photograph. There was the explanation! It was this image that your consciousness, your intuition, had dimly identified with the young woodcutter, your new Mataiea friend.

The photograph was taken by Charles Spitz, photographer for *L'Illustration,* and Paul had seen it for the first time at the Paris International Exposition of 1889, in the South Seas section that Spitz had helped to organize. The image had so bemused him that he stood looking at it for a long time. He returned to see it the next day, and at last he begged the photographer, whom he had known years ago, to sell him a print. Charles gave it to him as a gift. Its title, "Plant Life in the South Seas," was misleading. It wasn't the giant ferns or the ropes of vines and tangled leaves on a mountainside down which cascaded a small waterfall that were most important, but the person with naked torso and legs, in profile, who, clinging to the foliage, bent to drink or perhaps just to contemplate the falling water. A young man? A young woman? The photograph suggested the two possibilities equally strongly, without excluding a third: that the figure was both, alternatively or simultaneously. Some days, Paul was sure that the silhouette was a woman's; other days, a man's. The image intrigued him, stirred his imagination, unsettled him. Now he had no doubt: there was a mysterious likeness between the figure in the photograph and Jotefa, the Mataiea woodcutter. Discovering it gave him a surge of pleasure. The spirits of Tahiti were beginning to let you into their secrets, Paul. That same day he showed Charles Spitz's photograph to Teha'amana.

"Is this a man or a woman?"

The girl studied the print for a while and at last shook her head, undecided. She couldn't be sure either.

He had long conversations with Jotefa as he carved his idols and the boy watched. He was respectful; if Paul didn't speak to him, he would sit still and silent, afraid of getting in the way. But when Paul initiated the exchange, there was no stopping him. His curiosity was boundless, childish. He wanted to know more than Paul could tell him about the paintings and sculptures, as well as many things about the sexual habits of Europeans. His queries were of the sort that, if not posed with such transparent innocence, might have seemed vulgar and stupid. Were the cocks of the *popa'a* the same shape and size as the Tahitians'? Was the sex of European women the same as that of women here? Did they have more or less hair between their legs? He didn't seem to be firing off these questions in his imperfect French, mixed up with Tahitian words and exclamations and expressive gestures, from an unhealthy curiosity but rather from an eager desire to enrich his knowledge, to learn what it was that united or divided Europeans and Tahitians in matters generally excluded from conversation among Frenchmen. "A true primitive, a real pagan," Paul said to himself. "Despite having been baptized and defamed with a name that is neither Tahitian nor Christian, he is still untouched." Sometimes, Teha'amana came to listen, but in front of her Jotefa was inhibited and fell silent.

For regular or large-sized carvings, Koké preferred the wood of breadfruit trees, pandanus palms, palmyra palms, and coconut palms; for small ones, always that of the balsa tree, from which the Tahitians made their canoes. Soft and malleable, almost a clay, with neither knotholes nor grain, balsa wood felt almost like flesh. But it was hard to find it around Mataiea. The woodcutter told him not to worry. Did he want a good supply of that wood? A whole trunk? He knew a little grove of balsa trees. And he gestured toward the steep side of the nearest mountain. He would take Paul there.

They left at dawn, with a bundle of provisions, wearing only loincloths. Paul had become accustomed to walking barefoot, like the natives, something he had also done in the summer in Brittany and, before that, in Martinique. Although he had traveled frequently in the months he had been on the island, he had always taken the coastal roads. This was the first time he had set out through the forest like a Tahitian, burying himself in the dense growth of trees, shrubs, and brush that tangled overhead and blocked out the sun; the paths were invisible to him, though Jotefa could follow them easily. In the glimmering green shade, livened by the song of birds he hadn't yet heard, breathing in a damp, oleaginous, vegetal scent that penetrated all the pores of his body, Paul had a feeling of intoxication, fullness, exultation, like something produced by a magic potion.

A few feet ahead of him, Jotefa followed the trail without faltering, swinging his arms rhythmically. At each step, the muscles of his shoulders, back, and legs flexed, flashing with sweat. Paul could see him as a warrior, a long-ago hunter, venturing deep into the jungle in search of the enemy whose head he would cut off and carry home over his shoulder, to offer to his merciless god. Koké's blood boiled; his testicles and phallus throbbed; he was choked with desire. But— Paul! Paul!—it wasn't exactly the familiar desire, of leaping on that fine body and possessing it, but rather of abandoning himself, of being possessed the way man possesses woman. As if he had guessed Paul's thoughts, Jotefa turned his head and smiled. Paul blushed violently: had the boy noticed your stiff cock, poking through the folds of your loincloth? He didn't seem to give it the slightest importance.

"The road ends here," he said, pointing. "It continues on the other side. We'll have to get wet, Koké."

He plunged into the stream, and Paul followed him. The cold water was soothing, freeing him from the unbearable tension. The woodcutter, seeing that Paul was lingering in the river, protected from the current by a big rock, left the bag of provisions and his loincloth on the other side and dove in again, laughing. The water sang, slapping and foaming against his neat body. "It is very cold," he said, coming so close to Paul that he brushed up against him. The space was green-blue, not a single bird cried, and except for the noise of the current against the rocks, the silence, tranquillity, and freedom were such that Paul believed this must be paradise on earth. His cock was stiff again, and he felt himself swoon from an unfamiliar desire: to abandon himself, to surrender, to be loved and treated roughly like a woman by the woodcutter. Conquering his shame, he allowed himself to back toward Jotefa, and rested his head on the young man's breast. With a bright little laugh, in which there was no hint of mockery, the boy put his arms around Paul's shoulders and drew him in, clasping him tight. Paul felt him settle himself, mold himself to his body. Seized by vertigo, he closed his eyes. Against his back he felt the boy's cock, also hard, rubbing against him, and instead of pushing him away and striking out, as he had so many times on the *Luzitano*, the *Chili*, and the *Jérôme-Napoléon* when his fellow sailors tried to use him like a woman, he let the boy have his way, feeling not disgust but gratitude, and—Paul! Paul!—pleasure. He felt one of Jotefa's hands groping underwater until it captured his sex. Almost as soon as he felt its touch, he ejaculated, groaning. Jotefa followed suit a moment later, against his back, laughing all the time.

They came out of the stream; with the fabric of the loincloths they rubbed away the water running down their bodies. Then they ate the fruit they had brought. Jotefa made no mention of what had happened, as if it were of no importance, or he had forgotten it already. Remarkable, Paul, wasn't it? He had done something with you that would provoke anguish and remorse, sentiments of guilt and shame, in Christian Europe. But for the woodcutter, who was free, it was a mere amusement, a diversion. What better proof that European civilization (a misnomer) had destroyed all freedom and happiness, depriving human beings of the pleasures of the flesh? The very next day you would start a painting of the third sex, the sex of Tahitians and pagans, still uncorrupted by emasculated Christian morality. It would be a painting about ambiguity and the mystery of the act that (thanks to this heavenly spot and Jotefa) had made you realize—at the age of forty-four, when you thought you knew yourself and everything about yourself—that in the depths of your heart, obscured by your enormous masculinity, a woman was crouched.

They came to the little balsa grove, cut a long, cylindrical branch from which Paul could carve the Tahitian Eve he was planning, and set off immediately back toward Mataiea, carrying the wood between them. It was nightfall when they reached the village. Teha'amana was already asleep. The next morning, Paul gave Jotefa one of his little idols. The boy tried to refuse it, as if by taking it he would spoil the generous gesture he had made in accompanying his friend to find the wood he needed. Finally, at Paul's insistence, he accepted it.

"How do you say 'mysterious waters' in Tahitian, Jotefa?"

"*Pape moe.*"

That was what it would be called. He began to paint it the next morning, early, after preparing himself the usual cup of tea. He had Charles Spitz's photograph at hand, but he barely consulted it, because he knew it by heart, and because a better model for his new painting was the naked back of the woodcutter walking before him in the thick undergrowth, in a magic sphere still intact in his mind's eye.

He worked for a week on *Pape moe*. For much of that time, he was in the rare state of euphoria and unrest that he hadn't experienced since painting *Manao tupapau*. Only a select few would realize what the true subject of *Pape moe* was; he planned never to reveal it, not to Teha'amana, with whom he didn't usually discuss his paintings, and certainly not in his letters to Monfreid, Schuffenecker, the Viking, or his Paris dealers. They would see, in the middle of a lush grove of flowers, leaves, water, and stones, a being standing in shadow on the rocks and inclining his beautiful body toward the thin stream of a waterfall, to quench his thirst or pay tribute to the invisible god of the place. Very few would guess the enigma, the sexual ambiguity of that little person in whom a different sex was incarnated, an option that morality and religion had fought, persecuted, denied, and exterminated until they believed it had disappeared. They were wrong! *Pape moe* was the proof. In those "mysterious waters" over which the androgynous subject of the painting bent, you were floating too, Paul. You had just discovered it, after a long process that began with the spell cast over you by Charles Spitz's photograph at the International Exposition of 1889 and ended at the stream where you felt Jotefa's cock against your back and agreed to become his *taata vahine*, in that lonely spot outside of time and history. No one would ever know that *Pape moe* was a self-portrait too, Koké.

Despite the fact that what had happened made him feel closer to being the savage he had wanted to be for years, it still troubled him. You, Paul, a faggot? If someone had told you so years ago, you would have beat him senseless. Ever since he was a boy he had bragged of his manliness and defended it with his fists. He had done so often in his distant youth as a sailor in the holds and cabins of the *Luzitano* and the *Chili*, those merchant vessels aboard which he spent three years, and on the warship *Jérôme-Napoléon*, where he served another two years during the conflict with the Prussians. Who ever would have guessed then that you would end up painting and sculpting, Paul? Not once did it occur to you that you might be an artist. In those days you dreamed of a great shipboard career, visiting all the seas and ports of the world, every country, race, and landscape as you rose to captain. A whole ship and its vast crew at your command, Ulysses.

From the beginning aboard the *Luzitano*, the three-masted ship on which he was accepted as an apprentice in December 1865, too old to be admitted to the Naval Academy, it was necessary to use his fists and feet, to bite and brandish his knife, to keep his ass intact. Some didn't care. When they were drunk, many of his companions boasted of having endured that sailor's rite of passage. But you did care. You would never be anyone's faggot; you were a real man. On his first voyage as an apprentice—from France to Rio de Janeiro, three months and twenty-one days on the open sea—the other apprentice, Junot, a redheaded Breton covered in freckles, was raped in the boiler room by three stokers, who afterward helped him dry his tears, assuring him that he should feel no shame, that this was a common practice at sea, an initiation that no one could avoid and that, as a result, harmed no one, and in fact fostered fellowship among the crew. Paul did avoid it, which meant that he had to demonstrate to sailors desperate for lack of women that anyone who wanted to have his way with Eugène-Henri-Paul Gauguin had to be prepared to kill or die. His great strength and, above all, his determination and ferocity protected him. When he was released on April 23, 1871, after completing his military service on the *Jérôme-Napoléon*, his backside was as unscathed as it had been six years before. How your fellow sailors on the *Luzitano*, the *Chili*, and the *Jérôme-Napoléon* would have laughed if they had seen you in that forest stream, a grown man, the *taata vahine* of a Maori!

Sex hadn't been important to him at the time it most commonly is for ordinary mortals—in youth, the age of lust and ardor. In his six years as a sailor, he visited the brothels in every port—Rio de Janeiro, Valparaíso, Naples, Trieste, Venice, Copenhagen, Bergen, and others he scarcely remembered—more to accompany his friends, to avoid seeming odd, than to experience pleasure. It was hard for you to feel enjoyment in those squalid, stinking haunts crowded with drunks, fornicating with ruined, sometimes toothless women with dangling breasts, who yawned or dropped off to sleep from exhaustion as you mounted them. Only after several strong drinks could you manage one of those sad, hasty matings that left a taste of ashes in your mouth, a funereal melancholy. It was better to masturbate at night, on your pallet, rocked by the waves.

Neither as a sailor nor afterward—when, with a recommendation from his guardian, Gustave Arosa, he began to work as a stockbroker in the offices of Paul Bertin on the rue Laffitte, planning to make a bourgeois living for himself on the Paris Stock Exchange—was Paul obsessively preoccupied with sex. This preoccupation came later, when he began to alter the course of his life, to abandon his prosperous, disciplined, routine existence as a good husband and family man—at an age when a man's fate is usually settled—for that other, uncertain, adventurous life of poverty and dreams that had brought him to this place.

Sex began to be important to him at the same time as painting, an activity that at first seemed a mere hobby, taken up at the urging of Émile Schuffenecker, his friend and colleague at the firm of Paul Bertin, who one day showed him a notebook full of charcoal sketches and watercolors, and confessed that it was his secret desire to be an artist. Good old Schuff, who painted in his free time when he wasn't, like Paul, hunting down wealthy families who might entrust their investments in the Paris stock market to the wisdom of Paul Bertin, had encouraged him to take a night drawing class at the Colarossi Academy. Schuff was doing it, and it was great fun, more fun than playing cards or spending evenings at the tables outside the place Clichy cafés, nursing a glass of absinthe and trading theories on the rise and fall of stock prices. So began the adventure that had brought you to Tahiti, Koké. For good? Or for ill? Many times, in periods of hunger or distress, as in the days you spent in Paris caring for little Clovis, times of asking yourself how much longer you would go homeless, begging a bowl of soup from the nuns at the poorhouse, you had cursed good old Schuff for his advice, imagining how prosperous you would be now, and what a beautiful house you would have in Neuilly, in Saint-Germain, in Vincennes, if you had stayed on as a financial adviser on the Paris stock exchange. Perhaps by now you would be as rich as Gustave Arosa and, like your guardian, in the position of acquiring a magnificent collection of modern art.

By then he had already met Mette Gad, the Viking, an imposing Danish woman with faintly masculine features—Paul! Paul!—and had already married her, in November 1873, in a civil ceremony in the ninth arrondissement, and in a service at the Lutheran Church of the Redemption. And they had embarked on a very bourgeois life, in a very bourgeois apartment, in a neighborhood that was the zenith of bourgeois existence: the place Saint-Georges. Sex still mattered so little to Paul then that in the early days of his marriage he didn't mind complying with his wife's prudishness and making love to her as Lutheran morality counseled, Mette wrapped in her long buttoned-up nightdresses and in a state of total passivity, never permitting herself the slightest display of daring, merriment, or seductiveness, as if being loved by her husband were an obligation to be endured in the same way that a patient suffering from constipation endures taking cod-liver oil.

It was only some time later, when his mind began to churn out images suitable for painting and (without completely neglecting his work at the offices of Paul Bertin) he began to spend his nights drawing everything, in every sort of medium—pencil, charcoal, watercolors, oils—that he was suddenly racked at night by desire. Then he begged or ordered Mette to take liberties in bed that scandalized her, making her undress, pose for him, and let her jealously guarded private places be stroked and kissed. It had been the source of bitter conjugal disputes, the first shadow falling over a happy family that kept growing larger every year. Despite the Viking's resistance, and the growing urgency of his sexual desire, he didn't cheat on his wife. He had no lovers, he didn't visit houses of ill repute, he didn't rent flats for little seamstresses as his friends and colleagues did. None of the pleasures the Viking withheld from him were sought outside the marital bed. At the end of 1884, at the age of thirty-six, when his life had taken a Copernican turn and he had decided to be a painter, only a painter, never to return to business, and had begun his slow decline into poverty and bankruptcy, he was still faithful to Mette Gad. By then, sex had become a central preoccupation, a constant anxiety, a source of scandalous fantasies, of baroque exaggeration. As he gave up being bourgeois and began to lead the life of an artist—privation, informality, risk, creation, disorder—sex gradually came to dominate his existence, not only as a source of pleasure but also as a means of severing old ties and gaining new freedoms. Relinquishing bourgeois security caused you great hardship, Paul. But your life of the senses and spirit was the richer for it, more intense and luxuriant.

Now you had taken a new step toward freedom—from life as a bohemian and artist to life as a primitive, pagan, savage. This was great progress, Paul. Sex for you was no longer a refined form of spiritual decadence, as it was for so many European artists, but a source of health and energy, a way of renewing yourself and restoring your enthusiasm, drive, and will, to create better and live better. Because in the world to which you were finally gaining access, living was a perpetual process of creation.

Everything he had undergone had been necessary in order for him to conceive a painting like *Pape moe*. No reworking was needed. In the painting, Charles Spitz's photograph sparkled and quivered; the androgynous figure and Nature weren't two separate entities—they were integrated into a new form of pantheist life: water, leaves, flowers, branches, and stones pulsated, and the figure possessed the immutability of the elements. Skin, muscles, black hair, strong feet firmly set on rocks covered in dark moss, all signaled respect, reverence, love for that being of another civilization who, though colonized by the Europeans, preserved his ancestral purity in the hidden depths of the forest. It saddened you to have finished *Pape moe*. As always when you put the final touch on a good piece of work, you were beset by the question of whether this might be the beginning of your decline as an artist.

Two or three nights later, there was a full moon. Enchanted by the soft light falling from the sky, he clambered over Teha'amana's body—she was breathing deeply, snoring softly and regularly—and went down to the flat ground that surrounded the house, with *Pape moe* in his arms. He contemplated the painting bathed in the bluish-yellow glow that gave an enigmatic sheen to the pool, where tangled aquatic plants were growing, plants that might be mistaken for lights or reflections. Nature, too, was androgynous in the painting. You weren't prone to sentimentality, which was something you had to immunize yourself against in order to transcend the limits of your degraded civilization and become part of the old traditions, but you felt tears come to your eyes. It was one of the best paintings you had ever done, Paul. It wasn't quite a masterpiece, like *Manao tupapau*, but it was nearly as good. Something the mad Dutchman used to repeat over and over again with great conviction, back in Arles in those last fall days of 1888, before your friendship was overwhelmed by that mix of love and hysteria—the true revolution in painting would take place not in Europe but far away, in the tropics, where *Rarahu*, or *The Marriage of Loti*, the novel that had dazzled them both, had taken place—wasn't it a resounding reality in *Pape moe*? There was a vigor in it, a spiritual strength that came from the innocence and freedom with which a primitive soul, unencumbered by western culture, saw the world.

The night that Paul met the mad Dutchman, in the winter of 1887 at the Grand Bouillon, Restaurant du Chalet, in Clichy, Vincent didn't even let Paul congratulate him on the paintings he was showing. "It is I who should congratulate you," Vincent said, shaking Paul's hand vigorously. "I've seen your Martinique paintings at Daniel de Monfreid's. Astounding! Painted with the phallus, not the brush— paintings that are art and sin all at once." Two days later, Vincent and his brother Theo came to Schuffenecker's house, where Paul had been staying since his return from his adventures in Panama and Martinique with his friend Laval. The mad Dutchman examined the paintings from every angle and declared, "This is great painting, it comes from the guts, like blood, like sperm." He embraced Paul, entreating him, "I want to paint with my phallus, too. Show me how." And so began their ill-fated friendship.

The mad Dutchman, in one of his brilliant intuitive leaps, hit the nail on the head before you, Paul. It was true. Over the course of that painful sojourn, first in Panama, then on the outskirts of Saint-Pierre, in Martinique, from May to October of 1887, you became an artist. Vincent was the first to realize it. Compared to that, what did it matter that you had suffered so terribly, laboring as a digger on the canal works of Monsieur de Lesseps, devoured by mosquitoes and on the brink of dying from dysentery and malaria in Martinique? It was true: in that painting of Saint-Pierre illuminated by the splendid sun of the Caribbean, in which the colors burst like ripe fruits and the reds, blues, yellows, greens, and blacks clashed with the ferocity of gladiators, battling for control of the painting, life erupted at last like a blaze on the canvas, purifying it, redeeming it from the cowardliness your painting and sculpting had shown up until then. On that trip, in fact, despite having come close to dying of hunger and sickness—puking your guts out in a little hut, the rain pouring through the palm-leaf roof—you began to wipe the cobwebs from your eyes and see clearly: the health of painting was abandoning Paris, in search of new life under other skies.

Sex had burst into his life too, like the light in his paintings, with uncontainable belligerence, sweeping away all the scruples and prejudices that until then had kept it in check. Like his fellow shovel-wielders in the pestilent swamps where the locks of the future canal opened, he went in search of the mulattas and black women who flocked to the Panamanian camps. Not only could they be had for a modest sum, they could also be beaten while they were being fucked. If they cried and, frightened, tried to flee, what satisfaction, what cruel pleasure to fall upon them and subdue them, show them who was master. You never loved the Viking like that, Paul, not as you did those black women with enormous breasts, animal maws, and voracious sexes, who burned like braziers. That was why your painting had been so drab and stiff, so conformist and timid—because your spirit, your sensibility, your sex were. On one of those stifling nights in Saint-Pierre, when you could have had any of those hip-swaying black women who spoke impassioned Creole, you made yourself the promise—you wouldn't keep it, Paul—that when you saw the Viking again, you would teach her a belated lesson. You said so to Charles Laval, one night when you were drunk on cheap rum.

"The first time we're together, I'll do away with all the Nordic frigidity the Viking inherited at birth. I'll beat her and tear her clothes off, bite her and hold her tight until she screams and struggles, until she writhes and fights to survive. Like a black woman. She'll be naked and I'll be naked, and in the battle she'll learn to sin, to take pleasure, to give pleasure, to be ardent, submissive, and delectable like the bitches of Saint-Pierre."

Charles Laval stared at you, stunned, not knowing what to say. Koké laughed out loud, his eyes fixed on *Pape moe*, which was lit by the phosphorescent light of the moon. No, no. The Viking would never make love like a Martinican or a Tahitian; her religion and culture prohibited it. She would always be half human, a woman whose sex had withered before she was born.

The mad Dutchman understood perfectly, from the very beginning. The canvases Paul had painted in Martinique looked as they did, not because of the outrageous colors of the tropics, but because of the freedom of mind and body achieved by an apprentice savage, a painter who was learning all at once to paint, to make love, to obey his instincts, to accept what there was in him of nature and the devil, and to satisfy his appetites like man in his natural state.

Were you a savage when you returned from Paris after that unhappy trip to Panama and Martinique, still recovering from the malaria that whittled away your flesh, poisoned your blood, and robbed you of twenty pounds? You were beginning to be one, Paul. In any case, your behavior was no longer that of a civilized bourgeois. How could it be after you had sweated in the oppressive sun wielding your shovel in the jungles of Panama, and made love to mulattas and black women in the mud, the red earth, the dirty sand of the Caribbean? Then, too, you were carrying the unspeakable disease inside you, Paul, a mark of shame but also proof of your unbridled manhood. You didn't know that you were infected, and you wouldn't know for some time. But you were already a being freed of scruples, respectability, taboos, and conventions, proud of your impulses and passions. How else would you have dared to reach out and grope the breasts of the delicate wife of good old Schuff, your best friend, who was lodging you, feeding you, and even slipping you a few francs to buy absinthe at the café? Madame Schuffenecker paled, flushed, and fled, stammering a protest. But her modesty and shame were such that she never dared tell Schuff about the liberties taken by the friend he had helped so much. Or did she? Touching Madame Schuffenecker when circumstances left you alone with her became a dangerous game. You enjoyed it enormously, and it drove you to your easel, didn't it, Koké?

A small cloud dimmed the light of the moon, and Paul returned to the hut, carrying *Pape moe* very carefully, as if it might shatter. It was a shame that the mad Dutchman would never see this canvas. He would have fixed it with the stunned gaze he acquired on important occasions, and then he would have embraced you and kissed you, exclaiming in a choked voice, "You've fornicated with the devil, my friend!"

At last, in the middle of May 1893, the repatriation order sent by the government of France to the provincial government of French Polynesia arrived. It was Governor Lacascade himself who brought the news that, according to the instructions received—he read aloud the ministerial resolution—it had been agreed, in view of Paul's insolvency, to award him a second-class ticket from Papeete to Marseille. That same day, after five and a half hours of jostling in the public coach, Paul returned to Mataiea and announced to Teha'amana that he was leaving. He talked for a long time, explaining in great detail the reasons he was compelled to return to France. Sitting on one of the benches under the mango tree, the girl listened without a word or a tear, and without any sign of reproach. With her right hand she mechanically caressed her left foot, the one with the seven toes. Nor did she say anything when Paul stopped talking. After smoking a last pipe, he went up to bed and found Teha'amana already asleep. The next morning, when Koké opened his eyes, his *vahine* had gathered up her things and left.

When Paul set sail for France aboard the *Duchaffault*, at the beginning of June 1893, the only person on the dock in Papeete to bid him farewell was his friend Jénot, recently promoted to fleet lieutenant.

THE SHADOW OF CHARLES FOURIER

LYON, MAY AND JUNE 1844

In Chalon-sur-Saône as well as in Mâcon, where Flora spent the last week of April and the first few days of May 1844, her tour relied almost entirely on the help of her friendly foes, the Fourierists. They offered their assistance so generously that Flora's conscience pricked her. How to make plain her differences with these disciples of the deceased Charles Fourier, when they received her and saw her off at stagecoach stations and river landings, and did everything they could to arrange meetings and appointments for her, without offending them? Nevertheless, although it pained her to disillusion them, she did not hide her criticisms of their theories and conduct, which to her seemed incompatible with the task that consumed her: the salvation of humanity.

In Chalon-sur-Saône, the Fourierists organized a meeting for the day after her arrival, in the vast hall of the local Masonic lodge called Perfect Equality. A glance around the crowded room, into which two hundred people were crammed, was enough to make her heart sink. Hadn't you written them that the meetings should always be small, thirty or forty workers at most? A small number permitted dialogue, personal engagement. An audience like this was distant, cold, unable to participate, obliged merely to listen.

"But madame, there was enormous curiosity to hear you. You come preceded by such fame!" protested Lagrange, the head Fourierist in Chalon-sur-Saône.

"I care nothing for fame, Monsieur Lagrange. I seek effectiveness. And I cannot be effective if I am addressing an anonymous, invisible mass. I like to speak to human beings, and to do that I need to see their faces and make them feel that I want to talk to them, not impose my ideas the way the Pope imposes his on his Catholic flock."

More alarming than the number of listeners was the social composition of the audience. As Monsieur Lagrange introduced her from the stage, decorated with a little jar of flowers and a wall of Masonic symbols, Flora discovered that three-quarters of those present were bosses, and only a third workers. To come to Chalon-sur-Saône to preach the Workers' Union to these exploiters! There was no hope for the Fourierists despite the intelligence and honesty of Victor Considérant, who, since the death of the founder in 1837, had presided over the movement. Their original sin, which opened an unbridgeable chasm between you and them, was the same as that of the Saint-Simonians: not believing in a revolution waged by the victims of the system. Both distrusted the ignorant, poverty-stricken masses and maintained with beatific naïveté that society would be reformed thanks to the goodwill and money of bourgeois citizens enlightened by their theories.

The amazing thing was that even now, in 1844, Victor Considérant and his followers were still convinced that they would win over to their cause a handful of rich men who, once converted to Fourierism, would finance a "societary revolution." In 1826, Charles Fourier had announced in notices in the Paris press that he would be at home every day in Saint-Pierre Montmartre from twelve to two in the afternoon, to explain his social reform projects to noble-minded and justice-seeking industrialists or persons of independent means interested in providing financial assistance. Eleven years later, on the day of his death in 1837, the goodhearted old man with kindly blue eyes, in his eternal black frock coat and white tie—it saddened you to think of it, Andalusa—was still waiting punctually from twelve to two for the visit that never came. Never! Not a single rich man, not a single bourgeois, took the trouble to go and ask him questions or listen to his plans for ending human suffering. And none of the famous names to whom he wrote requesting support for his projects—among them Bolívar, Chateaubriand, Lady Byron, Dr. Francia of Paraguay, and all the ministers of the Restoration and King Louis Philippe—deigned to answer him. And the Fourierists, blind and deaf, continued to trust in the bourgeoisie and mistrust the workers!

Seized by a sudden access of retrospective indignation, imagining poor Charles Fourier sitting in vain every midday in his modest dwelling in the twilight of his life, Flora abruptly changed the subject of her talk. She had been describing the functioning of the future Workers' Palaces, and now she moved on to sketch a psychological portrait of the present-day bourgeoisie. As she declared that masters were ungenerous, narrow-minded, petty, fearful, mediocre, and wicked, she noticed with glee that her listeners were squirming in their seats as if they were being attacked by squadrons of fleas. When it came time for questions, there was a barbed silence. At last, a furniture factory owner, Monsieur Rougeon, still young but already sporting the comfortable belly of the victor, stood up and said that, given the opinion Madame Tristán had of bosses, he couldn't explain to himself why she bothered to invite them to join the Workers' Union.

"For a very simple reason, monsieur. The bourgeoisie has money and the workers don't. To realize its plans, the Workers' Union will need funds. It is money we want from the bourgeoisie, not the bourgeoisie themselves."

Monsieur Rougeon reddened. Indignation made the veins in his forehead stand out.

"Am I to understand, madame, that if I join the Union, I won't have the right to enter the Workers' Palaces or use their services, despite paying my dues?"

"Exactly, Monsieur Rougeon. You don't need those services, because you are able to pay from your own pocket for the education of your children, medical care, and an old age without worries. That isn't true of the workers, is it?"

"Why should I give my money without receiving anything in return? I'd have to be a fool."

"Out of generosity, altruism, a spirit of solidarity with the down-trodden. Sentiments that you have difficulty comprehending, I see."

Monsieur Rougeon left the lodge in a huff, muttering that such an organization would never count him among its supporters. Some people followed him, in accord with his sentiments. From the door, one of them remarked, "It's true: Madame Tristán is a subversive."

Later, at a dinner hosted by the Fourierists, upon seeing their hurt and disappointed faces, Flora made a gesture to pacify them. Whatever her differences with Charles Fourier's disciples, she said, she had so much respect for the learning, intelligence, and integrity of Victor Considérant that once the Workers' Union was established, she wouldn't hesitate to put his name forward as a candidate for Defender of the People, the first paid representative of the working class, chosen to defend workers' rights in the National Assembly. Victor would be a popular spokesman, she was sure, as good as the Irishman O'Connell in the English Parliament. This show of deference toward their leader and mentor lifted their spirits. When they bade her farewell at the inn, they had made peace, and one of them said jokingly that, hearing her speak that night, he had at last understood why she was called Madame-la-Colère.

She couldn't sleep well. She was upset by what had happened at the Masonic lodge, and she lamented having let herself be carried away by the urge to insult the bourgeoisie rather than concentrating on bringing her message to the workers. You had a foul temper, Florita; at the age of forty-one, you were still unable to control your outbursts. But it was your stubbornness and fits of ill humor that had allowed you to maintain your freedom, and win it back each time you lost it. When you were Monsieur André Chazal's slave, for example. Or when you became little more than an automaton, a beast of burden, living with the Spence family, at a time when you still knew nothing about the Saint-Simonians, Fourierism, Icarian communism, or the work of Robert Owen in New Lanark, Scotland.

The four days she spent in Mâcon, home of Lamartine, the celebrated poet and member of parliament, her bodily ills beset her again, as if to test her fortitude. To the crippling pains in her uterus and stomach was added fatigue; she was tempted to cancel appoint-

ments, visits to the newspapers, and meetings to recruit workers—
who were more elusive here than elsewhere—and simply fall onto
the little flowered bed in her room at the lovely Hôtel du Sauvage.
She resisted the temptation with a Herculean effort. At night, exhaustion and nerves kept her awake, remembering—she liked to torture herself with these thoughts sometimes, as penance for not being
more successful in her struggle—her three years of calvary in the
service of the Spences. The family must have been well-to-do, but
except on trips its members hardly enjoyed their prosperity, due to
thrift, puritanism, and lack of imagination. The husband and wife,
Mr. Marc and Mrs. Catherine, must have been in their fifties, and
Miss Annie, the younger sister of the former, around forty-five. All
three were thin, gawky, rather forbidding in their perpetually black
attire, and entirely devoid of curiosity. They hired her as a companion
to accompany them on a trip to the Swiss mountains, where they
would breathe pure mountain air and scour their lungs, blackened by
the soot of London factories. The salary was good; it allowed her to
pay the wet nurse for the care of her children and left her something
for her personal needs. Her designation as a companion proved to be
a euphemism; in truth, she was the trio's servant. She served them
breakfast in bed—their inedible porridge, their toast, and the weak
cups of tea that all three drank three or four times a day—washed
and ironed their clothes, and helped the horrible sisters-in-law, Mrs.
Spence and Miss Annie, to dress after their morning ablutions. She
ran errands, took their letters to the post office, and went to the market to buy the insipid biscuits they took with their tea. But she also
dusted rooms, made beds, emptied chamberpots, and at mealtimes
suffered the daily humiliation of seeing that her portions were half the
size of the Spences'. Some staples of the family diet, like meat and
milk, were perpetually denied her.

But the worst part of those three years in the Spences' service
wasn't the mindless drudgery or the numbing routine that kept her
on her feet from dawn until dusk. Rather, it was the feeling she began
to have soon after she started working for them that the three were
making her vanish, robbing her of her status as a woman, a human being, rendering her a lifeless instrument without any sense of dignity
or even a soul, to whom the right of existence was granted only in

the brief instants she was given orders. She would have preferred that they mistreat her, that they hurl dishes at her head—this, at least, would have made her feel alive. Their indifference—she couldn't remember if they had ever asked her how she felt, or ventured a kind remark or a single affectionate gesture—offended her in the depths of her soul. In her relationship with her employers, it was her job to work like an animal, perform routine duties all day long, and resign herself to abandoning all dignity, pride, and emotion—to renounce even the feeling of being alive. Nevertheless, when the Spences' time in Switzerland came to an end and they proposed bringing her back with them to England, she accepted. Why, Florita? Well, of course, how else were you to continue supporting your children, all three of whom were still alive then? It would be difficult, too, for André Chazal to find you in London, and report you to the police there for running away from home. The fear of prison shadowed you all those years.

Dismal memories, Florita. Her three years as a servant shamed her so much that she expunged them from her life story until, much later, André Chazal's lawyer brought them to public light at the accursed trial. Now the memories assailed her in Mâcon: because she felt so ill, because she was so frustrated by this hideous city of ten thousand souls, all of whom seemed as ugly to her as the houses and streets they inhabited. Although she visited the four trade unions, leaving at each her address and a pamphlet about the Workers' Union, only two people came to visit her: a cooper and a blacksmith. Neither was of interest. Both confirmed that Mâcon's trade unions were on the verge of extinction, since now the workshops had found a way to pay lower wages, by hiring farmers and migrant harvest laborers for brief periods of intensive work rather than keeping permanent forces. The workers had left en masse to seek employment in the factories of Lyon. And the farmer-laborers didn't want to be bothered by union problems because they didn't consider themselves members of the proletariat but rather country men occasionally employed in the workshops to supplement their income.

The only source of entertainment in Mâcon was Monsieur Champvans, the head of the newspaper *Le Bien Public*, which the illustrious Lamartine edited from Paris by correspondence. A distinguished, cultured man, Champvans treated her with a refinement and courtesy that delighted her despite her political and moral reservations about the bourgeoisie. Politely he hid his yawns as she described the Workers' Union and explained the ways in which it would transform society. But he treated her to an exquisite lunch at the best restaurant in Mâcon and took her to the country to visit Lamartine's estate, Le Monceau. The castle of the great democrat and man of letters struck her as an irritating and tasteless ostentation. She was beginning to tire of the visit when Madame de Pierreclos, widow of the poet's illegitimate son—who, shortly after marrying, had died from tuberculosis at the age of twenty-eight—appeared to show her the grounds. The comely young widow, still a girl, talked to Flora about her tragic love and the state of grief in which she had lived since her husband's death, determined never to enjoy anything again, and to lead a cloistered life of self-sacrifice until death liberated her from her sufferings.

Hearing such talk from this lovely young woman, whose eyes were filled with tears, annoyed Flora beyond measure. As they strolled among Le Monceau's flowerbeds, she immediately began to lecture her.

"It saddens me to hear you talk so, madame, but it angers me, too. You are not a victim of misfortune, but a monster of egotism. Excuse my frankness, but you'll see that I am right. You are young, beautiful, rich—and rather than thanking the heavens for such bounty and making the most of it, you bury yourself alive because a turn of fate saved you from marriage, the worst servitude a woman can endure. Thousands, millions of people are left widows or widowers, and you believe your widowhood is an earth-shattering catastrophe."

The girl stopped walking and turned as pale as death. She stared at Flora incredulously, wondering if she was insane, or had at just that moment gone mad.

"An egotist because I am loyal to the great love of my life?" she asked.

"No one has the right to squander an opportunity like yours," Flora retorted. "Forget your mourning, abandon this mausoleum. Start to live. Study, do good, help the millions of human beings who, unlike you, suffer from very real and concrete problems—hunger, sickness, unemployment, ignorance—and are unable to face them. What you have isn't a problem—it's a solution. Widowhood saved you from having to discover the slavery that matrimony means for women. Don't play at being the heroine of a romance novel. Follow my advice: return to life and concern yourself with more generous things than the cultivation of your own pain. And finally, if you don't want to devote yourself to doing good, enjoy yourself, travel, take a lover. It's what your husband would have done if you had died of tuberculosis."

From being cadaverously pale, Madame de Pierreclos flushed bright red. And all at once she began to laugh hysterically, and couldn't stop for some time. Flora watched her, amused. When she took her leave, the little widow, still stunned, stuttered that although she wasn't sure whether Flora had been speaking seriously or in jest, her words would cause her to reflect.

Upon boarding the ship for Lyon, Flora felt freed of a great weight. She was tired of towns and villages, anxious to be in a great city once again.

Her first impression of Lyon, with its grim mansions like barracks, following one upon the other as in a nightmare, and its cobbled streets, which hurt the soles of her feet, was not pleasant. The grayness of the city, the contrast in it between the extremely rich and the desperately poor, and the way it seemed to serve as a monument to the exploitation of workers reminded her of London with the Spences. This depressing first-day sensation would gradually vanish as she attended more and more gatherings, meetings, and appointments, and as she was, for the first time in her life, hounded by the police. Here at last she had innumerable meetings with workers from every sector: weavers, shoemakers, stonemasons, blacksmiths, carpenters, velvet makers, and others. Her fame had preceded her— many people knew who she was and looked at her on the street with admiration or disapproval; some eyed her as a queer fish. But the reason she would remember her six weeks in Lyon all through the remaining months of her tour—in Lyon she marked two months since her departure from Paris—was that, in the crowded schedule of those weeks, she overwhelmingly confirmed not only the excessive exploitation of the poor but also the reserves of decency, moral purity, and heroism of the working classes despite the absolute degradation of their living conditions. "In six weeks in Lyon I learned more about society than in all the rest of my life," she wrote in her journal.

In the first week she gave more than twenty lectures in the workshops of the Croix-Rousse silkworkers, the famous *canuts* who, a short time before—in 1831 and 1834—had led two workers' revolutions that the bourgeoisie crushed with terrible bloodshed. In the narrow, dark, and dirty workshops perched on the mountain of Croix-Rousse, its interminable steps making her gasp for breath, Flora had difficulty associating the men half hidden in the shadowy dark, barely illuminated by an oil lamp—the meetings took place at night, after the day's work—with the fighters who had faced with sticks and stones the soldiers' bayonets, bullets, and cannon blasts. They were timid, barefoot, dressed in rags, their faces blank with exhaustion; they worked from five in the morning until eight at night, with a small break at midday. Many doubted that she had written *The Workers' Union*. Prejudice against women had permeated all social classes. Because she wore skirts, they believed her incapable of conceiving ideas for the redemption of the working class. After a certain awkwardness, due to their surprise at discovering she was a woman, they asked many questions, and when she quizzed them about their problems, they generally expressed themselves with great self-assurance. There were plenty of limited types among them, but also intelligences in the rough who were prevented by society from polishing themselves. She left these meetings nearly collapsing from exhaustion, but in a state of spiritual incandescence. Your ideas were taking hold, Florita—the workers were adopting them, the Workers' Union was beginning to become a reality.

On the ninth day of her stay, four police officers and the police commissioner of Lyon, Monsieur Bardoz, appeared at the Hôtel de Milan with a search warrant. After spending a few hours rummaging through her things, they took away her papers, notebooks, and private letters—among them a passionate one from Olympia—and the copies of *The Workers' Union* that she hadn't yet distributed to bookstores. As they left, they handed her a summons to appear before the King's Counsel, Monsieur A. Gilardin.

Gilardin was a man as thin as a knife, dressed in a suit like a religious habit. He didn't rise to greet her when she entered his office.

"The work you are doing in Lyon is subversive," he said icily. "An investigation has been opened, and you may be charged as an agitator. Consequently, while we await the results of the investigation, I prohibit you to continue your meetings with the *canuts* of Croix-Rousse."

Flora studied him slowly from head to toe, with disdain. She made a great effort not to explode. "Do you consider it subversive to exchange ideas with the people who weave the cloth for the elegant suits you wear? I'd like to know why."

"Those filthy holes are no place for ladies. And it is a dangerous business to speak to the workers when one has inflammatory ideas about the social order." The lipless mouth of the King's Counsel barely moved as he spoke. "I must warn you: so long as this investigation continues, you will be under observation. But if you like, you may leave Lyon immediately."

"The only way you'll make me leave is by force. I like this city very much. And I must warn you of something too: I will move heaven and earth so that the press here and in Paris let the people know the outrage that is being perpetrated upon me."

She left the office of the King's Counsel without bidding him farewell. The three opposition newspapers—*Le Censeur, La Démocratie*, and *Le Bien Public*—reported the search and the seizure of her papers, but none of them dared to criticize the measure. And from that day on, two police officers were stationed at the door of the Hôtel de Milan, taking note of the visitors Flora received and following her in the street. But they were so lazy and clumsy that it was easy to give them the slip, thanks to the complicity of the chambermaids at the hotel, who helped her leave through a kitchen window that opened onto a back alley. Therefore, despite the prohibition, she continued to hold meetings with the workers, taking every possible precaution, always fearing that the police would appear, alerted by some traitor. They never did.

At the same time, she undertook an intense labor of social research, visiting workshops, hospitals, poorhouses, madhouses, orphanages, churches, schools, and finally brothels in the neighborhood of La Guillotière. On this last expedition, accompanied by two Fourierists—they had behaved very well, finding her a lawyer to defend her case before the King's Counsel—she was not disguised as a man, as in London, but covered in a cape and a rather ridiculous hat that hid half her face. Although it wasn't as Dantean as the enormous Stepney Green in London, La Guillotière presented a spectacle that unnerved her: prostitutes clustered on corners and in the doorways of taverns and bawdy houses with cheery names—The Bride's House, The Warm Arms. She asked the ages of many of the youngest: twelve, thirteen, fourteen. Children, barely developed, playing at being women. How was it possible that men could be aroused by these creatures of skin and bone, who were not yet out of childhood and were threatened by consumption and syphilis, if they hadn't already contracted them? Her heart shrank; rage and sorrow struck her dumb. Just as in London, here too there was something part monstrous and part comic: in the midst of depravity, children two, three, and four years old crawled among the prostitutes and their clients (many laborers among them), playing on the dirt floors of the houses of ill repute, left there by their mothers while they worked.

Though profoundly disgusted, she made these visits out of a sense of moral obligation—she couldn't reform what she didn't know. From the early days of her marriage to André Chazal, sex had repelled her. Even before she acquired political awareness or an understanding of social problems, she had intuited that sex was one of the primordial weapons for the exploitation and control of women. This was why, although she didn't preach chastity or monkish reclusion, she had always distrusted theories that extolled the sexual life and the pleasures of the flesh as the objectives of a future society. It was one of the reasons she had distanced herself from Charles Fourier, for whom she nonetheless felt admiration and fondness. Curious, the case of the master; he had always led, at least in appearance, a life of complete austerity. He was thought to be a misogynist. But in his design of the society of the future—the coming Eden, the period of harmony to follow civilization—sex took pride of place. It was hard for her to accept this. Such a project could end in true chaos, despite the master's good intentions. It was unnecessary, absurd, impossible to organize society around sex, as certain Fourierists pretended to do. In the phalansteries, according to Fourier's design, there would be young virgins who would entirely forgo sex; and vestals, who would practice it moderately with the vestels or troubadours; and women with even more freedom, the damsels, who would pair off with the minstrels; and so on, up a rising scale of freedom and excess—odalisques, fakiresses, bacchantes—up to the bayaderes, who would make love as a charitable act, sleeping with the old, the sick, travelers, and in general beings who were otherwise condemned by an unjust society to masturbation or abstinence. Although every aspect of this system might be free and voluntary—each person could choose which sexual body of the phalanstery they wanted to belong to, and abandon it at will—to Flora it seemed improper. It made her fear that under its shelter new injustices would spring up. The plans for her Workers' Union included no sexual formulas. Except for establishing the absolute equality of men and women and the right to divorce, it avoided the subject of sex.

What alarmed her most about Fourier's doctrine were his claims that "all fantasies are good in matters of love" and "all passionate obsessions are just, because love is essentially unjust." His defense of the "noble orgy" made her dizzy, as did his espousal of coupling in groups and his assertion that in the society of the future, minority tastes—unisexual, as he called them—like sadism and fetishism shouldn't be suppressed but rather encouraged so that each person might find his perfect match and be satisfied in his weakness or whim. All this, of course, would harm no one, since everything would be freely chosen and approved. These ideas of Fourier scandalized her so much that she secretly rather agreed with Proudhon, the puritanical reformer who not long before, in his 1840 pamphlet *What Is Property?*, had accused the Fourierists of "immorality and pederasty." The scandal had recently led Victor Considérant to temper the sexual theories of the movement's founder.

Although she recognized and admired his revolutionary daring, Flora was intimidated by Fourier's libertine tolerance in sexual matters. She was also amused at times. She and Olympia had laughed until they cried one afternoon in the midst of lovemaking, remembering the master's confession that he had an "irresistible passion for lesbians," and his claim that, according to his calculations and research, he could prove that there were twenty-six thousand "like-minded individuals" in the world, with whom he could form an "association" or "body" in the future world of Harmony, in which he and those like him would freely and unabashedly enjoy sapphic displays. The lesbians exhibiting themselves before these happy voyeurs would do so of their own accord, because the performance would allow them to exercise their exhibitionistic talents. "Shall we invite him to join us, my dear?" Olympia laughed.

You could poke fun at Fourier's classificatory mania now, Florita, but ten years ago, upon returning from Peru, how overjoyed you were to discover his teachings, which recognized the unjust situation of women and the poor, and proposed to alleviate it by encouraging the formation of a new society, which would emerge with the establishment of more and more phalansteries. Humanity had progressed beyond its early stages—Savagery, Barbarism, Civilization—and now, thanks to new ideas, it would soon enter the last: Harmony. The phalanstery, with its four hundred families of four members each, would constitute a perfect society, a small paradise organized in such a way that all sources of unhappiness would disappear. Justice was useless, at least in bringing happiness to human beings. Fourier had foreseen this and prescribed everything. In each phalanstery the most tedious, stupid, and unrewarding jobs would pay best, while the most enjoyable and creative would pay least, since working at the latter would constitute a pleasure in and of itself. As a result, a coalman or a tinsmith would be better recompensed than a doctor or an engineer. Each limitation or vice would be turned to its best advantage for the good of society. Since children liked to play in the mud, they would be assigned the task of picking up garbage in the phalansteries. At first, this seemed the height of wisdom to Flora. So did Fourier's formula for ensuring that men and women did not tire of always doing the same thing: they would rotate from job to job, sometimes in a single day, to keep routines from growing stale. From gardener to professor, from bricklayer to lawyer, from laundress to actress, no one would ever be bored.

And yet she ultimately found alarming many of the categorical statements made by the kind and compassionate Fourier. To maintain that "on my own I have managed to gainsay twenty centuries of political imbecility" was an exaggeration. The master presented unverifiable assertions as scientific truths: that the world would last exactly eighty thousand years, and that in that time each human soul would transmigrate between the earth and other planets 810 times and live 1,626 different lives. Was this science or sorcery? Wasn't it ludicrous? By the same token, though she knew that she was not nearly as wise as the founder of Fourierism, she said to herself that the Workers' Union program was more realistic than its Fourierist counterpart, precisely because it was more modest.

After her visit to the brothels, her tour of La Antigualla, a madhouse and hospital for prostitutes suffering from shameful diseases, was even worse. The ill and the insane, intermingled, were supervised by cruel, moronic warders who beat the madmen when they screamed too much as they walked half naked and in chains around a courtyard full of filth, amid clouds of flies. In the corners, ruined women spat blood or displayed the pustules of syphilis as they tried to sing hymns under the direction of the Sisters of Charity, who ran the infirmary. The hospital's director, a pleasant man with modern ideas, admitted to Flora that in the majority of cases it was poverty that caused the alienation of these wretches.

"It makes perfect sense, doctor. Do you know how much a working woman earns in Lyon for fourteen or fifteen hours in the workshop? Fifty centimes—a third or a quarter of what a man makes for the same job. How are they to live on that much a day, if they have children to feed? That is why many turn to prostitution, and are driven mad."

"Don't let the sisters hear you." The doctor lowered his voice. "In their view, madness is a punishment for sin. Your theory would seem hardly Christian to them."

It wasn't only at La Antigualla that Flora encountered priests and nuns. They were everywhere. Lyon, city of rebellious workers, was also a clerical city, stinking of incense and the sacristy. She went in and out of many churches, which were full of poor fanatics praying on their knees or listening passively to the obscurantist tripe spilled out by priests who preached resignation and obedience to the powerful. Saddest of all was to see that the poor made up the immense majority of the faithful. To study fetishism, she climbed up to Lyon's highest point, nearly expiring in the process, where Notre Dame de Fourvière was worshiped in a small chapel. The ugly figure of the Virgin impressed her much less than did the abject idolatry of the mass of parishioners who had climbed so high and were now on their knees pushing and elbowing to approach the glass case holding the statue of the Virgin and touch it with a fingertip. It was the Middle Ages in the heart of one of the most industrialized and modern cities in the world!

Returning to the center of Lyon, halfway down the mountain she tried to visit a poorhouse where old people with no home or job could take refuge and be given a roof over their heads, a bowl of soup, and a Christian burial. She couldn't get in. The place was guarded by policemen with muskets. Through the bars, she saw the Sisters of Charity, who also ran schools for the poor in the city. Of course! Nuns and officers arm in arm, keeping the poor trapped from childhood to old age, teaching them submission through prayers and sermons, or imposing it by force.

Compared to these research forays, how different were her meetings with the small groups of *canuts* from the silk factories, and other Lyonnais workers. Sometimes the discussions were violent. Flora always left them strengthened in her convictions, feeling rewarded for her efforts. One night, at a meeting with some Icarian workers, followers of Étienne Cabet—whose novel, *Travels in Icaria*, had converted many in the region to his doctrine, called communist—Flora fainted in the middle of an ardent dispute. When she opened her eyes, it was dawn. She had spent the night in a weavers' workshop, lying on the ground. The workers who slept there had taken turns watching over her, massaging her hands and wetting her forehead. She had seen one of the workers, Eléonore Blanc, at other meetings. Flora had noticed that the young woman listened devotedly and had an agile mind. Something told her that she might become one of the leaders of the Workers' Union in Lyon. She invited her to the Hôtel de Milan for tea, and they talked for hours under the placid gaze of the policemen charged with watching her. Yes, Eléonore Blanc was an exceptional woman, and she would form part of the organizing committee of the Lyon Workers' Union.

By the time the examining magistrate called her in, Flora had become even more famous in Lyon. People flocked to her in the streets, and although some men averted their eyes and some women dared to say, "Go away and leave us alone," most greeted her with friendly words. Perhaps it was this popularity that made the magistrate, Monsieur François Demi, decree—after interrogating her for two hours in a most agreeable conversation—that there were no grounds on which to charge her, and that the police should return the papers they had seized.

"These last few weeks I've been simply superb," Flora said to herself upon recovering her notebooks, letters, and diaries, which Commissioner Bardoz himself sullenly delivered. Yes indeed, Florita. In five weeks in Lyon you had preached to hundreds of workers, enriched your knowledge of social injustice, set up a committee of fifteen people, and on the suggestion of the workers themselves ordered a third edition of *The Workers' Union*, to be sold at a very low price in order to put it within the reach of the humblest of pocketbooks.

Her words had even reached the heart of the enemy, the Church. Her last meeting in the region came as a surprise. In great secrecy, some priests who lived in a community in Oullins, under the leadership of Abbot Guillemain de Bordeaux, invited her to visit, since "many of our ideas are the same as yours." She went out of curiosity, expecting little of the meeting. But to her astonishment, she was received in the castle of Perron at Oullins by a group of religious revolutionaries. They called themselves the rebel priests. They had read and discussed Proudhon, Saint-Simon, Cabet, and Fourier. But their guiding spirit and mentor was Father Lamennais, who had lived a generation before. Rejected by the Vatican, he had been a supporter of the Republic, an opponent and scourge of the monarchy and the bourgeoisie, a defender of freedom of worship and social reform. Like Saint-Simon and like Flora, these rebel priests believed that the revolution should preserve Christ and a Christianity untainted by the authoritarianism of the Church and the privileges of power. The evening was pleasant, and as Flora took her leave, she told the rebel priests that there would be a place for them in the Workers' Union too. She counseled them, half in jest and half seriously, that since they had taken so many important steps they should take one more and rebel against ecclesiastical celibacy.

Her parting with Eléonore Blanc, on the day she left Lyon, was very hard. The girl burst into tears. Flora embraced her and whispered in her ear something that frightened her even as she said it. "Eléonore, I love you more than my own daughter."

6

ANNAH FROM JAVA

PARIS, OCTOBER 1893

ᝈ

When one fall morning in 1893 a knock came at the door of his studio in Paris at number 6, rue Vercingétorix, Paul stood open-mouthed in astonishment: the tiny dark-skinned woman-child in front of him was dressed in a tunic like the habit of a Sister of Charity, with a little monkey on her arm, a flower in her hair, and around her neck a sign that read: "I am Annah from Java. A gift for Paul, from his friend Ambroise Vollard."

As soon as he saw her, before he had even recovered from his bewilderment at receiving such a present from the young dealer, Paul wanted to paint. It was the first time he had felt the urge since his return to France, on August 30, after his ill-fated three-month voyage from Tahiti. Everything had gone wrong. He had disembarked in Marseille with only four francs in his pocket and arrived dazed and half dead of hunger in a blazingly hot Paris deserted by his friends. In the two years he had been away in Polynesia, the city had become strange and hostile. The exhibition of his forty-two "Tahitian paintings" at Paul Durand-Ruel's gallery had been a failure. Only eleven were sold, and the proceeds didn't make up for what he had been required to spend on frames, posters, and publicity, going into debt again. Although some of the reviews were favorable, he had felt ever

81

since that the Paris art world was shutting him out, or treating him with disdainful condescension.

Most depressing had been the blunt way in which Camille Pissarro, your old teacher and friend, had summarily dismissed your Tahitian theories and paintings. "This art isn't yours, Paul. Go back to being what you used to be. You are a creature of civilization, and it is your duty to paint harmonious things, not to imitate barbarous cannibal art. Listen to me. Turn back now; stop pillaging from the savages of Oceania and be yourself again." You hadn't argued. You had just said goodbye with a bow. Not even the affectionate gesture of Degas, who bought two paintings, could lift your spirits. Many artists, critics, and collectors shared Pissarro's harsh opinions: What you had painted while you were away in the South Seas was a cheap imitation of the superstitions and idolatry of primitive beings, light years away from civilization. Was that what art was supposed to be? A return to the scrawls, blots, and magic of cave dwellers? But it wasn't just a rejection of the new themes and techniques of your painting, acquired with so much sacrifice over the last two years in Tahiti. It was also a stifled, murky, twisted rejection of you personally. Why? Because of the mad Dutchman, no less. After the tragedy at Arles, Vincent's stay in the Saint-Rémy madhouse, and his suicide—and especially after the death of his brother, Theo van Gogh, also at his own hand—Vincent's paintings (which no one was interested in while he was alive) began to attract notice, to sell, to rise in value. A morbid fashion for van Gogh was born, and with it everyone in the painting community began to retroactively reproach you for having been incapable of understanding and helping the Dutchman. Bastards! Some added that you might even have provoked the mutilation in Arles, with your proverbial lack of tact. You didn't need to hear them to know that they were pointing at you and whispering behind your back at parties, social gatherings, galleries, cafés, salons, and studios. The calumnies filtered through in magazines and newspapers, in the oblique way in which the Paris press generally commented on the news of the day. Not even the providential death of your father's brother, Uncle Zizi, a bachelor in his eighties in Orléans, who left you several thousand francs, which arrived in time to rescue you for a while from poverty and debts, could revive your enthusiasm. How long would you continue in this state, Paul?

Until the morning that Annah from Java, with that picturesque sign around her neck, and with Taoa, her scampering, sarcastic-eyed monkey on a leather leash, came swaying like a palm to share the exotic, light-filled retreat into which Paul had converted the studio he rented on the second floor of an old building in a corner of Montparnasse. Ambroise Vollard had sent her to be his servant. That was what Annah had been before in an opera singer's house. But that same night, Paul made her his lover. She soon became his companion in games, fantasies, and pranks, and finally his model. Where was she from? Impossible to say. When Paul asked her, Annah told him a story riddled with so many geographic contradictions that doubtless it was all a fabrication. Maybe the poor girl didn't even know and was inventing a past as they spoke, revealing her prodigious ignorance of the planet's countries and continents. How old was she? She said seventeen, but he calculated that she was younger, perhaps only thirteen or fourteen, like Teha'amana; at the age—which so aroused you— when the early-blooming girls of primitive countries enter adulthood. Her breasts were developed and her thighs firm, and she was no longer a virgin. But it wasn't the clean-limbed little body of the companion he was vouchsafed by ungrateful Paris—a slip of a thing, a perfect miniature, beside the bulk of forty-five-year-old Paul—that immediately seduced him.

It was her dark, ashy mixed-blood face; her fine, sharp features— the little turned-up nose, the thick lips inherited from her Negro ancestors—and the liveliness and insolence of her eyes, which showed unrest, curiosity, mockery of everything she saw. She spoke a foreigner's French, exquisitely flawed, with such vulgar utterances and expressions that Paul was reminded of the port-city brothels of his sailor youth. Despite having absolutely nowhere to go, not knowing how to read or write, and possessing nothing but her monkey Taoa and the clothes on her back, she exhibited a regal arrogance in her self-possession, her posturing, and the sarcastic remarks she made about everyone and everything, as if nothing deserved her respect and society's conventions did not apply to her. When she didn't like something or someone, she would stick out her tongue and make a face that Taoa imitated, screeching.

In bed, it was hard to tell if she was enjoying herself or pretending. In any case she gave you pleasure, and she entertained you at the same time. Annah gave you back what you were afraid you had lost since your return to France: your desire to paint, your sense of humor, your will to live.

The day after Annah appeared in his studio, Paul took her to a shop on the boulevard de l'Opéra and bought her clothes, which he helped her to choose. They bought boots, too, and half a dozen hats, which Annah loved. She even wore them inside, and they were the first thing she put on when she got out of bed. Paul would shake with laughter when he saw her dancing naked toward the kitchen or the bathroom with a stiff *canotier* on her head.

Thanks to Annah's gaiety and inventiveness, the studio on the rue Vercingétorix became a place for gatherings and festivities on Thursday afternoons. Paul would play the accordion, sometimes dressing in a Tahitian pareu and covering his body with fake tattoos. Old friends came to the soirees with their wives and lovers: Daniel de Monfreid and Annette, Charles Morice with a daring countess who was sharing his poverty, the Schuffeneckers, the Spanish sculptor Paco Durrio, who sang and played the guitar, and a pair of neighbors, two Swedish expatriates—the sculptor Ida Molard and her husband, William, a composer—who sometimes brought along a countryman of theirs, a half-mad playwright and inventor called August Strindberg. The Molards had an adolescent daughter, Judith, a restless, romantic girl who was fascinated by the painter's studio. Paul had hung yellow wallpaper, painted the window frames in shades of amber, and crowded the room with his Tahitian paintings and sculptures. Spikes of vegetation, bright blue skies, emerald seas and lagoons, and voluptuous naked bodies seemed to leap from the walls. Before Annah appeared, Paul had kept a certain distance from his Swedish neighbors' daughter, amused by her obvious infatuation and never touching her. But since the arrival of exotic Annah, who roused his senses and fantasies, he began to play teasingly with Judith, too, when her parents were nowhere near. He would catch her around the waist, brush her lips, and squeeze her budding breasts, whispering, "This will all be mine, won't it, young lady?"

Terrified and pleased, the girl would nod. "Yes, yes, all yours."

And so it occurred to him to paint the Molards' daughter nude. He proposed it to her, and Judith, white as a sheet, didn't know what to say. Nude, entirely nude? Of course—weren't artists always painting and sculpting nude models? No one would know because, after completing it, Paul would hide the painting until Judith grew up. Only when she was a full-grown woman would he show it. Would she accept? In the end, she did. They had only three sessions, and the adventure almost ended in disaster. Judith would come up to the studio when her mother, Ida, who nourished a charitable passion for animals, went out with Annah on expeditions around Montparnasse in search of sick or hurt abandoned dogs and cats, which they would bring home, care for, cure, and find adoptive parents for. The girl, naked on some brightly colored Polynesian blankets, never lifted her eyes from the floor; she shrank and curled into herself, trying to make herself as invisible as possible to the eyes probing her secrets.

By the third session, when Paul had sketched Judith's spindly silhouette and little oval face with big frightened eyes, Ida Molard burst into the studio shrieking like a player in a Greek tragedy. It was hard work to calm her down, to convince her that your interest in the child was purely aesthetic (was it, Paul?), that you had respected her, that your desire to paint her nude was thoroughly innocent. Ida would be pacified only when you swore that you would abandon the project. In front of her you drenched the unfinished canvas with turpentine and scraped it with a palette knife, obliterating the image of Judith. Then Ida forgave you and you had tea together. Sulky and scared, the girl listened in silence as they talked, without joining in their conversation.

When, some time later, Paul decided to do a nude portrait of Annah, he had a brilliant idea: he would superimpose the image of his lover over the unfinished study of Judith. And so he did. The painting took him a long time because of the incorrigible Annah. She was the fidgetiest and most unmanageable model you would ever have, Paul. She was always moving, changing her pose, or, when she was bored, pulling faces to try to make you laugh—the favorite Thursday-evening game, along with spiritism—or, tired of posing, she would simply get up, toss on some clothes, and run outside, as Teha'amana would have done. There would be nothing else to do but put your brushes away and stop work until the next day.

Painting this portrait was your response to the offensive reviews and talk about your Tahitian paintings that you had been reading and hearing everywhere since the Durand-Ruel exhibition. It was a canvas painted not by a civilized man, but by a savage, by a wolf on two feet, without a collar, only passing through the prison of cement, asphalt, and prejudices that was Paris before returning to your true home in the South Seas. The refined artists of Paris, its finicky critics, its polite collectors, would feel their sensibilities, their moral standards, their tastes assaulted by this frontal nude of a girl who not only was not French, European, or white but also had the gall to show her breasts, navel, mound of Venus, and tuft of pubic hair as if defying anyone to confront her, to face her with a life force, exuberance, or sensuality as strong as hers. Annah hadn't asked to be what she was; she didn't even realize the incandescent power she derived from her origins, her blood, the untamed forests where she was born, just like a panther or a cannibal. How superior you were to ossified Parisian women, Annah!

It wasn't only the body gradually appearing on the canvas—the head darker than the burnished ocher and gold of the torso and thighs, and the big feet with nails like the claws of a beast—that was provocative; it was also the surroundings, as inharmonious as it was possible to imagine, with Annah arranged in a sacrilegious and obscene pose in a Chinese armchair of blue velvet. The wooden arms of the chair were two Tahitian idols you had invented, one on each side of Annah, like an abjuration of the West and its insipid Christian religion in the name of lusty paganism. And there was the unexpected presence, on the green cushion where Annah's feet rested, of those luminous little flowers that had been straying into your paintings ever since you discovered Japanese prints, when you first began to paint. Studying the symbolism and subtlety of those prints, you had had your first inkling of what you now saw clearly at last: that European art was ailing, infected by the consumption that killed so many artists, and that only a revitalizing bath in the primitive cultures not yet exterminated by Europe, where an earthly paradise still existed, would rescue it from decadence. The presence on the canvas of Taoa, the red monkey looking half pensive and half lackadaisical at Annah's feet, reinforced the nonconformity and stifled sexuality that suffused the whole painting. Even the apples floating on the pink background over Annah's head skewed the symmetry, conventions, and logic fervently worshiped by the artists of Paris. Bravo, Paul!

Though it proceeded extremely slowly because of Annah's tendency to wander, the work was stimulating. It was good to paint with conviction again, knowing that you were painting not only with your hands but also with your memories of the landscapes and people of Tahiti—you missed them terribly, Paul—with their ghosts, and, as the mad Dutchman liked to say, with your phallus, which sometimes, in the middle of a session, would swell at the sight of the naked girl and compel you to take her in your arms and carry her to bed. Painting after making love, with the smell of semen in the air, made you feel young again.

Since coming back from Tahiti, he had written to tell the Viking that as soon as he sold a few paintings and had enough money for the ticket, he would travel to Copenhagen to see her and the children. Mette answered with a letter in which she declared herself surprised and hurt that he hadn't rushed to see his family as soon as he set foot in Europe. Inertia got the better of him each time a picture of his wife and children came to his mind. That again, Paul? You, a family man again? The legal proceedings required to claim the small inheritance from Uncle Zizi, the appearance of Annah in his life, and the desire she awakened in him to paint again made him keep postponing the family reunion. When spring came, he decided impetuously to take Annah to Brittany, to his old retreat of Pont-Aven, where he had spent so many seasons and had begun to be an artist. It wasn't just a return to his origins. He wanted to reclaim the works painted there in 1888 and 1890, left with Marie Henry in Le Pouldu in exchange for room and board; since he was always penniless, he had invariably paid late, only in part, or never. Now, thanks to Uncle Zizi's francs, he could settle his debt. You remembered those canvases with apprehension, because you were a more mature painter now than the simpleton who went to Pont-Aven believing that in the depths of mysterious, religious, tradition-bound Brittany he would find the roots of the primitive world dessicated by civilized Paris.

His arrival in Pont-Aven caused true commotion, not so much on his account but because of Annah and the capering and shrieks of Taoa, who had learned to leap from her mistress's arm to Paul's shoulder and back, waving her arms. As soon as he arrived, he learned that Charles Laval—his companion on his adventures in Panama and Martinique—had died in Egypt, and that his wife, the beautiful Madeleine Bernard, was very ill. This news depressed you, as did memories of your old friends, the artists with whom you had lived out your Brittany dreams years ago: Jacob Meyer de Haan, a recluse in Holland where he was devoted to mysticism; Émile Bernard, also in retreat from the world, immersed in religion and now speaking and writing against you, and good old Schuff, back in Paris, spending his days arguing with his wife instead of painting.

But in Pont-Aven he met new friends, young painters who knew and admired him for his paintings and his fame as an explorer of the exotic who had left Paris to seek inspiration in far-off Polynesia: Armand Seguin, Émile Jourdan, and the Irishman Roderic O'Conor, who, like their lovers and wives, received him with open arms. They vied to pay him compliments, and they were as obsequious with Annah as they were with Paul. In contrast, Marie Henry—Marie the Doll—from the inn at Le Pouldu, stood firm, despite having greeted him affectionately: the paintings were not on loan or pawned. They had been given in payment for room and board. She would not return them. Though it was said now that they weren't worth much, in the future they might be. There was nothing to be done.

As the days went by, the cordial welcome that Paul and Annah had received from the townspeople of Pont-Aven gradually shifted to reticence and then mute hostility. This was because of the childish antics, the mischief making, and the sometimes astonishingly tasteless pranks with which O'Conor, Seguin, Jourdan, and some of the other young artists living in Pont-Aven amused themselves, egged on by Annah, who was delighted by the excesses of her bohemian companions. They got drunk and went out into the streets to torment the local women; they invented ridiculous plays in which Annah was always the heroine. Her shameless poses, silly grimaces, and torrential laughter stunned the townspeople, who scolded the group from their windows at night for their behavior, ordering them to be quiet. Paul participated from a distance in these farces, as a passive spectator. But his presence was a silent endorsement of his disciples' misbehavior, and the people of Pont-Aven considered him responsible, as the oldest and most important.

Most notorious was the chicken scandal, conceived by the incorrigible Annah. She convinced Paul's young disciples—that was what they called themselves—to sneak into old man Gannaec's henhouse, the best stocked in the region, and replace the chicks' water with cider to make them drunk. Then they dripped paint on the birds, opened the henhouse door, and shooed them toward the main square, where, as the town band played its Sunday concert, there burst an incredible stream of multicolored fowl that cackled raucously and turned in circles or fell over, discombobulated. The villagers' indignation was immense. The mayor and the parish priest presented their complaints to Paul, and urged him to rein in his rash friends. "Any day now this will come to a bad end," the priest declared.

And so it did. Weeks after the episode of the drunken, paint-spattered chickens, on the sunny day of May 25, 1894, the whole group—O'Conor, Seguin, Jourdan, and Paul, as well as their respective lovers and wives and Taoa—took advantage of the beautiful weather to walk to Concarneau, an ancient fishing port twelve kilometers from Pont-Aven, where the old walls and stone houses of the medieval quarter were still preserved. From the moment they stepped onto the seaside promenade along the port, Paul had the feeling that something unpleasant was going to happen. The taverns were full of fishermen and sailors who, sitting outside in the splendid sunlight, lowered their mugs of cider and beer in astonishment at the sight of the outlandish group—long-haired men in garish attire and flamboyant women, among whom, strutting like a circus performer, was a black woman leading a screeching monkey on a string and baring her teeth at them. There were exclamations of surprise and disgust, and the group noticed threatening gestures. "Begone, clowns!"

Unlike the residents of Pont-Aven, the people of Concarneau weren't used to artists. And much less to a tiny black woman making faces at them.

Halfway down the promenade a cloud of children surrounded them, staring curiously, some smiling and others saying things in their crusty Breton that didn't sound very friendly. All at once, they began to throw little stones, pebbles they took from their pockets. They aimed especially at Annah and the monkey, which huddled against its mistress's skirts, frightened. Paul saw Armand Seguin move away from the group, catch up with one of the stone throwers, and seize him by the ear.

Then everything happened so fast that Paul would later remember it as vertiginous. Some fishermen from the nearest tavern got up and came running toward them. A few seconds later, Armand Seguin was flailing, shoved repeatedly by a big man in clogs and a sailor's cap who roared: "Only I am allowed to hit my son." Stumbling and falling, Armand was pushed back, back, and finally tumbled into the foamy sea that beat against the parapet. In a youthful impulse, Paul swung his fist at Armand's attacker and watched him collapse, bellowing, with both hands over his face. It was the last thing he saw, because seconds later, a windmill of men in clogs threw themselves at him, hitting and kicking from every direction all over his body. He defended himself as well as he could, but he slipped and felt his right ankle, crushed and cut open, buckle under him. The pain made him lose consciousness. When he opened his eyes, women's cries sounded in his ears. Kneeling at his feet, a medic showed Paul his naked leg—he had slit his trousers to examine it—where a splintered bone showed through the bloody flesh. "They've broken your tibia, sir. You'll have to spend a long time in bed."

Dizzy, in pain, nauseated, he remembered the return to Pont-Aven in a horse-drawn carriage like a bad dream, each pothole or bump making him howl. To help him sleep, he was given little swallows of a bitter cordial, which scratched his throat.

He spent two months in bed at the Pension Gloanec, in a little room with a very low roof and pygmy windows, which was turned into an infirmary. The doctor's verdict was disheartening: with his tibia broken, it was out of the question to return to Paris, or even to try to stand. Only with complete bed rest would the bone return to its proper place and knit; in any case, he would always limp and in the future he would have to use a cane. For the rest of your life you would remember the pains you felt in those eight weeks spent motionless in bed, Paul. Or rather, the single pain, blind, intense, animal, that drenched you in sweat or made you shiver, sob, and rave, certain that you had lost your mind. Tranquilizers and painkillers didn't help at all. Only alcohol, which you drank almost ceaselessly, numbed you and afforded you brief intervals of peace. But soon not even alcohol could ease the torment, which made you beg the doctor when he came each week, "Cut off my leg, please!" Anything to put an end to your infernal sufferings. The doctor decided to prescribe laudanum. The opium made you drowsy; in your stupor, that slow, spinning calm, you forgot your ankle and Pont-Aven, the Concarneau affair, and everything else. Only a single thought occupied your mind: "This is a sign. Leave as soon as possible. Return to Polynesia and never come back to Europe again, Koké."

After an unfathomably long time, and after a night in which he at last slept without nightmares, he awoke one morning with a clear head. The Irishman O'Conor was on guard beside his bed. Where was Annah? He had the feeling it had been many days since he had seen her.

"She went back to Paris," the Irishman told him. "She was very sad. She couldn't stay here after the neighbors poisoned Taoa."

That, at least, was what Annah assumed had happened—that the villagers of Pont-Aven, who hated Taoa as much as they hated her, had prepared the mess of bananas that gave Taoa the stomachache that killed her. Instead of burying her, Annah gutted the monkey with her own hands, sobbing, and took the remains away with her to Paris. Paul remembered that Titi Little-Tits, when she grew bored of Mataiea, had left him to return to the exciting nightlife of Papeete. Would you ever see naughty Annah again? Not a chance.

When he could get up—he did limp, and couldn't move without a cane—he had to attend several police hearings about the fight in Concarneau before he returned to Paris. He expected nothing from the judges, fellow countrymen of the attackers, and probably just as hostile as the fishermen toward bohemians who disturbed the peace.

The fishermen were acquitted, of course, in a sentence that was an insult to common sense, and made to pay only a symbolic sum in damages, which didn't cover even a tenth of the cost of his care. Away, away, as soon as possible. Away from Brittany, France, Europe. This world had turned against you, and if you didn't hurry, it would be the death of you, Koké.

The last week in Pont-Aven, as he was learning to walk again—he had lost twenty-five pounds—Alfred Jarry, a young poet and writer from Paris, came to visit him. Jarry called him maestro and made him laugh with his drolleries. He had seen Paul's paintings at Durand-Ruel's and in the homes of collectors, and he was extravagantly admiring, reading aloud several poems he had written about them. He listened raptly to Paul's rantings about French and European art. Paul invited him and the other Pont-Aven disciples, who saw him off at the station, to follow him to Oceania. Together they would form the Studio of the Tropics that the mad Dutchman had dreamed of in Arles. Working in the open air, living like pagans, they would revolutionize art, restoring to it the strength and daring it had lost. They all swore they would come. Together, they would travel to Tahiti. But on the train back to Paris, he suspected that they, like his old friends Charles Laval and Émile Bernard, would fail to keep their word. You'd never see your new Pont-Aven friends again, either, Paul.

In Paris, everything went from bad to worse. It seemed impossible that things could deteriorate even further after those months of convalescence in Brittany. In the art world, because of despicable politics, suspicion and uncertainty ruled. Since the assassination of President Sadi Carnot by an anarchist, the climate of repression, the denunciations, and the persecutions had led many of his acquaintances and friends (or ex-friends) who sympathized with the anarchists (like Camille Pissarro), or who opposed the government (like Octave Mirbeau), to leave. There was panic in artistic circles. Would you have problems because you were the grandson of revolutionary and anarchist Flora Tristán? The police were so stupid they might have you classified as a hereditary subversive.

Quite a surprise awaited him upon his return to number 6, rue Vercingétorix. Not content with moving away and leaving him half dead in Brittany, Annah, that devil in skirts, had ransacked the studio, taking furniture, rugs, curtains, clothing, jewelry, and keepsakes that she had surely already auctioned off at the flea market and in the dens of Paris usurers. But—the supreme humiliation, Paul!—she hadn't taken a single painting, drawing, or notebook. She left them behind as useless junk in the otherwise empty room. After a burst of rage and cursing, Paul began to laugh. You felt no hostility toward that magnificent savage. She really was one, Paul. A true savage to the marrow, in body and soul. You still had much to learn before you could match her.

In those last few months in Paris, while preparing for his definitive return to Polynesia, he missed the little whirlwind who called herself Javanese but might have been Malaysian, Indian, or anything at all. To console himself for her absence, he had his nude portrait of her, which he devoted himself to retouching until he felt that it was finished, as Judith, the Molards' daughter, watched in a state of trance.

"Do you see yourself there, Judith, in the background, showing through that pink wall, like Annah's white and blond double?"

No matter how hard she stared, or how long she studied the canvas, Judith couldn't distinguish the silhouette behind Annah that Paul pointed out to her. But you weren't lying. The outline of the girl, which you had erased with turpentine and scraped away with a palette knife to pacify her mother, Ida, hadn't entirely disappeared. It showed through briefly, like magic, a fleeting apparition, at certain hours of the day, in a certain light, charging the painting with secret ambiguity, a mysterious undercurrent. He painted the title over Annah's head around some floating fruits, in Tahitian: *Aita tamari vahine Judith te parari*.

"What does that mean?" the girl asked.

"The woman-child Judith, still untouched," translated Paul. "You see, although at first glance this seems to be a portrait of Annah, you're the real heroine of the painting."

Lying on the old mattress that the Molards had lent him so he wouldn't have to sleep on the floor, he said to himself many times that the canvas would be the only good memory of his return to Paris, so pointless, so painful. He had finished the preparations for his departure to Tahiti, but he had had to postpone the trip because—"It never rains but it pours," his mother used to say in Lima, when she lived on the charity of the Tristán family—his legs were covered with eczema. The burning and itching tormented him, and the blotches turned into a solid expanse of pus-filled sores. He had to spend three weeks on the infectious disease ward at La Salpêtrière. Two doctors confirmed what you already knew, although you never accepted the truth. The unspeakable illness, again. It would retreat from time to time, giving you respites of six or eight months, but beneath the surface it continued its deadly work, poisoning your blood. Now it manifested itself on your legs, stripping the skin from them, making them erupt in bloody craters. Later, it would move up to your chest, your arms, your eyes, and leave you in shadows. Then your life would be over, even if you were still alive, Paul. The cursed thing wouldn't stop there, either. It would continue until it had penetrated your brain, robbed you of your senses and memory, driven you mad—until you were a contemptible ruin, at whom people would spit, from whom all would shrink. You would become a mangy dog, Paul. To ward off his depression, he secretly drank the alcohol brought to him in coffee jugs or soda bottles by chivalrous Monfreid and generous Schuff.

When he left La Salpêtrière, his legs were dry, although they were crisscrossed with scars. His clothes hung on him, he was so thin. With his long chestnut hair, now liberally streaked with gray and held back by a big astrakhan hat; his jutting broken nose above which his blue eyes twitched, in perpetual agitation; and the goatee on his chin, he was still imposing, and so were his movements and gestures and the profanities with which he salted his talk when he met his friends at their houses or on the terrace of some café, since he could no longer receive anyone in his empty studio. People turned to stare at him, and point, because of his appearance and his eccentricities: the reddish black cape that he wore flying behind him, his shirts in Tahitian colors and his Breton vest, his blue velvet trousers. They thought him a magician, an ambassador from an exotic country.

The inheritance from Uncle Zizi was much reduced by the cost of hospital stays and doctors, so he bought himself a third-class ticket on the *Australian*, which, setting sail from Marseille on July 3, 1895, would cross the Suez Canal and arrive in Sydney at the beginning of

August. From Sydney he would take a connection to Papeete, via New Zealand. Before he left, he tried to sell his remaining paintings and sculptures. He held an exhibition in his own studio, to which, with the help of his friends and a cryptic invitation composed by the Swede August Strindberg, whose plays were now very popular in Paris, he managed to attract some collectors. Sales were meager. An auction of all his remaining work held at the Hôtel Drouot was somewhat more successful, although it didn't live up to his expectations. He was in such a hurry to reach Tahiti that he couldn't hide his eagerness. One night, at the Molards', the Spaniard Paco Durrio asked him why he was nostalgic for a place so terribly far from Europe.

"Because I am no longer a Frenchman or a European, Paco. Although my appearance might suggest otherwise, I am a tattooed native, a cannibal, a black islander."

His friends laughed, but he was telling them something true, though exaggerating as usual.

While he was preparing his baggage—he had bought an accordion and a guitar to replace those taken by Annah, many photographs, and a good stock of canvases, stretchers, brushes, and paint—he received a furious letter from the Viking, in Copenhagen. She had learned of the public sale of his paintings and sculptures at the Hôtel Drouot, and she was claiming her share. How could he treat his wife and five children so unnaturally, children whom she, working miracles—teaching French, translating, begging for help from her relatives and friends—had spent so many years supporting? It was his obligation as father and husband to help them, by sending them money from time to time. Now he was in the position to do so, selfish beast.

Mette's letter exasperated and saddened him, but he didn't send her a cent. Stronger than the remorse that sometimes assaulted him—especially when he thought of his daughter Aline, a sweet and delicate girl—was his overpowering desire to go away, to get to Tahiti, which he should never have left. Hard luck, Viking. He needed the little money he had made at the public sale to return to Polynesia; he wanted his bones to be buried there, not on this continent of freezing winters and frigid women. Let her get by with the paintings of his that she still had, and let her be consoled by her belief—it wasn't yours, Paul—that the sins her husband had committed by neglecting his family he would pay for by burning in hell for all eternity.

On the eve of his voyage there was a going-away party at the Molards' apartment. They ate and drank, and Paco Durrio danced and sang Andalusian songs. When Paul forbade his friends to accompany him to the station the next morning, where he would take the train to Marseille, little Judith burst into tears.

7

NEWS FROM PERU

ROANNE AND SAINT-ÉTIENNE,

JUNE 1844

◆

The sky was full of stars and a richly scented summer breeze was blowing the night that Flora arrived in Roanne from Lyon, on June 14, 1844. At her boardinghouse, unable to sleep, she sat staring out the window at the blazing firmament, but her thoughts were all of Eléonore Blanc. If every poor woman were as energetic, intelligent, and thoughtful as the little Lyonnais worker of whom she had grown so fond, the revolution would be over in a matter of months. With Eléonore on it, the Workers' Union committee would function perfectly as the engine of the great workers' alliance of the south of France.

You missed the girl, Florita. On this calm and starry night in Roanne, you would have liked to hold her tight and feel her slender body again, as you felt it the day you went looking for her at her wretched hovel on the rue Luzerne, and found her crying.

"What's wrong, my child? Why are you crying so?"

"I fear not being strong or worthy enough to do everything you expect of me, madame."

Hearing the girl talk like that, stricken with emotion, and seeing the affection and reverence in her gaze, Flora had to make a great effort not to cry, too. She threw her arms around her and kissed her on her forehead and cheeks. Eléonore's husband, a dye worker with stained hands, understood nothing.

"Eléonore says you've taught her more in these last few weeks than she's learned in her whole life so far. And instead of being happy, she cries! Who's to understand her!"

Poor girl, married to such a fool. Would she be destroyed by marriage, too? No, you would make sure to protect and rescue her, Andalusa. She imagined a new kind of human relationship, in a society transformed by the Workers' Union. Marriage as it existed—the buying and selling of women—would give way to the free choice of partners. Two people would be united because they loved each other and had common goals; if they came to disagree, they would separate on friendly terms. Sex would not dominate, as it did even in Fourier's concept of Phalansteries; it would be moderated, held in check by the love for humanity. Desires would be less selfish, since couples would devote much of their affection to others, to the improvement of life in common. In such a world, you and Eléonore could live together and love each other like mother and daughter, or two sisters, or lovers, united by a single cause and by solidarity with your fellow human beings. And your relationship would not have the exclusivist and egotistic slant that your affair with Olympia had had (which is why you ended it, giving up the only pleasurable sexual experience of your life, Florita); on the contrary, it would be sustained by a shared love for justice and social action.

The next morning she began her work in Roanne, setting out very early. The journalist Auguste Guyard—a liberal and a Catholic but an admirer of Flora, whose books on Peru and England he had reviewed enthusiastically—had organized two meetings for her of thirty workers each. They weren't very successful. Compared to the shrewd and restless *canuts* of Lyon, the Roannais seemed exceedingly passive. But after visiting three cotton textile factories—the major local industry, which employed four thousand workers—Flora was surprised that the wretches weren't even more backward, given the conditions in which they worked.

Her worst experience was in the textile workshops of a former laborer, Monsieur Cherpin, who was now one of the region's richest men and an exploiter of his erstwhile brethren. Tall, strong, hairy, vulgar, with coarse manners and an odor from his armpits that made her head swim, he greeted her with a mocking stare, looking her up and down without bothering to hide his disdain—he, after all, was a successful man and she was an insignificant woman committed to the unnecessary salvation of humanity.

"Are you sure you want to go down there?" He gestured toward the basement workshop. "You'll regret it, I warn you."

"We'll speak later, Monsieur Cherpin."

"If you come out alive," he chuckled.

Eighty unfortunates were squeezed into a stifling cave crowded with three rows of looms, in which it was impossible to stand upright because the roof was so low, or to move because it was so cramped. A rathole, Andalusa. She thought she was going to faint. The fiery heat of the furnace, the pestilence, and the deafening noise of eighty looms working at once made her ill. She could barely form questions to put to the half-naked, dirty, skeletal beings crouched over their looms, many of whom barely understood her since they spoke only the Burgundian dialect. A world of ghosts, apparitions, the living dead. They worked from five in the morning until nine at night, and the men made two francs a day, women eighty centimes, and children (under the age of fourteen) fifty centimes. She returned to the surface drenched in sweat, her temples throbbing, and her heart racing, clearly feeling in her breast the chill of her uncomfortable lodger. Monsieur Cherpin handed her a glass of water, laughing obscenely all the while.

"I warned you it was no place for a decent woman, Madame Tristán."

Struggling to keep her composure, Madame-la-Colère spoke slowly and precisely. "As someone who began as a weaver, do you think it fair to make your fellow human beings work in such conditions? That workshop is worse than any sty I've ever seen."

"It must be fair, because dozens of men and women crowd in here every morning begging me to give them work," boasted Monsieur Cherpin. "You're pitying the lucky ones, madame. If they were paid more, they'd spend it in the taverns, getting drunk on the cheap wine that addles their brains. You don't know them. I do, precisely because I used to be one of them."

The next evening, after an exhausting day spent delivering copies of the cheap edition of *The Workers' Union* to Roanne's bookshops and visiting two other textile factories, just as dreadful as Monsieur Cherpin's, Flora was taken by Auguste Goyard to visit the thermal springs of Saint-Alban. Their owner, Dr. Émile Goin, was a faithful reader of her books, especially her account of her travels in Peru, *Peregrinations of a Pariah*, which he made her sign. A handsome man in his fifties with graying sideburns, sharp eyes, and a courtly but pleasant demeanor, Dr. Goin lived with his placid wife and three crinolined daughters in a manor house full of paintings and sculptures and surrounded by gardens. At the dinner to which she was invited, Flora noticed that the master of the house was gazing at her admiringly. It was not only your intellectual accomplishments that attracted him but also the blackness of your ringlets, the charm and liveliness of your eyes, and the harmoniousness of your features, Andalusa. She felt flattered. "Here is a man you might have been able to bear living with," she thought. Dr. Goin wanted to know whether everything Flora had written in *Peregrinations of a Pariah* was true, or whether it had been colored by her imagination. No, no, nothing had been altered; she had tried to tell only the truth, like Rousseau in his *Confessions*. Was it true, then, that her incredible adventure had begun purely by chance, upon her encounter in a Paris boardinghouse with a ship's captain who was returning to Peru?

Indeed, that was how the story began that made you what you were today, Florita. The noble Captain Chabrié saved you from being a dreary parasite, from living a borrowed life like Dr. Goin's fat, cow-eyed wife. Yes, it had happened at that boardinghouse in Paris where you took refuge with your daughter, Aline, after three years of servitude and moral degradation working as a maid for the Spence family. A place where you thought André Chazal, the husband from whom you had been fleeing and hiding for so long, would never find you. What a tangle of coincidence and happenstance decided people's fates, didn't it, Flora? How different your life might have been if your table companion hadn't spoken to you that night in the small dining room where the boarders took their evening meal.

"Excuse me, madame, but I just heard the landlady call you

Madame Tristán. Is that your last name? You wouldn't by chance be related to the Tristán family of Peru?"

The captain, Zacharie Chabrié, often traveled to faraway Peru, and there, in Arequipa, he had met the Tristán family, the region's wealthiest and most influential clan. Patrician kin! For three days, Flora interrogated the amiable seaman at lunch and dinner, extracting from him everything he knew about the family—your family, since Don Pío, its head, was none other than the younger brother of your father, Don Mariano. After she was widowed, your mother had written many times to this Don Pío, your flesh-and-blood uncle, asking him for help and never receiving a response. The strange turns life takes, Florita. If you hadn't had those talks with Captain Chabrié in 1829, it would never have occurred to you to write that loving and dramatic letter to your uncle in Arequipa, the extremely powerful Don Pío Tristán y Moscoso, telling him—with a naïveté for which you would pay dearly—the situation in which you and your mother had been left at Don Mariano's death, as a result of your parents' irregular marriage.

Ten months later, when Flora had lost hope, a reply came from Don Pío. It was a clever and calculated letter in which, while calling her "dear niece," he let her know in no uncertain terms that as an illegitimate daughter—alas, the unyielding rigor of the law!—she had no right to any part of the inheritance of his "dear brother Don Mariano." In any case, there was no such inheritance, since after debts and taxes were paid, Flora's father's fortune had vanished. Nevertheless, Don Pío Tristán, in a magnanimous gesture, was sending his unknown niece in Paris, through Don Mariano de Goyeneche, a cousin of his living in Bordeaux, a gift of twenty-five hundred francs and another offering of three thousand piastres, this from the mother of Don Pío and Don Mariano, Flora's grandmother, a hardy matron of ninety-nine springs.

The money fell into Flora's lap like a blessing from heaven. Those were difficult times, because André Chazal was pursuing her relentlessly. He had discovered her whereabouts in Paris, and brought a suit against her before the courts, accusing her of being a deficient wife and mother. He also claimed the two children who were still living (the oldest, Alexandre, was dead by then). Flora was able to pay for a lawyer, provide for her defense, extend the process, and delay a verdict that, as her lawyer warned her, would be unfavorable, given the existing laws against women who abandoned their homes. There was an attempt to reach a friendly settlement at the home of one of Flora's maternal uncles, Major Laisney, in Versailles. André Chazal, whom she hadn't seen in six years, appeared reeking of alcohol and full of rage and reproaches, his eyes glassy. He was half mad with resentment and bitterness. "You have dishonored me, madame," he kept repeating, shakily. After controlling herself for some time, as her lawyer had begged her to, Madame-la-Colère could bear no more: she seized a china plate from the nearest shelf and smashed it over her husband's head. He toppled to the floor, bellowing with surprise and pain. In the midst of the confusion, Flora seized the hand of little Aline—whom the law had consigned to her father's custody—and fled. Her mother refused to take her in, scolding her for behaving like a madwoman. Not content with that, she revealed (you were sure of it) Flora's hiding place to André Chazal—a dingy little hotel on the rue Servandoni, in the Latin Quarter, where Flora had taken shelter with Aline and Ernest-Camille. One morning, as Flora was leaving the hotel with the boy, her husband came striding toward her. She ran, but Chazal caught up with her at the doors of the Sorbonne's Faculty of Law. Descending upon her, he began to beat her. Flora defended herself as best she could, trying to block his blows with her bag, and Ernest-Camille screamed, terrified, clutching his head. A group of students separated them. Chazal howled that this woman was his legitimate wife, and that no one had the right to interfere in a conjugal dispute. The future lawyers hesitated. "Is that true, madame?" When she confessed that she was indeed married to the gentleman, the young men, crestfallen, stood aside. "If he is your husband, we can't defend you, madame. The law is on his side."

"You are worse swine than this swine," Flora screamed at them as André Chazal dragged her to the police station on the place Saint-Sulpice. There the captain booked her, reprimanded her, and warned her not to leave her hotel on the rue Servandoni. Soon she would receive a summons from the judge. Appeased, André Chazal left, with little Ernest-Camille wailing in his arms.

Hours later, Flora was a fugitive again, with Aline, who was just six years old. Thanks to the francs and piastres from Arequipa, she was able to wander the French countryside for nearly six months, avoiding Paris assiduously. She lived a makeshift existence, under false names, in extremely modest hostelries or peasants' homes, never staying anywhere too long. She was sure that there was an order of arrest out against her. If the police laid their hands on her, she would lose Aline, too, and go to jail. She pretended to be a widow distraught by the death of her husband, a Spanish woman in political exile from her country, an English tourist, the wife of a sailor on his way to China who was distracting herself from her loneliness by traveling. To make her money last, she barely ate, and searched for cheaper and cheaper lodgings. One day, in Angoulême, the fatigue, dread, and uncertainty overcame her. She fell ill, with such a high fever that she became delirious. Madame Bourzac, the owner of the farm where she was staying, became her guardian angel, and the savior of little Aline. She cared for Flora, cured her, and rallied her, and when Flora, between sobs, told her her true story, Madame Bourzac was infinitely kind and reassuring.

"Don't you worry, madame. The little girl can't keep living like this, on the road, like a Gypsy. Leave her with me until your situation is settled. I've grown fond of her, and I'll care for her like a daughter."

"The noblest and most generous soul I've ever known," exclaimed Flora. "Without her, Aline and I would have died in that terrible time. Madame Bourzac! A humble peasant, who scarcely knew how to write her own name."

"Had you already decided to leave for Peru?" Dr. Goin gazed at her with such fascination that Flora blushed.

"What else was there for me to do? Where could I go to be free of André Chazal and the so-called justice of the French?"

From Angoulême she wrote a letter to Don Mariano de Goyeneche, the cousin of Don Tristán who lived in Bordeaux. Flora had already been in contact with him, to receive the money from Arequipa. She begged him for an audience, in order to confide in him a delicate matter of the utmost urgency. They must speak in person. Don Mariano de Goyeneche answered immediately, very cordially. The daughter of his cousin Mariano Tristán could come to Bordeaux whenever she liked. She would be received with open arms and all the loving-kindness in the world. Don Mariano had no family, and he would be happy to have her stay as long as she liked.

"Here I must interrupt my story," said Flora abruptly, rising to her feet. "It is very late, and I leave for Saint-Étienne early tomorrow."

When Dr. Goin kissed her hand goodbye, Flora felt his wet lips linger insinuatingly on her skin. "He desires me," she thought, repulsed. Her displeasure kept her from sleeping on her last night in Roanne, and made her tense and ill-humored the next day on the train to Saint-Étienne. And in a way, it lingered, plaguing her, and she was unable to shake it off the whole week she spent in that city of cretinous and semicretinous soldiers, and pious, idiot workers, impervious to any intelligent idea, altruistic sentiment, or social initiative. The only happy event that week in Saint-Étienne was the arrival of two long and affectionate letters from Eléonore Blanc, which she answered with equally lengthy missives. As she had expected, the committee in Lyon was moving full sail ahead.

In the four weavers' workshops that she visited—two for men, one for women, and one mixed—she was surprised to learn that the workers prayed at the beginning and end of each day. At one of the shops she was invited to pray with them. When she explained that she wasn't a Catholic, because in her view the Church was a repressive institution, they looked at her with such horror that she feared they would attack her. She left every meeting convinced that she was wasting her time. Despite her efforts, she would recruit hardly anyone for the Workers' Union. In the end she couldn't gather the usual ten members for the organizing committee; she had to form it with seven, and she suspected that half would desert as soon as she left.

So that her visit to Saint-Étienne would not be entirely fruitless, she devoted herself to the social researches that, second only to political action, were her favorite pursuit. From a table at the pleasant Café de Paris, where she took her breakfast and midday meal, and with whose owner she had grown friendly, she watched the officers of the garrison who had made the Café de Paris an extension of the barracks.

She soon came to the conclusion that the rank-and-file soldiers were born dolts, and that the artillery officers, though they attained the level of normal human beings, were nauseatingly arrogant and snobbish. Apparently these officers, the sons of wealthy families of the haute bourgeoisie or the aristocracy, had nothing better to do than to come to the Café de Paris, play dominoes or cards, drink, smoke, tell jokes, and flirt with the women who passed by on the pavement while they waited for war to come and give them something to do. They pretended to flirt with Flora, too, at first. But they soon stopped, because her confident and ironic manner made them uncomfortable. They preferred their women to be submissive, like their orderlies and horses. Flora said to herself that she had been very wise to follow the teachings of Saint-Simon and prohibit the production of weapons and the creation of armies in the Workers' Union plans for a new society.

The blaze of memories ignited at the dinner with the Goins in Roanne smoldered on throughout her visit to Saint-Étienne. That stay in Bordeaux, at the mansion of the incredibly rich Don Mariano de Goyeneche, who insisted that she call him Uncle Mariano, and himself always called her Niece Flora, was a dream come true. Never had you been in such a sumptuous house, or seen so many servants, or imagined what it was like to live like a rich person. Never had you been treated with such deference, or lavished with so many compliments and comforts. Nevertheless, Andalusa, those months in Bordeaux were not as happy as they might have been, because you were not yet used to lying. You lived in fear, trepidation, and uncertainty, terrified of contradicting yourself, of saying the wrong thing, of being discovered, humiliated, and returned to your true state by Don Mariano de Goyeneche and his right-hand man, secretary, sacristan, and constant companion—Ismaelillo, the Holy Eunuch.

Don Mariano de Goyeneche swallowed Flora's lies without suspecting a thing. He believed her when she said that since the recent death of her mother she was alone in the world, with no relatives or friends in Paris, and that under the circumstances she had had the idea—the yearning, the dream—of traveling to Peru, to Arequipa, to see her father's homeland, to meet her father's family, to visit the house where her father was born. Only there would she feel safe, consoled in her abandonment and loneliness. Flora wiped her eyes with a little silk handkerchief, made her voice quaver, and faked a sob. The stern-faced, white-haired old man in his dark suit like a monk's robes was moved, and as she told her unhappy story, he took her hand several times, nodding his head. Certainly, Florita, it would not do for a young woman like her to be left alone in the world. The daughter of his cousin Mariano Tristán should travel to Peru, where her uncle, grandmother, and cousins would provide enough warmth and affection to fill the void left by her mother's death. He would write to Pío of her journey, and he himself would find her a good ship and advise her so that she would be safe along the way. While they waited for news from Arequipa, Florita should stay here in Bordeaux, in this very house, which would be gladdened by her youth. Don Mariano de Goyeneche would be happy to have his niece's company for a few months.

You spent almost a year in Don Mariano de Goyeneche's mansion—the house of a man who, if he still lived, must hate and despise you as thoroughly as he cherished and protected you eleven years ago; a man who believed you to be unmarried and a virgin when in fact you were a fugitive wife, a mother, a woman whose own mother was still alive in Paris—although, because of the way she took André Chazal's side, she was dead to you, and you would never see her or write to her again. What must the expression on Don Mariano de Goyeneche's face have been when he read, in *Peregrinations of a Pariah*, the truth about the stories you told him? The pure and innocent niece, for whom he bought passage to Peru, was really a no-good runaway, wanted by the police! He must surely have hurried to confession and, that night, wrapped his gaunt body more tightly in his hairshirt.

He was, along with Ismaelillo, the Holy Eunuch, the most Catholic person Flora had ever known. So utter and obsessive a Catholic was Don Mariano that, more than a believer, he seemed a caricature. His greatest pride (perhaps fueled by secret envy) was that his younger brother was the archbishop of Arequipa. "A prince of the Church in the family, Florita! What an honor, what a responsibility!" He had remained a bachelor in order to better serve God and the

Church, although he hadn't taken the vows of chastity, poverty, and obedience that it seemed Ismaelillo had. He went to Mass at the cathedral every day, and several days a week he returned to church in the afternoons for the benediction and rosary. He dragged Flora to masses, vespers, novenas, incense-perfumed ceremonies, and processions. She made extraordinary efforts to feign devotion like Don Mariano's when it came time to pray: kneeling not on the prie-dieu but on the cold stone floor, her hands folded on her breast, eyes closed, her whole body expressing contrition and humility, and her face absorbed in prayer. Priests, parish priests, directors of charitable works, Sisters of Charity, and parishioners all visited the house, and Don Mariano gave each and every one of them a warm welcome, offering them cakes and sweets with steaming cups of chocolate "from Cuzco," and sending them off with generous donations.

His giant stone mansion, in the neighborhood of Saint-Pierre at the center of Bordeaux, looked like a convent. It was full of crucifixes, sacred images, religious-themed tapestries, and paintings; besides the old chapel, in the corners there were small altars, niches, and shrines to saints and the virgin, where incense burned. Since the heavy curtains were usually drawn, an eternal dusk reigned in the vast old house, an air of devotion and earthly renunciation that struck fear into Flora. Affected by the somber and ceremonious atmosphere, people tended to speak in low voices, afraid of causing offense by making noise in such a mournful and spiritual place.

The Holy Eunuch was a young Spaniard extremely well versed in Don Mariano's financial affairs. At present, he was managing Don Goyeneche's assets and income, but in the future he would perhaps enter a seminary. He lived in a separate wing of the mansion, and his office and bedroom were as austere as the cells of a cloister. At dinner, Don Mariano asked God's blessing for their fare; at lunch Ismaelillo did it, in such a pompous tone, and with such an exalted and seraphic expression on his face, that Flora could scarcely keep from laughing. More than handsome, he was pretty, with his rosy, clean-shaven face, his slim waist, and his hands, soft as the skin of a newborn baby, his nails trimmed and glossy. He wore the same drab clothing as the master of the house, but unlike Don Mariano de

Goyeneche, who seemed perfectly comfortable with the complete surrender of his body and soul to the love of God and the practice of religion, the young Spaniard—he was probably about the same age as Flora, thirty or thirty-two at most—betrayed in his gestures, mannerisms, and behavior an unresolved conflict, a divide between his outward conduct and inner life. Sometimes he struck Flora as an angelic being, whose ardent faith made him deny himself all pleasures and desires and withdraw from the world to devote himself to God and the salvation of his soul. But other times she suspected him of being a duplicitous being, a dissembler concealing his cynicism behind a mask of modesty, austerity, and goodness, pretending to be what he wasn't and to believe things he didn't in order to win the confidence of Don Mariano, thrive in his shadow, and inherit his fortune.

Suddenly she began to notice a suspiciously greedy glitter in Ismaelillo's eyes. Sometimes she provoked it, not without malice, carelessly lifting her skirt when they were sitting together so that her slender ankle was revealed, or, seemingly anxious not to miss a syllable of what Ismaelillo was saying, moving so close to him that the young Spaniard must have been able to smell her and feel the brush of her skin. Then he would lose control, turning pale or flushing; his voice would change and he would trip over his words, leaping confusedly from subject to subject. He had taken a liking to her as soon as he saw her, in that old house with its smells of wax and incense. Flora knew it from the first day. He had fallen in love with her, and it must have caused him great anguish. But he never dared say anything that went beyond the most conventional of friendly remarks. Still, his eyes betrayed him, and Flora often surprised in them the eager little light which meant: How I'd like to be free, to be able to tell you what I feel, to take your hand and kiss it, to beg you to let me court you, to love you, to ask you to be my wife and let you teach me to be happy.

In the year she spent in that house, while her voyage to Peru was being arranged, Flora lived like a princess, though she was bored by the incessant religious obligations. Without her reading—never had she read so much as in those months, in Don Mariano's big library— and the companionship and devotion of the Holy Eunuch, it would have been much worse. Ismaelillo took long walks with her along the banks of the Garonne, or in the neighboring countryside, where the vineyards spread as far as the eye could see, and entertained her by telling her about Spain, Don Mariano, and the intrigues of the great Bordeaux families, which he knew in great detail. One day, when they were playing cards next to the fire, Flora noticed that he kept nervously slapping at his trousers, as if to shoo away an insect, or as if he were being stung. Surreptitiously, she began to spy on his movements. Yes, there could be no doubt about it: he was pleasuring himself, aroused by Flora's proximity, and he was doing it right there, shamelessly, almost within sight of Don Mariano, who was reading a parchment-covered book in his rocking chair. To torment him, she suddenly asked him to bring her a glass of water. Ismaelillo turned fiery red and stalled by pretending he hadn't quite heard her; finally he got up, hunched over and turned sideways, but even so, glancing furtively, Flora could see a bulge in his trousers. That night she heard him sob, kneeling in the chapel. Could he be flogging himself? From that moment on, she felt a mixture of compassion and disgust for the young Spaniard. You pitied him, Florita, but he repulsed you, too. He was a good man and he suffered, surely. But how determined he was to heap more sufferings upon those that life doled out of its own accord. What must have become of him?

Flora's most picturesque experience in Saint-Étienne was her visit to the munitions factory adjoining the garrison. She was given permission to visit it thanks to three Fourierists who were friends of the colonel heading the regiment, who designated one of his assistants, a captain with a coquettish little mustache, to escort her. His descriptions of the weapons that were made there bored her so much that she let her mind wander. But at the end of the visit, the civilian director of the factory and several artillery officers offered her refreshments. The conversation was proceeding innocuously when suddenly the captain who had been her escort asked her, after much hemming and hawing, what truth there was in the rumors that Madame Tristán had pacifist leanings. She was going to answer evasively—she was expected at a ribbon makers' workshop in the neighborhood of Saint-Benoît, and didn't want to waste time on a pointless discussion—but seeing the surprise, frank reproach, and derision on the faces of the officers around her, she couldn't help herself.

"Plenty of truth, Captain! I *am* a pacifist, of course. Which is why my plan for the Workers' Union states that in the society of the future weapons will be prohibited and armies abolished."

Two hours later, she was still arguing heatedly with her scandalized interlocutors when one of them dared to say, furiously, that it was "unworthy of a Frenchwoman" to have such ideas.

"My loyalty is to humanity first and France second, gentlemen," she said, ending the conversation. "Thank you for your company. I must go."

She left exhausted by the argument, but amused at having unsettled those pretentious artillerymen with her subversive ideas. How you had changed, Florita, since, lodged in the Girondin mansion of Don Mariano de Goyeneche, you prepared to leave for Peru to escape the persecution of André Chazal. You were rebellious then, true, but confused and ignorant, and not revolutionary at all yet. It never occurred to you that it might be possible to fight in an organized way against a society that permitted female slavery in the guise of marriage. What good your Peruvian adventures would do you! You were truly changed by that year in Arequipa and Lima.

Don Pío Tristán consented to Flora's voyage, though unenthusiastically. She was invited by the family to stay in the house where her father was born and spent his childhood and youth. Don Mariano de Goyeneche and Ismaelillo looked into ships sailing for South America in the coming weeks. They found the *Carlos Adolfo*, the *Fletes*, and the *Mexicain*. All three were to leave in February 1833. Don Mariano went personally to inspect them. He eliminated the first two; the *Carlos Adolfo* was old and full of patches; the *Fletes* was a good ship, but it traveled halfway down the African coast before turning toward South America. The *Mexicain* was the best choice. A small ship, it would make a single stop before sailing to Valparaíso through the Straits of Magellan. The crossing would take just over three months.

Once the ship was chosen and the cabin reserved, all that remained was to await the day of departure. Ever since Flora had come to live in Bordeaux, Don Mariano and Ismaelillo had insisted on making her practice her bad Spanish, of which Flora remembered a few words and sentences spoken by her father when she was a child in the

Vaugirard house. They both took their roles as teachers very seriously, and in a few months, Flora could follow their conversation and stumble along in Spanish.

It wasn't from Don Mariano's servants that she learned the insulting nickname that Ismaelillo was called in Bordeaux society, but from the victim himself. It was on one of those long walks they took along the banks of the broad Garonne or in the countryside just outside the city, during which Flora thought she could feel his struggles, the fierce and silent battle he was fighting in his heart to confess—or not confess—the passion he felt for her.

"You will doubtless have heard what they call me behind my back—the people of Bordeaux, that is."

"No, I've heard nothing. A nickname, you mean?"

"A vulgar and profane one," said the young man, biting his lips. "The Holy Eunuch."

"It is vulgar," Flora exclaimed, confused. "And slightly profane. But stupid, mostly. Why are you telling me this?"

"I don't want there to be any secrets between us, Flora."

Head bowed, he fell silent for the rest of the walk, as if overcome by fatalism. It was, you believed, the moment at which he came closest to breaking his vows and letting you know that he was human, not divine, and that he dreamed of holding a beautiful and intelligent woman like you in his arms. Better that he hadn't. Despite the disgusting things you saw him do sometimes, you had come to feel affection for him, mixed with compassion.

Visiting the Saint-Benoît ribbon makers infuriated and depressed her. These twenty or so mute, illiterate, ignorant workers lacked even the most basic curiosity. It was like talking to trees or stones. It would have been easier to turn the preening officers of the Café de Paris into revolutionaries than these wretches, who were numbed by hunger and exploitation, and had had the last particles of intelligence squeezed out of them by the bourgeoisie. When, while she was taking questions, one of the workers alluded to a rumor that she was getting rich selling copies of *The Workers' Union*, she didn't even have the heart to be angry.

The day she learned the date that the *Mexicain* would set sail from

Bordeaux to Peru—April 7, 1833, at eight in the morning, high tide—she also learned that the captain of the ship she was about to take was Zacharie Chabrié. When she heard Don Mariano de Goyeneche say his name, she felt as if she had been struck by lightning. Zacharie Chabrié! The captain from the Paris boardinghouse who had told her about the Tristán family of Arequipa. He had met Aline, and as soon as he saw Flora appear with Don Mariano and Ismaelillo, he would call her madame and ask about her "lovely daughter." All your lies would come tumbling down and crush you, Andalusa.

She spent a sleepless night, her chest tight with dread. But by the next morning, she had come to a decision. On a pretext, she went out, claiming a vow to Saint Clara that she had to fulfill alone, and drove to the port in a hired carriage. It was easy to find the company's offices. After she had waited for half an hour, Captain Chabrié appeared at the door. She recognized his tall figure, his thinning hair, his gentlemanly and provincial round Breton face, his benevolent eyes. He recognized her instantly.

"Madame Tristán!" He stooped to kiss her hand. "I asked myself, upon seeing the list of passengers, if it might be you. You're traveling with me on the *Mexicain*, aren't you?"

"Can we speak in private for a moment?" asked Flora, adopting a dramatic expression. "It is a matter of life or death, Monsieur Chabrié."

Taken aback, the captain led her into an office, and gave her what must have been his seat, a broad sofa with a little footstool.

"I am going to confide in you because I believe you are a gentleman."

"I won't disappoint you, madame. How can I help?"

Flora vacillated for a few seconds. Chabrié had the look of one of those old-fashioned Breton men who, though they've traveled the world, still hold fiercely to their traditional beliefs, morals, and religion.

"I beg you not to ask me any questions," she implored, her eyes filling with tears. "I'll explain everything once we're at sea. On the day we set sail, when you see me come accompanied, I need you to greet me as if you were meeting me for the first time. Don't fail me.

I beg you by everything you hold dear, Captain. Do you promise me you'll do it?"

Zacharie Chabrié nodded, very serious.

"I need no explanation. I don't know you, I've never seen you. I'll have the pleasure of meeting you on Tuesday, at eight, the hour of our departure."

8

PORTRAIT OF ALINE GAUGUIN

PUNAAUIA, MAY 1897

On July 3, 1895, Paul boarded the *Australian* in Marseille, exhausted but happy. For weeks he had been living in a state of dread, fearing sudden death. He didn't want his remains to molder in Europe, but in Polynesia, his adopted land. In that respect at least you shared your grandmother Flora's internationalist manias, Koké. A person's birthplace was an accident; his true homeland he chose himself, body and spirit. You had chosen Tahiti, and you would die like a savage, in that beautiful land of savages. The thought took a great weight off his mind. Didn't you care if you never saw your children again, Paul, or your friends? Monfreid, good old Schuff, the last of the Pont-Aven disciples, the Molards? Bah, you didn't care a bit.

At Port Said, the last port of call before the ship crossed the Suez Canal, he went down to wander around the makeshift little market by the ship's gangplank. Suddenly, amid the tumult of voices and the shouts of Arab, Greek, and Turkish peddlers hawking fabric, trinkets, dates, perfumes, and honeyed sweets, he spotted a Nubian in a red turban who winked at him obscenely, showing him something half hidden in his big hands. It was an astounding collection of erotic photographs, in fine condition, depicting every position and union imaginable, even a woman being sodomized by a hound. He bought all forty-five immediately. They would be a great addition to the chest of prints, objects, and curiosities that he had left in storage in Papeete. Gleefully, he imagined the reaction of the Tahitian girls when he showed them his outrageous new possessions.

Studying those photographs and concocting fantasies inspired by them was one of his few entertainments during the two endless months it took him to get to Tahiti, with stops in Sydney and Auckland, where he was stranded for three weeks waiting for a ship on its way to the islands. He arrived in Papeete on September 8. The ship entered the lagoon in the great orgy of light at dawn, and he felt indescribable happiness, as if he were coming home and a swarm of relatives and friends were gathered at the dock to greet him. But there was no one waiting, and he had a miserable time finding a wagon big enough to carry all of his bundles, packages, rolls of canvas, and paints to a small boardinghouse he knew on the rue Bonard, in the center of the city.

Papeete had been transformed in the two years he was gone: now there were electric lights, and the nights no longer had the half-mysterious, half-gloomy air they once did, especially the port and its seven little bars, now ten. The Military Club, frequented by colonists and tradesmen as well as soldiers, boasted a brand-new tennis court behind its fence of stakes. The sport was one that you, Paul, who had had to walk with a cane ever since the beating in Concarneau, would never play.

The pain in his ankle had lessened on the voyage, but no sooner did he set foot on Tahitian soil than it returned worse than ever, so much so that some days it kept him howling in bed. Tranquilizers had no effect; only alcohol helped, when he drank until his speech slurred and he could barely stand. And laudanum, too, which a Papeete druggist agreed to sell him without a prescription, for an exorbitant gratuity.

The drowsy stupor into which he was plunged by the opium kept him sprawled in his room, or in the armchair on the terrace of the modest boardinghouse where he continued to stay in Papeete while a hut was built for him in Punaauia, some eight miles from the capital, on a piece of land that he had bought for practically nothing. It was a bamboo hut, with a roof of plaited palm leaves, and later he decorated and furnished it with objects left from his previous stay, the few items he had brought with him from France, and other things he bought in the Papeete marketplace. He divided the single room with a simple curtain, so that one side would be his bedroom and the other his studio. Once he had set up his easel and arranged his canvases and paintings, his spirits rose. To make light, he cut an opening in the roof himself, with difficulty because of the chronic pain in his ankle. Still, for several months he was unable to paint. He carved some wooden panels which he hung on the walls of the hut, and when the pain and itching of his legs allowed it—the unspeakable illness had returned again, like clockwork—he made sculptures, idols that he baptized with the names of ancient Maori gods: Hina, Oviri, the Arioi, Te Fatu, Ta'aora.

All this time, day and night, whether he was lucid or swimming in the gelatinous sea into which the opium dissolved his brain, he thought of Aline. Not his daughter Aline—the only one of his five children with Mette Gad whom he occasionally remembered—but his mother, Aline Chazal, later Madame Aline Gauguin when his grandmother Flora's political and intellectual friends, eager upon Flora's death to assure the future of the orphan girl, married her in 1847 to the republican journalist Clovis Gauguin, his father. A tragic marriage, Koké; yours was a tragic family. This torrent of memories was unleashed the day that Paul began to pin the Port Said photographs up in rows on the walls of his new studio in Punaauia. One of the models, looking straight at the photographer from the arms of another naked girl, had the kind of black hair that the Parisians called *andalousienne*, and enormous, languid eyes; she reminded him of someone, and without knowing why, he felt uncomfortable. Hours later, he realized. It was your mother, Paul. The features, the hair, the sad eyes made the whore in the photograph look a little like Aline Gauguin. He laughed, then grew distressed. Why were you remembering your mother now? He hadn't thought of her since 1888, when he painted her portrait. Seven years, and now she was lodged in his consciousness day and night, an obsession. And what was that feeling, the lacerating sadness that dogged you for weeks, even months, at the beginning of your second stay in Tahiti? The strange thing wasn't that he should think of his mother, dead for so long, but that the memory should come accompanied by this sensation of sorrow and despair.

He learned of the death of his widowed mother in 1867—twenty-eight years ago, Paul!—at anchor in the harbor of an Indian city aboard the merchant ship *Chili*, on which he was employed as a seaman second class. Aline had died in faraway Paris at forty-one, the same age at which Grandmother Flora had died. You didn't feel then the terrible grief you felt now. "Well," you kept repeating, assuming a properly bereaved expression as you received the condolences of the *Chili*'s officers and sailors, "all of us have to die. Today, my mother; tomorrow, the rest of us."

Did you ever love her, Paul? Not when she died, true. But when you were a child, living with your great-great-uncle Pío Tristán in Lima, you loved her very much. One of your clearest childhood memories was how sweet and pretty the young widow looked in the big old house where you lived like royalty, in the central Lima neighborhood of San Marcelo, when she dressed like a Peruvian lady and draped her slender body in a big silver-bordered mantilla, covering her head and half her face with it and leaving only one of her eyes visible. How proud Paul and his little sister, María Fernanda, felt when the vast family clan of Tristáns and Echeniques complimented Aline Gauguin. "So pretty!" "A picture, a vision."

Where was the portrait you painted of her in 1888, working from memory and the only photograph of her you had kept, buried in your chest of odds and ends? It was never sold, as far as you knew. Did Mette have it in Copenhagen? You should ask her in your next letter. Was it among the canvases in the possession of Daniel de Monfreid or good old Schuff? You'd ask them to send it to you. You remembered it in great detail: a greenish-yellow background, like that of a Russian icon, the color highlighting Aline Gauguin's long and lovely black hair. It fell to her shoulders in a graceful sweep, and was tied at the neck with a violet ribbon, arranged in the shape of a Japanese flower. Real Andalusian hair, Paul. You worked hard to make the eyes look the way you remembered them: big, black, curious, a little shy, and quite sad. Her very white skin came to life at the cheeks with the blush that rose on them when someone spoke to her, or she entered a room where there were people she didn't know. Shyness and quiet strength were her prevailing character traits; the capacity for suffering silently and without complaint; the stoicism that so infuriated Grandmother Flora, Madame-la-Colère—your mother had told you so herself. You were absolutely certain that your *Portrait of Aline Gauguin* revealed all of that and brought to the surface the prolonged tragedy that was your mother's life. You had to find it and get it back, Paul. It would keep you company here in Punaauia, and you wouldn't feel so lonely anymore, with the open sores on your legs and the ankle those idiot doctors in Brittany didn't fix right.

Why did you paint that portrait, in December 1888? Because in the last futile attempt you and Gustave Arosa had made to mend your relationship, you had just learned about that hideous trial. The revelation posthumously reconciled you with your mother; not with your guardian, but with her. But did it really, Paul? No. You were already such a barbarian that even hearing about your mother's martyrdom when she was a girl—Gustave Arosa let you read all the trial documents because he thought you would feel friendlier toward him if you shared his sorrow—didn't relieve you of the resentment that had been gnawing at you ever since Aline, after you returned from Lima and had been living for a few years with Uncle Zizi in Orléans, left you as a boarder at Monsignor Dupanloup's Catholic school and went to Paris. To be Gustave Arosa's lover and kept woman, of course! You had never forgiven her for it, Koké. Not for leaving you in Orleáns, or for being the lover of that millionaire dilettante art collector. So what kind of savage were you, Paul? A hypocrite with bourgeois prejudices, that's what you were. "I forgive you now, Mother," he bellowed. "Forgive me, too, if you can." He was thoroughly drunk, and his thighs burned as if a small inferno were blazing in each one. He thought of his father, Clovis Gauguin, dying at sea on the voyage to Lima as he was fleeing France for political reasons, and buried at ghostly Port Hunger, near the Straits of Magellan, where no one would ever go to put flowers on his grave. And of Aline Gauguin, arriving in Lima widowed and with two small children, on the brink of despair.

It was then, feeling so forlorn, unable to leave his hut because of the pain in his ankle, that he remembered his mother's prophecy, made in the will in which she left him her few paintings and books. She wished you success in your career. But she added a sentence that galled you still: "Since Paul has made himself so disliked by all my friends, one day my poor son will be utterly alone." Your prophecy came true, Mother. Your son was a lone wolf, a lonely dog. She guessed at the savage inside of you before your true nature was revealed, Paul. Yet it wasn't true that you had been rude to all of Aline Gauguin's friends, only to Gustave Arosa, your guardian. And you *had* been rude to him. You could never smile at him or make him believe you loved him, no matter how kind he was to you or how many gifts and how much good advice he gave you, or how he supported you when you gave up the sea to make your way in the world of finance. He got you a job at the firm of Paul Bertin so that you could try your luck on the Paris stock exchange, and he did you many other favors. But he could never be your friend, because if he loved your mother, it was his duty to leave his wife and publicly proclaim his love for Aline Chazal, widow of Gauguin, instead of secretly keeping her as his mistress for the sporadic satisfaction of his desires. Yet a savage shouldn't be troubled by such foolish matters. What sort of prejudices were these, Paul? Though of course you weren't a savage then, but simply a bourgeois who made his living on the stock exchange and dreamed of being as rich as Gustave Arosa. His great burst of laughter shook the bed and knocked down the mosquito net, which wrapped itself around him, trapping him like a fish.

When the pains subsided, he made inquiries about his old *vahine*, Teha'amana. She had married a young man from Mataiea called Ma'ari, and she was still living in the village with her new husband. Although he had few hopes, Paul sent a message with the boy who cleaned Punaauia's little Protestant church, begging her to come back to him and promising her many presents. To his surprise and satisfaction, in a few days Teha'amana appeared at the door of his hut. She was carrying a small bundle of clothes, as she had been the first time. She greeted him as if they had just seen each other the day before. "Good morning, Koké."

Though plumper now, she was still a beautiful, graceful girl, with a sculptural body and ripe breasts, buttocks, and belly. Her arrival cheered him so much that he began to feel better. The pain in his ankle disappeared, and he started to paint again. But the reunion with Teha'amana didn't last long. The girl couldn't hide her revulsion at his sores, though Paul almost always kept his legs bandaged, after smearing them with a salve of arsenic that soothed the itch. Making love with her now was a pale imitation of the celebrations of the body that he remembered. Teha'amana balked, sought excuses, and when there was no way out of it, Paul saw—divined—how her face screwed up in distaste, and she played along though repugnance prevented her from feeling any pleasure. No matter how he showered her with gifts and swore that his eczema was a passing infection, soon to be cured, the inevitable occurred: one morning Teha'amana picked up her little bundle and left, without saying goodbye. Some time later, Paul learned that she was living again in Mataiea with her husband Ma'ari. What a lucky man, you thought. She was an exceptional young woman and it wouldn't be easy to replace her, Koké.

It wasn't. Sometimes mischievous local girls would come to watch him paint or sculpt after their catechism classes at Punaauia's Protestant and Catholic churches (equidistant from his hut), amused by the half-naked giant surrounded by brushes, paints, canvases, and half-carved pieces of wood. Although he occasionally managed to drag a girl into his bedroom and take his pleasure with her wholly or in part, none of them agreed to be his *vahine*, as he was always proposing. The coming and going of girls brought him trouble, first with the Catholic priest, Father Damian, and then with the minister, Reverend Riquelme. Both came, separately, to reproach him for his shameless, immoral behavior and his corruption of the native girls. Both threatened him: he might bring the law down upon himself. To both he responded that there was nothing he would like better than to have a permanent companion, because these teasing games were a waste of his time. But he was a man with needs. If he didn't make love, his inspiration dried up. It was as simple as that, gentlemen.

Then, six months after Teha'amana's departure, he found another *vahine*: Pau'ura. She was—naturally—fourteen years old. She lived near the village, and she sang in the Catholic choir. Two or three times after the evening practices, she made her way to Koké's hut. Stifling her giggles, she stared for a long time at the pornographic postcards displayed on a wall of the studio. Paul gave her presents and went to buy her a pareu in Papeete. At last, Pau'ura agreed to be his *vahine*, and came to live in the hut. She wasn't as pretty, bright, or passionate as Teha'amana, and she neglected her household duties; instead of cleaning or cooking, she ran off to play with the village girls. But her feminine presence in the hut did him good, especially at night, lessening the anxiety that kept him from sleeping. Hearing Pau'ura's steady breathing and seeing the shape of her sleeping body in the dark calmed him and gave him back a measure of security.

What was keeping you awake at night? Why were you in this perpetual nervous state? It wasn't the vanishing of your inheritance from Uncle Zizi and the meager profits of the auction at the Hôtel Drouot. You had grown used to living without money; that never prevented you from sleeping. It wasn't the unspeakable illness either. Because now the sores had closed again, after tormenting you for so long. The pain in your ankle was bearable for the moment. What was it, then?

Thoughts of his father, the political fugitive whose heart stopped in the middle of the Atlantic as he was fleeing France for Peru; and memories of the *Portrait of Aline Gauguin*. Where was it? Neither Monfreid nor Schuff had it; they had never even seen it. Mette was hiding it in Copenhagen, then. But he had asked for news of its whereabouts in two letters, and in her one response she hadn't mentioned the portrait. He asked a third time. When would you receive a reply, Paul? There would be a six-month wait, at least. Hopelessness got the better of him: you would never see it again. Aline Gauguin's likeness became another irritation, something you couldn't get out of your head.

It was the memory of the flesh-and-blood Aline Chazal, not just that of her image, that besieged him. Why was it now that you kept remembering over and over again the misfortunes that marked the life of your grandmother's only surviving child? It would've been better if the unfortunate daughter of Flora Tristán had died like her two brothers.

At that last meeting with his guardian, Paul saw how Gustave Arosa's eyes filled with tears as he described Aline Chazal's ordeal. That this man knew every detail confirmed Paul's suspicions about the relationship between his mother and the millionaire. She was so close-mouthed, so jealous of her secrets—to whom if not a lover would she have confided her shameful history? As you learned the macabre details of Aline Gauguin's life, instead of weeping like your guardian, you were overcome by jealousy and shame. Now, however, on this warm, windless night, the air sweet with the smells of trees and plants, the light of the big yellow moon like the color you used for the background of Aline Gauguin's portrait, you wanted to cry, too. For yourself, for the unfortunate journalist Clovis Gauguin, but especially for your mother. Hers was a terribly sad childhood, certainly. Born after Grandmother Flora had already fled your grandfather's house—that heartless monster André Chazal, that revolting hyena, was your grandfather, much as it chilled your blood to admit it—she spent the first years of her life as a fugitive, not knowing what a home or a family was. Under the skirts of fast-moving Grandmother Flora, fleeing the persecution of the abandoned husband, Aline was kept in boardinghouses, small hotels, and seedy inns or, even worse, left with peasant wet nurses. Without father or mother, her childhood must have been dismal. When Grandmother Flora was away for two years in Arequipa, in Lima, crossing the sea, she left Aline with a kindhearted woman from the Angoulême countryside who took pity on her, as Grandmother Flora herself told it in *Peregrinations of a Pariah*. How you regretted not having that memoir here with you, Paul.

Upon returning to France, Flora rescued Aline, who was able to enjoy her mother's company for just three years. This period after being taken from Angoulême to Paris, to the little house at number 42, rue du Cherche-Midi, when she was enrolled as a day student at a girls' school on the nearby rue d'Assas, was the happiest time of Aline's life. Gustave Arosa said so, and it must have been true, since she had told him so herself: it was the only time she had her mother, a home, a cozy routine approximating normality. Until October 31, 1835, when the nightmare began that would only end three years later, with the pistol shot in the rue du Bac. The day it began, Aline Chazal was on her way home from school, accompanied by a maid. A drunk, carelessly dressed man, his red eyes bulging, stopped her in the middle of the street. In a single motion he shoved the terrified maid aside and pushed Aline into a waiting carriage, shouting, "A girl like you should be with her father, a good man, not with a degenerate like your mother. I tell you, I am your father, André Chazal." October 31, 1835: the beginning of Aline's torments.

"What a way to discover the existence of her father," Gustave Arosa said, with deep sadness. "Your mother was just ten years old, and she had no memory of André Chazal." It was the first of three kidnappings the girl would suffer, events that had made her the sad, melancholy, wounded being she was ever after, the woman you painted in that missing portrait, Paul. But worse than the kidnapping itself, worse than the cruel, brutal way her father made himself known to Aline, were the motives, the reasons that drove that loathsome creature to abduct her. Greed! Money! The illusion of a ransom to be paid in Peruvian gold! How did the rumor, the myth, that the woman who abandoned him had returned from Peru swimming in the riches of the Tristáns of Arequipa reach that worthless scum, your grandfather André Chazal? He didn't kidnap Aline out of fatherly love, or the pride of a wronged husband. Rather, he intended to blackmail Grandmother Flora and strip her of the fortune he imagined she had brought back from South America. "There is no limit to the vileness and depravity of some human beings," lamented Gustave Arosa. And indeed, André Chazal's behavior resembled that of the worst kinds of animal: crows, vultures, jackals, vipers. The wretch had the law on his side; women who fled their homes were, under the pious moral code of Louis Philippe's reign, as contemptible as whores, and had fewer legal rights.

Madame-la-Colère handled the situation well, didn't she, Paul? It was such things that suddenly made you feel visceral sympathy and limitless admiration for the grandmother who died four years before you were born. She must have been crushed, destroyed, by her daughter's kidnapping. But she didn't lose her presence of mind. With the help of relatives on her mother's side of the family, the Laisneys (and especially her uncle, Major Laisney), she arranged a meeting with her husband—because Aline's kidnapper was still her husband in the eyes of the law. The meeting took place four weeks after the kidnapping, at Major Laisney's house in Versailles. You could easily imagine the scene, and once you had made a few quick sketches depicting it. The cold conversation, the reproaches, the shouts. And all of a sudden, your magnificent grandmother hurling a flowerpot—

a basin, a chair?—at André Chazal's head and, in the confusion, taking Aline by the hand and running away with her down the empty, flooded streets of Versailles. A providential rainstorm aided her escape. Your grandmother was an incredible woman, Koké!

After that amazing rescue, the story grew tangled, opaque, and looped back on itself in Paul's memory, like a bad dream. Denounced and persecuted, Grandmother Flora went from police station to police station, from prosecutor to prosecutor, from courtroom to courtroom. Since scandal makes lawyers famous, Jules Favre, an ambitious, detestable young attorney who would later go into politics, assumed André Chazal's defense in the name of order, the Christian family, and morality, and set himself to ruining the reputation of the escaped housewife, unworthy mother, unfaithful wife. And the girl? Where was your mother while all of this was happening? She had been sent by the court to a chilly boarding school, where Chazal and Grandmother Flora could visit her separately, just once a month.

On July 28, 1836, Aline was kidnapped for the second time. Her father took her by force from the boarding school run by Mademoiselle Durocher at number 5, rue d'Assas, and secretly shut her up in a disreputable boardinghouse on the rue du Paradis-Poissonnière. "Can you imagine the girl's state of mind after such upheavals, Paul?" whimpered Gustave Arosa. After seven weeks, Aline escaped from her confinement, climbing out a window, and managed to make her way to Grandmother Flora, who was now living on the rue du Bac. For a few months, she was able to be at home with her mother.

But Chazal, with the help of the devious Jules Favre, got the law and the police to hunt down the girl and return her to his custody. On November 20, 1836, Aline was kidnapped for the third time, this time by a police commissioner at her front door, and turned over to her father. At the same time, the King's Counsel informed Grandmother Flora that any attempt to snatch Aline from her father would mean prison for her.

Now came the foulest and ugliest part of the story. So foul and ugly that on the afternoon that Gustave Arosa, thinking to ingratiate himself with you, showed you the letter that the girl managed to get to Grandmother Flora in April 1837, you had hardly begun to read it when you closed your eyes, sickened by disgust, and returned it to your guardian. That letter played a role in the trial, was printed in the newspapers, became part of the legal record, and fueled gossip in Paris's salons and watering holes. André Chazal lived in a squalid lair in Montmartre. In her letter, with spelling mistakes in every line, the girl desperately begged her mother to rescue her. At night she felt fear, pain, and panic, because her father—"Monsieur Chazal," she said—usually drunk, made her lie down naked with him on the only bed in the room, while he, naked too, held her, kissed her, rubbed himself against her, and wanted her to hold him and kiss him as well. So foul, so ugly was this episode that Paul preferred to gloss over it, as well as over the charge his grandmother Flora levied against André Chazal, accusing him of rape and incest. Terrible, enormous accusations, and they sparked the expected scandal, but—thanks to the consummate skill of that other monster, Jules Favre—they landed the incestuous rapist in jail for only a few weeks, since although all signs indicated that he was guilty, the judge decreed that "the material fact of incest" could not be "irrefutably proved." Furthermore, the verdict condemned the girl to live apart from her mother once again, at a boarding school.

Had you put all that drama, with its tincture of Grand Guignol, in your *Portrait of Aline Gauguin*, Paul? You weren't sure. You wanted the canvas back so that you could find out. Was it a masterpiece? Maybe it was. In it, you remembered your mother's shy gaze burning dark and steady, gleaming blue, piercing the spectator and losing itself at some indeterminate point in space.

"What are you looking at in my painting, Mother?"

"My life, my poor wretched life, my son. And yours, too, Paul. I would have liked your life to be different—not like your grandmother's or mine or that of your poor father, who died at sea and was buried at the ends of the earth, but the life of someone normal, settled, safe; a life without hunger, fear, flight, or violence. It wasn't to be. I bequeathed you my bad luck, Paul. Forgive me, son."

When, some time later, Koké's sobs awakened Pau'ura and she asked him why he was crying, he lied to her.

"My legs are burning again, and the ointment is all used up."

It seemed to you that the moon—radiant Hina, goddess of the Arioi, the ancient Maori—was sad, too, motionless in the sky of

Punaauia, shining through the leaves intertwined in the square of the window.

Now there was hardly a cent left of the inheritance from Uncle Zizi, and the money Paul had brought from Paris. Neither Monfreid, nor Schuff, nor Ambroise Vollard, nor the other dealers with whom he had left paintings and sculptures in France showed any signs of life. His most faithful correspondent, as always, was Daniel de Monfreid. But Monfreid couldn't find a buyer for a single canvas or sculpture, not even a miserable sketch. Food grew scarce, and Pau'ura complained. Paul proposed an exchange to the Chinese owner of the only shop in Punaauia: he would give drawings and watercolors in return for food for himself and his *vahine* until he received money from France. At last, the grocer grudgingly agreed.

A few weeks later, Pau'ura told him that the Chinaman, instead of keeping the drawings, hanging them on the wall, or trying to sell them, was using them to wrap his wares. She showed him what was left of a scene of Punaauia mango trees, stained, wrinkled, and spotted with fish scales. Limping, leaning on the cane that he now needed to move anywhere at all, even inside the hut, Paul went to the shop and berated the owner for his lack of sensitivity. He was so loud that the Chinaman threatened to go to the police. From then on, Paul's hatred of the Punaauia shopkeeper began to extend itself to all the Chinese living in Tahiti.

Ill health and lack of money were not the only things that kept him in a state of frustration, always on the verge of exploding in rage. There was also his obsessive preoccupation with his mother and her portrait, lost without a trace. Where was it? And why was it the disappearance of that particular canvas—you had lost so many, without blinking an eye—that plunged you into depression, filling you with foreboding? Were you going mad, Paul?

For a while he stopped painting, instead just sketching in his notebooks and sculpting small masks. He worked without conviction, distracted by his worries and his physical ills. His left eye became infected and was always weeping. The Papeete druggist gave him some drops for conjunctivitis, but they had no effect at all. When the vision of the infected eye began noticeably to deteriorate, he was frightened: were you going blind? He went to the Vaiami Hospital, and the physician, Dr. Lagrange, made him stay. From the hospital, Paul wrote a letter full of bitterness to the Molards, his old neighbors on the rue Vercingétorix, in which he told them, "Ever since my infancy misfortune has pursued me. Never any luck, never any joy. Everyone always against me, and I exclaim: God Almighty, if You exist, I charge You with injustice and spitefulness."

Dr. Lagrange, who had lived in the French colonies for a long time, never liked him. He was a man in his fifties, too bourgeois and formal—with his little bald spot, rimless spectacles pinching the end of his nose, stiff collar and bow tie despite the heat of Tahiti—to be friendly with a bohemian of outrageous habits who mingled with the natives, and about whom the worst kind of stories circulated around Papeete. But he was a conscientious professional, and he submitted him to a rigorous examination. The diagnosis came as no surprise to Paul. His eye infection was another manifestation of the unspeakable illness, which had moved into a more serious stage, as the rash and suppurating sores on his legs indicated. Would it keep getting worse, then? How much longer, Dr. Lagrange?

"It is an illness of long duration, as you know," said the doctor, evading the question. "You must continue to adhere strictly to the treatment. And be careful with the laudanum; don't exceed the dosage I've prescribed."

The doctor hesitated. He wanted to add something but didn't dare, doubtless fearing your reaction, since in Papeete you had become known for your temper.

"I'm the kind of man who can stand bad news," Paul encouraged him.

"You know, too, that this is a very contagious illness," murmured the doctor, wetting his lips with the tip of his tongue. "Especially if one has sexual intercourse. In that case, the transmission of the malady is inevitable."

Paul almost responded with a crude remark, but he restrained himself in order not to aggravate the problems he already had. After he had been in the hospital for eight days, the administration presented him with a bill for 118 francs, warning him that if he didn't pay at once, his treatment would be suspended. That night he climbed out a window and jumped the hospital gate to reach the street. He returned to Punaauia in the public coach. Pau'ura announced that she was four months pregnant. She also told him that the Chinese grocer, in retaliation for his shouting, had started a rumor in the village that Paul had leprosy. The neighbors, alarmed by the idea of such a horrifying illness, were uniting to petition the authorities to make him leave town, shut him up in a leper colony, or rule that he keep away from the populated places of the island. Father Damian and Reverend Riquelme were backing them up because, although they probably didn't believe the Chinaman's gossip, they were happy to seize the chance to free the village of a lecher and a heathen.

None of this frightened or worried him much. He spent most of the day dozing in the hut, his mind emptied of all memories and longing. Since his only source of provisions had dried up, he and Pau'ura ate mangoes, bananas, coconuts, and breadfruit, which she picked nearby, and the fish that the girls who had befriended him sometimes brought, behind their families' backs.

Around this time, Paul finally began to forget the portrait of his mother. Another obsession replaced Aline Gauguin: his conviction that the Arioi secret society still existed. He had read about it in Moerenhout's book about ancient Maori beliefs, lent to him by the colonist Auguste Goupil. And one day he set out to prove that the natives of Tahiti were keeping the existence of this mythical society hidden, guarding it jealously from foreigners, European or Chinese. Pau'ura told him that he was imagining things; the Maori villagers who still came to visit him assured him that he was mad. Most of them had never even heard of the secret society of the Arioi, gods and lords of the ancient Tahitians. And the few who had heard of it swore that no natives believed in such antiquated notions anymore, that they were beliefs lost in the mists of time. But Paul, stubborn and single-minded, persisted day and night for several months on the subject of the Arioi. And he began to paint canvases and carve idols and wooden statues inspired by the imaginary beings. The Arioi made him want to paint again.

They're lying to me, you thought; they still see me as a European, a *popa'a*, not the barbarian I have become inside. A few dozen years of French colonization couldn't have wiped out centuries of beliefs, rituals, myths. In order to defend their religious traditions, the Maori must surely have hidden them away in a holy place, out of reach of the Protestant ministers and Catholic priests, enemies of their gods. The secret society of the Arioi, foundation of the most glorious phase of Maori life on all the islands, was still alive. Its members probably met in the depths of the forest to perform the old dances and sing; the permanent expression of their beliefs was in their tattoos. Though prohibited, and not as elaborate and mysterious as those of the Marquesas, tattoos flourished in Tahiti, hidden under pareus. To those who knew how to read them, they revealed the position of the individual in the Arioi hierarchy. When Paul began to claim that sacred prostitution, anthropophagy, and human sacrifices were still practiced in the brooding silence of the forests, the word spread in Punaauia that although it might not be true that the painter had leprosy, he had probably lost his mind. In the end, people laughed at him when he asked them, sometimes imploring, sometimes furious, to reveal the secret of the tattoos and to initiate him into the society of the Arioi: Koké had paid his dues, Koké was a Maori now.

A letter from Mette ended this ominous stage with a final blow. Written two and a half months previously, it was dry and cold: his daughter Aline, just twenty, had died that January of pneumonia, which she had caught after being exposed to the cold as she returned from a dance in Copenhagen.

"Now I know why I've been troubled by the memory of my mother and her portrait ever since I came back from Europe," Paul told Pau'ura, with Mette's letter in his hand. "It was a sign. My daughter was named Aline after my mother. She was delicate, too, a little shy. I hope she didn't suffer as much in her childhood as the other Aline Gauguin."

"I'm hungry," Pau'ura interrupted him, touching her stomach with a comical expression on her face. "No one can live without food, Koké. Haven't you noticed how thin you are? You have to do something so we can eat."

9

THE CROSSING

AVIGNON, JULY 1844

As she was packing her bags to travel from Saint-Étienne to Avignon, at the end of June 1844, an unpleasant event obliged Flora to change her plans. A progressive Lyon newspaper, *Le Censeur*, accused her of being a "secret government agent" sent to the south of France with the mission of "castrating the workers" by preaching pacifism and informing the monarchy about the activities of the revolutionary movement. The page of slander included a boxed editorial by the paper's publisher, a Monsieur Rittiez, exhorting workers to redouble their vigilance so as not to be deceived by "the pharisaic trickery of false apostles." The committee of the Lyon Workers' Union asked her to come in person to refute these falsehoods.

Flora, incensed by the indignity, did so at once. In Lyon she was received by the full committee. Distressed though she was, it was wonderful to see Eléonore Blanc, who trembled in her arms, her face bathed in tears. At the inn, Flora read and reread the outrageous accusations. According to *Le Censeur*, her duplicity had been discovered when the objects confiscated at the Hôtel de Milan by Monsieur Bardoz, Lyon's commissioner, reached the hands of the King's Counsel; among them was a copy of a report sent by Flora Tristán to the authorities about her meetings with the leaders of the workers' movement.

So shocked and angry was she that she couldn't sleep all night, despite the orange-blossom water that Eléonore Blanc made her sip in bed. The next morning, after a quick cup of tea, she stationed herself at the door of *Le Censeur*, demanding to see the publisher. She asked her friends on the committee to let her go alone, because if Monsieur Rittiez saw that she had come accompanied, he would surely refuse to meet with her.

Monsieur Rittiez, whom Flora had met in passing on her previous stay in Lyon, made her wait outside for nearly two hours. Out of prudence or cowardice, he received her in the company of seven writers, who remained in the crowded and smoky room throughout the interview, supporting their employer in such servile fashion that Flora felt ill. And these poor wretches were the pens of Lyon's progressive paper!

Did Rittiez, diligent former pupil of the Jesuits, who wriggled like an eel out of answering Flora's questions about the lying reports, believe that he could intimidate her by surrounding himself with thugs? She had the urge to tell him straight away that eleven years ago, when she was an inexperienced young woman of thirty, she had spent five months on a ship alone with nineteen men, without being discomfited in the least by so many trouser wearers. She was hardly intimidated now by seven cowardly, calumny-slinging intellectual lackeys; rather, their presence filled her with fighting spirit.

Instead of responding to her protests ("From where does the monstrous lie come that I am a spy?" "Where is this proof allegedly found among my papers by Commissioner Bardoz, when it appears nowhere on the list of everything that was confiscated from me and later returned by the police—a list signed by the commissioner himself?" "How dare your newspaper cast such aspersions on someone who devotes all her energies to fighting for the workers?"), Monsieur Rittiez just kept repeating the same thing over and over again like a parrot, behaving as if he were in Parliament. "I don't publish slander. I simply take issue with your ideas, because pacifism disarms the workers and delays the revolution, madame." And every so often he attacked her with another lie, saying that she was a Fourierist, and as such preached a collaboration between masters and workers that only served the interests of capital.

You would later remember those two hours of absurd debate, Florita—a dialogue of the deaf—as the most depressing episode of your entire tour of France. It was very simple. Rittiez and his entourage of hacks hadn't been taken unawares or tricked; they had concocted the false information, possibly out of envy, because of the success you had had in Lyon, or because discrediting you by accusing you of being a spy was the best way to vanquish your revolutionary ideas, with which they disagreed. Or did they hate you because you were a woman? They couldn't stand to see a woman set out to save mankind, which seemed to them an exclusively male endeavor. And the perpetrators of such villainy called themselves progressives, republicans, revolutionaries. In two hours of argument, Flora never managed to get Monsieur Rittiez to tell her where the specious information spread by *Le Censeur* had come from. She left in disgust, slamming the door behind her and threatening to bring a libel suit against the newspaper. But the Workers' Union committee dissuaded her: *Le Censeur*, newspaper of the opposition to the monarchy, had prestige, and a legal suit against it would hurt the popular movement. Better to counter the false information with public denials.

That was what she did in the following days, giving talks in workshops and meeting halls, and visiting all the other newspapers until two, at least, published letters of rectification. Eléonore didn't leave her side for an instant, showing such love and devotion that Flora was deeply moved. How lucky she had been to meet her, and how fortunate it was that the Lyon Workers' Union could count on such an idealistic and determined young woman.

The uproar and unpleasantness did their part to weaken her physically. From the second day of her return to Lyon, she began to feel feverish, her stomach queasy and her body racked by shivers that tired her enormously. But she refused to slacken her frenetic pace. Wherever she went, she accused Rittiez of sowing discord in the popular movement from his paper.

At night, the fever kept her awake. It was strange. You felt just as you had eleven years ago, in your five months aboard the *Mexicain*, the ship commanded by Captain Zacharie Chabrié on which you crossed the Atlantic. Rounding Cape Horn and sailing up the coast toward Peru, toward the meeting with your father's family, you hoped that not only would they welcome you with open arms and give you a new home, they would turn over to you a fifth part of your father's fortune. Then all your money problems would be solved, you would no longer be poor, you could educate your children and lead a peaceful life free of want and risk, and never again fear falling into the clutches of André Chazal. Of those five months at sea—in the tiny cabin in which you could barely stretch your arms; surrounded by nineteen men (sailors, officers, the cook, the cabin boy, the ship's owner, and four passengers)—you remembered your terrible sea-sickness. Like the stomachaches you were having now in Lyon, it sapped your energy, equilibrium, and ability to think logically, and plunged you into confusion and doubt. You were living now as you had then, certain that at any moment you might collapse, incapable of standing upright, of moving in step with the irregular swaying of the floor beneath your feet.

Zacharie Chabrié behaved like the perfect Breton gentleman Flora had guessed him to be the night they had met at that Paris boarding-house. He waited on her assiduously, himself bringing to her cabin the herbal teas that were supposedly a remedy for nausea and order-ing the construction of a small bunk on the deck, next to the chicken coops and crates of vegetables, because in the fresh air Flora's sea-sickness subsided and she had brief periods of relief. It wasn't only Captain Chabrié who showered her with attentions. The second in command—Louis Briet, another Breton—did too, and even the ship's owner, Alfred David, who pretended to be a cynic and issued fierce denunciations of the human species and predictions of disaster, softened in her presence and became amiable and obliging. Everyone on the ship, from the captain to the cabin boy, from the Peruvian pas-sengers to the Provençal cook, did all they could to make the crossing pleasant, despite the agonies of seasickness she suffered.

But nothing happened as you expected it to on that journey,

Florita. You weren't sorry to have made it—on the contrary, it was as a result of that experience that you were what you were now, a fighter for the welfare of humanity. Your eyes were opened to a world where cruelty, evil, poverty, and suffering were infinitely worse than anything you could have imagined—you, who, because of your little marital troubles, believed you had known the depths of misfortune.

After twenty-five days at sea, the *Mexicain* dropped anchor in the bay of La Praia, off the island of Cape Verde, to caulk the ship's bilge, which had sprung a few leaks. And you, Florita, who had been so happy to hear that you would spend a few days on solid ground, not feeling everything moving under your feet, discovered that being in La Praia was even worse than being seasick. In that city of four thousand inhabitants, you saw the true, horrifying, indescribable face of an institution that you had only heard talked about before: slavery. You would always remember your first sight of La Praia, which the newly arrived passengers of the *Mexicain* reached by crossing a black, rocky stretch of ground and scaling the tall cliff along which the city spread. There, in the small main square, two sweaty soldiers, swearing between blows, flogged two naked black men tied to a post, amid swarms of flies, under a molten sun. The cries of the men and the sight of the two bloody backs stopped you in your tracks. You grasped Alfred David's arm.

"What are they doing?"

"Flogging two slaves who have stolen something, or worse," the ship's owner explained, with a gesture of indifference. "The masters set the punishment and pay the soldiers to carry it out. Flogging in this heat is terrible. Poor slavers!"

All the white and mixed-blood residents of La Praia earned their living hunting, buying, and selling slaves. The slave trade was the only business of the Portuguese colony, where everything that Flora saw and heard, and all the people she met in the ten days it took to caulk the *Mexicain*'s hold, aroused pity, fright, rage, and horror in her. You would never forget the widow Watrin, a tall, portly matron the color of milky coffee, whose house was full of engravings of her hero Napoleon and the generals of the Empire. After offering you pastries and a cup of chocolate, she proudly showed you the most original object on display in her salon: two black fetuses, floating in fish bowls full of formaldehyde.

The principal landowner of the island, Monsieur Tappe, was a Frenchman from Bayonne, a former seminarian who, sent by his order to the African missions to win converts, had left the Church to devote himself to the less spiritual but more profitable work of selling slaves. He was a stout, red-faced man in his fifties, with a bull neck, prominent veins, and lewd eyes, which settled so brazenly on Flora's breasts and neck that she nearly slapped him. She held back, though, listening in fascination as Monsieur Tappe railed against the cursed English, who with their foolish puritan prejudices against the slave trade were driving the slave traders to ruin. Tappe came to eat with them on the *Mexicain*, bringing jugs of wine and cans of preserved food as gifts. Flora felt sick to her stomach seeing how voraciously the slave driver gobbled mouthfuls of lamb and other roasted meat, between long swallows of wine that made him belch. He presently owned twenty-eight black men, twenty-eight black women, and thirty-seven black children, who "behaved themselves," he said, thanks to "Monsieur Valentin," the whip he kept coiled at his waist. When he was drunk, he confessed that out of fear that his servants would poison him, he had married one of his slaves (fathering three children upon her "who came out as black as coal") and made his wife taste all his food and drink.

Another character who would be forever fixed in Flora's memory was the toothless Captain Brandisco, a Venetian whose schooner was anchored in the bay of La Praia next to the *Mexicain*. He invited them to dine on his ship, and received them dressed like a comic opera player, in a hat topped with peacock feathers, the boots of a musketeer, tight red velvet trousers, and a shirt of shot silk studded with precious stones. He showed them a chest of glass beads that, he boasted, he bartered for blacks in the villages of Africa. His hatred of the English surpassed even that of the ex-seminarian Tappe. The English had surprised the Venetian at sea with a ship full of slaves, and confiscated his own vessel, his slaves, and everything he had on board, and sent him to prison for two years, where he had contracted the pyorrhea that made him lose his teeth. At dessert, Brandisco tried to sell Flora an alert-looking black boy to be her page. In order to convince her that the boy was healthy, he ordered him to remove his loincloth, and the adolescent immediately uncovered himself, smiling as he displayed his private parts.

Only three times did Flora leave the *Mexicain* to visit La Praia, and on each visit she saw soldiers from the colonial garrison flogging slaves by order of their masters in the scorchingly hot little square. The spectacle saddened and enraged her so much that she decided not to endure it anymore, and told Chabrié that she would remain on board ship until the day of their departure.

It was the first great lesson of your trip, Florita: the horrors of slavery, supreme injustice in this world of injustices that had to be remedied in order to make the world human. And yet, in *Peregrinations of a Pariah*—the book, published in 1838, in which you told the story of your journey to Peru—your account of your visit to La Praia included phrases like "the smell of the negro, which defies comparison, making one ill and lingering everywhere" for which you could never be sorry enough. The smell of the negro! How you later lamented that silly, stupid remark, the repetition of a commonplace among Parisian snobs. It wasn't the "smell of the negro" that was repugnant on that island, but the smell of poverty and cruelty, the fate of those Africans whom the European merchants had turned into commodities. Despite everything you had learned about injustice, you were still ignorant when you wrote *Peregrinations of a Pariah*.

Her last day in Lyon was the busiest of the four. She woke up with severe pains in her stomach, but to Eléonore, who advised her to stay in bed, she replied, "People like me aren't allowed to be sick." Half dragging herself, she went to the meeting that the Workers' Union committee had organized for her in a workshop with thirty tailors and cutters. They were all Icarian communists, and their bible (although many only knew it from hearing it discussed, since they were illiterate) was *Travels in Icaria*, Étienne Cabet's last book, published in 1840. In it, the old Carbonarist, under the guise of relating the adventures of a fictional English aristocrat, Lord Carisdall, in a fabulous, egalitarian country with no bars, cafés, prostitutes, or beggars—but with public toilets!—illustrated his conception of a future society in which economic equality would be achieved, money and business abolished, and collective property established through progressive taxation of income and inheritance. The tailors and cutters of Lyon were prepared to travel to Africa or America, like Robert Owen, to found Étienne Cabet's perfect society, and were saving to purchase land in the New World. They showed little enthusiasm for the project of a worldwide Workers' Union, which seemed a mediocre alternative when compared to their Icarian paradise, where there would be no poor, no social classes, no idlers, no servants, no private property; where all belongings would be held in common, and the State, "the sovereign Icar," would feed, clothe, educate, and entertain all citizens. By way of farewell, Flora resorted to sarcasm: it was selfish to turn one's back on the rest of the world to flee to a private Eden, and utterly naive to believe word for word what was written in *Travels in Icaria*, a book that was neither science nor philosophy—no more than a literary fantasy! Who, with the least bit of sense in his head, would take a novel as a book of doctrine and a guide to revolution? And what kind of revolution was it that held the family sacred and preserved the institution of marriage—the buying and selling of women to their husbands?

The bad feeling that she was left with by the tailors was erased at the farewell dinner organized for her by the Workers' Union committee at a weavers' meeting hall. The vast room was filled to overflowing with three hundred workers, who, over the course of the evening, gave Flora several ovations and sang "The Workers' Marseillaise," composed by a cobbler. The speakers said that *Le Censeur*'s slander had served only to strengthen Flora Tristán's cause, and to expose the envy that she awakened in those who had failed. She was so moved by this tribute that, she told them, it was worth being insulted by the Rittiezes of the world if the reward was such a night. This packed hall proved that the Workers' Union was unstoppable.

Eléonore and the rest of the committee members saw her off at the wharf at three in the morning. The twelve hours in the little boat on the Rhône—watching the mountains loom behind the riverbanks and seeing the sun rise over the cypress-covered peaks as they slipped toward Avignon—brought back memories of the crossing from Cape Verde to the coasts of South America in the *Mexicain*. For four months she never set foot on solid ground, seeing only the sea and the sky and her nineteen companions, convulsed by seasickness day after day in that floating prison. Worst was the crossing of the equator, in torrential rain that buffeted the ship and made it creak and groan as if it were about to come to pieces. Sailors and passengers had to be shackled to the bars and rings on deck so the waves wouldn't sweep them away.

Had the nineteen men on the *Mexicain* fallen in love with you, Florita? Probably. In any case, it was clear that all of them desired you, and that, in their forced captivity, they were agitated and tormented by being so near a woman with big black eyes, long Andalusian hair, a tiny waist, and gracious ways. You were sure that not only the adolescent cabin boy but also some of the sailors thought of you as they pleasured themselves in private, employing the same filthy methods you had discovered Ismaelillo, the Holy Eunuch, using in Bordeaux. The close quarters and forced deprivation heightened your charms, and they did all desire you, but none was ever disrespectful, and only Captain Zacharie Chabrié formally declared his love for you.

It had happened at La Praia, on one of those afternoons when everyone went ashore except for Flora, who didn't want to see the slaves being flogged. Chabrié stayed behind to keep her company. It was pleasant to talk to the polite Breton in the ship's prow, watching the sun set in a blaze of colors far off on the horizon. The sweltering heat had eased, a cool breeze blew, and the sky was phosphorescent. The frustrated tenor, not yet forty, was slightly stout, but he was so perfectly groomed and exquisitely courteous that at moments he seemed almost handsome. Despite your horror of sex, you couldn't help flirting with him, amused by the emotions you stirred in him when you threw your head back and laughed, or made a witty retort, fluttering your eyelashes, exaggerating the graceful motion of your hands, or extending a leg under your skirt to reveal a glimpse of your slender ankle. Chabrié would flush happily and sometimes, to entertain you, he would intone a ballad or an aria by Rossini, or a Viennese waltz in a strong, melodious voice. But that afternoon, perhaps emboldened by the forgiving dusk, or because you were being more charming than usual, the gentlemanly Breton couldn't restrain himself and, gently taking one of your hands between his, he lifted it to his lips, murmuring, "Forgive my boldness, mademoiselle. But I can wait no longer. I must tell you: I love you."

His long, tremulous declaration of love exuded sincerity and decency, courtesy, good breeding. You listened, taken aback. Did such men exist, then? Gallant, sensitive, considerate men, convinced that women should be treated with kid gloves, as they were in romance novels? The seaman was trembling, so mortified by his forwardness that you took pity on him and, though you did not formally accept his love, allowed him to hope. A serious mistake, Florita. You were impressed by his integrity and the purity of his intentions, and you told him that you would always love him as the best of friends. In an impulse that would bring you trouble later, you took Chabrié's blushing face in your hands and kissed him on the forehead. Crossing himself, the captain of the *Mexicain* thanked God for making him the happiest man on earth at that moment.

Over the next eleven years, Florita, did you ever regret having toyed with the affections of the good Zacharie Chabrié on that voyage? She asked herself this as the little ship on the Rhône approached Avignon. The answer was no, as it had been before. You didn't regret the games, flirtations, and lies that kept Chabrié on tenterhooks all the way to Valparaíso, believing that he was making progress, that at any moment Mademoiselle Flora Tristán would give him the definitive yes. You manipulated him shamelessly, tantalizing him with your ambiguous responses and those calculated moments of abandon when you permitted him to kiss your hands while he was visiting you in your cabin when the sea was calm for a moment; or when, all at once, in a rush of emotion, you allowed him to rest his head on your knees and stroked his thinning hair, encouraging him to keep telling you his life story: his travels, his dreams of being an opera singer as a young man in Lorient, the disappointment he suffered with the only woman he loved in his life before meeting you. More than once, you even let Chabrié's lips brush yours. Weren't you sorry? No.

The Breton had firmly believed that Flora was an unwed mother ever since she explained the silence she asked him to keep before the day she came aboard ship in Bordeaux. Since he was a committed Catholic, she thought that he would be scandalized to hear that she had had a child out of wedlock. But on the contrary, learning of her "disgrace" prompted Chabrié to propose marriage to her. He would adopt the girl, and they would go and live far from France, where no one could remind Florita of the despicable man who had besmirched her youth: Lima, California, Mexico, even India if she preferred. Although you never loved him, the truth was—wasn't it, Florita?—that sometimes you were tempted by the idea of accepting his offer. They would marry, and settle in a remote and exotic spot where no one knew you or could accuse you of bigamy. There you would lead a quiet, bourgeois life, without fear or hunger, under the protection of an impeccable gentleman. Could you have stood it, Andalusa? Absolutely not.

The Avignon wharf was before them. There would be no more probing of the past. Back to the present. To work! There was no time to waste, Florita. The salvation of mankind permitted no delays.

It wasn't easy to save the workers of Avignon, with whom she could barely communicate, since most of them spoke the regional tongue and hardly any French at all. In Paris, Agricol Perdiguier, that beloved veteran of the workers' associations, had given her some letters of introduction to people in his native city—he was called the Good Man of Avignon—despite being in disagreement with her Workers' Union theories. Thanks to his letters, Flora was able to hold meetings with the textile workers and the laborers on the Avignon-Marseille railroad, who were the best paid in the region (at two francs a day). But the meetings were not very successful because the men were so astoundingly ignorant. Despite being cruelly exploited, they never reflected on their situation but instead sat idle, resigned to their fate. At the meeting with workers from the textile factories, she sold just four copies of *The Workers' Union*, and at the gathering of railroad workers, ten. The people of Avignon had little desire to wage revolution.

When she learned that the workday in the five textile factories belonging to the richest industrialist of Avignon was twenty hours long, three or four hours longer than usual, she wanted to meet the man responsible. Monsieur Thomas was perfectly happy to see her. He lived in the ancient palace of the Dukes of Crillon, on the rue de la

Masse, where he arranged to meet her very early in the morning. Inside the gorgeous building was a jumble of furniture and paintings of different eras and styles, and the office of Monsieur Thomas—a bony man, bristling with nervous energy—was old and dirty, with unpainted walls and stacks of papers, boxes, and files on the floor, among which she could barely move.

"I demand no more of my workers than I demand of myself," he barked at Flora, when she, after explaining her mission, reproached him for giving the workers only four hours to sleep. "I work from dawn until midnight, personally overseeing the operation of my factories. A franc a day is a fortune for those worthless wretches. Don't be fooled by appearances, madame. They live like beasts because they don't know how to save. They spend what they make on alcohol. I, for your information, never touch a drop."

He explained to Flora that he didn't force them to accept his schedule. Anyone who didn't like the system could look for work elsewhere. For him it was no problem; when labor was lacking in Avignon, he imported it from Switzerland. He never had any difficulties with those brutes from the Alps: they worked quietly and gratefully on the wages he paid them. Slow-witted though they were, the Swiss did know how to save.

Without even considering it for an instant, he told Flora that he didn't intend to give her a cent for her Workers' Union project, because although he didn't know much about her ideas, there was something about them that struck him as anarchistic and subversive. For the same reason, he wouldn't buy a single book from her.

"I appreciate your frankness, Monsieur Thomas," said Flora, getting to her feet. "Since we'll never see each other again, allow me to tell you that you are neither a Christian nor a civilized being but a cannibal, a devourer of human flesh. If someday your workers hang you, you will have earned it."

The industrialist burst into laughter, as if Flora had paid him a compliment.

"I like women of character," he said, gleefully. "If I weren't so busy, I'd invite you to spend a weekend at my country estate in the Vaucluse. You and I would get along famously, my lady."

Not all the businessmen of Avignon were so crude. Monsieur Isnard received her courteously, listened to her, pledged twenty-five francs to the Workers' Union, and ordered twenty books to distribute among his "most intelligent" workers. She realized that unlike Lyon, which was a modern city in every sense, Avignon was politically prehistoric. The workers were apathetic, and the ruling classes were either monarchists or supporters of Napoleon, essentially the same thing in different guises. It didn't augur well for her crusade to eliminate injustice, but she still hoped for success.

Flora refused to let herself be demoralized by bad omens, or by the pains in her lower abdomen that tormented her remorselessly all ten days in Avignon. At night at her boardinghouse, The Bear, since it was hot and she couldn't sleep, she opened the window to feel the breeze and see the Provence sky clotted with stars. They were as numerous and brilliant as the stars you watched from the *Mexicain* on calm nights after the ship crossed the equator, at those dinners on deck at which Captain Chabrié provided the entertainment, singing Tyrolese songs and arias by Rossini, his favorite composer. Alfred David, the ship's owner, drew on his knowledge of astronomy to tell Flora the names of the stars and constellations, with the patience of a good schoolteacher. Captain Chabrié turned pale from jealousy. The Peruvian passengers who diligently helped you practice your Spanish must have made him jealous too; Fermín Miota from Cuzco, his cousin Don Fernando, and the old soldier Don José and his nephew Cesáreo competed to teach you verbs, correct your syntax, and demonstrate for you the phonetic variations of Peruvian Spanish. But although all the attentions the others lavished on you must have bothered Chabrié, he never said so. He was too proper and polite to make scenes. Since you had told him that you would give him your final answer when you arrived in Valparaíso, he was waiting, doubtless praying every night that you would say yes.

After the equatorial heat and a few weeks of dead calm and good weather, in which your seasickness subsided and the voyage became more bearable—you were able to devour the books by Voltaire, Victor Hugo, and Sir Walter Scott that you had brought with you—the *Mexicain* faced the worst part of its journey: Cape Horn. To round it in July or August was to risk shipwreck at any moment. The gale-force winds seemed to strive to toss the ship against the mountains of ice that loomed to meet them, and snow and hail fell, inundating the cabins and the hold. Day and night they lived half-frozen and in terror. Flora couldn't sleep for fear of drowning in those terrible weeks, and she admired the way the officers and sailors of the *Mexicain*, Chabrié first among them, managed to be everywhere at once, hoisting or lowering the sails, bailing water, protecting the machines, and repairing damages for twelve or fourteen hours straight without resting or eating. Most of the crew had little warm clothing. The sailors shivered with cold and were often overcome by fever. There were accidents—an engineer slipped from the mizzenmast and broke his leg—and a skin infection causing itching and boils swept half the ship. When they were at last around the cape and the ship began to sail up the coast of South America through the waters of the Pacific, toward Valparaíso, Captain Chabrié held a ceremony in which he gave thanks to God for bringing them through their trials alive. With the exception of Alfred David, who declared himself agnostic, passengers and crewmen hung on the captain's words. Flora did too. Until Cape Horn, you had never felt so close to death, Andalusa.

It was precisely that ceremony and the heartfelt prayers of Zacharie Chabrié that she was thinking of when it occurred to her to spend her few free hours one morning in Avignon on a visit to the old church of Saint-Pierre. The citizens of Avignon considered it one of the jewels of the city. Mass was being held, and Flora sat on a bench at the back of the nave in order not to disturb the faithful. Soon she felt hungry—because of her intestinal troubles, her meals were frugal—and since she had a roll in her pocket, she took it out and began to eat it, discreetly. Her discretion didn't do her much good, because almost immediately she was surrounded by a chorus of furious women with kerchiefs on their heads and missals and rosaries in their hands, who scolded her for disrespecting a sacred place and offending the worshipers during Holy Mass. She explained that it hadn't been her intent to offend anyone, that she had to eat something when she was tired because she had a stomach ailment. Instead of placating them, her explanations irritated them even more, and several of them began to call her "Jew," or "blasphemous Jew," in French and Provençal. Finally she left the church to keep the altercation from getting out of hand.

Was the incident she was subjected to the next day as she entered a weavers' workshop the result of what had happened in the church of Saint-Pierre? Blocking her way menacingly at the door to the workshop was a group of female workers, or the wives and relatives of workers, to judge by the extreme poverty of their attire. Some were barefoot. Flora's attempts to talk to them and discover why they were displeased with her, why they wanted to keep her from entering the workshop to meet with the weavers, were fruitless. The women, gesticulating furiously and shouting in a mix of French and the regional tongue, drowned her out. In the end, she managed more or less to understand them. They were afraid that their husbands would lose their jobs because of her, or that they might even be sent to prison. Some even screamed "Seductress!" and "Whore, whore!" shaking their fists at her. The two men who were accompanying her, disciples of Agricol Perdiguier, advised her to cancel her meeting with the weavers. With tempers at such a pitch, a physical attack couldn't be ruled out. If the police came, Flora would take the blame.

She opted instead to visit the papal palace, now turned into a barracks. She had no interest in the ponderous, ostentatious building, and even less in the paintings by Devéria and Pradier that adorned its massive walls—when one was fighting a war against society's ills there wasn't much time or energy to spare for the appreciation of art—but she was captivated by Madame Gros-Jean, the old doorkeeper who led visitors around the palace that so resembled a prison. Fat, blind in one eye, bundled up in blankets despite the fierce summer heat that made Flora sweat, full of energy, and a ceaseless talker, Madame Gros-Jean was a fanatical monarchist. Her commentary served as a pretext for her rant against the Great Revolution. According to her, all of France's misfortunes had begun in 1789, with those godless demons the Jacobins, especially the monstrous Robespierre. With macabre relish and violent condemnation, she listed the black deeds of the Robespierrian bandit Jourdan, dubbed the Beheader, who personally beheaded eighty-six martyrs in Avignon, and wanted to demolish this very palace. Fortunately, God hadn't let him and instead caused Jourdan to end his days on the guillotine. When Flora, just to see the look on the doorkeeper's face, said suddenly that the Great Revolution was the best thing to happen to France since the time of Saint Louis, and the most important event in human history, Madame Gros-Jean had to clutch a column, struck dumb by shock and indignation.

The last stretch of the *Mexicain*'s trip, along the South American coast, was the least unpleasant. Living up to its name, the Pacific Ocean was always calm, and Flora could read in greater tranquillity, not just her own books but those in the ship's little library, which held authors like Lord Byron and Chateaubriand, whom she read now for the first time. As she did, she took notes, studying diligently and discovering riveting ideas on every page. She also discovered the lapses in her education. But you had not really had an education, had you, Florita? That, not André Chazal, was your life's tragedy. What kind of education did women receive, even today? Would those women at Saint-Pierre have called you Jew, or the women at the weavers' workshop accused you of being a whore, if they had received an education worthy of the name? That was why the obligatory Workers' Union schools for women would revolutionize society.

The *Mexicain* dropped anchor in the port of Valparaíso 133 days after setting sail from Bordeaux, almost two months behind schedule. Valparaíso was a single long street, running parallel to the black sand beaches that lined the coast, and on it a multifarious crowd bustled, in which all the peoples of the planet seemed to be represented, to judge by the variety of languages that were spoken besides Spanish: English, French, Chinese, German, Russian. The city was the gateway to South America for all the world's merchants, mercenaries, and adventurers who came to make their fortunes on the continent.

Captain Chabrié helped her settle in a boardinghouse run by a Frenchwoman, Madame Aubrit. Her arrival caused a stir in the small port city. Everyone knew her uncle, Don Pío Tristán, the richest and most powerful man in the south of Peru, who for a while had been exiled here in Valparaíso. The news of the arrival of Don Pío's French niece—and she was from Paris, too!—threw the city into tumult. In the three first days, Flora had to resign herself to receiving a constant stream of visitors. The important families wanted to pay their regards to Don Pío's niece, each swearing that they were acquainted with Don Pío; at the same time, they wanted to see with their own eyes whether what legend said of Parisian women—that they were beautiful, elegant, and wanton—was really true.

With their visits came a piece of news that dropped on Flora like a bomb. Her old grandmother, Don Pío's mother, upon whom she had rested her hopes for being recognized and taken in by the family, had died in Arequipa on April 7, 1833, the same day Flora had turned thirty, the same day she had boarded the *Mexicain*. An inauspicious beginning to your South American adventure, Andalusa. Seeing her turn pale, Chabrié consoled her as best he could. Flora was going to seize the chance to tell him that she was too upset to give an answer to his offer of marriage, but he, guessing what she was about to say, wouldn't let her speak.

"No, Flora, don't say a thing. Not yet. This isn't the moment to discuss such an important matter. Continue your trip; go on to Arequipa to meet your family; settle your affairs. I'll come see you there, and then you can let me know your decision."

When Flora left Avignon for Marseille on July 18, 1844, she was more cheerful than she had been during her first few days in the papal city. She had established a Workers' Union committee of ten members—textile workers, railroad workers, and a baker—and attended two intense secret meetings with the Carbonarists, who, despite having been brutally suppressed, were still active in Provence. Flora explained her ideas to them, congratulated them on their courageous defense of their republican ideals, but managed to exasperate them by saying that it was childish foolishness to form secret societies; these were romantic fantasies as outdated as the Icarian plan to found a paradise in America. The fight had to be joined in the full light of day, in view of the whole world, here and everywhere, so that the ideas of the revolution would reach every worker and peasant—all of those who were exploited, without exception—because only they, by rising up, could transform society. The Carbonarists listened, taken aback. Some harshly reproached her for offering criticism no one had asked for. Others seemed impressed by her audacity. "After your visit, perhaps we Carbonarists will have to revise our prohibition on accepting women into our society," said their leader, Monsieur Proné, as he bade her farewell.

10

NEVERMORE

PUNAAUIA, APRIL 1897

When Pau'ura told him that she was pregnant, at the end of May
1896, Koké thought little of it. And neither did his *vahine*; in typical Maori fashion, she accepted her pregnancy with neither joy
nor bitterness, but placid fatalism. It had been a terrible time for
him, with the return of his sores, the pains in his ankle, and his financial woes after the last cent of Uncle Zizi's inheritance was spent. But
Pau'ura's pregnancy coincided with a change in his luck. Just as the
sores on his legs were beginning to heal again, he received a remittance of fifteen hundred francs from Daniel de Monfreid. Ambroise
Vollard had sold a few canvases and a sculpture, at last.

"Ever since they learned I was going to be the father of a Tahitian,
the Arioi have decided to protect me. From now on, with the help of
the gods of this land, all will be well," said Paul, half in jest and half
seriously, to the ex-soldier Pierre Levergos, a Frenchman who, after
turning in his uniform, had settled on a small orchard on the outskirts of Punaauia and sometimes came to smoke a pipe or drink rum
with Paul.

And all was well, for a while. With money and somewhat improved health—though he knew his ankle would always trouble him,
and he would limp for the rest of his life—he could, after paying his

debts, once again buy the casks of wine that sat greeting visitors at the door of his hut, and organize those Sunday meals at which the pièce de résistance was a runny, almost liquid omelet that he made himself with all the fanfare of a master chef. The parties again provoked the wrath of Punaauia's Catholic priest and Protestant minister, but Paul paid them no heed.

He was in good humor, cheerful, and, to his own surprise, moved to see how his *vahine*'s waist and belly had begun to thicken. In her first few months, the girl suffered none of the nausea and vomiting that had accompanied all of Mette Gad's pregnancies. On the contrary, Pau'ura went about her usual routine as if she hadn't even noticed there was a being germinating inside her. Beginning in September, when her belly began to swell, she acquired a kind of placidity, a cadenced slowness. She spoke slowly, breathed deeply, moved her hands in slow motion, and walked with her feet far apart so she wouldn't lose her balance. Koké spent much time watching her surreptitiously. When he saw her breathe deeply, bringing her hands to her belly, as if trying to feel the baby's heartbeat, he was overcome by an unfamiliar feeling: tenderness. Were you getting old, Koké? Maybe. Could a savage be stirred by the universally shared experience of paternity? Yes, evidently, since you were excited about this child of your seed that would soon be born.

His state of mind was reflected in five paintings that he finished quickly, all on the subject of motherhood: *Te arii vahine* (The Noblewoman), *No te aha oe riri* (Why Are You Angry?), *Te tamari no atua* (The Son of God), *Nave nave mahana* (Delightful Day), and *Te rerioa* (The Dream). Paintings in which you scarcely recognized yourself, Koké, since in them life showed itself without drama, tensions, or violence; apathy and tranquillity reigned in sumptuously colored landscapes, and human beings seemed mere reflections of the paradisiacal vegetation. The work of a contented artist!

The baby, a girl, was born three days before Christmas 1896, at sunset, the birth attended by the village midwife in the hut where they lived. It was a delivery without complications, the sound of the children of Punaauia practicing Christmas carols at the Protestant and Catholic churches in the background. Koké and Pierre Levergos celebrated the event with glasses of absinthe, sitting outside, singing Breton songs accompanied by the painter on his mandolin.

"A raven," said Koké suddenly. He stopped playing, and pointed into the big mango tree nearby.

"There are no ravens in Tahiti," the ex-soldier exclaimed, surprised, jumping up to see. "No ravens and no snakes, either. Maybe you didn't know?"

"It is a raven," Koké insisted. "I've seen many in my life. At Marie Henry's house—the Doll's house—in Le Pouldu, one came to sleep on my windowsill every night, to warn me of some misfortune I couldn't fathom. We became friends. That bird is a raven."

But they couldn't settle the matter beyond a doubt, because as they approached the mango tree, the dark shape took flight, its winged shadow vanishing.

"The raven is a bird of ill omen, as I know very well," said Koké. "The one in Le Pouldu came to bring me tidings of a tragedy. This one has come with news of another catastrophe. My eczema will return, or this hut will be struck by lightning in the next storm and burn down."

"It was another kind of bird, who can say what kind," maintained Pierre Levergos. "No raven has ever been seen on Tahiti, or Moorea, or any of these islands."

Two days later, as Koké and Pau'ura were arguing over where to take the baby to be baptized—she wanted the Catholic church, but he didn't, because Father Damian was a worse enemy than Reverend Riquelme, who was more tractable—the child stiffened, began to turn blue as if she couldn't breathe, and lay still. When they reached the clinic in Punaauia, she was already dead, "of a congenital defect in the respiratory system," according to the death certificate signed by the public health official.

They buried the child in the Punaauia cemetery, with no religious ceremony. Pau'ura didn't cry, not that day or any of the following days, and little by little she resumed her daily life, never mentioning her dead daughter. Paul didn't speak of her either, but he thought day and night about what had happened. The reflection began to torment him as the *Portrait of Aline Gauguin* had months before, the whereabouts of which he had never discovered.

You thought about the dead child, and the sinister bird—it was a raven, you were sure of it, no matter how many times natives and colonists assured you that there were no ravens in Tahiti. The winged silhouette stirred up old memories from a time that now seemed impossibly distant, though it wasn't so long ago. In the modest library of the Military Club of Papeete, and in Auguste Goupil's private library—the only collection worthy of the name on the island—he tried to find some publication in which the French translation of "The Raven," by Edgar Allan Poe, might appear. You had heard the poem read aloud by the translator, your friend the poet Stéphane Mallarmé, in his house on the rue de Rome, at those Tuesday gatherings you once attended. You vividly recalled slim, elegant Stéphane's description of the grim period of Poe's life in which—ravaged by alcohol, drugs, hunger, and family troubles in Philadelphia—he wrote the first version of the text. In Stéphane's translation, so stark and at once so harmonious, sensual, and macabre, Poe's tremendous poem pierced you to the marrow, Paul. After the reading you were inspired to do a portrait of Mallarmé, in homage to the man who had been capable of rendering Poe's masterwork so cleverly in French. But Stéphane didn't like the painting. Maybe he was right; maybe you hadn't managed to capture his elusive poet's face.

At the farewell dinner his friends had held for him at the Café Voltaire on March 23, 1891, on the eve of his first trip to Tahiti—it was hosted by Stéphane Mallarmé himself—he remembered that the poet read two translations of "The Raven," his own and that of the fearsome poet Baudelaire, who boasted of having spoken with the devil. Later, in thanks for the portrait, Stéphane gave Paul a signed copy of the small private edition of his translation, published in 1875. Where was that little book? He searched through his chest of odds and ends but couldn't find it. Which of your friends had taken it? On which of your innumerable moves had you lost the poem you now urgently wanted to read again, as urgently as you craved alcohol and laudanum when your pains returned? The discouraging memory of your failed attempts to recover your mother's portrait kept you from begging your friends to search for Stéphane's book.

He didn't remember the lines, only the refrain—"Nevermore"—and also the tale and the way it unfolded. It was if it had been written for you, Koké, as a Tahitian, at precisely this moment of your life. You felt yourself to be—you were—the student who, on that stormy midnight, absorbed in his reading and reflections, his heart broken by the death of his beloved Lenore, is interrupted by a raven. It bursts in through the window, blown by the gale or sent from some dark place, and perches on the white marble bust of Pallas that guards the door. You remembered with fervent clarity the poem's melancholy and its macabre shadings, its allusions to death, horror, misfortune, hell ("night's Plutonian shore"), darkness, the uncertainty of the beyond. To all the questions the student asks about his beloved and the future, the bird responds with its sinister croak ("Nevermore") until an anguished consciousness of eternity, of time come to a standstill, is forged. And then come the final lines, when the tale abandons the student and his black visitor, condemned to sit face to face until the end of time.

You had to paint, Koké. The flicker deep inside that you hadn't felt for so long was there again, urging you on, galvanizing you, making you incandescent. Yes, yes, of course you must paint. And what would you paint? Feverish, consumed by excitement and the rush of blood that lifted the hair on his skin, rose to his head, and made him feel confident, powerful, triumphant, he stretched a canvas and clamped it to the easel. He began to paint the dead child, trying to resuscitate her out of old Maori beliefs and superstitions, of which no trace remained, or which the present-day Maori kept so hidden, so secret, that they were veiled from you, Koké. He worked for whole days, morning and afternoon, with a break at midday for a short nap, reinventing the tiny body, the mottled face. At dusk on the third day, when he could no longer work comfortably in the fading light, he slashed a brushful of white paint across the image he had so carefully constructed. A livid disgust pulsed behind his ears and eyes—the kind of rage that possessed him when, after a fit of enthusiasm spurred him to work, he realized he had failed. What the canvas showed you was tripe, Koké. Then, in addition to his disappointment, frustration, and sense of impotence, he felt a sharp pain in his joints and bones. He left his brushes next to the palette and decided to drink himself senseless. As he was crossing the bedroom toward the front door and the cask of bordeaux, he saw, without seeing, Pau'ura lying naked on her side, her face turned toward the rectangular openings in the wall through which, in a cobalt blue sky, the first stars were showing. His *vahine*'s eyes rested on him for an instant, indifferent, and then turned back toward the sky, serenely or perhaps dully. There was something mysterious and hermetic about Pau'ura's chronic disengagement, something that intrigued him. He stopped short, went to her, and stood there watching her. You had a strange feeling, a premonition.

What you were seeing was what you had to paint, Koké. That very instant. Without speaking, he went to his studio, retrieved his sketchbook and a few pieces of charcoal, returned to the bedroom, and sat down on the mat beside the bed, facing Pau'ura. She didn't move or ask any questions as he, with a sure hand, made two, three, four sketches of the girl lying on her side. Every once in a while, Pau'ura closed her eyes, overwhelmed by sleepiness, then opened them again and rested them on Koké for a moment, without the least curiosity. Motherhood had made her hips broader and rounder, and lent her belly a majestic heaviness that made you think of the bellies and hips of Ingres's languid odalisques, and the queens and goddesses of Rubens and Delacroix. But no, no, Koké. This marvelous body, the skin matte with golden highlights, the solid thighs extending into strong, well-shaped legs, wasn't European or Western or French. It was Tahitian. It was Maori. This was evident in the carelessness and freedom with which Pau'ura lay, in the unconscious sensuality she exuded from all her pores, even her locks of black hair made blacker by the yellow cushion—its color a gold so rich that it made you think of the mad Dutchman's intense golds, which the two of you spent so much time discussing in Arles. The air was thick with an arousing, inviting smell. At the sight of your *vahine*, naked, in the providential pose that had rescued you from depression, thick desire began to intoxicate you more than the wine you had been about to drink.

His cock stiffened, but he didn't stop drawing. To interrupt his work now would be sacrilege; the same spell would not descend again. By the time he had what he needed, Pau'ura had fallen asleep. He felt drained, but possessed of a sense of well-being and great peace. Tomorrow you would begin the painting again, Koké, this time without hesitation. You knew exactly what you would paint.

And you knew, too, that behind the golden nude lying on a bed, her head resting on a yellow cushion, there would be a raven. And the painting would be called *Nevermore*.

At noon the next day, his friend Pierre Levergos came up to the hut as he often did, to drink and talk. Koké dismissed him abruptly. "Don't come back until I call you, Pierre. I don't want to be interrupted, not by you or anyone."

He didn't ask Pau'ura to lie in the same position again; it would have been like asking the sky to reproduce the half-light in which he had seen his *vahine*, a light just beginning to dissolve and blur objects, plunging them into shadow, making them indistinct shapes. Never again would she fall into that spontaneous blankness, that absolute lassitude in which he had surprised her. The picture was so vivid in his mind that he was able to re-create it easily, without wavering for a second in sketching the outline of the figure. It was uncommonly difficult, however, to bathe her image in that fading, slightly bluish light, the eerie, magical, miraculous aura that you were convinced would give *Nevermore* its hallmark, its character. He worked the shape of the feet carefully, just as he remembered them, distended, terrestrial, the toes separated, conveying a sense of solidity, of always having been in direct contact with the earth, of carnal commerce with nature. And he labored over the bloody smudge of discarded cloth next to Pau'ura's right foot and leg: a flickering flame, a clot trying to make its way through that sensual body.

He noticed that there was a close correspondence between this canvas and the one he had painted of Teha'amana in 1892, *Manao tupapao*, his first Tahitian masterpiece. This would be another masterpiece, Koké. Deeper, more mature than the first; colder, less melodramatic, perhaps more tragic. Instead of Teha'amana and her fear of the specter, here Pau'ura, after the ordeal of losing her daughter shortly after birth, lies passive and resigned in the knowing Maori attitude before fate, here represented by the crow without eyes, taking the place of the demon in *Manao tupapao*. When you painted that other canvas five years ago, you were still encumbered with much of the residue of the Romantic fascination with evil, the macabre, and the lugubrious, like Baudelaire, poet enamored of Lucifer, whom

Baudelaire one night claimed to have recognized sitting in a Montparnasse bistro, striking up a conversation with him about aesthetics. Those Romantic-literary trappings had disappeared. The crow was tropicalized, turned a greenish color, with a gray beak and smoke-spotted wings. In this pagan world, the reclining woman accepted her limitations, knowing herself to be powerless before the secret, cruel forces that descend suddenly upon human beings to destroy them. Against such forces, primitive wisdom—the wisdom of the Arioi—doesn't rebel, weep, or protest. It faces them philosophically, consciously, resignedly, as the tree and the mountain face the storm, and the sand on the beach confronts the sea that washes over it.

When the nude was finished, he furnished the surrounding space lavishly, making it rich in detail and using many different colors in subtle combinations. The mysterious, shifting evening light charged each object with ambiguity. All the motifs of your private world appeared, giving your personal stamp to a composition that was, nevertheless, unequivocally Tahitian. As well as the sightless crow in tropical colors, on different panels there were imaginary flowers, swollen tuberous shapes, plantlike ships with sails spread, a sky of floating clouds that might be painted on a canvas covering the wall, or might be the sky showing through an open window of the room. The two women talking behind the reclining girl, one with her back turned, the other facing sideways—who were they? You didn't know; there was something ominous and menacing about them, something that made them seem crueler than the shadowy demon of *Manao tupapao*, masked by the ordinariness of their appearance. It was enough to take a closer look at the reclining girl to realize that, despite the tranquillity of her pose, her eyes were slanted to the side: she was trying to listen to the conversation taking place behind her, a conversation that made her uneasy. The little Japanese flowers that had come automatically to your brush ever since you discovered the Japanese printmakers of the Meiji period appeared on different objects in the work: the cushion, the sheet. But now the secret ambiguities of the primitive world were expressed in those little flowers, too, since they changed depending on the viewer's perspective, becoming butterflies, comets, drifting shapes. When he finished the painting—he spent nearly ten days polishing it and reworking the details—he felt happy, sad, empty. He called Pau'ura. After looking at it for a while in a blank way, she shook her head without much enthusiasm.

"I don't look like that. That woman is old. I'm much younger."

"You're right," he replied. "You're young. That woman, she's eternal."

He slept for a while, and when he woke up, went looking for Pierre Levergos. He invited him to Papeete, to celebrate the masterpiece he had just completed. In the little port bars, they drank anything they could, all night without stopping—absinthe, rum, beer—until they both collapsed. They tried to go into an opium den near the cathedral, but the Chinese threw them out; they slept on the floor of a tavern. The next day, returning to Punaauia in the public coach, Paul's guts churned; he retched, and the contents of his stomach were poisonously acidic. But even in this wretched state, he packed up the canvas carefully and sent it to Daniel de Monfreid, with a brief message: "Since this is a masterpiece, if you can't get a good price for it, I'd prefer that you not sell it."

When a response came four months later from Monfreid, saying that Ambroise Vollard had sold *Nevermore* for five hundred francs on the first day he showed the painting in his gallery, Paul had left Punaauia and was living in Papeete. He had found a job as an assistant draftsman in the colonial administration's Department of Public Works, for which he earned 150 francs. It was enough for him to live on, modestly. He had stopped going around half naked, in just a pareu; now he dressed Western-style and wore shoes, like a functionary. Pau'ura had left him—she disappeared one day with her handful of things, without saying a word—and depressed by her departure and the death of his daughter, Aline, which troubled him more the more time passed, he had sold the house in Punaauia and sworn publicly, before a group of friends, that he would never paint so much as a stroke again, even on a scrap of paper, or sculpt anything, even from a breadcrumb. From now on, he would devote himself simply to surviving, without making any kind of plans. When they asked why he had made such a radical decision, not sure whether he was serious or whether this was alcohol-induced delirium, he replied that after *Nevermore* anything he could paint would be worthless. *Nevermore* was his swan song.

There then began a period of his life in which everyone in Papeete was always watching him, asking themselves how much longer his agonies would be prolonged; he seemed to have entered the final stage of his existence and to be doing everything possible to speed his death. He lived in a boardinghouse on the outskirts of Papeete, where the city disappeared, swallowed up by the forest. Each morning he left home very early on his way to the Department of Public Works; because of his limp, the trip took him twice as long as it would have taken a man walking normally. His work was little more than symbolic—Governor Gustave Gallet had hired him as a favor—since he drew the plans he was assigned so clumsily and with such lack of enthusiasm that they had to be redone. No one said anything to him. They all feared his temper, those fits of rage that now seized him not just when he was drunk but when he was sober, too.

He ate almost nothing, and grew very thin; there were purplish circles under his eyes, and his face was so haggard that his broken nose seemed even bigger and more crooked, like the noses of the idols he once liked to carve in wood, claiming that they were ancient gods of the Maori pantheon.

From work he proceeded directly to the little port bars, of which there were now twelve. He moved slowly alone along the wharf road, the quai du Commerce, limping, leaning on his cane, with clear evidence of physical suffering on his face, brooding, surly, never returning anyone's greeting. He who had had periods of great sociability with the natives and colonists became withdrawn, remote. One day he would choose the tables of one bar, the next day another. He would drink a glass of absinthe, rum, wine, or beer, and after two or three swallows his eyes would turn glassy, he'd stumble over his words, and his gestures would become slow and clumsy, like those of a confirmed drunkard.

Then he would talk to the barmen, the prostitutes, the loafers, or the drunks around him, or to Pierre Levergos, who came from Punaauia to keep him company, pitying his loneliness. According to the ex-soldier, those who thought Paul was about to die were wrong.

In his opinion, something even worse was happening to him: he was losing his mind; his thoughts were muddled. He spoke of his daughter, Aline, dead in Copenhagen at the age of twenty before he could even say goodbye to her, and he hurled vicious blasphemies and imprecations against the Catholic Church. He accused it of having exterminated the local gods, the Arioi, and of poisoning and corrupting the healthy, free, openhearted customs of the natives, imposing upon them the prejudices, prohibitions, and mental vices that had reduced Europe to its current state of decadence. His hatreds and rages had many targets. Some days he focused on the Chinese living in Tahiti, whom he accused of wanting to extend their yellow empire and eliminate the Tahitians and colonists. Or he became caught up in long, incomprehensible soliloquies on art's need to exchange the Western model of beauty created by the Greeks, with its harmoniously proportioned white men and women, for the unharmonious, asymmetrical, and bold aesthetic values of primitive peoples, whose prototypes of beauty were more original, varied, and impure than European prototypes.

It didn't matter to him whether anyone was listening or not, because if someone interrupted him with a question, he gave no sign that he had noticed, or silenced them with an obscenity. He remained immersed in his own world, becoming progressively less open to conversation with others. Worst were his rages, which led him to suddenly insult random sailors recently arrived in Papeete, or try to clout with a chair any unlucky patron who happened to glance his way. Then, the gendarmes would haul him off to the police station and make him sleep in a cell. Although those who knew him ignored his taunts, the same was not true of sailors passing through, who sometimes came to blows with him. And this time it was Paul who had the worst of it, his face bruised and his body battered. He was only forty-nine years old, but he was as ruined in body as he was in spirit.

Another of Koké's obsessions was going to live in the Marquesas. Anyone who had been to those distant colonies, the nearest more than fifteen hundred kilometers from Tahiti, tried to dissuade him of the fantastic idea he had conceived of the islands, but soon gave up, realizing he wasn't listening. His mind no longer seemed capable of distinguishing between fantasy and reality. He said that everything that had been corrupted and annihilated in Tahiti and the other islands in the archipelago by Catholic priests and Protestant ministers, as well as French colonists and Chinese tradesmen, was still intact, virgin, pure, authentic in the Marquesas. There, the Maori people were still what they had always been: a proud, free, barbaric, hardy, primitive people living in harmony with nature and their gods, still innocently enjoying nudity, paganism, feasts, music, sacred rites, the art of communicating through tattoos, collective and ritual sex, and the life-giving practice of cannibalism. He had been seeking all this since he broke free of the bourgeois shell binding him since childhood, and he had spent a fruitless quarter of a century on the trail of that earthly paradise. He had looked for it in tradition-bound, Catholic Brittany, proud of its faith and customs, but there it was already sullied by tourist painters and Western modernism. Nor had he found it in Panama, Martinique, or here in Tahiti, where the displacement of primitive culture by European ways had already dealt a death blow to the vital core of the island's higher civilization, of which just a few miserable shreds remained. That was why he had to leave. As soon as he got some money together, he would buy a ticket for the Marquesas. He would burn his Western clothes, his guitar and accordion, his canvases and brushes. He would walk into the forest until he came to an isolated village, and there he would make his home. He would learn to worship the bloodthirsty gods who sharpened man's instincts, dreams, imagination, and desires, who never sacrificed the body to reason. He would study the art of tattoo making, and master its labyrinthine system of symbols, the coded knowledge that preserved intact a marvelously rich cultural history. He would learn to hunt, dance, and pray in the elemental Maori language even older than Tahitian, and he would regenerate himself by eating the flesh of his fellow man. "I'll never put myself within reach of your teeth, Koké," said Pierre Levergos, the only person he allowed to joke with him.

Behind his back, everyone laughed at him. They repeated his mad ravings, and when they weren't calling him "the Barbarian" or "the Cripple" they called him "the Cannibal." The way he mixed things up when he set about recalling his past made it clear that he wasn't quite right in the head anymore. He boasted of being a direct descendant of Moctezuma, the last Aztec emperor, and if anyone respectfully reminded him that a few days before he had claimed that he was descended in a straight line from a viceroy of Peru, he said it was quite true, that he had also had a grandmother, Flora Tristán, who was an anarchist in the days of Louis Philippe and that, as a boy, he helped her prepare the bombs and gunpowder for her terrorist attacks on bankers. He wasn't afraid to make nonsensical claims or grossly anachronistic assertions; his memories were the momentary inventions of someone disconnected from reality, of a mind that had fabricated a past for itself because its real past was eroded by illnesses, remedies, madness, and drink.

No colonist, tradesman, or officer from the small garrison ever invited him home, nor was he permitted to enter the Military Club. To the families of the small colonial society of Tahiti-nui, he became a leper: because he had publicly cohabitated with native women; because he had consorted with prostitutes and engaged in openly scandalous and depraved behavior, in Mataiea as well as in Punaauia (behavior wildly exaggerated by Papeete's rumor mills); and because of the bad name he was given by the island's priests and ministers (especially Father Damian) who, although they maintained an intense rivalry in the contest for native souls for their respective churches, were agreed in considering the drunken and degenerate painter a public menace, a disgrace to society, and a source of immoral behavior. He might commit a crime at any moment. What else could one expect of the sort of person who publicly praised cannibalism?

One day a pregnant native girl appeared at the Department of Public Works, asking for him. It was Pau'ura. Casually, as if they had last seen each other only yesterday—"Hello, Koké"—she showed him her belly, a half-smile on her face. She had her little bundle of clothes in her hand.

"Have you come to stay with me?"

Pau'ura nodded.

"Is that my child in your belly?"

The girl nodded again, quite certain, a playful gleam in her eye.

He was very happy. But complications immediately arose, inevitable in any business in which you were involved, Koké. The owner of the boardinghouse refused to let Pau'ura share Paul's room, saying that her boardinghouse was modest but decent, and she would permit no unmarried couples under her roof, much less a white man and a native woman. The couple then made a dismal round of all the private homes in Papeete that took in guests. All refused to accept them. Paul and Pau'ura had to take refuge in Punaauia, on Pierre Levergos's little property. The ex-soldier agreed to put them up until they could find a place to live, an offer that earned him the enmity of Father Damian and Reverend Riquelme.

Living in Punaauia and working in Papeete made Koké's life difficult. He had to take the first public coach before the sun had risen, and he still arrived at the Department of Public Works half an hour late. To make up for his tardiness, he offered to stay half an hour after the office had closed.

As if he didn't have enough problems already, he became consumed by a mad idea: to sue the pensions and boardinghouses of Papeete that had refused him lodging with his *vahine*, accusing them of having violated French law, which prohibited discrimination against its citizens on grounds of race or religion. He wasted hours, days, consulting lawyers and speaking to the public prosecutor about the amount of compensation that he and Pau'ura might request for their grievances. They all tried to dissuade him, pointing out that he would never win such a case, since the law upheld the right of the owners and managers of hotels and boardinghouses to refuse people who, in their judgment, were not respectable. And what kind of respectability could he claim, he who lived in flagrant adultery, illegitimate union, or bigamy—with a native woman, no less—had been involved in countless drunken brawls, as documented in police records, and was also accused of having fled the hospital without paying what he owed? It was out of pity that the doctors of the Vaiami Hospital hadn't pressed charges; but if he persisted in going to court, the matter would come to light and Koké would be the one to suffer.

It wasn't these arguments that made him give up his efforts, but a joint letter from his friends Daniel de Monfreid and good old Schuff, which reached him in the middle of 1897 like manna from heaven. It came accompanied by a remittance of fifteen hundred francs, and it announced that there would soon be another installment. Ambroise

Vollard was beginning to sell his paintings and sculptures, not just to one customer, but to many. He had promises from purchasers that could be cemented at any minute. All of this seemed to herald a change in his fortunes. His two friends were pleased that collectors were at last beginning to recognize what some critics and painters were already admitting in low voices: that Paul was a great artist, that he had revolutionized contemporary aesthetics. "We don't disregard the possibility that the same thing could happen to you that happened to Vincent," they added. "After having systematically ignored him, now everyone is fighting over his paintings, and paying astonishing sums for them."

On the same day he received the letter, Paul resigned from the Department of Public Works. In Punaauia, he bought a small plot of land, not far from Pierre Levergos's little property, where, since Pierre's house was tiny, he and his *vahine* slept in an open-walled shelter, next to the orchard. With the letter and the check from his friends, he convinced the Bank of Papeete to give him a loan for his new house, the plans for which he drew himself, and whose construction he closely monitored.

Since Pau'ura's return, his improvement was noticeable. He began eating again, his color returned, and above all, he recovered his spirits. Once again he was heard laughing and being sociable with his neighbors. It wasn't just the presence of his *vahine* that cheered him; it was also the prospect of being the father of a Tahitian. That would mean he finally belonged to this land, and would be evidence that the Arioi accepted him at last.

In a few months, the new dwelling was habitable. It was smaller than the old one but more solid, with walls and a roof that would withstand the wind and rain. He hadn't resumed painting, but Pierre Levergos no longer believed that he would keep his promise of never taking up his brushes again. Art and painting were frequent topics of conversation. The ex-soldier listened, pretending greater interest than he felt, as Paul criticized painters he had never heard of, and defended incomprehensible ideas. How was it possible for there to be a "revolution" in painting, in any sense of the word? The ex-soldier sat stunned when Paul, at his most inspired moments, claimed that Europe's—and France's—tragedy had begun when painting and sculpture stopped being part of people's lives as they had been until the Middle Ages, and in every ancient civilization: Egyptian, Greek, Babylonian, Scythian, Inca, Aztec, and here, too, among the ancient Maori. Life was still lived the old way in the Marquesas, where he and Pau'ura and the child would move soon.

The unspeakable illness cut short Koké's recuperation, returning suddenly in the month of March with more fury than ever. The sores on his legs opened again, oozing pus. This time, the salve of arsenic failed to ease the burning. At the same time, the pain in his ankle grew worse. The druggist in Papeete refused to continue selling him laudanum without a doctor's prescription. With his head hanging, utterly humiliated, he had to let himself be taken to the Vaiami Hospital. They refused to admit him until he paid what he still owed from the time he escaped out the window. He also had to leave a deposit as guarantee that this time he would pay his bill.

He spent eight days in the hospital. Dr. Lagrange agreed to prescribe laudanum for him again, but warned Paul not to continue abusing the narcotic, which was largely responsible for his loss of memory and the episodes of disorientation of which he was now complaining—not knowing who he was, where he was, or where he was going. Then, approaching the matter in a very roundabout way so as not to hurt his feelings, the doctor ventured to suggest that given the state of his health it might be better for him to return to France, his native land, where he could spend his last years—years which would be very painful, he had to understand—among people he knew, people of his own language, blood, and race. Paul's response was to raise his voice.

"My language, my blood, and my race are those of Tahiti-nui, doctor. I'll never set foot in France again, a country to which I owe only failure and heartache."

There were still sores on his legs when he left the clinic, and the pain in his ankle hadn't subsided. But laudanum dulled the itching and burning, and blunted his despair. It was quite an experience to be detached bit by bit from his surroundings, to sink into a state of pure sensation, imagery, and spiraling fantasy, freed from the pain and revulsion he felt at knowing he was rotting alive, that the wounds on his legs, their stench not masked by the ointment-coated bandages, were bringing to the surface all the sins, filth, shameful deeds, cruelties, and mistakes of a lifetime. A lifetime that apparently was nearing its end, Paul. Would you die before you reached the Marquesas?

On April 19, 1898, Koké and Pau'ura's son was born, a good-sized, healthy boy who by mutual agreement they called Émile.

II

AREQUIPA

MARSEILLE, JULY 1844

◈

There are cities one hates instinctively, thought Flora the moment
she stepped down from the coupé that had brought her from Avignon with a priest and a salesman as her traveling companions. She
eyed the buildings of Marseille with displeasure. Why did you hate a
city you hadn't even seen yet, Florita? Later, she would say it was because it was prosperous: a little Babylon of greedy adventurers and
immigrants, overpopulated by the well-to-do. Excessive commerce
and wealth had produced in its inhabitants a mercantile spirit and
fierce individualism that afflicted even the poor and downtrodden,
among whom she detected no inclination toward solidarity but rather
a stony indifference to the ideas of workers' unity and universal fra-
ternity that she had come to instill in them. Cursed city, whose people thought only of lucre! Money was society's poison; it corrupted
everything and made human beings greedy and rapacious beasts.

As if Marseille wanted to give her reasons to justify her dislike of
it, everything went wrong from the moment she set foot on Marseillais soil. The Hôtel Montmorency was horrid and full of fleas, re-
minding her of her arrival in Peru in September 1833, at the port of
Islay, where on her first night—at the home of Don Justo, the postmaster—she was bitten so much she thought she would die. The next

day she escaped to an inn in the center of Marseille, run by a Spanish family; they gave her a big, plain room and didn't object to her receiving groups of workers there. The poet-bricklayer Charles Poncy, composer of the Workers' Union anthem, whom Flora had counted on to be her guide in her meetings with the workers of Marseille, had gone to Algiers, leaving a little note behind: his nerves were frayed and his body weary; he needed rest. What could one expect of poets, even if they were workers, too? They were simply monsters of egotism, blind and deaf to the fortunes of their fellows, narcissists mesmerized by the sufferings they invented only in order to immortalize them in verse. Perhaps, Andalusa, for the Workers' Union of the future, you should consider outlawing not just money but poets, as Plato did in his Republic.

To crown it all, beginning the first day in Marseille her ailments, especially her stomach troubles, returned. As soon as she ate anything, bloating and cramps made her double over in pain. Resolved not to acknowledge defeat, she carried on with her visits and meetings, taking in nothing but clear broth or gruel, which her aching belly managed to digest.

On her second day in Marseille, after a meeting with a group of shoemakers, bakers, and tailors organized by two Fourierist hairdressers whom she had written from Paris on the recommendation of Victor Considérant, she witnessed a scene at the docks that made her blood boil. From the wharf, she was watching a recently docked ship unload. This allowed her to see with her own eyes the workings of the white-slave system that she had just been told about at the hairdressers' meeting. "The longshoremen won't come to see you, madame," they had told her. "They treat the poor worse than anyone." The dockworkers had a license that gave them the sole right to work in the holds of the ships, loading or unloading goods and helping passengers with their baggage. Many preferred to subcontract their jobs to the Genoese, Turks, or Greeks who crowded at the head of the wharf, waving and shouting, begging to be called. The dockworkers received a franc and a half for each trip, which was a good wage, and they gave the subcontracted laborers fifty centimes, so that without lifting a finger they pocketed a franc of commission. What drove Flora mad was noticing one of the longshoremen pass an enormous valise—almost a chest—to a Genoese woman, tall and strong, but heavily pregnant. Hunched over with the load on her shoulder, the woman grunted as she crept toward the passenger's carriage, her face flushed and dripping with sweat at the effort. The longshoreman handed her twenty-five centimes. And when she, in broken French, began to demand the other twenty-five, he threatened and swore at her.

Flora strode up to him as he was returning to the ship with a group of companions.

"Do you know what you are, you wretch?" she asked, beside herself. "A traitor and a coward. Aren't you ashamed to treat that poor woman the same way you and your brethren are treated by those who exploit you?"

The man stared at her uncomprehendingly, doubtless wondering whether she was mad. At last, amid the others' laughter and jeering, he asked her, with a show of offense, "Who are you? And what right do you have to meddle with me?"

"My name is Flora Tristán," she said angrily. "Remember it well. Flora Tristán. I've devoted my life to fighting the ill-treatment of the poor. Not even the bourgeoisie are as despicable as workers who exploit other workers."

The man's eyes—he was big, with a sloping belly, bow legs, and eyebrows that met in the middle—kindled in indignation.

"Try whoring—you'll have better luck at it," he exclaimed, moving away and making a rude gesture at the gawkers on the wharf.

Flora was shivering and had a high fever when she returned to the inn. After taking a few spoonfuls of broth, she got into bed. Though she was well covered and it was the middle of summer, she was cold. For several hours she was unable to fall asleep. Oh, Florita, this miserable body of yours couldn't keep pace with your anxieties, your obligations, your plans, your will. Were you really so old? At forty-one a human being should be full of life. How you had deteriorated, Andalusa. Just eleven years ago, you were able to stand that terrible voyage from France to Valparaíso so well, and then the trip from Valparaíso to Islay, and finally the assault of those fleas that bit you all night. What a welcome Peru gave you!

Islay: a single street of bamboo huts, a beach of black sand, and a harbor without a pier, where passengers were brought ashore just like freight and animals, lowered on pulleys from the ship's deck onto wooden lighters. The arrival in Islay of the French niece of powerful Don Pío Tristán caused a commotion in the little port town of one thousand. That was why you stayed in the best house in town, which belonged to postmaster Justo de Medina. It may have been the best, but it was still infested by the fleas that reigned everywhere in Islay. On the second night, upon seeing that you were bitten from head to toe and scratching ceaselessly, Don Justo's wife divulged the formula that allowed her to sleep. Five chairs in a row, the last of which must touch the bed. Standing on the first, remove your dress and make the slave carry it—and the fleas on it—away. Take off your undergarments on the second chair, and rub the exposed parts of your body with a mixture of warm water and cologne to dislodge the fleas on your skin. And so on, removing the rest of your clothes on each new chair and rubbing the respective body parts uncovered, until you reached the fifth chair, where a nightdress soaked in cologne was waiting; for as long as it was damp, it would keep the tiny insects away. This allowed one to fall asleep. Two or three hours later, the fleas would return to the attack, emboldened, but by then you were already asleep, and with habit and a little luck, you wouldn't feel them.

It was the first lesson you learned in your father's homeland, Florita, the country of your uncle Pío and your vast paternal family, which you had come to explore in hopes of recovering some part of Don Mariano's inheritance. You would spend a year in Peru, and it was there that you would discover almost fantastical opulence, learning what it was like to live in the midst of a family that gave itself airs and had no material worries.

How strong and healthy you were then, Andalusa, at the age of thirty. If you hadn't been, you couldn't have borne those forty hours on horseback, scaling the Andes and crossing the desert between Islay and Arequipa. From the edge of the sea to eighty-six hundred feet above sea level, along precipices and up steep mountainsides—you could see clouds beneath your feet—where the horses sweated and whinnied, overcome by the effort. The cold of the peaks was succeeded by the heat of an interminable desert of scorched stones and sand dunes where death cropped up suddenly in the form of the skeletons of cattle, mules, and horses; there were no trees, not a single patch of leafy shade, not a stream or a well. It was a desert without birds or snakes or foxes, without living creatures of any species. To the torment of thirst was added a general uneasiness. There you were, all alone, surrounded by the fifteen men of the mule train who looked at you with undisguised greed—a doctor, two merchants, the guide, and eleven mule drivers. Would you make it to Arequipa? Would you survive?

You made it to Arequipa, and you survived. In your present physical condition, you would have died in that desert and been buried there like the young student whose tomb, with its rough wooden cross, was the only sign of a human presence on the lunar two-day journey from the port of Islay to the majestic volcanoes of the White City.

Because she felt so ill, she lost patience very quickly with the stupid questions she was sometimes asked at the gatherings in Marseille, when workers came to meet with her at the Spanish inn. Compared to the workers of Lyon, the workers of Marseille were cavemen, ignorant, crude, with no interest at all in social questions. They listened to her indifferently, yawning, as she explained that the Workers' Union would promise them steady jobs, and the ability to give their children an education as good as the education the bourgeois provided for their own children. What irritated Flora most was the sullen suspicion, the sometimes open hostility, with which they listened to her inveigh against money, declaring that commerce would disappear with the revolution, and that men and women would work, as in early Christian communities, not for material gain but out of altruism, to satisfy their own needs and the needs of others. And that in this future world everyone would live simply and without slaves, whether white or black. And that no man would have mistresses or be a bigamist, or a polygamist, as so many men were in Marseille.

Her diatribes against money and commerce alarmed the workers. She noticed it in their looks of surprise and disapproval. And it seemed absurd to them that Flora should consider it wicked or shameful for men to have mistresses, visit prostitutes, or keep harems like a Turkish pasha. One of them dared to tell her so.

"Maybe you don't understand the needs of men, madame, because you are a woman. Women are happy with one husband, which is more than enough for them. But for us, having just one woman all our lives is dull. You may not realize it, but men and women are different. Even the Bible says so."

You felt ill when you heard these commonplaces, Florita. Nowhere had you seen such a cynical display of lust and sexual exploitation as in this city of merchants flaunting their wealth, or so many prostitutes so openly and shamelessly soliciting clients. Your attempts to talk to the whores on the narrow streets near the port crowded with little bars and brothels—less squalid than those of London, you had to admit—were a failure. Many didn't understand you, since they were Algerians, Greeks, Turks, or Genoese who could speak barely a few words of French. All fled you, frightened, fearing that you were a proselytizer or a government agent. You would have had to disguise yourself as a man, as you did in England, to gain their trust. In your meetings with journalists, professionals with Fourierist, Saint-Simonian, or Icarian sympathies, and even with common workers, you thought you were dreaming when you heard them speak with open admiration of the bankers, shipowners, shipping agents, and tradesmen who took mistresses, about the houses they set up for them, the clothing they dressed them in, the jewels they adorned them with, and the way they pampered them. "Monsieur Laferrière keeps his mistresses in fine style." "No one treats them as well as he does; he's a wonderful man." What kind of revolution could she undertake with such people?

In their exhibitionistic displays of power and wealth, these merchants were less like the rich men of Paris or London than those of distant Arequipa. It was in Peru in September 1833, after her journey from Islay, that Flora learned for the first time what privilege and wealth meant—on a vertiginous scale—when a horseback procession of dozens of people, all dressed in the fashions of Paris, and almost all of them her relatives by blood or marriage (the principal families of

Arequipa were biblical in their vastness, and all interrelated), came out to meet her at the Tiabaya heights. They escorted her to Don Pío Tristán's house on Calle Santo Domingo, in the center of the city. She remembered that triumphal entrance into her father's land as other-worldly: the green beauty of the valley watered by the Chili River, the flocks of llamas with their tall ears, and the three proud volcanoes crowned with snow at the foot of which were scattered the little white houses, made of the light-colored stone called *sillar*, of Are-quipa, a city of thirty thousand. Peru had been a republic for some years, but everything about this city, where white men played at be-ing lords and dreamed of truly attaining such status, spoke of colonial life. It was a city full of churches, convents, monasteries, barefoot In-dians, and blacks. Down the middle of straight streets of chipped cobblestones there ran channels into which all threw their garbage, the poor pissed and defecated, and from which mules, dogs, and street children drank. Among wretched dwellings and hovels of rub-bish, planks, and straw, great houses suddenly rose, majestic and pala-tial. Don Pío Tristán's was one of them. He was away from Arequipa, at his Camaná sugar refineries, but the grand mansion faced in white *sillar* awaited Flora in full splendor, amid bursting fireworks. Pitch torches lit the great courtyard, and the entire household staff, ser-vants and slaves, was grouped there to welcome her. A woman in a mantilla, wearing many rings and necklaces, embraced her. "I'm your cousin Carmen de Piérola, Florita—welcome home." You couldn't believe your eyes: you felt like a beggar in the midst of such luxury. In the grand reception hall, everything glittered; besides the immense crystal chandelier there were candelabra with colored candles all along the walls. Dazed, you moved from one person to the next, pre-senting your hand. The gentlemen kissed it, bowing gallantly, and the women embraced you in the Spanish fashion. Many spoke to you in French, and all asked for news of a France you had never known, a France of theaters, dress shops, horse races, balls at the Opéra. Also present were several Dominican monks in white habits, attached to the Tristán family—the Middle Ages, Florita!—and in the middle of the reception, the prior suddenly asked for silence in order to speak a few words of greeting to the recent arrival, praying that heaven bless her stay in Arequipa. Cousin Carmen had arranged a dinner. But you excused yourself, half dead of fatigue, surprise, and emotion: you were exhausted, you preferred to rest.

Cousin Carmen—extremely cordial and effusive, with no neck and a face pitted with smallpox scars—led you to your chambers, in a back wing of the house: a spacious dressing room and a bedroom with a soaring ceiling. At the door she presented a little black girl with lively eyes, who was waiting for them still as a statue.

"This slave is for you, Florita. She has prepared a bath of warm water and milk for you, to refresh you before you sleep."

Just like the rich of Arequipa, the merchants of Marseille didn't seem to notice what an obscene spectacle of plenty they represented, surrounded by the destitute. It was true that the poor of Marseille were rich in comparison to the little Indians who begged in the doorways of the churches of Arequipa, huddled in their ponchos and raising their blind eyes or their crippled limbs to arouse pity; or those who trotted beside their flocks of llamas, bringing their produce to market on Saturdays beneath the arches of the Plaza de Armas. But here in Marseille many people were poverty-stricken too, almost all of them immigrants; and because they were immigrants, they were exploited in the workshops, at the port, and on the farms in the surrounding countryside.

Not a week had passed since she came to Marseille, and she had already—despite feeling so unwell—held many meetings and sold fifty copies of *The Workers' Union*, when she had an experience that she would later remember sometimes with a laugh, and sometimes indignantly. A woman who identified herself only as Madame Victoire stopped by to see her several times at the Spanish inn. The fourth or fifth time, they finally met. She was a woman of uncertain age, lame in her left foot. Despite the heat, she was dressed in dark clothing, with a scarf covering her hair; a big cloth bag dangled from her arm. She insisted so vehemently that they speak in private that Flora brought her into her room. By her accent, Madame Victoire seemed to be Italian or Spanish, though she might also have been from the countryside around Marseille, since its inhabitants spoke French in a way that Flora sometimes found incomprehensible. Madame Victoire praised her so lavishly—such jet black hair, those eyes must glitter like fireflies in the dark, what a fine profile, what tiny little feet—that Flora could not help but blush.

"You are very kind, madame," she interrupted. "But I have many engagements, and I can't linger. What did you wish to see me about?"

"To make you rich and happy," said Madame Victoire, stretching her arms and eyes wide, as if encompassing a universe of luxury and good fortune. "This little visit of mine could change your life. You'll never be able to thank me enough, my pretty."

She was a procuress. She had come to tell Flora that a very rich, generous, handsome man, of Marseillais high society, had seen her and fallen in love with her—the gentleman was a romantic soul, who believed in love at first sight—and was prepared to whisk her away from this dingy inn, set her up in her own house, and satisfy her every need and whim so that from now on she would lead a life befitting her beauty. Did you like the idea, Florita?

Overcome with astonishment, Flora laughed so hard she choked. Madame Victoire laughed too, thinking the deal was done. Thus it came as a great surprise when Flora's laughter turned to fury and she flew at the procuress, shouting insults and threatening to report her to the police if she didn't leave immediately.

Madame Victoire left, muttering that once she recovered she would regret her childish reaction. "You have to seize your chances, my pretty, because they won't come twice."

Flora sat pondering this turn of events. Her indignation gave way to a sense of vanity, of secret coquetry. Who was it who aspired to be your lover and protector? A doddering old man? You should have faked interest, coaxing his name from Madame Victoire. Then you could have gone to see him and scolded him. But such a proposal, from one of the rich and lascivious men of Marseille, suggested that despite your many misfortunes, the relentless demands of your life, and your illnesses, you must still be an attractive woman, capable of beguiling men, of driving them to commit rash acts. Your forty-one years sat lightly on you, Florita. Hadn't Olympia said to you more than once, at your moments of great passion, "I suspect you are immortal, my love"?

In Arequipa, the young woman newly arrived from France was considered by all to be a beauty. She was told so from the very first day by her aunts, uncles, cousins, nieces, nephews, and the tangled array of relatives of relatives, family friends, and inquisitive members of Arequipan society who came to pay her their respects in the first few weeks, bringing little gifts, and to satisfy the frivolous, gossipy, unhealthy curiosity that was an endemic affliction of fashionable society in Arequipa. How coolly and disdainfully you saw them now, all those people who were born and lived in Peru but dreamed only of France and Paris, those recently minted republicans who pretended to be aristocrats, those very respectable ladies and gentlemen whose lives could not have been more empty, parasitic, selfish, or shallow. Now you could make such stern judgments. Then, you couldn't. Not yet. In those first few months in your father's homeland you lived happily, flattered by all those rich bourgeois. With their kindnesses, invitations, affectionate gestures, and gallantries, those wealthy bloodsuckers made you feel rich, too, Florita, and respectable, bourgeois, aristocratic.

They thought you were a virgin and unmarried, of course. No one suspected the dramatic married life you had fled. How wonderful it was to rise in the morning and be attended, to have a slave always awaiting your orders; never to worry about money, because so long as you lived in this house there would always be food, a roof over your head, affection, and a wardrobe that soon grew many times larger, thanks to the generosity of your relatives, and especially your cousin Carmen de Piérola. Did this treatment mean that Don Pío and the Tristán family had decided to forget that you were an illegitimate child and recognize your rights as a legitimate daughter? You wouldn't know for sure until Don Pío returned, but the signs were encouraging. Everyone treated you as if you had never been separated from the family. Perhaps your uncle Pío's heart had softened. He would recognize you as his brother Mariano's legitimate daughter, and give you the part of your father's and grandmother's inheritance that you were due. You would return to France with an income permitting you to live the rest of your life like a bourgeoise.

Alas, Florita! It was all for the best that it hadn't happened, wasn't it? You would have become one of those rich, stupid women you hated so much now. Better by far for you to have suffered that disappointment in Arequipa, and learned by dint of setbacks to recognize injustice, hate it, and fight it. You didn't return a rich woman from your father's homeland; instead, you became a rebel, an avenger, a "pariah," as you would proudly call yourself in the book in which you decided to tell your story. In the end, you had many reasons to be grateful to Arequipa, Florita.

The most interesting meeting in Marseille was held at a leather workers' guild. Some twenty people were gathered in the hall, which was permeated with the smell of leather, dyes, and damp wood, when Benjamin Mazel, gallant and flamboyant disciple of Charles Fourier, suddenly appeared. He was a man in his forties, of exalted speech and boundless energy, wrapped in a cape spotted with stains and dandruff, with the unruly hair of a Romantic poet. With him he had brought a heavily annotated copy of *The Workers' Union*. His opinions and criticisms won you over immediately. Gesticulating like an Italian, Mazel—who reminded you, with his big athletic body and irrepressible enthusiasm, of Colonel Clemente Althaus, of Arequipa—said that the Workers' Union project of social reform was missing a key element, which should be included along with the right to work and the right to an education—the right to free daily bread. He expounded in detail on his idea, and in the process convinced the twenty leather workers, and Flora herself. In the society of the future, bakeries would all belong to the State, and would perform a public service, like schools and the police; they would no longer be profit-making institutions and would supply bread free to all citizens. The cost would be subsidized by taxes. Thus no one would die of hunger, no one would be idle, and all children and young people would receive an education.

Mazel wrote pamphlets and had been running a little newspaper that was shut down for being subversive. Later, over tea and refreshments, Flora listened to him recount his political mishaps—he had been arrested several times as an agitator—and she couldn't stop thinking of Clemente Althaus, who, along with La Mariscala, had impressed her most of all the people she met in Peru in 1833. Like Mazel, Althaus radiated energy and vitality from every pore of his body, and was the embodiment of adventure, risk, and action. But unlike Mazel, he cared nothing about injustice, nor that so many people were poor and so many rich, nor that the latter were so cruel to those who had nothing. Althaus's only concern was that there be wars in the world so that he could take part in them, shooting, killing, giving orders, devising strategies and putting them into practice. Making war was his vocation and his profession. A tall, blond German with the body of an Apollo and eyes of blue steel, Althaus seemed much younger than his forty-eight years when Flora met him. He spoke French as well as he spoke German and Spanish. He had been a mercenary since adolescence, and he grew up fighting on battlefields from one end of Europe to the other in the ranks of the coalition forces during the Napoleonic wars. When these were over, he came to South America in search of other wars in which he could sell his services as a military engineer. Hired by the government of Peru and named colonel of the Peruvian army, he had spent fourteen years fighting in the civil wars that shook the young republic from the day of its independence, changing sides time and again according to the offers he received from the combatants. Flora would soon discover that from her uncle on down—Don Pío Tristán had been viceroy of the Spanish colony, and then president of the Republic—changing sides was Peruvian society's most popular sport. The funny thing was that everyone boasted of it, as the sophisticated art of avoiding danger and exploiting the chronic state of armed conflict in which the country was sunk. But no one touted their lack of principles, ideals, and loyalties, or the pure quest for adventure and pay when it came time to decide whose side to join, with more wit and audacity than Colonel Clemente Althaus. He was in Arequipa—where he had first come when it was part of Simón Bolívar's Greater Colombia—because it was in Arequipa that he had fallen in love with Manuela de Flores, Flora's cousin and the daughter of a sister of Don Pío and Don Mariano, whom he had married. Since his wife was in Camaná with Don Pío and his court, Althaus became Flora's constant companion. He showed her all the interesting places in the city, from its churches and centuries-old convents to the religious mystery plays that were performed outdoors in the Plaza de las Mercedes before a motley crowd that followed the miming and recitations of the actors for hours on end. He took her to see cockfights in Arequipa's two coliseums, to bullfights in the Plaza de Armas, to the theater where anonymous farces or classic plays by Calderón de la Barca were staged, and to the very frequent processions that made Flora imagine this was what bacchanals and saturnalias must have been like: indecent buffoonery to entertain the common folk and keep them lulled. With bands of musicians preceding them, half-castes and blacks dressed as Pierrots, harlequins, fools, and in masks performed acrobatic feats and amused the plebes with their clowning. Next, wreathed in incense, came the penitents dragging chains, bearing crosses, and flagellating themselves, followed by an anonymous mass of Indians praying in Quechua and wailing. The men carrying the saint's platform fortified themselves with hard liquor and a drink made of fermented corn—they called it *chicha*—and were thoroughly drunk.

"These people are so superstitious they make the worst soldiers in the world," said Althaus, laughing, and you listened, mesmerized. "Cowards, half-wits, dirty, undisciplined. The only way to keep them from fleeing combat is by terrorizing them."

He told you that he had managed to establish in Peru the German custom whereby the officers themselves, and not their subordinates, administered corporal punishment to the troops.

"It's the officer's whip that makes a good soldier, just as the lion tamer's whip makes the circus beast," he continued, overcome by mirth.

You thought, He's like one of those German barbarians who trampled the Roman Empire.

One day, when they had gone to Tingo with some friends to see the thermal baths (there were several in the countryside near Arequipa), she and Althaus went off on their own to visit some caves. All at once, the German took her in his arms—you felt as fragile and vulnerable as a bird caught in his grasp—caressed her breasts, and kissed her on the mouth. Flora had to make a real effort not to surrender to his touch, because he exercised a charm over her that she had never experienced with any other man. But the repugnance that she had conceived for sex ever since her marriage to Chazal prevailed.

"I very much regret that you've destroyed the fondness I felt for you with this offense, Clemente," she said. Then she slapped him, though without much force, barely turning his surprised, fair-skinned face.

"It is I who am sorry, Florita," Althaus apologized, clicking his heels. "I swear on my honor, it will never happen again."

He kept his word, and in all Flora's remaining months in Arequipa, he never forgot himself or made an advance again, although sometimes she detected flickers of desire in his pale blue eyes.

A few days after the episode at the baths, she experienced the first earthquake of her life. She was in her dressing room, writing a letter, when she heard a terrible din of barking in the city—she had been told that the dogs were the first to feel what was coming—and a second later she saw her slave Dominga fall to her knees and, with her arms upraised and her eyes terrified, begin to pray aloud to the Lord of Earthquakes:

> Have mercy on us, O Lord
> Temper, O Lord, your wrath
> your justice and your judgment
> Sweet Jesus of mine
> By your holy wounds
> Have mercy on us, O Lord

The earth shook for two full minutes, with a deep, muffled rumbling, while Flora, frozen in place, forgot to run to the shelter of the doorway, as her relatives had taught her. The earthquake didn't do much damage in Arequipa, but it destroyed two cities on the coast, Tacna and Arica. The three or four tremors that came later were insignificant compared to the quake. You would never forget the feeling of impotence and doom you had during that interminable shaking. Here in Marseille, eleven years later, it still sent a shiver up your spine.

She spent the rest of her time in the Mediterranean port in bed, oppressed by the heat, the pains in her stomach, her general weakness, and spells of neuralgia. Her impression of the workers of Marseille improved a little then. When they saw that she was ill, they did their utmost to care for her. They filed through the inn in small groups, bringing fruit and bunches of flowers, and they stood at the foot of the bed with their caps in their hands, attentive and shy, waiting to be asked to do something, eager to serve her. Thanks to Benjamin Mazel, she was able to form a Workers' Union committee of ten people, all of whom were manual laborers except for the pamphleteer and agitator: a tailor, a carpenter, a bricklayer, two leather workers, two hairdressers, a seamstress, and even a longshoreman.

The meetings in her bedroom at the inn were informal. Because of her weakness and discomfort, Flora spoke little. But she listened carefully, and found herself amused by the naïveté and the enormous ignorance of her visitors, or angered by the bourgeois prejudices they had acquired. They believed Turkish, Greek, and Genoese immigrants were responsible for all thefts and crimes, for example, and they were unwilling to consider women as their equals, with the same rights as men. So as not to irritate her, they pretended to accept her ideas about women, but Flora saw by their expressions and the little glances they exchanged that she hadn't convinced them.

At one of these meetings she learned from Mazel that Madame Victoire was not only a procuress but also a police informant, and that she had been inquiring about Flora for days in the gathering places of Marseille. So here, too, the authorities were on her trail. When he heard this, Salin, a carpenter who visited her every day, was alarmed, and feared that the police would arrest Madame Tristán and lock her up in a dungeon with prostitutes and thieves; he offered to dress her up in his National Guard uniform and hide her in a shepherds' hut he knew of in the mountains. The proposal made everyone laugh. Flora informed them that she had already lived an adventure like the one Salin was proposing, and told them about her exploits in London five years before, where she had spent four months almost continually dressed as a man in order to move about freely and carry out her social research. As she was talking, her strength failed her and she fainted.

In Arequipa, you had dressed up as a man, too—as a hussar, with a sword, plumed helmet, boots, and mustache—at carnival time, to attend a costume ball. At night, the members of Arequipan society entertained themselves by pelting each other with confetti, streamers, and perfume, but during the day, they celebrated just like the common folk, with buckets of water and *cascarones*—eggshells full of colored water—in real street battles. From the roof terrace of Don Pío's house, you watched the spectacle with all the fascination you felt for this strange land, so different from any other you had known.

Everything about Arequipa surprised you, disconcerted you, and sharpened your understanding of human beings, society, and life. There were the religious orders, for example, which had made a lucrative business out of selling their robes to the dying, since it was an Arequipan custom to bury the dead in religious garments. And there was the fact, too, that this worldly little city's social life was more intense than that of Paris. Families paid and received visits all day, and at noon they ate the delicious cakes and sweets made by the cloistered nuns of Santa Catalina, Santa Teresa, and Santa Rosa, drinking chocolate from Cuzco, and smoking constantly—the women more than the men. Gossip, tittle-tattle, confidences, slander, and the indiscreet discussion of family secrets and scandal were the stuff of dinner conversation. At all of these gatherings, of course, everyone spoke nostalgically, enviously, and desperately of Paris, which for them was an outpost of Paradise. They devoured you with questions about life in Paris, and you, knowing less about it than they did, had to invent all kinds of stories in order not to disappoint them.

A month and a half into your stay in Arequipa, Uncle Pío was still in Camaná and showed no signs of returning. Was this prolonged absence a strategy to discourage your aspirations? Did Don Pío fear that you had brought fresh proof with you that would force the law to declare you a legitimate daughter and therefore the primary heiress of Don Mariano Tristán? She was absorbed in these reflections when it was announced that Captain Zacharie Chabrié, recently arrived in Arequipa, would come that afternoon to visit her. The appearance of the Breton seaman, whom she hadn't thought of once since she said goodbye to him in Valparaíso, shook her like another earthquake. There was no doubt that he would insist upon marrying her.

The first day of her reunion with Chabrié was friendly, thanks to the presence in the drawing room of half a dozen relatives, which prevented the captain from discussing the passionate business that had brought him there. But his eyes told Flora what his words could not. The next day, he came in the morning, and Flora couldn't avoid being left alone with him. On his knees, kissing her hand, Zacharie Chabrié begged her to accept him. He would devote the rest of his life to making her happy, and he would be a model father for Aline; Flora's daughter would be his daughter, too. Overwhelmed, not knowing what to do, you almost told him the truth: that you were a married woman, not with a single daughter but with two surviving children, legally and morally barred from marrying again. But you were held back by the fear that Chabrié would betray you to the Tristáns in a fit of spite. What would happen then? The society that had opened its arms to you would expel you as a fraud and liar, a fugitive wife and heartless mother.

How to free yourself of him, then? In bed in Marseille, fanning herself against the heat of the October evening and listening to the buzz of the cicadas, Flora again felt an uneasiness in the pit of her stomach, a swelling of guilt and bad conscience. It always happened when she remembered the scheme she had employed to disappoint Chabrié and free herself from his hounding. Now you felt the cold metal of the bullet, too, close to your heart.

"Very well, Zacharie. If you truly love me, prove it to me. Get me an official document, a birth certificate, showing that I am my parents' legitimate daughter. Then I'll be able to claim my inheritance and with what I inherit we'll be able to live safe and sound in California. Will you do it? You have acquaintances, influence in France. Will you get me a certificate, even if you have to bribe an official?"

Turning pale, the honest man and staunch Catholic stared wide-eyed at her, unable to credit what he had just heard.

"But Flora, do you realize what you're asking?"

"When true love is at stake, nothing is impossible, Zacharie."

"Flora, Flora. Is this the proof of love you require? That I commit a crime? That I break the law? You ask me to do such a thing? To become a criminal to secure your inheritance?"

"I see. You don't love me enough to be my husband, Zacharie."

You watched as he grew even paler; then he turned so red he seemed apoplectic. He swayed where he stood, on the verge of collapse. Finally, he moved away, his back to you, dragging his feet like an old man. At the door, he turned and said, with one hand held high, as if exorcising you, "Know that now I hate you as much as I once loved you, Flora."

What must have become of the noble Chabrié after you parted? You never heard from him again. Perhaps he read *Peregrinations of a Pariah*, and thus discovered the real reason for your ugly ruse to rebuff his love. Might he have forgiven you? Did he still hate you? What would your life have been like, Florita, if you had married Chabrié and buried yourself in California with him, never setting foot in France again? Peaceful and sheltered, no doubt. But then you never would have opened your eyes to the world, or written books, or become the standard-bearer of the revolution destined to liberate women from slavery and the poor from exploitation. In the end, you were right to make the poor man undergo that terrible ordeal in Arequipa.

When, somewhat recovered from her ailments, Flora was packing her bags to continue on to Toulon, the next stop on her tour, Benjamin Mazel brought her an amusing piece of news. The poet-bricklayer Charles Poncy, who had left her in the lurch with the excuse of a rest trip to Algiers, had never crossed the Mediterranean. He had boarded the ship, but before it set sail he was seized by terror at the prospect of shipwreck and suffered a nervous attack, blubbering, shouting, and demanding that they put down the gangway and let him ashore. The ship's officials opted for the English navy's method of curing recruits of their fear of the sea: they tossed him overboard. Mortally ashamed, Charles Poncy had been hiding in his little house in Marseille, waiting for time to pass so that everyone would think he was in Algiers, following his muse. A neighbor had given him away, and now he was the laughingstock of the city.

"Just like a poet," said Flora.

12

WHAT ARE WE?

PUNAAUIA, MAY 1898

᪣

H e arrived in Papeete early in the morning, before the heat grew too intense. The mail boat from San Francisco, announced the evening before, was in the lagoon now, and had docked. Drinking a beer at one of the port bars, he waited for the men from the post office to appear. He saw them pass along the quai du Commerce, in a carriage pulled by a weary horse, and the oldest of the postmen, Foncheval or Fonteval—you always got it wrong, Koké—nodded at him. Sitting quietly, speaking to no one, sipping the beer on which he had spent his last few cents, he waited until the two men were lost from sight beneath the royal poincianas and acacias of the rue de Rivoli. He whiled away the time calculating how long it would take them to sort the packages and letters spread out over the floor of the little post office onto shelves and into mailboxes. His ankle didn't hurt, and he didn't feel the burning itch of his shins that had kept him awake all night, in a cold sweat. You would have better luck now than you had with the boat a month ago, Koké.

He headed slowly toward the post office, not hurrying the pony that pulled his little cart. The sun, which he felt licking at his head, would blaze hotter and hotter as the minutes and hours passed, until the heat reached its intolerable height, between two and three in the afternoon. The rue de Rivoli was half-deserted, although some people were out in the gardens and on the balconies of its big wooden houses. Through the green of the tall mango trees, he glimpsed the tower of the cathedral in the distance. The post office was open. You were the first visitor that morning, Koké. Behind the counter, the two postmen were busying themselves filing letters and packages, already ranged in alphabetical order.

"There's nothing for you," Foncheval or Fonteval said to him in greeting, with an apologetic gesture. "I'm sorry."

"Nothing?" He could feel the scorching pain in his shins, the throbbing of his ankle. "Are you sure?"

"I'm sorry," repeated the old postman, shrugging his shoulders.

He knew immediately what he had to do. Without haste, he returned to Punaauia, at the leisurely pace of the pony that pulled the little cart on which half was still owing, cursing the Paris gallery owners he hadn't heard from in half a year at least. It would be more than a month before the next boat arrived from Sydney. What would you live on until then, Koké? The Chinaman Teng, the only storekeeper in Punaauia, had cut off his credit because it had been two months since he settled the debt he had run up for canned food, tobacco, and alcohol. That wasn't the worst of it, Koké. You were used to owing money to half the world and still preserving your confidence in yourself and your love of life. But a feeling of emptiness, of exhaustion, had gripped you in the last three or four days, when you realized that your enormous painting, thirteen feet long and almost seven feet tall, the biggest you had ever painted and the one that took you the longest—several months—was finished at last. An extra brushstroke would spoil it. Wasn't it a shame that you had painted the best work of your life on sackcloth that would soon rot in the damp and the rain? He thought, Does it matter whether it disappears before anyone sees it? No one will recognize that it's a masterpiece anyway. No one would understand it. How could it be that even your loyal friend Daniel de Monfreid, whom you had begged for help three months ago with the desperation of a drowning man, hadn't written you?

He arrived in Punaauia around midday. Fortunately, Pau'ura and little Émile weren't home. Not because Pau'ura might have hindered your plans, for the girl was a true Maori, accustomed to obeying her husband no matter what he did or asked, but because you would've had to talk to her, answer her stupid questions, and just now you didn't have the time or the patience for foolishness, much less for the child's wailing. He remembered how intelligent Teha'amana had been. Talking to her had helped him endure hard times; talking to Pau'ura didn't. He climbed the swaying outside staircase of the hut to the bedroom, in search of the bag of powdered arsenic he kept to rub on the sores on his legs. Picking up his straw hat and the staff with the head he had carved in the shape of an erect phallus, he left the house, without so much as a farewell glance at the mess of books, notebooks, clothes, postcards, glasses, and bottles, amid which the cat was dozing. He didn't even look into his studio, where he had lived closeted in a state of incandescence for the last few weeks, working on the enormous painting that had consumed his entire existence. Without a glance he passed by the little school next door, from which came the sound of running and shouting, and he hurried across the orchard belonging to his friend, the ex-soldier Pierre Levergos. Wading across the stream, he set out along the valley of Punaruu, which threaded its way into the steep and densely forested mountains, leaving the coast behind.

By now it was very hot, the summer sun fierce enough to cause anyone foolish enough to spend long bareheaded to lose consciousness. In some of the few native huts he passed he heard laughter and singing. The New Year festivities, begun a week ago. And twice before he left the valley he heard someone shout in greeting, "Koké, Koké," calling him by the nickname that was the Tahitian attempt to say his last name. He raised his hand in reply without stopping, trying to quicken his step, which aggravated the itching of his legs and the stabbing pains in his ankle.

In reality, he was moving very slowly, leaning on his staff, limping. Every so often, he wiped the sweat from his brow with his fingers. Fifty years old—a decent age to die. Would the posthumous glory you had trusted in so firmly when you were younger, in Paris, Finistère, Panama, and Martinique, be granted you? When the news of your death reached France, would Parisian whim serve to kindle an interest in your work and life? Would your fate be the same as the mad Dutchman's after his suicide? Curiosity, recognition, admiration, oblivion: none of it mattered to you in the slightest.

He had begun to climb the mountain along a narrow path, shaded by an intricate canopy of coconut palms, mango trees, and breadfruit trees half buried in the undergrowth. He had to beat his way through using his staff as a machete. I don't regret anything I've done, he thought. Not true. You regretted having contracted the unspeakable illness, Koké. As the path became steeper, he climbed more slowly, shaken by the effort. The last thing you wanted was for your heart to fail you now. Your death would come as you had planned it, not when and where the unspeakable illness decided. Walking protected by the foliage of the mountain slopes was a thousand times preferable to walking through the valley under the sky's skull-boring glare. He stopped several times to catch his breath before reaching the little plateau. He had climbed there a few months earlier, guided by Pau'ura, and had scarcely stepped onto that raised bit of earth—treeless but thick with ferns of all sizes, with a view of the valley, the white line of the coast, the clear blue lagoon, the rosy glow of the coral reefs, and beyond, the sea merging with the sky—when he decided, "I want to die here." It was a beautiful spot, quiet, perfect, unspoiled—possibly the only place in all of Tahiti that still looked exactly like the refuge you had in mind seven years ago, in 1891, when you left France for the South Seas, announcing to your friends that you were fleeing European civilization and its corruption by the golden calf in search of a pure and primitive world, a land of skies without winter where art wouldn't be just another business venture but a sacred, vital, and sporting task, and where to eat an artist would need only to raise his arm and pluck fruit from heavily laden trees, like Adam and Eve in the Garden of Eden. Reality hadn't lived up to your dreams, Koké.

Borne on the soft breeze, an intense fragrance rose up to the little natural balcony suspended from the mountainside, the sort of fragrance that was given off by the foliage in the rainy season and that the Tahitians called *noa noa*. Inhaling with delight, for a few seconds he forgot his ankle and his legs. He sat on a patch of dry earth, at the foot of a clump of ferns that hid the sky. Coolly, his hand steady, he opened the bag and swallowed all the powdered arsenic, helping it down with saliva, and taking small pauses so he wouldn't choke. He licked the last grains from the bag. It had an earthy taste, slightly acidic. Feeling no fear and not conjuring up any of his favorite gruesome scenarios, he waited with distant curiosity for the poison to take effect. Almost at once, he began to yawn. Were you going to fall asleep? Would you slip gently, unconsciously, from life to death? You had thought that death by poison would be dramatic, with horrific pains, convulsions, a cataclysm in your guts. Instead, you sank into a hazy world and began to dream.

He dreamed of that black woman in Panama, in April or May of 1887, with her red sex like a clot. At the door of her plank shack there was always a line longer than the line for any other Colombian prostitute in the camp. The workers on the canal under construction preferred her because of her *perrito*; it took Paul some time to learn that this was the benign Panamanian version of the terrifying, mythical *vagina dentata*. According to the canal laborers, this woman's *perrito* didn't castrate those who mounted her, but only nibbled at them affectionately; the startling tickle gave them pleasure. Curious, he stood in line on payday, just like the other diggers on his squad, but he didn't notice anything special about her sex. You remembered the powerful scent given off by her sweaty body, the warm invitation of her belly, thighs, and breasts. Had she given you the unspeakable illness? The suspicion had plagued him ever since the raging fevers that nearly killed him in Martinique. Was it because of the black woman in Panama that your vision had weakened, your heart was failing, and your legs were covered in pustules? The thought made him sad, and suddenly he was weeping for his daughter, Aline: it had been so many years since you saw her, and you would never see her again, because she had died far away in Denmark, felled by pneumonia. Surely she had become a lovely young Danish lady who spoke French as badly as Pau'ura. Now you, too, were dying, on this faraway little South Seas island, Tahiti-nui. And then he dreamed of his companion and friend Charles Laval. You had met him when times were good in Pont-Aven, and together the two of you traveled to Martinique and Panama, in search of Paradise. It wasn't there; instead, you and Charles walked straight into hell. Charles came down with yellow fever and tried to kill himself. But why grieve now for Charles Laval, Koké? Hadn't he been cured of the pestilence? Hadn't he survived his suicide attempt? Hadn't he returned to France to tell of his deeds like a crusader home from Jerusalem? Hadn't he achieved respectable success as a painter? And above all, hadn't he married the beautiful, delicate, ethereal Madeleine, sister of Émile Bernard, whom you had been in love with back in Brittany? Abruptly, his dream became a nightmare. He was choking. Something thick and hot was rising up his esophagus and blocking his throat. He couldn't spit it out. He lay this way for a long time, agonizing, choking, struggling, gripped by nausea. When he opened his eyes, he had vomited on himself, and a line of red ants was marching across his chest, around the vomit stains.

Were you alive? You were. But you were confused, dazed, and ashamed, without the strength even to lift your arms. It was evening, and in the distance the last light of day glowed. From time to time he lost consciousness, and a series of scenes paraded through his head. One especially kept recurring, in which he was on the deck of the *Jérôme-Napoléon*. An officer asked, "Where did you break your nose, Seaman Gauguin?" "It isn't broken, sir; it was always that way. I may have blue eyes and a French last name, but I am an Inca, sir. My nose is the proof." It was night now; when he opened his eyes he saw stars and shivered in the cold. He slept, awoke, fell asleep again, and suddenly he realized with utter clarity what title he should give the painting on which he had been working for the last few months, after half a year without touching a brush or making a single sketch in his notebooks. The certainty flooded him with soothing security and eclipsed the shame he felt at having failed to commit suicide, just as Laval had failed in the Caribbean in April or May 1887, when he was infected by the pox. With the first gleams of dawn he recovered the strength and presence of mind to get to his feet and stand. His legs trembled but they didn't burn, and his ankle didn't ache at all anymore. Before starting back, he spent a while brushing away the red ants that were crawling all over him. How frustrated they must be that you hadn't died, Koké; what a feast they might have had on your rotting body. Rotting or not, it was so stubborn and stupid that it had insisted on staying alive.

Although he was tortured by thirst—his tongue was as petrified as a lizard's—he didn't feel bad, in body or spirit, as he headed down the mountain toward the valley; rather, he was filled with eager anticipation. You were anxious to be home, to plunge into the river in Punaauia where you bathed each morning before starting work, to drink plenty of water and some nice hot tea with a dash of rum (was there any rum left?). Then, lighting your pipe (was there any tobacco left?), you would go into the studio and immediately paint the title that had come to you thanks to your frustrated suicide attempt, in black letters in the upper-left corner of that thirteen-foot-long stretch of sackcloth to which you had been riveted these last few weeks. Was it a masterpiece? It was, Koké. In that upper corner, those tremendous questions would preside over the canvas. You hadn't the slightest idea what the answers might be. But you were sure that anyone who knew how to look could find them in the painting's twelve figures, which traced, in a counterclockwise arc, the human trajectory from the beginning of life in infancy to its end in ignominious old age.

Just before he reached the valley, he came upon a small waterfall flowing in a mossy crevice down the mountainside. He drank, happily. After wetting his face, head, arms, and chest, he rested, sitting on the edge of the path, his legs dangling in space, sunken in a pleasant daze. The rest of the way back he was drunk with fatigue, but in high spirits.

He arrived home around midday, as if he had just circled the earth. Little Émile was sleeping naked on his back in his cot, and Pau'ura, sitting on the mat on the floor with the cat curled around her legs, was trying to coax a melody from the guitar. She looked at him and smiled, still strumming the strings of an instrument she would never master. Every note was out of tune.

"I tried to kill myself and I didn't succeed; I swallowed so much poison that it made me vomit, which saved me; but now I have no arsenic for my legs," he said slowly, in French, which Pau'ura understood perfectly well, although she spoke it with difficulty. "I'm not only a failed artist and a penniless wretch, I'm also a failed suicide. Go on, make me a cup of tea."

Pau'ura's absent expression didn't alter. Mechanically, she sketched a smile, while her hands kept up their attempt to pluck pleasant chords from the much-abused guitar.

"Koké," she said, without moving. "A cup of tea."

"A cup of tea!" he repeated, lying down on the bed and shooing her with his hands. "Now!"

Untangling herself from the cat, she left the guitar on the floor, and walked to the door, her hips gently swinging. She looked older than her sixteen or seventeen years. She was shapely and not very tall, with long blue-black hair that swept her shoulders, and silky skin that seemed to glow against her red pareu. A lovely girl, perhaps the prettiest *vahine* you had lived with since you came to Tahiti. She had given birth twice, and it hadn't changed her body for the worse at all; her silhouette was still slender and youthful. You had been with her for years now, but you had never come to love her the way you loved Teha'amana, whom you still thought of sometimes with irrepressible longing. And why hadn't you come to love her, Koké, since she was not only beautiful but also meek and obliging? Because she was too stupid. Recently, he had reduced his conversation with his Tahitian wife to the bare essentials. If Pau'ura was quiet, he was able to feel a certain fondness for her; she kept him company, she was a help, and when he was assailed by desire, which occurred less often than it once had, she was a firm, sensual young body. But when she opened her mouth to speak, in her poor French or in a Tahitian he couldn't always understand, he was depressed by the banality of her questions and her inability to comprehend the explanations he tried to give her. But most of all he was exasperated by her utter apathy concerning anything spiritual, intellectual, artistic, or simply intelligent. Had she understood that you tried to kill yourself? She had understood it very well. But since everything her husband did was right, what could she possibly have to say about it? Did she have a voice or a vote in matters concerning her lord and master? She wasn't a woman, Koké. She was a pretty little adolescent body, a cunt and breasts, nothing more.

He fell asleep. But not for long, because when he opened his eyes the cup of tea that Pau'ura had left for him beside the bed was still hot. He went looking for the last bottle of rum in the larder. It was almost empty, but the few drops he shook into his tea enlivened the drink. He sipped it slowly as he went fearfully into his studio and took a long look at the immense canvas on the easel that he had built especially for it, like the scaffolding of a building. Arrows of sunlight filtering through the bamboo set the painting in motion, creating a curious sense of vibration; a flurry of butterflies, as in the leafy glade of Punaruu on the hottest days of the year. Yes, Koké, the title was right. Taking up his palette and one of his finest brushes, he wrote in the upper-left corner: Where do we come from? What are we? Where are we going?

Was this the work you intended to paint? Now, seeing it upon your return from the dead—a pretty phrase, Koké—with the perspective and serenity of having come back from the great beyond, you were no longer so sure. Was it Paradise as reinvented by a painter-savage settled on the island of Tahiti? That had been your vague original intention. Or rather, to paint a Garden of Eden that wasn't abstract, European, or mystical but Maori, from the hell into which you had been plunged in these last months of unrelenting misfortune. A real-life Eden, incarnated here and now. But that wasn't what you saw before you. Who was that big central figure in a white loincloth, plucking a fruit from the invisible tree over her head and dividing the canvas in two? Not Eve, surely. He wasn't even certain it was a woman, because although something about the skin, waist, and arms could be considered feminine, the bulges that swelled the loincloth weren't a woman's: they were a goodly pair of testicles and a substantial phallus, possibly in the process of becoming erect.

He began to laugh. A *taata vahine*! A *mahu*! That was what you had painted, Koké: a man-woman. Seven years ago, upon arriving in Tahiti in June 1891, when Lieutenant Jénot (what must have happened to him?) told you that the natives thought you were a *taata vahine*, a *mahu*, because of your long, loose hair and your cowboy hat, it made you shudder. You, a man-woman? Hadn't you given ample proof of your virility ever since you reached the age of reason? Uncomfortable, you cut your long hair and replaced the Buffalo Bill hat with a straw one. But later, upon discovering that Tahitians, unlike Europeans, considered a *taata vahine* as acceptable as an ordinary man or woman, you changed your mind. Now you were proud of having been mistaken for a *mahu*. It's the one thing the missionaries haven't been able to take away from them, he thought. Weren't there *taata vahines* in the villages, and in the bosom of many families, despite the fierce preaching of priests and pastors determined to impose a strict sexual symmetry, with men on one side, women on the other, and everything ambiguous that lay in between eliminated? No one had yet been able to make the natives give up their sexual wisdom. Amused, he remembered his adventure with the woodcutter Jotefa, by the waterfall: it hadn't been so long ago, yet it seemed centuries, Koké. Yes, there were still many *taata vahines* in Tahiti. Not in Papeete, but inland, where the European influence had come late, haphazardly, or never. Often he had seen the boys who wore flowers in their hair like women and cooked, wove, and cleaned house being fondled by men at gatherings when everyone was drunk, and sometimes being taken like women, as if it were the most natural thing in the world. And in the same circumstances, he had also seen girls and women embracing and caressing one another, with no one seeming the least bit surprised. These were the last traces of the lost civilization you had come looking for in vain, Koké, the last gasp of that primitive, healthy, pagan, happy culture, unashamed of the body and untainted by the decadent notion of sin. It was all that was left of what had brought you to the South Seas, that wise acceptance of the need for unfettered love, love in all its incarnations, including hermaphroditism. It wouldn't last much longer. Europe would eliminate the *taata vahine*, too, as it had eliminated the old gods, the old beliefs, the old customs, the old nudity, the tattoos, the anthropophagy, the healthy, joyful, vibrant civilization that had existed once upon a time. But it was still alive in the Marquesas. You had to go there, before you expired.

Without realizing or intending it, you had painted a *taata vahine* in the middle of your greatest work. An homage to what used to be, to what had been stolen from the Tahitians. In all your years here, you hadn't found a single person who could remember what his people's traditions, relations, and daily life used to be like. Even the splendid nudity in which they appeared in your paintings had been denied them. The missionaries had clad their copper bodies in gowns like religious habits. What a crime! Hiding those lovely ocher, ash-gray, or bluish-black forms that for centuries they must have proudly flaunted in the sunlight, with animal innocence. The gowns they were made to wear obscured their gracefulness, ease, and strength, branding them with the degrading mark of the serf. Koké, Koké: in order to make that vanished culture exist you had had to create it from scratch. Had there ever been Maori like the ones in your paintings? Creatures of nature, at one with their bodies, brother and sister to the trees that bestowed their fruits upon them, to the sea and the lagoon where they fished and bathed and where their swift canoes split the waters, protected from misfortune by the forbidding goddess, Hina, whom you had also had to invent for them, since no Tahitian could remember what it was like when their ancestors worshiped her. The missionaries had stolen their memory, made them into amnesiacs.

It had been a good idea to paint the upper corners that tarnished yellow, to suggest an ancient fresco whose borders were beginning to crumble with age. And the regular shading of the landscape was right, too, underlaid by the soft blue and Veronese green of the background, upon which dancing branches and trunks coiled like tentacles and snakes. The trees were the only aggressive beings in the painting. The animals, in contrast, were peaceful: cats, goat, dog, birds, all living in harmony with the humans. Even the old woman kneeling on the left, who was about to die or perhaps was already dead, and had assumed the pose of the Peruvian mummies that you had never been able to forget, seemed resigned to her demise.

And those two figures in pink robes in the middle ground, who were walking backward through time, from death to life, beside the tree of knowledge? While you were painting them, you thought they might be you yourself and the unfortunate Aline. But no—those whispering figures weren't you and your dead daughter. They weren't Tahitians, either. There was something sinister, sullen, scheming, hollow, in the way they exchanged confidences, the way they were absorbed in each other, uninterested in their surroundings. Closing his eyes, he searched the depths of his soul. What did those two represent, Koké? You didn't know. You would never know. A good sign. It was not simply with your hands, your ideas, your fantasies, and your old skill that you had painted your greatest work, but also with the dark forces deep in your soul, the seething of your passions, the fury of your instincts, the urgency that surfaces in exceptional paintings. Paintings that never die, Koké. Like Manet's *Olympia*.

He was immersed for a long time in the study of his painting, trying to fully understand it. When he came down from the studio,

Pau'ura had prepared supper, and was waiting for him in the space below that was open to the elements on two sides and served as a dining room. She had Émile in her arms, and the child—for whom you had never come to feel the same fondness you felt for his sister who died soon after she was born—was silent and absolutely still, though his eyes were wide open. Just as well. There was a dish of fruit on the table, and the omelette you had taught your *vahine* to make the way you liked it: very soft and yielding, almost liquid. The pounding of the invisible sea could be heard close by.

"So Chinaman Teng gave us credit again," he said, smiling. "How did you persuade him?"

"Koké," she nodded. "Chinaman. Eggs. Salt."

There was something calm, sweet, childish in her eyes that contrasted with the adult roundness of her body.

"If I love you tonight, I'll feel truly resuscitated," he said aloud, sitting down to eat.

"Truly," said Pau'ura, pouting.

13

THE NUN GUTIÉRREZ

TOULON, AUGUST 1844

F lora's first impression of Toulon, where she arrived at dawn on July 29, 1844, could not have been worse. "A city of soldiers and criminals. I'll accomplish nothing here." Her pessimism was inspired by Toulon's dependence on the naval armory, where five thousand city workers were employed alongside prisoners sentenced to hard labor. Then, too, her stomach pains and neuralgia had given her no peace since Marseille.

Her hosts in Toulon were bourgeois Saint-Simonians, very modern so long as they were discussing technical matters, scientific progress, and the organization of the production of industrial goods, but terrified that Flora's outbursts would bring them trouble with the authorities. Their leader, a foppish captain called Joseph Corrèze, wearied her with his counsels of prudence and moderation.

"If I had intended to be prudent and moderate, I would never have set out on this tour," Flora said, putting him in his place. "That's what you're here for. I've come to start a revolution, and I'll have to tell some hard truths, that's all there is to it. If it angers the authorities, it'll improve my standing with the workers."

And it did anger the authorities, even before Flora opened her mouth in public. The day after her arrival, the commissioner of

Toulon, a bearded man in his fifties who smelled of lavender, came to see her at her hotel and questioned her for half an hour about what she intended to do in the city. Any act that subverted public order would be vigorously punished, he warned her. Hours later, she received a summons from the King's Counsel ordering her to appear at his office.

"Tell your master I won't go," exploded Madame-la-Colère, indignant. "If I've committed a crime, let him have me arrested. But if all he wants is to intimidate me and make me waste my time, he won't succeed."

The Counsel's assistant, a well-mannered young man, looked at her with surprise and apprehension, as if this woman who was raising her voice and shaking a menacing index finger under his nose might proceed to physically attack him. Ten years ago, Florita, on a morning a few days after first meeting you, your uncle Pío Tristán looked at you with the same astonishment, bewilderment, and fright when the two of you finally addressed the thorny question of your inheritance, in the big house on Calle Santo Domingo in Arequipa. Don Pío, a slight, elegant, suave gentleman with blue eyes and gray hair, had prepared his arguments well. After a friendly preamble, he deluged you with Latinisms and legalese, informing you that since you were the illegitimate daughter of parents whose marriage had no verifiable legal status—as you had confessed in your letter to him—you couldn't hope to receive a cent of his dear brother Mariano's inheritance.

Don Pío had been delayed three months in returning from his Camaná sugar refineries, as if he feared meeting his young niece from France. You, at first sight of this younger brother of your father, whose features reminded you so much of his, were moved to tears. You were still a sentimentalist, Andalusa. You threw your arms around your uncle, trembling, whispering that you wanted to love him and for him to love you; you were so happy to have recovered your father's family, to once again enjoy the warmth and security you hadn't known since your childhood in Vaugirard. You said it and you meant it, Florita! And your uncle seemed to be moved, too, embracing you and, his blue eyes clouded with emotion, murmuring, "Good Lord, but you're the living image of my brother, child."

In the next few days, the old man, marvelously well preserved at the age of sixty-four—with an income of three hundred thousand francs, he was the richest of the rich in Arequipa—lavished attentions and affection on his niece. But when he at last consented to speak to her in private, and Flora explained her wish to be recognized as the legitimate daughter of Don Mariano and, as such, to receive an income of five thousand francs from her grandmother's and father's legacies, Don Pío was transformed into an icy juridical being, the unyielding representative of legal norms: the law was sacred and must prevail over feelings; if not, there would be no such thing as civilization. According to the law, Florita was owed nothing; if she didn't believe him, she could consult any number of judges and lawyers. Don Pío had already done so, and he knew of what he spoke.

Then Flora exploded in one of her rages, the kind that had just caused the young assistant of the King's Counsel in Toulon to turn pale and depart, nearly fleeing. Ungrateful, ignoble, selfish man— was this how he repaid the efforts of Don Mariano, who had cared for him, protected him, and provided for his education in France? By taking advantage of his helpless daughter, refusing to recognize her rights, condemning her to a life of poverty, when he was an incredibly rich man? Flora's voice rose to such a pitch that Don Pío, white as a sheet, dropped into an armchair. He seemed defeated and tiny in this room, whose walls were hung with portraits of his ancestors, high officials and court favorites of the colonial administration: magistrates, field marshals, bishops, viceroys, mayors, generals. Later, he confessed to Flora that it was the first time in his sixty-four years, whether inside or outside the family, that he had seen a woman forget her place and disrespect a paterfamilias. Was this common practice in France now?

Flora burst out laughing. No, Uncle, she thought. Where women are concerned, customs in France are even more reactionary than they are in Arequipa.

When her Saint-Simonian friends in Toulon heard about the visit from the commissioner and the summons from the Counsel, they were alarmed. Her hotel room would certainly be searched. Captain Joseph Corrèze hid in his house all of Flora's papers having to do with the operations of the Workers' Union in the provinces. But for some mysterious reason, there was no search and the King's Counsel didn't request Flora's presence again on her visit.

To distract her from these upsets, the Saint-Simonians took her to the port to watch the "sea jousting," an annual entertainment attracting visitors to Toulon from every region of France, and even Italy. Perched on small platforms in the prows of boats that served as seagoing warhorses, two lancers armed with long, sharp-pointed poles and protected by wooden shields were propelled toward each other at full speed in a spirited charge by the dozen rowers in each boat. At the violent collision, one or often both of the lancers fell into the water, amid the roars of the crowd packed on the wharfs and the seaside promenade. After the show, the Saint-Simonians were rather irked when Flora informed them that what had struck her most was seeing that those poor men, attacking each other with lances to amuse the common folk and the bourgeoisie, were falling into filthy water, where the city's sewers emptied. They would surely catch some disease.

You had never liked mass entertainments, at which individuals, emboldened by the crowd, were turned into animals, losing control of their instincts and behaving like savages. That was why you were so deeply disgusted when Clemente Althaus took you to see the bullfights in Arequipa's Plaza de Armas, and the cockfights at which throngs of frenzied men bet on the bleeding birds and urged them on. You went because it was your natural inclination to want to see and know everything, even though it meant you often swallowed some unpleasant drafts.

Colonel Althaus, who claimed that he, too, was a victim of Don Pío's greed, tried to console her—and to dissuade her from taking any legal action to secure recognition as a legitimate daughter. She would never find a good lawyer willing to stand up to the most powerful man in Arequipa, he assured her, nor a judge who would dare to declare Don Pío guilty of any crime. "This isn't France, Florita! This is Peru!" Even the German cherished illusions of France's superiority.

And in fact, the half dozen lawyers you consulted were unequivocal: you hadn't the slightest chance. By writing that naive letter to Don Pío in which you told him the truth about your parents' marriage, you had sealed your own fate. You would never win the suit if you were so rash as to file it. Flora even consulted a radical lawyer who had been shunned by Arequipan society as a priest-baiter ever since he had dared, two years before, to defend the nun Dominga Gutiérrez, a scandal that was still furnishing grist for the city's rumor mills. Young, ardent Mariano Llosa Benavides delivered the final blow: "I'm sorry to disappoint you, Doña Flora, but legally, you'll never win this case. Even if your papers were in order and your parents' marriage was legitimate, we'd lose it anyway. No one has ever won a lawsuit against Don Pío Tristán. Don't you realize that one half of Arequipa owes him their livelihood, and the other half dreams of suckling from his teat, too? Although in theory we're a republic now, the colony lives and thrives in Peru."

Brooding over her defeat, she had to give up her dreams of becoming a prosperous little bourgeoise. But wasn't it all for the best, Flora? It was. And therefore, even though Arequipa had dashed so many of your hopes, you still harbored a stubborn fondness for that city of volcanoes. It was there your eyes were opened to inequality, racism, the blindness and selfishness of the rich, and the inhumanity of religious fanaticism, the source of all oppression. The story of the nun Dominga Gutiérrez—a cousin of yours, of course, in this city of infinite silent acts of incest—disturbed, astounded, and outraged you. To understand the story, you had to ask a thousand questions. It was also necessary to know the convents, another feature of Arequipa, distinguished not only by its churches and houses of white *sillar*, its earthquakes, and its revolutions but by its reputation as the most Catholic city in Peru, America, and perhaps the entire world. And you determined to get to know them.

With her tremendous force of will, powerful enough to move mountains, she begged, pleaded, and conspired with friends and relatives until Bishop Goyeneche gave her the necessary permission to visit Arequipa's three main convents for cloistered nuns: Santa Rosa, Santa Teresa, and Santa Catalina. The last, where Flora spent five nights, was a small Spanish city hidden away in the center of Arequipa, behind fortified walls: exquisite little streets with Andalusian and Extremaduran names, peaceful squares riotous with carnations and rosebushes, tinkling fountains, and flocks of women circling through the refectories, oratories, recreation halls, chapels, and living quarters with gardens, terraces, and kitchens, where each nun had the right to keep four slaves and four servants cloistered with her.

Flora couldn't believe her eyes at the sight of such ostentation. She had never imagined that a convent would be the scene of such luxury. Besides the riches in art—paintings, sculptures, and tapestries; silver, gold, alabaster, and marble objects of worship—the cells were furnished with rugs and cushions, linen sheets, and embroidered coverlets. Refreshments and meals were served on dishes imported from France, Flanders, Italy, and Germany, with cutlery of chased silver. The nuns of Santa Catalina gave her a lively welcome. They were self-assured, cheerful, charming, and as feminine as it was possible to imagine. To learn "how the women in France dress," they were not satisfied to have Flora take off her blouse and show them her corset and bodice; she had to remove her skirts and sash too, because they were itching with curiosity to touch a Frenchwoman's intimate garments. Bright-red and mute with shame, Flora, in underthings and stockings, had to subject herself for some time to the nuns' noisy scrutiny, until the prioress came to rescue her, herself shaking with laughter.

She spent several instructive and certainly enjoyable days at the aristocratic convent, which only well-born novices, able to pay the high dowries demanded by the order, could enter. Despite the perpetual confinement and the long hours devoted to meditation and prayer, the nuns were never bored. The rigors of the cloister were leavened by its comforts and the nuns' social activities: they spent a good part of the day feting one another, playing like children, or visiting in the little houses that the black and mixed-blood slaves and Indian servants kept immaculately clean. All the nuns she questioned in Santa Catalina firmly believed that Dominga Gutiérrez was possessed by the devil, and they all said that nothing so grotesque could ever have happened at Santa Catalina.

It was, of course, at the convent of Santa Teresa that Dominga's story took place. Run by the Discalced Carmelites, it was more austere and more rigorous than Santa Catalina. Flora spent four days and three nights there, too, stiff with anguish. Santa Teresa had three beautiful cloisters, with neatly clipped climbing vines, tuberoses, jasmine, and rose bushes as well as henhouses and an orchard that the nuns tended with their own hands. But the informal, worldly, playful, and frivolous atmosphere of Santa Catalina did not reign here. At Santa Teresa, no one enjoyed herself; all prayed, meditated, worked in silence, and suffered in body and soul for the love of God. In the tiny cells where the nuns were shut up to pray—they weren't their bedrooms—there was no luxury or comfort, just naked walls, an ascetic straw-backed chair, a rough wooden table, and, hanging from a nail, the scourge with which the nuns flogged themselves to offer the sacrifice of their mortified flesh to the Lord. From her cell, Flora, horrified, could hear the cries that accompanied the nightly slap of the scourges, and understood what life must have been like for her cousin Dominga Gutiérrez in the ten years she spent here, from the time she was fourteen.

That was how old she was when, at her mother's insistence, and after a romantic disappointment—the young man she loved married someone else—she entered Santa Teresa as a novice. After just a few weeks, or maybe even a few days, she realized that she could never adapt to the regimen of sacrifice, extreme austerity, silence, and total isolation, in which one hardly slept, ate, or lived because every moment was devoted to praying, singing hymns, flagellation, confession, and working the earth with one's own hands. Through the visiting-room screen, she begged and pleaded with her mother to remove her from the convent, but her entreaties were in vain. Her confessor's arguments reinforced her mother's, and confused Dominga: she must resist her impulses; the devil was trying to make her abandon her true religious vocation.

A year later, after taking the vows that would bind her to this place and its routine until her death, Dominga heard—in the reading at a meal of a few pages from Saint Teresa's *Life*—the story of a case of possession, of a nun from Salamanca who was inspired by the devil to devise a macabre strategy for fleeing the convent. Dominga, who had just turned fifteen, experienced a moment of illumination. So there was a way to escape, after all. In order to succeed, she had to proceed with infinite caution and patience. It took her eight years to carry out her plan. When you thought what those eight years must have been like for your cousin Dominga, years of plotting the complex scheme step by tiny step, taking infinite precautions, retreating each time she was overcome by fear of discovery, only to begin again the next day—tireless Penelope, weaving, unraveling, and weaving her shroud again—your heart seized. Visited by destructive urges, you dreamed of burning down convents and hanging or guillotining the fanatical oppressors of body and spirit who ran them, like the revolutionaries of 1789. Later, you repented of these secret massacres wrought by your indignation.

At last, on March 6, 1831, at the age of twenty-three, Dominga Gutiérrez was able to execute her plan. The day before, two of her servants had procured the corpse of an Indian woman, with the complicity of a doctor at the San Juan de Dios Hospital. Under cover of night, they brought it in a sack to a shop rented for the purpose across from Santa Teresa. After the last stroke of midnight, they dragged it into the monastery through the main door, which was left open by the doorkeeper sister, who was also part of the scheme. There Dominga was waiting for them. She and the maids carried the body to the small niche where the nun slept. They dressed the Indian in Dominga's habit and scapulars. Then they doused the body with oil and set fire to it, making sure that the flames ate away the face until it it was unrecognizable. Before they fled, they left the cell in disarray, to make the feigned accident seem more believable.

From her hiding place in the rented room, Dominga Gutiérrez observed the funeral service celebrated by the nuns of Santa Teresa before they buried her in the cemetery next to the orchard. It had worked! The young ex-nun didn't seek refuge at home, for fear of her mother, but at the house of an uncle and aunt who had been very fond of the girl. The couple, frightened by the responsibility, ran to tell Bishop Goyeneche the incredible story. Two years had passed since then, and the scandal still had not abated. Flora found the city divided between those who sympathized with Dominga and those who condemned her. Dominga herself, after being asked to leave her aunt and uncle's house, had been given refuge by one of her brothers on a small farm in Chuquibamba, where she was living in a different sort of confinement while the legal and ecclesiastical actions against her took their course.

Did she regret what she had done? Flora went to Chuquibamba to find out. After an arduous journey through the Andean highlands, she came to the simple little country house that served as a lay prison for Dominga. Her cousin received her unhesitatingly. She seemed far older than her twenty-five years. Suffering, fear, and uncertainty had disarranged her face with its chiseled features and high cheekbones; a nervous tremor shook her lower lip. She was dressed simply, in a flowered peasant's dress fastened at the neck and wrists, and her hands were callused from working the earth, her fingernails cut short. There was something evasive and frightened in her deep, serious eyes, the foreboding of some catastrophe. She spoke softly, searching for her words, afraid of making a mistake that would aggravate her situation. At the same time, when she talked about her case, at Flora's urging, she was firm in her resolve. She had gone about things wrong, undoubtedly. But what else could she have done to escape the imprisonment against which her mind and soul rebelled every second of her life? Succumb to despair? Go mad? Kill herself? Was that what God would have wanted? What saddened her most was that her mother had sent word to tell her that since her apostasy, Dominga was dead to her. What plans did she have? Her dream was that the whole process—the tangled cases before the courts and the curia—would come to an end, and she would be permitted to go and live in anonymity in Lima, in freedom, even if she had to work as a servant. When they parted, she whispered in Flora's ear, "Pray for me."

What must Dominga Gutiérrez have done these past eleven years? Would she at last be living far from Arequipa, where she would always be an object of controversy and public curiosity? Would she have managed to travel to Lima and disappear there as she yearned to do? Would she have learned of the love and solidarity with which you had told her story in *Peregrinations of a Pariah*? You would never know, Florita. Since Don Pío Tristán had had your memoirs publicly burned in Arequipa, you had never received another letter from the acquaintances and relatives you came to know on your adventures in Peru.

In her visit to Toulon's naval armory, which took a full day, Flora had the opportunity to see the prison world from up close again, as she had in England. It wasn't the kind of prison her cousin Dominga experienced, but something worse. The thousands of inmates who were sentenced to hard labor in the armory works wore chains around their ankles that often tore the skin and left scars. It wasn't just the chains that distinguished them from the ordinary laborers, with whom they worked side by side in workshops and quarries; it was also the striped smocks they wore and their caps, whose color indicated the sentence they were serving. It was hard to repress a shudder upon seeing an inmate wearing the green cap of perpetual servitude. Like Dominga, these poor wretches knew that unless they escaped, they would live out the rest of their lives in thrall to their soul-destroying routine, watched over by armed guards, until death came to free them from their nightmare.

As in the English prisons, here, too, she was surprised by the number of prisoners who at first glance seemed to be feeble-minded—miserable creatures suffering from cretinism, delirium, or other forms of alienation. They stared at her spellbound, with the empty, glassy eyes of those who have lost all use of reason, their mouths open and threads of saliva hanging from their lips. It must have been a long time since many of them had seen a woman, to judge by the expressions of ecstasy or terror on their faces as they watched Flora pass. And some of the idiots lowered their hands to their private parts and began to masturbate, with animal naturalness.

Was it right for the mentally unfit, the impaired, and the insane to be tried and convicted like individuals who were in full possession of their faculties? Was it not a monstrous injustice? What responsibility for his acts could a deranged person have? Instead of being imprisoned here, many of these men sentenced to hard labor should be sent to asylums. Although, remembering England's psychiatric hospitals and the treatment madmen were obliged to undergo, it was preferable to be convicted as a "normal" delinquent. Here was a subject on which to reflect and seek a solution for the society of the future, Florita.

The officials of the Toulon armory warned her not to speak to the laborers—prisoners or ordinary workers—because uncomfortable situations could arise. But, true to her nature, Flora approached various groups, asking questions about their working conditions and the relations between the men in chains and the workingmen; suddenly, to the dismay of the two naval officers and the civil servant accompanying her, she was presiding over a heated open-air debate about the death penalty. She defended the abolishment of the guillotine as a means of administering justice, and announced that the Workers' Union would outlaw it. Many of the workers protested, incensed. Considering the number of crimes and robberies that were already committed despite the existence of the guillotine, what would happen when criminals were no longer deterred by the threat of death? The debate was interrupted in ludicrous fashion when a group of madmen, drawn by the discussion, tried to join in. Overexcited, they gestured wildly, bounced up and down, talked all at once—each rivaling the next in outrageousness—or sang and capered to call attention to themselves, amid general laughter, until the guards imposed order, brandishing their batons.

For Flora, the experience was extremely useful. Many workers, on the basis of what they had heard on her visit to the armory, became interested in the Workers' Union and asked where they could speak with her at greater length. From that day on, and to the surprise of her Saint-Simonian friends who had scarcely been able to organize a few gatherings with a handful of bourgeois, Flora was able to congregate two or three times a day with groups of workers who, full of curiosity, came to meet this strange person in skirts who was determined to bring about justice for all in a world where there were no exploiters or rich men, and where, among other peculiarities, women would have the same rights as men before the law, in the family, and even in the workplace. From the pessimism she had felt upon her arrival in this city of soldiers and sailors, Flora proceeded to an enthusiasm that even brought her relief from her maladies. She felt refreshed, and possessed with the energy of her best years. From dawn until midnight she was engaged in frenetic activity. As she undressed—oh, the constricting corset, against which you had launched a diatribe in your novel *Méphis*, and which would be prohibited in the society of the future as an unworthy garment, since it made women feel cinched like mares!—and took stock of her day, she was happy. The results could not have been better: fifty copies of *The Workers' Union* sold—she would have to order more from the printer—and more than a hundred new members for the movement.

To the meetings in private houses, workers' societies, Masonic halls, or artisans' workshops there sometimes came immigrants who spoke no French. With the Greeks and Italians it was no problem, since some bilingual person always appeared to act as interpreter. It was more difficult with the Arabs, who remained squatting in a corner, infuriated by their inability to participate.

At these gatherings of people of different races and languages, incidents often arose that Flora had to stifle by speaking out forcefully against racial, cultural, and religious prejudices. You were not always successful, Florita. How difficult it was to convince many of her compatriots that all human beings were alike, regardless of the color of their skin, the language they spoke, or the god they prayed to! Even when they seemed to accept this, scorn, contempt, insults, and racist and nationalist declarations flowed forth the moment some disagreement arose. In one of these arguments, Flora indignantly reproached a French caulker for asking that "Mahometan pagans" be barred from the meetings. The worker got up and left, slamming the door behind him and shouting, "Nigger slut!" Flora took the opportunity to encourage the group to exchange ideas on the subject of prostitution.

It was a long, complicated discussion, in which, owing to Flora's presence, the men in attendance took a while to gather their courage and speak frankly. Those who condemned prostitution did so without conviction, more to flatter Flora than because they truly believed what they were saying, until a gaunt ceramicist with a slight stutter—he was called Jojó—dared to contradict his companions. With his eyes cast down, in the midst of a dead silence followed by malicious giggles, he said that he didn't approve of all these attacks on prostitutes. They were, after all, "the mistresses and lovers of the poor." Did the poor have the means of the bourgeoisie to keep women? Without prostitutes, the lives of the humble folk would be even drearier and duller.

"You say that because you are a man," Flora interrupted him, indignant. "Would you say the same if you were a woman?"

A violent argument broke out. Other voices spoke up in defense of the ceramicist. During the debate, Flora learned that the bourgeois of Toulon had the habit of forming societies to keep mistresses jointly. Four or five businessmen, industrialists, or men of independent means would establish a common fund for the maintenance of a corresponding number of lovers, whom these scoundrels would share. Thus they saved money, and each enjoyed a little harem. The session ended with a speech by Flora, her listeners skeptical if not derisive, in which she expounded her idea—diametrically opposed to Fourierist notions—that in the society of the future, thieves and prostitutes would be sent to remote islands, far from everyone else, so that they could no longer corrupt others with their bad behavior.

Your long-standing hatred of prostitution had to do with the distaste and repugnance sex aroused in you from the time you married Chazal until you met Olympia Maleszewska. No matter how often you told yourself rationally that it was hunger and desperation that drove so many women to spread their legs for money, and that therefore prostitutes like the poor creatures you had seen in London's East End were more deserving of pity than disgust, something instinctive, a visceral repudiation, a burst of rage, surged through you, Florita, when you thought how women who sold their bodies to satisfy men's lustful desires abdicated all moral standing and renounced their dignity. "At bottom you are a puritan, Florita," joked Olympia, nibbling your breasts. "I defy you to say you aren't enjoying yourself at this instant."

And yet, in Arequipa, during the civil war between Orbegosistas and Gamarristas that Flora observed in the first months of 1834, she came—for the first and last time in her life—to feel respect and admiration for the female camp followers, who were, after all, a kind of prostitute. You wrote as much in *Peregrinations of a Pariah*, in your fervent homage to them.

What a journey it was to your father's native land, Andalusa! You were fortunate to have witnessed a revolution and a civil war, and you even participated in the conflict, in a way. You hardly remembered the causes and circumstances, which anyway were a mere cover for the insatiable appetite for power that afflicted all the generals and petty tyrants who had been disputing the presidency of Peru since independence—by legal means and, more frequently, with gunfire and cannon blasts. This time, the revolution began when the National Convention in Lima chose Grand Marshal Don Luis José de Orbegoso to succeed President Agustín Gamarra, who was finishing up his term, rather than General Pedro Bermúdez, protégé of Gamarra and, especially, of Gamarra's wife, Doña Francisca Zubiaga de

Gamarra. This woman, known as Doña Pancha but also called La Mariscala (the Lady Marshal), possessed an aura of adventure and legend that had fascinated you ever since you first heard talk of her. She dressed in military attire, had fought on horseback alongside her husband, and governed beside him. While Gamarra was president, La Mariscala wielded as much power or more in government affairs than the marshal did, and she never hesitated to draw her pistol or flourish her whip to uphold her authority, or strike anyone who disobeyed her or failed to treat her with respect, like the most aggressive of men.

When the National Convention chose Orbegoso instead of Bermúdez, the Lima garrison, at the urging of Gamarra and La Mariscala, staged a military uprising on January 3, 1834. But it was only partially successful, because Orbegoso managed to escape Lima with part of the army to organize the opposition. The country was divided into two camps, according to which garrisons declared themselves on Orbegoso's side, and which on Bermúdez's. Cuzco and Puno, headed by General San Román, chose to support the coup, or in other words Bermúdez, Gamarra, and La Mariscala. Arequipa, meanwhile, went to Orbegoso, the legitimate president, and, under the military command of General Nieto, began preparing to repel the attack of the upstarts.

Exciting times, weren't they, Florita? Carried along by the thrill of events, she never felt herself to be in danger, even during the battle of Cangallo, three months after the beginning of the civil war, which decided the fate of Arequipa. From her uncle Pío's roof terrace, Flora watched the battle with binoculars, as if she were at the opera, while her uncle, her other relatives, and all of Arequipan society crowded into the monasteries, convents, and churches, fearing the sack of the city—which would inevitably follow the action no matter who won—more than they feared bullets.

By then, Flora and Don Pío had made peace, miraculously. Once Florita accepted that she couldn't take any legal action against her uncle, he took pains to pacify her, afraid of the scandal she had threatened him with the day of their fight, rallying his wife, children, nieces, and especially Colonel Althaus to convince her to abandon her plans to leave the Tristán household. She should stay here, where she would always be treated as Don Pío's beloved niece, cherished and cared for by the whole clan. She would never lack for anything, and everyone would love her. You consented—what choice did you have?

And you never regretted it. What a pity it would have been to miss those three months of indescribable ferment, upheaval, turmoil, and social unrest in Arequipa, from the outbreak of revolution to the Battle of Cangallo.

General Nieto had hardly begun to militarize the city and prepare it to resist the Gamarristas when Don Pío was seized by hysterics. For him, civil war meant the combatants would pillage his fortune under the guise of collecting contributions for the defense of freedom and the nation. Sobbing like a child, he told Florita that General Simón Bolívar had extracted a sum of twenty-five million pesos from him, and General Sucre had taken ten thousand more, and of course neither blackguard had returned a cent. What would he be expected to pay now to General Nieto, who was, besides, the puppet of that diabolical revolutionary priest, the ruthless Dean Juan Gualberto Valdivia, who, in his newspaper *El Chili*, accused Bishop Goyeneche of stealing from the poor and protested the celibacy of priests, which he intended to abolish? Flora advised him to go in person and donate five thousand pesos in an act of spontaneous allegiance, before General Nieto fixed a sum. In doing so, he would win over the general and be safe from new revolutionary bleedings.

"Do you think so, Florita?" murmured the miser. "Wouldn't two thousand be enough?"

"No, Uncle, you must give him five thousand, to disarm him completely."

Don Pío did as she said. And after that, he consulted Flora on every action he took in a conflict in which his only concern, like all the wealthy citizens of Arequipa, was not to be stripped bare by the warring factions.

Colonel Althaus obtained the post of chief of staff under General Nieto after he considered the possibility of entering the service of Nieto's adversary, General San Román, who was on his way from Puno with the Gamarrista army to invade Arequipa. Delighted by the prospect of war, Althaus shared all sorts of confidences with Flora. He cruelly mocked General Nieto, who, with the funds he had raised in hard cash from Arequipa's men of means—Flora watched as the downcast gentlemen filed along Calle Santo Domingo toward the general headquarters, the prefecturate, carrying their sacks of money—had bought "twenty-eight hundred sabers for an army of just six hundred soldiers, rounded up by force on the streets, who don't even have shoes to wear."

The military encampment was set up at a league's distance from the city. Under Althaus's command, some twenty officers instructed the recruits in the arts of war. In their midst, mounted on a mule and wrapped in a purple cape, with a rifle on his shoulder and a pistol on his hip, the solemn Dean Valdivia paraded. Though he was only thirty-four, he looked much older. After exchanging a few words with him, Flora came to the conclusion that this swashbuckling priest was probably the only person fighting the revolution in the service of an ideal, not petty interests. After they had finished their drills, Dean Valdivia addressed the yawning soldiers in ringing speeches, exhorting them to fight to the death for freedom and the Constitution, incarnated in the person of Marshal Orbegoso, and inveighing against "Gamarra and his slut, La Mariscala," those coup plotters and subverters of democratic order. Judging by the conviction with which he spoke, Dean Valdivia believed wholeheartedly in everything he said.

Besides the regular army, made up of the recruits levied against their will, there was a battalion of young volunteers from the well-to-do families of Arequipa. They had baptized themselves "the Immortals," another proof of the spell cast by all things French. As young men of the upper classes, they had brought with them to the camp their slaves and servants, who helped them dress, prepared their meals, and carried them in their arms across muddy fields and the river. When Flora visited the camp, they threw a banquet for her, with bands of musicians and native dances. Would these society boys be capable of fighting, when at first glance they seemed to regard the camp as just another of the genteel parties at which they whiled away their lives? Althaus said that half of them would fight and be killed, not out of idealism but because they wanted to be like the heroes of French novels; and the other half would run like hares as soon as they heard the whistle of the bullets.

The camp followers were something else. Concubines, mistresses, wives, or lovers of the recruits and soldiers, these Indian and mixed-blood women—barefoot, in brightly colored skirts, and with long braids hanging down under their picturesque country hats—made the camp work. They dug trenches, built barricades; cooked meals for their men, washed their clothes, and deloused them; acted as messengers, lookouts, nurses, and healers; and were always available for the sexual relief of the combatants. Many of them, despite being pregnant, continued to work as hard as the others, followed by small children in rags. According to Althaus, when it came time to fight the women were the most warlike, and were always on the frontlines, escorting, assisting, and spurring on their men, and taking their places when they fell. On marches, the military commanders sent them ahead to occupy villages and confiscate foodstuffs and supplies to assure the provision of the troops. They might be whores—but wasn't there a great difference between whores like these Indian women and whores like the ones who prowled the environs of the naval armory in Toulon as soon as night fell?

When Flora left for Nîmes on August 5, 1844, she told herself that her stay in Toulon had been more than profitable. The Workers' Union committee had not only a board of eight but also a membership of 110, among them eight women.

WRESTLING WITH THE ANGEL

PAPEETE, SEPTEMBER 1901

When Paul called a meeting of the Catholic Party in Papeete's city hall on September 23, 1900, against "the Chinese invasion," many people, among them the ex-soldier Pierre Levergos, his Punaauia friend and neighbor, and even Pau'ura, his wife, concluded that the eccentric, scandal-rousing painter had finally lost his mind. Teng, the Chinese storekeeper of Punaauia, had stopped greeting him long ago, and refused to sell him anything. But otherwise, even Paul himself, in his intervals of rationality and lucidity, realized that his disease and the remedies for it had impaired his thinking, and that often he was no longer capable of controlling his actions; he made decisions by instinct or intuition, like a small child or a senile old man. Truly, you weren't what you used to be, Koké. It had been months, perhaps even years, since you painted *Where Do We Come From? What Are We? Where Are We Going?*, and you hadn't finished a single new work. When you weren't laid low by illness, alcohol, or drugs, you spent all your time working on the satirical, demagogic little monthly paper *Les Guêpes* (The Wasps), mouthpiece of François Cardella's Catholic Party, in which you fiercely attacked Governor Gustave Gallet, the Protestant colonists headed by your old friend Auguste Goupil, and the island's Chinese tradesmen, against whom you worked yourself into a rage, accusing them of being the advance guard of a "barbarian invasion worse than Attila the Hun's" that intended to supplant French rule of Polynesia with "the yellow plague."

What madness was this? Neither Pierre Levergos nor his other friends could understand it. How had Paul come to serve—so stridently, not to say abjectly—the interests of Monsieur Cardella, pharmacist and owner of the sugarcane plantation Atimaono, and the other colonists of the Catholic Party, whose only reason for hating Governer Gallet was that he wanted to restrain their high-handedness and their abuse of power and make them obey the law, instead of behaving like feudal lords? It was absurd and incomprehensible, because for as long as he had lived in Tahiti, Paul had been considered an outcast by the colonists he now served; until just a few months ago, they had scorned him for being a bohemian, for his anarchist views, for being friendly with the natives who appeared in his paintings. How could it be that the Maori, whom you had once praised so highly, lamenting the disappearance of their traditions and ancient beliefs, were now accused in *Les Guêpes* by their old defender of being thieves, and of a thousand other sins? In each issue, *Les Guêpes* reproached judges for their tolerant attitude toward natives who stole from the families of colonists, and for turning a blind eye or handing down sentences so light that they were a travesty of justice. Pau'ura received complaints every day from their neighbors in Punaauia. "Is it true that Koké hates us now?" "What have we done to him?" She was at a loss for a response.

It was money that had brought about this change in him. The Catholic colonists had bought you, Koké. Before, you were always in great difficulties, making those desperate trips to the post office in Papeete to see if your friends in Paris had sent you a remittance, and borrowing money from half the world so that you, Pau'ura, and Émile wouldn't starve to death. Now, with what you were paid by the Catholic Party to fill the four pages of *Les Guêpes* with caricatures and invective, you had no material worries. Once again you were able to stock your little house in Punaauia with provisions and liquor and, when your ill health permitted it, to organize those Sunday dinners that ended in orgies and brought a blush even to the cheeks of Pierre Levergos, ex-soldier who thought there was nothing he hadn't seen.

So it was your material needs and the gradual disintegration of your brain from the cursed disease and its cursed remedies that explained your incredible change from one year to the next. Was that it, Koké? Or was this another way of killing yourself, slower but more effective than the previous attempt?

The meeting on September 23, 1900, was even worse than Pierre Levergos feared it would be. He went knowing that he wouldn't enjoy himself, but not wanting to disappoint Paul, whom he liked, and perhaps pitied. Pierre, who prided himself on being more French than anyone else (he had proved it by wearing a uniform and bearing arms for France), did not support the war declared by the Corsican Cardella and other wealthy colonists on the Chinese merchants of Tahiti in the name of patriotism and racial purity. What fool would swallow that lie? Pierre Levergos, like everyone in Tahiti-nui, knew that the Chinese were hated because they had upset the monopoly on the import of goods for local consumption. Their stores were cheaper than the shops owned by Cardella and the other colonists. Paul was the only one who seemed wholeheartedly to believe that the Chinese, who had been settled in Tahiti for two generations, constituted a threat to France; that the forces of yellow imperialism wanted to snatch France's holdings in the Pacific—and that the dream of all yellow men was to rape a white woman!

It was outrageous ideas like this and worse that Pierre Levergos heard Paul proclaim in the meeting at Papeete's town hall, which was attended by fifty Catholic colonists. Several of them, though firmly behind François Cardella in his fight against Governor Gallet, showed discomfort at certain passages in Paul's racist, chauvinistic speech, as when, speaking of the Chinese on the island, he dramatically proclaimed, gesturing emphatically: "The yellow blot on the French flag turns me red with shame."

After the members of the audience filed past the stage to congratulate the speaker, Paul and Pierre went to have a drink at one of the little portside bars before returning to Punaauia. Koké was very pale, exhausted. They had to walk slowly, Paul leaning on the staff whose head was no longer an erect phallus but a naked Tahitian woman. He was limping more than usual, and it seemed that any moment he might collapse from fatigue. Once they reached Les Îles, he slumped down at a table on the terrace, shaded by a big umbrella, and ordered absinthe. How he had aged since Pierre Levergos had first met him upon his return from Paris, in September 1895! Only five years had passed, but Paul seemed to have endured ten or more. He was no longer yesterday's big, strong, handsome figure, but a stooped old man, his hair full of gray. An angry bitterness shone on his face, which was creased with wrinkles and covered with a grizzled beard. Even his nose seemed to have become more broken and twisted, like an old vine. From time to time he grimaced, in pain or exasperation. His hands shook like those of an inveterate drunkard.

Pierre Levergos was afraid that Paul would ask him what he thought about the speech, but he was lucky, because neither in all the time they spent at the port, nor on the trip back to Punaauia, nor later that night, as they were eating outside at Paul's hut, watching Pau'ura play with little Émile, did Paul once refer to politics, his obsession of late. Instead, he talked ceaselessly about religion. Incredible, Koké—you would never stop surprising people. Now he was telling the astonished Pierre that upon his death, humanity would remember him as a painter and a religious reformer.

"That's what I am," he declared, confidently. "When the essay I'm about to finish is published, you'll understand, Pierre. In 'Modern Thought and Catholicism' I put Catholics in their place, in the name of true Christianity."

Pierre Levergos was blinking rapidly. What the devil? Was this the same Paul who, in *Les Guêpes*, had called for the removal of all Protestant teachers from the island's schools, and their replacement by Catholic missionaries? Now he had written an essay tightening the screws on Catholicism. There could be no doubt: he was out of his head and his right hand no longer knew what the left was doing. He continued along on the same theme: sooner or later, humanity would understand that *le sauvage péruvien* had been a mystical artist, and that the most religious painting of modern times was *The Vision After the Sermon*, which he had painted back in Pont-Aven, a little town in Breton Finistère, at the end of the summer of 1888. The work revived in modern art a sense of spiritual and religious inquiry that had languished ever since the height of its glory in the Middle Ages.

After that, Pierre Levergos couldn't understand a word of Koké's monologue—Paul had had a lot to drink, and his tongue was somewhat tangled—which was full of the names of people, things, places, and events that meant nothing to him. They must have come from memories that for some reason were stirred up on this quiet, moonless night in Punaauia, pleasantly cool and free of insects.

"This is 1900, isn't it?" Paul patted his neighbor on the knee. "I'm talking about the summer of 1888. Just twelve years ago. A grain of sand in the path of Chronos. But yes, it's as if centuries had passed since then."

This was what your body was telling you—the sick, tired, mistreated, and rage-filled body you dragged about with you—now that you were fifty-two. How different it was from the body you had had at forty, when, hale and hearty despite the privations and hardships you suffered for lack of money after you abandoned the world of business for painting, you exuded an invincible optimism about your calling, your talent, the beauty of life, and art as religion, a conviction that swept all obstacles aside. Weren't you idealizing the past, Paul? That summer of 1888, on your second stay in Pont-Aven, you were hardly in perfect form. Not your body, anyway, though perhaps your spirit was. Your body was still racked by the aftereffects of the fevers and malaria you had caught in Panama, although it had been ten months since you returned to France, in November 1887. The truth was that you painted *The Vision After the Sermon* while suffering from terrible dysentery, enduring the spasms of pain that were caused by the bile concentrated in your stomach before it came out your anus, escorted by thunderous farts that made you the laughingstock of the whole Pension Gloanec. How embarrassed you were to think that the young, beautiful, pure, ethereal Madeleine Bernard might hear those uncontainable strings of farts, legacy of the malarial fevers (perhaps the first symptoms of the unspeakable illness, Paul?) contracted on your ill-fated adventures in Panama and Martinique!

Now, as your tongue, which had become an unruly little beast, tried to explain all of this to the good Pierre Levergos, who was dozing in his chair, you no longer felt angry at Émile Bernard—although since your split in 1891, he had been proclaiming from streetcorners and rooftops that you grudged him credit for having been the first to develop the concept of synthetism. As if you had any interest in founding schools that it was likely no one remembered anymore. You were more hurt by other things Bernard had said—that handsome, fine-featured, slender boy, twenty years younger than you, and the brother of the beautiful Madeleine. He had appeared one day at the Pension Gloanec at the unspoiled age of eighteen, and said, stammering, "Your friend Schuffenecker sent me from Concarneau to meet you. He says you're the only person in the world who can help me be a real artist." Now he claimed that you had plagiarized the ideas and composition of *The Vision After the Sermon*, and the caps of its ecstatic Breton women, from a painting he had done previously called *Breton Women in a Meadow*.

"Nonsense, my dear Pierre," Paul declared, pounding the table. "The only thing I remember about *Breton Women in a Meadow* is the title. What could it have been that made my best disciple suddenly envy me and hate me so much?"

Something very human, Paul: Bernard realized that *The Vision After the Sermon* was a masterpiece, and the realization was too much for him. In revenge, he began to hate the person he had once so loved and admired. Poor Émile! What must have become of him? Perhaps, upon reflection, his accusations weren't entirely unfounded. Without Bernard, you might never have painted—in your tiny room at the Pension Gloanec, the inn crammed with painter friends who considered you their mentor: Bernard, Laval, Chamaillard, Meyer de Haan—the work in which you captured a miracle, or possibly simply a vision. A group of pious Breton women, after hearing the Sunday sermon of a tonsured priest (he is tucked into a corner of the painting and has a profile like yours), are absorbed in prayer and caught up in a state of bliss when they see before them—or perhaps imagine— that disturbing episode from Genesis: Jacob wrestling with the angel, the scene restaged in a Breton meadow bisected by an apple tree and colored an impossible shade of vermillion. The true miracle of the painting wasn't the apparition of biblical characters in real life, Paul, or in the minds of those humble peasants. It was the insolent colors, daringly antinaturalist: the vermillion of the earth, the bottle green of Jacob's clothing, the ultramarine blue of the angel, the Prussian black of the women's garments and the pink-, green- and blue-tinted white of the great row of caps and collars interposed between the spectator, the apple tree, and the grappling pair. What was miraculous was the weightlessness reigning at the center of the painting, the space in which the tree, the cow, and the fervent women seemed to levitate under the spell of their faith. The miracle was that you had managed to vanquish prosaic realism by creating a new reality on the canvas, where the objective and the subjective, the real and the supernatural, were mingled, indivisible. Well done, Paul! Your first masterpiece, Koké!

At the time, you didn't understand that kind of Catholic faith. You had lost it, if you ever possessed it. You hadn't gone to Brittany in search of the Catholicism the Bretons had preserved through their stubborn opposition to modernity and their veneration of the past, at a time when they were silently and firmly resisting the Third Republic's efforts to root out clericalism and institute radical secularism in France. You went, as you explained to good old Schuff, in search of the savagery and primitivism that seemed to you fertile ground for the flourishing of great art. Rural Brittany seduced you from the first as a backward, superstitious place, clinging to its ancestral rites and customs—a land that had happily turned its back on the government's modernizing efforts and responded to secularization by holding more processions, filling its churches to overflowing, and celebrating sightings of the Virgin everywhere. You loved all of that. To blend into the landscape, you began to wear an embroidered Breton vest and wooden clogs that you carved and decorated yourself. You attended the *pardons*, ceremonies that were particularly popular in Pont-Aven, at which the faithful, many on their knees, circled the church asking forgiveness for their sins; you visited all the calvaries of the region, beginning with the most revered, in Nizon, and you made a pilgrimage to the small chapel of Tremaló, with its ancient wooden multicolored Christ that would inspire you to paint another religious work: *The Yellow Christ*.

Yes, all the elements of the antinaturalist painting you dreamed of attempting were present in Brittany; you had even pontificated to good old Schuff, "When my clogs resound on this granite soil, I hear the dull, matte, powerful tone that I'm after in my paintings." You couldn't have done it without Bernard and his sister, Madeleine. Without them, you never would have begun to feel, little by little, not even noticing it at first, that you, too, were being suffused with the faith that came naturally to them, no more and no less than their delicate features, their comely figures, and the grace with which they moved and spoke. The brother and sister lived and breathed religion twenty-four hours a day. Émile had been all over Brittany and Normandy on foot, visiting churches, convents, shrines, monasteries, holy spots, and places of worship in search of traces of the Middle Ages, which he considered the supreme period of human civilization because of its nearness to God and the presence of religion in all its public and private activities. Bernard wasn't rigidly devout; he was a believer, the kind of person you rarely encountered, and after mocking him for his ardent religious passion, you unconsciously began to let yourself be infected by the intensity with which he lived his Christian faith.

An unforgettable summer, wasn't it, Paul? "It was!" he exclaimed, pounding the table again. Pau'ura had gone into the hut with the child in her arms, and by now both would likely be placidly asleep, curled up with the cat. Pierre Levergos dozed, hunched over in his chair, snoring from time to time. The night had been dark when they sat down to eat, but the wind had scattered the clouds, and now a half-moon cast its light all around. As you smoked your pipe, you could see the golden sunflowers ringing the hut. You'd been told that European sunflowers wouldn't adapt to the tropical humidity of Tahiti. But stubbornly you had asked Daniel de Monfreid for the seeds, and with Pau'ura you had planted them, watered them, and lovingly tended them. And there they were now, alive, standing tall, luminous, exotic. They were less dazzling than the sunflowers of Provence that the mad Dutchman painted with such zeal, but they kept you company and—why was it, Paul?—they gave you a kind of spiritual solace. Pau'ura, on the other hand, laughed at your exotic flowers.

Extraordinary things had happened to you that summer of 1888, in the small Breton village bathed by the Aven. You came to understand the Catholic faith, you read Victor Hugo's *Les Misérables*, you painted a masterpiece, *The Vision After the Sermon*, you fell chastely in love with Madeleine Bernard, the Virgin Mary incarnate, and you grew fond of her brother, Émile. It was that summer that the mad

Dutchman urged you, in a flood of letters, to come at last and live with him in Arles. And it was that summer, because of Panama—because of some fly in a bottle of milk—that you were constantly shitting and explosively farting.

Of all those things, which was the most important? *Les Misérables*, Koké. Charles Laval, Jacob Meyer de Haan, Émile Bernard, Ernest de Chamaillard—all the painters living with you at the inn run by the widow Marie-Jeanne Gloanec had read Victor Hugo's novel (even Marie-Jeanne had read it), and all had praised it. You resisted immersing yourself in the massive tome that was winning hearts all over France, from doorkeepers to dukes, dressmakers to intellectuals, artists to bankers. But you gave in to Madeleine's pleading when she confessed to you that the book had "made her soul quake" and that she had read the whole thing "through a mist of tears." The adventures of Jean Valjean didn't make you weep, but they did move you, more than any other book you had read before. So much so that when you exchanged self-portraits with the mad Dutchman, at his request and as a prelude to coming to live with him at Arles, you painted yourself as the novel's hero, Jean Valjean, the ex-convict who becomes a saint through the infinite mercy of Bishop Monsignor Bienvenu, who wins him over to the side of good the day he hands him the candlesticks that Valjean intended to steal from him. The novel awed you, alarmed you, unsettled you. Did such moral purity, capable of withstanding human filth, and such generosity and selflessness, truly exist in this base world? Gentle Madeleine, on the afternoons when it didn't rain and it was possible to sit and wait for nightfall on the terrace of the Pension Gloanec, had a name for it: grace. But if it was God's life-giving power that, through Bishop Bienvenu and later Jean Valjean, made good triumph over evil—evil that, pooled deep in the soul of the implacable Javert, is carried to the bottom of the Seine at the end of the novel—then what was the worth of the human animal?

In the portrait of yourself as Jean Valjean that you sent the mad Dutchman, you painted the misunderstood artist, doomed to social exile because of the blindness, materialism, and philistinism of his fellow citizens. But it may also have been in that self-portrait that you began to paint something that would only take full shape months later, in *The Vision After the Sermon*: the passage from the historic to the transcendent, the material to the spiritual, the human to the divine. Did you remember the congratulations and praise of your Pont-Aven friends when the painting was finished? And the words of the lovely Madeleine: "This work of yours will be with me until the end of my days, Monsieur Gauguin"?

Would the spiritual Madeleine have remembered *The Vision After the Sermon* as she lay dying of tuberculosis in Cairo, a year after poor Charles Laval? Of course not. She had surely forgotten all about you, the painting, and probably even that summer of 1888 in Pont-Aven. You never thought you would fall in love with anyone again after Mette Gad, Paul. True, by that time you were living apart, she in Copenhagen with your five children, and you in Pont-Aven, and the only thing left of your marriage was a piece of paper and some meager correspondence. But despite that, and despite your suspicion that you and Mette would never live together as a family again, you hadn't felt emotionally free. Until then, Koké. By 1888 you had come to the conclusion that Western-style love was a hindrance; that love, for artists, should be exclusively physical and sensual, as it was for primitive peoples, that it should not involve the emotions or the soul. Therefore, when you gave in to the temptations of the flesh and made love—with prostitutes, mostly—it felt like a hygienic act, a diversion without consequences. Madeleine Bernard's arrival at the Pension Gloanec in Pont-Aven that summer twelve years ago reminded you what it was like to be flustered, struck dumb, and thrown into confusion, so smooth and white was the skin of her youthful face, so melting her blue gaze, and so graceful and fragile her little body, which radiated innocence and goodness when she came into the dining room, went out onto the terrace, or walked on the banks of the Aven, lost in thought, watching the fishing boats set sail, as you spied on her, hidden in the trees.

You never spoke a word of love to her, or let fall a single hint. Because she was too young, because you were twice as old as she was? Rather, out of a strange moral self-censorship, the presentiment that by wooing her you would sully her integrity, her spiritual beauty. That was why you concealed your love, playing the role of an older brother who offers advice from a position of experience to the girl taking her first steps in the adult world. Not everyone suppressed the feelings aroused by her milky beauty. Charles Laval, for example. Was he already courting her that cool summer of 1888, reciting love poems to her while you, in your little room, gave shape and color to *The Vision After the Sermon*? Was theirs a beautiful romance? You hoped so. It was sad that they had died so young, a year apart, and she in exotic Egypt, so far from her native land. As you would die, Paul.

These experiences—*Les Misérables*, his pure love for Madeleine, the discussions with his painter friends in which the subject of religion frequently cropped up (like Émile Bernard, the Dutchman Jacob Meyer de Haan, a Jew converted to Catholicism, was obsessed with mysticism)—were crucial in preparing you to paint *The Vision After the Sermon*. When you had finished it, you sat up several nights in a row, writing letters to your friends by the light of the bedroom's tiny oil lamp. You told them that at last you had achieved the rustic, superstitious simplicity of the common folk, who drew no clear distinction in their daily lives and their ancient beliefs between reality and dreams, truth and fantasy, or sight and vision. Writing to Schuff and the mad Dutchman, you assured them that *The Vision After the Sermon* dynamited realism, ushering in an era in which art, instead of imitating the natural world, would be abstracted from the immediate experience of life through sleep; thus it would follow the example of the Divine Lord, creating as he had created. This was the obligation of the artist: to create, not imitate. In the future, freed from their bonds, artists could dare anything in their efforts to forge worlds different from the real world.

In whose hands must *The Vision After the Sermon* have come to rest? At the auction to raise money for your first trip to Tahiti, on Sunday, February 22, 1891, at the Hôtel Drouot, *The Vision After the Sermon* went for the highest price, nearly nine hundred francs. In what bourgeois Paris dining room must it be languishing now? You had wanted a religious setting for *The Vision After the Sermon*, and you offered to make a gift of it to the church in Pont-Aven. The priest turned it down, arguing that the colors—where in Brittany was there earth the color of blood?—would disturb the quiet decorum that was necessary in places of worship. And the priest at Nizon rejected it, too, even more angrily, claiming that such a painting would shock and scandalize his parishioners.

How things had changed in the last twelve years, Paul, since you wrote to tell good old Schuff that "with the problems of intercourse and hygiene solved, and now that I am able to focus wholly on my work, my life is settled." It was never settled, Paul. Nor was it settled now, although your articles, drawings, and caricatures for *Les Guêpes* had ended the anguish of wondering each day whether you would eat or not. Now, thanks to François Cardella and his Catholic Party cronies, you could eat and drink with a regularity you hadn't known in all your years in Tahiti. Often, the powerful Cardella invited you to his grand two-story mansion on the rue Bréa, with its carved-railing terraces and its sprawling gardens behind a wooden fence, and to political gatherings at his pharmacy on the rue de Rivoli. Were you happy? No. You were bitter and resentful. Because it had been more than a year since you painted even a simple watercolor or carved a tiny *tupapao*? Maybe, maybe not. What was the sense in painting anymore once you knew that all your works of lasting value were behind you? Should you take up your brushes to produce a testimony to your demise and ruin? Shit, no.

Better to pour all the creativity and aggression left in you into *Les Guêpes*, attacking the administrators sent from Paris, the Protestants, and the Chinese, who gave Cardella and his friends so many headaches. Did you ever feel any remorse at having become a mercenary in the service of people who once despised you, and who you yourself considered to be despicable? No. Many years ago you had decided that to be an artist it was necessary to rid yourself of every sort of bourgeois prejudice, and remorse was one of those encumbrances. Does the tiger regret the toothmarks it leaves on the deer it kills to eat? Does the cobra feel scruples when it hypnotizes a little bird and swallows it alive? Not even when you announced with great fanfare the wild claim that the Chinese had brought leprosy to Tahiti—an invention borrowed from Pierre Loti's *Marriage of Loti*, the novel that so enthused the mad Dutchman—in one of the first issues of *Les Guêpes*, in April or May of 1899, did you feel a bit of remorse for spreading slander.

"A good whore does her job well, my dear Pierre," he raved, too weak to rise from his chair. "I'm a good whore, deny it if you dare."

A deep snore came in response from Pierre Levergos. Once again, clouds had covered the moon, and the two men were plunged into an intermittent darkness, interrupted by the glow of fireflies.

Grandmother Flora would not have approved of what you were doing, Paul. Certainly not. That meddlesome madwoman would have been on the side of justice, not the side of François Cardella, principal producer of rum in Polynesia. What was justice on this wretched island, which every day looked less like the world of the ancient Maori and more like festering France? Grandmother Flora would have tried to find out, poking her nose into the mess of disputes, intrigue, and sordid interests disguised as altruism and then delivering a stern verdict. That was why you died when you were only forty-one, Grandmother! He, on the other hand, who didn't give a damn about justice, had, at fifty-three, lived twelve years longer than Grandmother Flora. But you wouldn't last much longer, Paul. In fact, with regard to what really mattered—beauty and art—your life story was already at an end.

When he was awakened at dawn on the following day by a downpour that soaked him to the skin, he remained sitting in his chair, exposed to the elements, with a terribly stiff neck. Pierre Levergos had left at some point during the night. He let the rain fall on him until he was entirely awake, and then he dragged himself into the hut, where he lay down in bed and slept. Pau'ura and the child had gone out.

Since he had given up painting, he no longer got up early as he used to. He tossed in bed until late in the morning, and then went to take the public coach to Papeete, where he stayed until dark, preparing the next issue of *Les Guêpes*. The magazine was monthly and only four pages long, but since everything in it was his—articles, caricatures, drawings, festive verses, gibes and gossip, funny stories—each issue required plenty of work. Then, too, he carried the materials to the printer, corrected the colors, proofs, and printing, and made sure that the magazine reached its subscribers and public places. He enjoyed all of this, and he tackled his work with enthusiasm. But he was bored by the constant meetings with François Cardella and Cardella's Catholic Party friends, who financed the magazine and paid him. They were always annoying him with bits of advice that were really orders in disguise. And they weren't afraid to reproach him, whether for going too far in his criticisms of Governor Gallet or for not being virulent enough. Sometimes he listened to them resignedly, his mind on other things. Other times he lost patience, interrupting with comments of his own, and on two occasions he offered his resignation. They didn't accept it. Who could those scum find to replace him, when they were barely able to scrawl a letter?

And so his life would have gone on indefinitely, if his physical ills, which had eased for some time, hadn't struck again at the beginning of 1901, with more fury than ever. One evening in January of the first year of the new century, at François Cardella's house on the rue Bréa, when his host offered him a cup of coffee with a splash of brandy, Paul's heart went mad. It beat fast, furiously, and his chest rose and fell like a bellows. He could scarcely breathe. All week he suffered from shortness of breath and choking attacks; finally, a vomit of blood drove him to the Vaiami Hospital.

"Well, Dr. Lagrange, does this mean I have heart problems now, too?" he joked to the physician examining him.

Dr. Lagrange shook his head. It wasn't a new illness, my friend. It was the same one as always, continuing its inexorable march. Now, just as it had done to his skin, blood, and mind, it began to ravage his heart. Between January and March of 1901, he had to check into the hospital three times, each time for several days, and finally for two weeks. They treated him well at the Vaiami, because most of the doctors, beginning with Dr. Lagrange, who was now the head of the hospital, supported Cardella in his campaign against the authorities sent from France. They even found him a drawing board so he could prepare issues of Les Guêpes from his bed.

But these obligatory stays in the hospital had an unexpected effect. He thought a great deal, and after a long period of sleeplessness, he suddenly came to the following conclusion: he was tired of what he was doing, and the people he was doing it for. He didn't want to die working for fools. It was sad to have come to such a pass, you, who had traveled to Tahiti fleeing money and—as you dreamed with the mad Dutchman in Arles, when you were still on good terms—yearning to build a little Eden devoted to freedom, beauty, creation, and pleasure, without European civilization's dependence on money. The House of Pleasure, Vincent called it! How strange and capricious fate was, Koké.

Had you forgotten, Paul? It all began a year and a half ago, after your frustrated suicide attempt, while you were painting *Where Do We Come From? What Are We? Where Are We Going?*, the last of your masterpieces. Things began to disappear from the hut—did they disappear, or were you imagining that they had?—and in your head you became certain that the thieves were the natives of Punaauia. Pau'ura told you that you were wrong, that you were dreaming. But the wheels of delusion were already turning and could not be stopped. You insisted that the court in Papeete prosecute the thieves, and since the judges reasonably refused to call a trial on the basis of such flimsy accusations, you wrote harsh public letters, full of fire and vitriol, accusing the colonial administration of colluding with the natives against the French. Thus was born *Le Sourire: Journal méchant*, whose venom amused the colonists. Delighted, they bought it, and sent you notes of congratulations. Then Cardella himself came to visit, and offered you the moon and the stars if you would take charge of *Les Guêpes*. Everything proceeded so smoothly, almost before you realized what was happening. For eighteen months, you had eaten and drunk, and caused a small earthquake on the island with your diatribes—and you had become distracted, forgetting in the confusion that you were a painter. Were you content with your fate? No. Would you continue working for Cardella? Certainly not.

What would you do, then? Leave this cursed island of Tahiti as soon as possible, since it was already ruined by Europe, which had destroyed everything that once made it a savage place, with room to breathe. Where would you take your tired bones and your ailing body, Paul? To the Marquesas, of course. The Maori people there were still free and untamed, and had preserved intact their culture, customs, and art of tattooing, as well as their sacred cannibalism, which they practiced deep in the forest, far from Western eyes. It would be a reawakening, Koké. In your new surroundings, fresh and unspoiled, the unspeakable illness would halt its progress. It was even possible that you would take up your brush again, Paul.

Once he had made the decision, everything began to fall into place. He had just been released from the Vaiami Hospital when, like a bombshell, the news came that Paris had removed Governor Gustave Gallet from his post. The colonists you worked for were so happy that it wasn't hard for you to convince them that after this triumph it no longer made sense to keep publishing the paper. They let you go with a nice bonus.

A few days later, when he was in one of those feverish states that always preceded his major life changes, and was investigating ships between Tahiti and the Marquesas, Pierre Levergos came to tell him that Axel Nordman, a Swedish gentleman recently settled in Tahiti, wanted to buy Paul's hut in Punaauia. He had seen it while passing by and had taken a liking to it. Paul closed the deal in forty-eight hours; after paying for his ticket and the shipping of his few possessions, he even had enough money over to give a little to Pau'ura and Émile. The girl categorically refused to come with him to the Marquesas. How could she live there, so far from her family? It was a very distant and dangerous place. Koké might die at any moment, and then what would she and the boy do? She preferred to return home to her family.

You didn't care much. Truthfully, Pau'ura and Émile would have been in the way as you embarked on your new existence. It irritated you, however, that Pierre Levergos refused to accompany you. You had offered to take him as your cook and share everything you had with him. Your neighbor was unyielding: he wouldn't leave here for all the gold in the world. Never would he be so mad as to follow you in your misguided decision. Then Paul called him bourgeois, cowardly, mediocre, and disloyal.

Pierre Levergos sat pensive for a while, without responding to these insults, chewing a blade of grass in a mouth from which half the teeth were missing. He and Paul were sitting outside, in the shade of the big mango tree. At last, calmly, without raising his voice, and enunciating each word clearly, Pierre spoke.

"Everywhere you go, you've been saying to people that you're leaving for the Marquesas because you'll be able to find cheaper models there, and virgin land, and a culture that isn't spoiled yet. I think you're lying to them. And you're lying to yourself, too, Paul. You're leaving Tahiti because of the rash on your legs. Here, no woman wants to sleep with you anymore because the smell is so bad. That's why Pau'ura doesn't want to go with you. You think that in the Marquesas, because they're poorer there, you'll be able to buy girls with a fistful of sweets. It's just another dream of yours that will turn into a nightmare, neighbor, mark my words."

No one came to see him off at the port in Papeete on September 10, 1901, when he boarded *La Croix du Sud* for Hiva Oa. With him he brought his harmonium, his collection of pornographic postcards, his chest of keepsakes, his self-portrait as Christ on the Mount of Olives, and a small painting of Brittany in the snow. Despite the new owner's insistence that he take everything away from the house in Punaauia, he left some rolled-up paintings there, and a dozen wooden carvings of his invented *tupapaos*. As he would learn a few months later in a letter from Axel Nordman, the hut's new owner threw all these trifles into the sea because they frightened his little son.

THE BATTLE OF CANGALLO

NÎMES, AUGUST 1844

In the stifling little room at the Hôtel du Gard in Nîmes, with its
smell of mustiness and cat urine, Flora spent the worst six days and
nights of her tour. Almost every night, from the fifth to the twelfth
of August 1844, she had a horrific nightmare. From their pulpits, the
city's priests rallied the fanatical masses packing the churches, sending them out into the streets of Nîmes in search of her, to kill her.
Trembling, she hid in doorways, vestibules, dark corners; from her
precarious refuge she could hear and see the throngs unleashed in
pursuit of the godless revolutionary, to avenge Christ their King.
When they found her and fell upon her with their faces distorted
by hatred, she awoke, drenched in sweat and paralyzed with fear,
smelling of incense.

From the first day, everything went badly in Nîmes. The Hôtel du
Gard was dirty and unfriendly, and the food was dreadful. (You,
Florita, who had never given much thought to food, now found yourself dreaming of a good homemade meal of thick soup, fresh eggs,
and newly churned butter.) Her stomach troubles, diarrhea, and the
pains in her uterus, along with the unbearable heat, made each day an
ordeal, aggravated by the feeling that her sufferings would be in vain,

since in this gigantic priest's-hole she wouldn't find a single intelligent worker to serve as a cornerstone for the Workers' Union.

In the end, she found one, though he wasn't from Nîmes but—naturally!—from Lyon. Out of forty thousand workers at this center for the production of silk, wool, and cotton shawls, he was the only one at the four meetings she managed to organize—with the unenthusiastic help of a pair of doctors recommended to her as philanthropists, modern thinkers, and Fourierists, Dr. Pleindoux and Dr. De Castelnaud—who didn't seem completely numbed by the narcotizing teachings of the priests, which the workers of Nîmes shamelessly swallowed. You thought you knew all there was to know about imbecility, Andalusa, but Nîmes showed you that its bounds could be extended indefinitely. The day she heard a mechanic at a meeting say, "Rich people are necessary because thanks to them there are poor people in the world, and we'll go to heaven and they won't," she first burst out laughing, and then suffered a dizzy spell. So disheartened was she to learn that the priests had convinced the workers it was good to be exploited—because by being poor they would gain entrance to Paradise—that she was speechless for some time, without even the heart to be angry.

Only during the tragicomic farce of the Battle of Cangallo, toward the end of her stay in Arequipa ten years before, had she seen such monumental idiocy and confusion—with one difference, Florita. A decade ago, as the Gamarristas and Orbegosistas enacted their pantomime complete with bloodshed and death on the outskirts of Arequipa, you, a privileged spectator, watched with emotion, sadness, irony, and compassion, trying to understand why Indians and men of mixed race, dragged into a civil war devoid of principles, ideas, or morals, a crude display of the ambitions of military leaders, allowed themselves to be used as cannon fodder, instruments in a struggle of factions that had nothing to do with them. In Nîmes, however, faced with a wall of religious prejudices and folly that blocked all prospects for the preaching of peaceful revolution, you reacted in a bitter, impassioned way, letting your rage cloud your judgment.

Was it your ill health that made you so impatient? Was it the fatigue of all these months living on the road, in shabby boardinghouses and inns, or squalid lodgings like the Hôtel du Gard, that was causing your depression? The nightmares in which the priests of Nîmes ordered the rabble to hunt you down left you exhausted. Better not to sleep at all than to dream. She spent much of the night with her window open, plotting apocalyptic ends for the city's priests. If you come to power, you'll teach them a terrible lesson, Florita. You'll drive them into the Roman coliseum they're so proud of and let them be devoured there by the same workers who've been turned into heartless beasts by their sermons. In the end, imagining these cruelties restored her good humor, making her laugh like a girl. Then, she would return to Arequipa.

What if all battles were as ridiculous as the one you happened to witness in the White City? Scenes of human chaos that afterward, to satisfy national patriotism, would be turned by the history writers into coherent demonstrations of idealism, courage, generosity, and principles, erasing all the fear, stupidity, avarice, egoism, cruelty, and ignorance of the many who were mercilessly sacrificed to the ambition, greed, and fanaticism of the few. It was possible that one hundred years from now, the travesty that was the Battle of Cangallo, that orgy of absurdity, would appear in Peruvian history books as an exemplary page in the country's glorious past, with heroic Arequipa, defender of General Orbegoso, the chosen president, fighting gallantly against the rebel forces of General Gamarra and losing, after deeds as bloody as they were brave (days later to be magically declared victorious). Yes, Florita: real history was a hideous mess, and written history was a maze of patriotic trickery.

General San Román's Gamarrista troops took so long to reach Arequipa that the Orbegosista army, led by General Nieto and Dean Valdivia, with Flora's cousin Clemente Althaus as chief of staff, nearly forgot about them, to such an extent that on April 1, 1834, General Nieto gave his soldiers permission to go into the city and get drunk. All night, from the Tristán house on Calle Santo Domingo, Florita could hear the clamor of singing, dancing, and shouting as the soldiers celebrated their free night at the city's *chicha* stands, downing the fermented corn drink and eating spicy stews. The music of guitars and the lutelike *charangos* rang through the streets. The next day, along the crest of the hills in the distance, in the crystalline air between the volcanoes on the horizon, General San Román's soldiers came into sight. Protected from the sun by a red parasol and armed with binoculars, Florita watched them appear and crawl closer, like a patch of ants. Meanwhile, in the midst of great uproar, her uncle Pío, cousin Carmen, aunt Joaquina, and everyone else—aunts, cousins, uncles, retainers, and friars—rushed around the house, filling bags and boxes with jewelry, money, clothing, and valuables, to take with them when they sought shelter in the city's monasteries, convents, and churches, like the rest of Arequipan society. At midmorning, when a great cloud of dust had completely obscured her view of General Román's soldiers, Flora saw Clemente Althaus appear on horseback, sweating and fully armed. The colonel had escaped the camp for a moment to warn them.

"All our men are drunk, including the officers, because of Nieto's stupid idea to give them the night free," he shouted angrily. "If San Román attacks now, we're lost. Go immediately to the monastery, to Santo Domingo."

And he rode off at full gallop, cursing in German. Although her aunts and female cousins urged her to accompany them, Flora stayed on the roof of the mansion with the men. They would move to nearby Santo Domingo when the battle began. The first bursts of musket fire sounded at seven in the evening. The shooting continued for several hours, sporadic and distant, without coming any nearer to the city. Around nine, a lone orderly appeared on Calle Santo Domingo. He had been sent by General Nieto to his wife, to tell her to hurry to the nearest monastery; things weren't going well. Don Pío Tristán had refreshment brought for him, while the orderly told them what had happened. Panting with fatigue, he described the battle as he gulped food and drink. General Román's square battalion was the first to attack. General Nieto's dragoons moved forward to meet it, and managed to hold it back. The struggle was even until, as night fell, Colonel Morán's artillery got its target confused, and instead of aiming at the Gamarristas, fired volleys of grapeshot at its own dragoons, wreaking havoc among them. The outcome was still undecided, but the triumph of San Román could no longer be ruled out. In anticipation of an invasion of the city by enemy troops, it would be best if "the gentlemen went into hiding." Did you remember the general terror this news produced, Florita? Minutes later, uncles and male cousins, followed by slaves, some loaded down with rugs and sacks of food and clothing, and many others carrying silver, china, and porcelain chamber pots, paraded toward the monastery and church of Santo Domingo, after boarding up the doors. The news must have spread like wildfire, because on their way to shelter, Florita recognized other families, running frantically for consecrated ground. In their arms they had all the riches and treasure they could carry, to keep it safe from the victor's grasp.

At the church and monastery of Santo Domingo, indescribable chaos reigned. The families of Arequipa could barely move, crammed into halls, passageways, naves, cloisters, and cells, with their children and slaves sprawled on the floor. There was a nauseating smell of urine and excrement, and a maddening din. Scenes of panic coincided with the prayers and psalms being sung by some groups, while the monks scurried back and forth, trying in vain to keep order. Because of their rank and fortune, Don Pío and his family had the privilege of occupying the prior's office; there, the vast clan, despite the closeness of the room, could at least take turns moving. The shooting stopped during the night, grew loud again at dawn, and ceased completely a little while later. When Don Pío decided to go and see what was happening, Flora went with him. The street was deserted; the Tristán house hadn't been invaded. From the roof, with her binoculars, the morning skies clear and the dust cloud swept away by a fresh breeze, Flora could see the shapes of soldiers embracing one another in the distance. What was happening? They soon found out, when Colonel Althaus came galloping down Calle Santo Domingo, blackened from head to toe, his hands covered in scratches, and his blond hair white with dust.

"General Nieto is even more of a fool than his officers and soldiers," he bellowed, beating the dust off his uniform. "He's accepted the truce requested by San Román, when we could have finished him off."

Colonel Morán's artillery, as well as causing losses among the army's own dragoons—between thirty and forty were killed, Althaus calculated—had bombarded the camp followers, mistaking them for Gamarristas; the colonel's cannons had crushed and crippled God knew how many of the women, irreplaceable as auxiliaries and provisioners of the troops. Despite this, after several bayonet charges, Nieto's soldiers, roused by the example of Dean Valdivia and Althaus himself, forced San Román's army to retreat. Then, instead of allowing the priest and the German to give chase and annihilate them, as they requested, Nieto accepted the enemy's appeal for a truce. He met with San Román, and they embraced and wept, kissing a Peruvian flag together. After the Gamarrista promised that he would recognize Orbegoso as president of Peru, that idiot Nieto sent him food and drink for his hungry soldiers. Dean Valdivia and Althaus had assured him it was a ploy by his adversary to gain time and regroup his forces. It was madness to accept a truce! Nieto stood firm: San Román was a gentleman; he would recognize Orbegoso as head of state, and thus the Peruvian family would be reconciled.

Althaus asked Don Pío, together with other Arequipa notables, to dismiss Nieto, assume command of the army, and order the resumption of hostilities. Flora's uncle turned as pale as death. He swore that he felt ill, and went away to bed. "The only thing that old miser cares about is his money," Althaus muttered. Florita asked her cousin whether, since the war had come to a halt, he would take her to the camp. After hesitating for a moment, the German agreed, hoisting her onto his horse's rump. The whole surrounding area was in ruins. Farms and dwellings had been sacked before being occupied by the camp followers and turned into shelters or infirmaries. Bloody women, half bandaged, were cooking on improvised hearths, and wounded soldiers still lay moaning on the ground, unattended, while others, exhausted by their endeavors, slept the sleep of the dead. Many dogs were roaming about, sniffing at corpses under clouds of vultures. While Florita was requesting details of the battle from some officers at Althaus's command post, an envoy arrived from San Román. By consensus of the general staff, he explained, his superior's promise to recognize Orbegoso as president could not be upheld: all his officers were opposed. Thus, action would begin anew. "Because of that cretin Nieto, we've lost a battle we had already won," Althaus whispered to Flora. He gave her a mule to return to Arequipa and tell the family that the war was starting up again.

Dawn found her laughing to herself in her miserable little room at the Hôtel du Gard at the memory of that battle, which proceeded from one mishap to the next on the way to its improbable conclusion. It was her third day in odious Nîmes, and at midmorning she had an appointment with the baker-poet Jean Reboul, whose poems had been praised by Lamartine and Victor Hugo. Would this bard, sprung from the world of the downtrodden, at last be the champion you needed to make the idea of the Workers' Union take hold in Nîmes and wake its people from their slumbers? Not a chance. Jean Reboul, famous worker poet of France, was, she discovered, a vain and prideful man—vanity was the poets' malady, Florita; it had been amply proved—whom she came to hate after spending ten minutes in his company. At one point she wanted to cover his mouth to silence his detestable flow of nonsense. He received her at his bakery and escorted her to the floor above. When she asked if he had heard of her crusade and the Workers' Union, the conceited tub of flesh began to list the dukes, professors, officials, and teachers who had written him, praising his inspired vision and thanking him for all he had done for French letters. When she tried to explain about the peaceful revolution that would end discrimination, injustice, and poverty, the fatuous pig interrupted her with a declaration that rendered her speechless. "But that is precisely what our Holy Mother the Church does, madame." Regaining her composure, Flora tried to enlighten him, explaining that all religious leaders—Jews, Protestants, and Mahometans, but especially Catholics—were allies of the exploiters and the rich because in their sermons they held out the promise of Paradise to keep suffering humanity resigned to its fate, when what was important wasn't some improbable heavenly reward after death but the free and just society that should be built here and now. The baker-poet recoiled as if the devil himself had appeared before him.

"You are evil, evil," he exclaimed, performing a kind of exorcism with his hands. "And you thought to come to me for help, with a project opposed to my religion?"

Madame-la-Colère finally exploded, calling Reboul a traitor to his origins, an impostor, an enemy of the working class undeserving of his high reputation, as time would make plain.

The visit to the baker-poet upset her so much that she had to sit on a bench in the shade of some plane trees until she was a little calmer. Next to her, she heard a couple, both very excited, saying they were going that afternoon to hear the pianist Liszt at the municipal auditorium. A curious thing; she and the pianist had coincided at nearly every stop on her tour. He seemed to be following on your heels, Florita. What if that night you took a rest and went to hear him play? No, impossible. You couldn't waste your time attending concerts like a bourgeoise.

It was only a month later, in Lima, that she heard how the Battle of Cangallo had ended, from the Gamarrista colonel Bernardo Escudero, with whom she may have embarked on a romance in her final days in Arequipa (did you, Florita?). The memory obliterated all thoughts of Jean Reboul. What a story! The day after the interruption of hostilities between Orbegosistas and Gamarristas, General Nieto ordered his army to set out in search of the conniving San Román. He found the Gamarrista soldiers in Cangallo, bathing in the river and resting. Nieto fell upon them, and victory seemed at hand. But once again, errors aided San Román. This time, it was Nieto's dragoons who mistook their target. Instead of firing their rifles at the enemy, they decimated their own artillery forces, even injuring Colonel Morán. Overwhelmed by what they imagined to be an unstoppable attack by the Gamarristas, Nieto's soldiers turned and ran in wild retreat toward Arequipa. At the same time, not knowing what was happening on the other side, and believing himself lost, General San Román also ordered his troops to retreat by forced marches, in view of the enemy's superior strength. In his flight, which was as desperate and ridiculous as Nieto's, he didn't stop until he reached Vilque, forty leagues away. The picture of the two armies running from each other with their generals at their heads, each believing it had been defeated, was something you would always remember, Florita—a symbol of the chaos and absurdity of life in your father's country, that endearing caricature of a republic. Sometimes the memory amused you, as it did now now, seeming to represent on a grand scale one of those Molièresque farces of entanglements and misunderstandings that here in France were thought to unfold exclusively on the stage.

The day after the battle, San Román learned that his rival had also fled, and once again he made an about-face and led his troops to occupy Arequipa. General Nieto had had time to enter the city, leave his wounded in the churches and hospitals, and with the troops still remaining to him, beat a retreat toward the coast. Florita said goodbye to her cousin, Colonel Clemente Althaus, with tears in her eyes. You suspected you would never see your darling blond barbarian again. You yourself helped pack his bags with changes of clean clothing, tea, bottles of bordeaux, and bags of sugar, chocolate, and bread.

When the soldiers of San Román, the inadvertent victor of the Battle of Cangallo, entered Arequipa twenty-four hours later, the feared plundering did not ensue. A commission of notables, led by Don Pío Tristán, welcomed them with flags and bands of musicians. In pledge of his solidarity with the conquering army, Don Pío gave Colonel Bernardo Escudero a donation of two thousand pesos for the Gamarrista cause.

Did Colonel Escudero fall in love with you, Andalusa? You were sure he did. And you fell in love with him too, didn't you? Well, maybe. But you were restrained by your better judgment before it was too late. According to the gossip, for the last three years, Escudero had been not only the secretary, deputy, and aide-de-camp but also the lover of the astonishing Doña Francisca Zubiaga de Gamarra, called Doña Pancha or La Mariscala, and the Virago by her enemies; the wife of Marshal Agustín Gamarra, ex-president of Peru, military leader, and professional conspirator.

Which parts of La Mariscala's story were truth, and which fiction? You would never be sure, Florita. The woman fascinated you, firing your imagination as no one ever had before; it might have been her warlike image, making her seem a character out of a novel, that awoke in you the determination and inner strength to become as free and forthright as in those days only men were allowed to be. La Mariscala had done it: why not Flora Tristán? She must have been the same age as you, perhaps thirty-three or thirty-four. She was from Cuzco, the daughter of a Spanish father and Peruvian mother; she met Agustín Gamarra, hero of Peru's struggle for independence—he fought alongside Sucre at the Battle of Ayacucho—in Lima, in a convent where she had been placed by her parents. In love, the girl ran away from the convent to be with him. They married in Cuzco, where Gamarra was prefect. The twenty-year-old wasn't the domestic, passive, child-bearing wife that most Peruvian ladies were, and were expected to be. She was her husband's most effective collaborator, his brains and right hand in all matters political, social, and even—this especially enhanced her legend—military. She served in his place as prefect of Cuzco when he was traveling, and on one such occasion, she crushed a conspiracy, appearing at the headquarters of the conspirators dressed as an officer, carrying a bag of money and a loaded pistol. "Which do you choose? Will you surrender and share the contents of this bag among you, or fight?" They preferred to surrender. More intelligent, courageous, ambitious, and audacious than General Gamarra, Doña Pancha rode on horseback alongside her husband, always dressed in boots, trousers, and army jacket, and fought in battles and skirmishes like the boldest of warriors. She became famous as an excellent shot. During the conflict with Bolivia, it was she, at the head of the troops, with her boundless daring and rash courage, who won the Battle of Paria. After the victory, she celebrated with her soldiers dancing *huaynos* and drinking *chicha*. She talked to them in Quechua, and she knew how to swear. After that, her influence over General Gamarra was absolute. In the three years that he was president of Peru, Doña Pancha wielded the true power. She was said to be embroiled in intrigues and to treat her enemies with unprecedented cruelty, because she was as lacking in scruples and restraint as she was brave. It was also said that she had many lovers, and that she alternately pampered and abused them, as if they were dolls or lapdogs.

Of all the stories told about her, there were two you had never forgotten, because—it was true, wasn't it, Florita?—you would have loved to have been the protagonist of both. La Mariscala was visiting the grounds of the Real Felipe Fort in Callao, in the president's stead. Suddenly, among the officers receiving her with full military honors, she noticed one who had boasted, or so it was rumored, of having been her lover. Without a moment's hesitation, she rushed at him, marking his face with a blow of her whip. Then, still seated on her horse, she ripped off his stripes with her own hand.

"You could never have been my lover, Captain," she declared. "I don't go to bed with cowards."

The other story took place in the palace. Doña Pancha was giving a dinner for four army officers. She was a charming hostess, joking with her guests and treating them with exquisite courtesy. When it came time for coffee and cigars, she dismissed the servants. Closing the doors, she turned to face one of her guests, assuming the cold voice and pitiless gaze common to all her rages.

"Did you tell these three friends of yours here present that you were tired of being my lover? If they have slandered you, you and I will give them their just deserts. But if it is true, and by your pallor I fear it is, these officers and I are going to whip you to within an inch of your life."

Yes, Florita, that woman—who, as you once witnessed, was plagued by epileptic attacks, which, together with her defeats and sufferings, would send her to her death before she was thirty-five—taught you an unforgettable lesson. There *were* women, then—and one in this backward, uncivilized country still in the making, at the ends of the earth—who refused to be humbled or treated like serfs, who managed to make themselves respected, who were worthy in and of themselves, not as appendages of men, even when it came to handling a whip or firing a pistol. Was Colonel Bernardo Escudero La Mariscala's lover? For three years, the Spanish adventurer—who, like Clemente Althaus, had come to Peru to enroll as a mercenary in the country's internal wars to try to make his fortune—had been Doña Pancha's shadow. When Florita asked him outright, he denied it, indignantly: lies of the Señora Gamarra's enemies, of course! But you weren't entirely convinced.

Escudero wasn't handsome, but he was very attractive. Thin, smiling, gallant, he had read more and seen more of the world than the other men around Flora, and she enjoyed herself thoroughly in his company as Arequipa adjusted, grudgingly, to its occupation by San Román's troops. They saw each other morning and evening, and rode together around Tiabaya, to the thermal springs of Yura, and to the slopes of the Misti, the volcano presiding benevolently over the city. Flora barraged him with questions about Doña Pancha, and Lima and its inhabitants. He answered with infinite patience and an abundance of wit. His remarks were intelligent, and his attentions subtle. In all, he was a supremely appealing man. What if you were to marry Colonel Bernardo Escudero, Florita? And what if, like Doña Pancha, you became the power behind the throne, using your intelligence and influence to institute from above the reforms society required in order to ensure that women would no longer be the slaves of men?

It wasn't a passing fancy. The temptation—to marry Escudero, stay in Peru, be a second Mariscala—took hold of you so thoroughly that you flirted with the colonel as you had never flirted with any man before, or ever would again, bent on seducing him. He suspected nothing, and was snared in an instant. Closing her eyes—a breeze had sprung up, bringing relief from the scorching summer heat of Nîmes—she relived that evening. She and Bernardo were alone together, at the Tristán house. Her words echoed under the vaulted ceiling. Suddenly, the colonel took her hand and lifted it to his lips, in great earnest. "I love you, Flora. I'm mad about you. You can do what you like with me. I'll always be yours." Were you pleased by this rapid victory? At first you were. Your ambitious plans were becoming reality, and it was all happening so fast. But a little while later, in the dark hallway of the house on Santo Domingo, when the colonel, as he was leaving, took you in his arms, pressed you to him, and lowered his mouth to yours, the spell was broken. No, no, my God, what madness! Never, never! To suffer that again? To feel, at night, a hairy, sweaty body on top of you, riding you like a filly? Not for all the gold in the world, Florita! The next day, you informed your uncle that you wanted to return to France. And on April 25, to Escudero's surprise, you bade farewell to Arequipa. Riding along with an English trader's mule train, you traveled to Islay, and then to Lima, where, two months later, you would take ship for Europe.

This tumult of Arequipan memories distracted her from the unpleasantness of her meeting with the poet-baker Jean Reboul. She walked slowly back to the Hôtel du Gard, along streets crowded with people speaking the regional language she didn't understand. Her tour had taught her that French was far from being the language of all Frenchmen, no matter what was thought in Paris. On many corners, she saw the tumblers, magicians, clowns, and fortune-tellers who in this city nearly outnumbered the beggars with outstretched hands offering to "pray a Hail Mary for the good lady's soul" in exchange for a coin. Begging was one of her chief frustrations: at every meeting, she tried to instill in the workers the idea that this sort of solicitation, a practice encouraged by the cassock-clad, was as repugnant as charity;

both morally degraded the poor and served only to soothe the conscience of the bourgeoisie. Poverty had to be fought by reform, not by alms. But her relief and good humor were short-lived, because on the way to the hotel, she decided to stop by the pool where washerwomen laundered the city's clothes. It was a spot that had filled her with rage ever since her first day in Nîmes. How was it possible that in 1844, in a country that prided itself on being the most civilized in the world, such a cruel and inhuman spectacle should exist, and that no one in this city of clerics and pious folk should do anything to put an end to it?

The pool, sixty feet long and one hundred feet wide, was fed by a spring that flowed from the rocks. It was the only laundering place in the city. In it, the clothing of the people of Nîmes was washed and wrung out by three or four hundred women, who, given the absurd shape of the pool, had to stand in water up to their waists in order to lather and scrub the clothes on the washboards, the only ones in the world that, instead of being tilted toward the water so that the women could remain kneeling on the shore, were set the opposite way. What stupid or wicked mind had conceived this design, which left the unfortunate women swollen and deformed like toads, and covered with rashes and blotches? The problem wasn't just that the washerwomen spent so many hours in the water, but that the water, which was also used for the local industry's dyeing of shawls, was full of soap, potassium, caustic soda, Javelle water, tallow, and dyes like indigo, saffron, and ruby. Several times Flora had spoken to some of these unhappy women, who suffered from rheumatism or infections of the uterus, and complained of miscarriages and difficult pregnancies. The pool was never empty. Many of the washerwomen preferred to work by night, when the absence of dye workers allowed them to choose a good spot. Despite their dramatic plight, and her efforts to explain that she was striving to improve their lot, she wasn't able to convince a single washerwoman to attend the Workers' Union meetings. They always seemed wary, and resigned. At one of her meetings with the doctors Pleindoux and Castelnaud, she mentioned the pool. They were surprised that Flora found the working conditions inhumane. Weren't clothes washed the same way everywhere? They saw no cause for alarm. Naturally, after discovering what the pool in Nîmes was like, Flora decided that while she was staying in the city, she would never send her clothes out to be cleaned. She would wash them herself, at the hotel.

The Hôtel du Gard wasn't exactly Madame Denuelle's guest house, was it, Andalusa? It was with Madame Denuelle, a former Parisian opera singer who had been stranded in Lima and had become an innkeeper, that Flora spent her last two months on Peruvian soil. Captain Zacharie Chabrié had recommended the place, and indeed, Madame Denuelle, who had heard about Flora from Chabrié, received her very graciously, offering her a comfortable room and excellent meals at a modest price (Don Pío had given her a parting gift of four hundred francs, as well as paying for her passage). In those eight weeks, Madame Denuelle introduced her to the cream of society, who came to the boardinghouse to play cards, converse, and engage in what Flora discovered were the principal pursuits of Lima's wealthy families: frivolity, social life, dances, luncheons, dinners, and worldly gossip. An odd city this Peruvian capital. Though its population was only eighty thousand, it could not have been more cosmopolitan. Along its little streets, intersected by channels into which residents tossed their refuse and emptied their chamberpots, there passed sailors from ships anchored in the harbor of Callao, hailing from all over the world—English, Americans, Dutch, French, Germans, Orientals—so that when Flora went out to visit the countless colonial monasteries, convents, and churches, or to walk around the Plaza Mayor, a sacred pastime of the well-dressed, she heard more languages around her than she had on the boulevards of Paris. Surrounded by groves of orange trees, banana trees, and palms, and built with spacious single-story houses, each with a large patio for sitting outside in the fresh air—it never rained here—and two courtyards, the first for the masters and the second for the slaves, this small, provincial-looking city, with its forest of steeples standing defiantly against the perpetually gray sky, had the most worldly, inviting, and sensual culture that Flora could have imagined.

Between Madame Denuelle's friends and her own relatives (she had brought letters for them from Arequipa), Flora was swamped every day of her two months in the city by invitations to sumptuous houses where lavish dinners were served. And then there were visits to the theater, the bullring (at one of the detestable fights a bull disemboweled a horse and gored a bullfighter), cockfights, the obligatory Paseo de las Aguas, where families went on foot or in calèches to see and be seen, to court, or to gossip, the hills of Amancaes, processions, services (women attended two or three every Sunday), and the beaches of Chorrillos; she also visited the dungeons of the Inquisition, and saw the horrifying instruments of torture that were used to wring confessions from the accused. She met everyone, from the president of the republic, General Orbegoso, and the most popular generals—some of them, like Salaverry, were little more than callow youths, amiable and gallant but shockingly ignorant—to an eminent thinker, the priest Luna Pizarro, who invited her to a session of Congress.

It was the Lima society women who impressed her the most. True, they seemed blind and deaf to the misery that surrounded them, the streets full of beggars and barefoot Indians who, squatting and motionless, seemed to be waiting for death, before whom the women shamelessly flaunted their elegant clothing and riches. But the freedom they enjoyed! In France, it would have been inconceivable. Dressed in *tapadas*, the typical garb of Lima, and the cleverest and most provocative attire ever devised—it consisted of a narrow skirt, the *saya*, and a shawl that, like a hood, covered shoulders, arms, and head, delicately tracing the outline of the body and covering three quarters of the face, leaving just one eye visible—the women of Lima, so arrayed (or so disguised), were able to pretend that they were beautiful and mysterious, and at the same time become invisible. No one could recognize them—least of all their husbands, as Flora heard them boast—and this made them uncommonly bold. They would go out alone, although followed at a distance by a slave, and they loved to play jokes or poke fun at acquaintances whose paths they crossed. They all smoked, bet heavily at cards, and were always flirting, sometimes outrageously. Madame Denuelle kept her informed about the secret love affairs, the romantic intrigues in which husbands and wives were embroiled, and which, if scandal erupted, would sometimes end in saber or pistol duels on the banks of the sluggish Rímac. As well as going out alone, the women of Lima rode horseback dressed like men, played the guitar, and sang and danced—even the old ladies—with bold insouciance. So emancipated were they that Florita found herself in difficulties at gatherings and soirees, when, with eager eyes and lips parted expectantly, they asked her to tell them "the terrible things Parisian women do." They had an unhealthy passion for satin slippers in daring shapes and every color, a key tool in their arsenal of seduction techniques. They gave you a pair, and you, Florita, would give them years later to Olympia, as a token of your love.

When Flora had been in Lima for four weeks, Colonel Bernardo Escudero appeared at Madame Denuelle's guest house. He was on his way through the capital, accompanying La Mariscala, who, taken prisoner in Arequipa, was waiting at the port of Callao for the ship that would carry her into exile in Chile, where she would of course also be escorted by Escudero. Her husband, General Gamarra, had fled to Bolivia after his uprising against Orbegoso ended in sorry fashion—in Arequipa, of course. La Mariscala and Gamarra had entered the city, conquered for them so buffoonishly by General San Román, just a few days after Flora left. The Gamarrista troops had multiplied the payments exacted from the residents of Arequipa, which inflamed the population. Then, two Gamarrista battalions, headed by Sergeant Major Lobatón, decided to rise up against Gamarra and pledge their loyalty to Orbegoso. They took over the command posts and raised a cheer to their former enemy, the rightful president. Upon hearing shots, the people of Arequipa misunderstood what was happening and, having had enough of the occupation, armed themselves with stones, knives, and hunting rifles and charged the rebel troops, thinking they were still Gamarristas. By the time they realized their error, it was too late, because they had already killed Sergeant Major Lobatón and his main collaborators. Then, more incensed than ever, they attacked the disconcerted army of Gamarra and San Román, which collapsed before the general onslaught. The soldiers changed sides or fled. General Gamarra managed to escape, disguised as a woman, and took asylum in Bolivia with a small entourage. La Mariscala, whom the furious masses were seeking to hang, jumped down from the roof of the house where she was staying and hid in the house next door, where hours later she was captured by Orbegoso's regular troops. Always skillful and quick at adapting himself to new political circumstances, Don Pío Tristán now presided over the Provisional Governing Committee of Arequipa, which declared itself Orbegosista and put the city under the command of the constitutional president. This committee had decreed that La Mariscala should be exiled, and the government in Lima had confirmed it.

Florita begged Bernardo Escudero to take her to see Doña Pancha. The two women met on board the English ship *William Rushton* that served as her prison. Although La Mariscala was defeated and half-destroyed (she would die a few months later), Flora had only to see her—a sturdy woman of medium height with wild hair and quicksilver eyes—and meet her proud, defiant gaze to feel the force of her personality.

"I am the savage, the fierce, the terrible Doña Pancha who eats children alive," she joked, in a gruff, dry voice. She was dressed with ostentatious elegance, wearing rings on all her fingers, diamond earrings, and a pearl necklace. "My family has asked me to dress this way in Lima, and I do it to indulge them. But the truth is that I feel more comfortable on horseback, in boots, jacket, and trousers."

They were talking cordially on deck, when Doña Pancha suddenly blanched. Her hands, lips, and shoulders began to shake, her eyes turned up in their sockets, and a white froth appeared on her lips. Escudero and the women traveling with her had to carry her into her cabin.

"Since the disaster in Arequipa, she has these attacks every day," Escudero told Flora that night. "Often several times a day. She was very sorry that she wasn't able to speak longer with you. She asked me to invite you to return to the ship tomorrow."

Flora returned, and was met with a shattered woman, a specter with bloodless lips, sunken eyes, and trembling hands. In a single night, Doña Pancha had aged terribly. She even had difficulty talking.

But this wasn't Flora's final memory of Lima. That was her visit to the Lavalle plantation, the largest and most prosperous in the region, at two leagues from the capital. The owner, Señor Lavalle, a man of exquisite refinement, spoke to her in good French. He took her to see the cane fields, the mills where the cane was ground, and the cauldrons at the refinery where the sugar was separated from the molasses. Flora desperately wanted to make him talk about his slaves. Finally, at the end of her visit, Señor Lavalle touched on the subject.

"The scarcity of slaves is ruining planters," he complained. "Imagine, I used to have fifteen hundred, and now I have scarcely nine hundred. They're so dirty and careless and idle, and their customs so barbaric, that they catch all sorts of illnesses and die like flies."

Flora dared to hint that perhaps the miserable existence they led, and their ignorance due to their complete lack of an education, might explain why the slaves were so liable to fall ill.

"You don't know these blacks," replied Señor Lavalle. "They're so lazy that they let their children die before their eyes. Their sloth is boundless. They're even worse than the Indians. Unless they're whipped, they can't be made to do anything."

Flora could contain herself no longer. She exclaimed that slavery was an aberration, a crime against civilization, and that sooner or later, it would be abolished in Peru as it had been already in France.

Señor Lavalle stood looking at her in puzzlement, as if he had discovered a different person beside him.

"Look at what's been happening in the old French colony of Santo Domingo since they freed their slaves," he replied at last, uncomfortably. "Absolute chaos and a return to barbarism. The blacks there are devouring each other."

And to demonstrate the extremes to which such people would go, he took her to the plantation's dungeons. In a shadowy cell, its floor covered in straw—it looked like the den of some beast—he showed her two young black women, completely naked, chained to the wall.

"Why do you think they are here?" he asked, with a glimmer of triumph. "These monsters killed their own newborn daughters."

"I understand them very well," replied Flora. "If I were in their place, I would have paid a daughter of mine the same favor. Even if it meant killing her, I would free her from living a life in hell, as a slave."

Was it there you began your career as an agitator and rebel, Florita, on that sugarcane plantation outside of Lima, before the feudal, Frenchified slaveowner? Whatever the case, if you hadn't traveled to faraway Peru and had the experiences you had there, you wouldn't be what you were now. What were you now, Andalusa? A free woman, yes. But a failed revolutionary from start to finish. Or at least here in Nîmes, this city of pious fools reeking of incense. On August 17, the day of her departure for Montpellier, when she took stock of her visit, the results couldn't have been more pathetic. Only seventy copies of *The Workers' Union* sold; she had to leave the other hundred that she had brought with Dr. Pleindoux. And she wasn't able to form a committee. At the four meetings she held, none of those present could be persuaded to campaign for the Workers' Union. No one, of course, came to see her off at the station on the morning she left.

But a few days later, in Montpellier, a frightened missive from the manager of the Hôtel du Gard informed her that someone had been interested in her in Nîmes after all, although happily only after her departure. The local commissioner, accompanied by two policemen, had arrived at the establishment with an order signed by the mayor of Nîmes, ordering her immediate expulsion from the city "for inciting the workers of Nîmes to demand an increase in wages."

The news made her laugh, and put her in a good humor all day. Well, well, Florita. So you weren't a complete failure as a revolutionary after all.

THE HOUSE OF PLEASURE

ATUONA (HIVA OA), JULY 1902

On the morning of September 16, 1901, when *La Croix du Sud* dropped anchor just off Atuona, on the island of Hiva Oa, and Paul, from the ship's bridge, spotted the cluster of people waiting for him at the little port—a gendarme in white uniform, missionaries in long robes and straw hats, a cluster of half-naked native children—he felt great happiness. At last his dream of reaching the Marquesas Islands had come true, and at last the horrible crossing of six days and six nights from Tahiti on that filthy, sweltering little ship was over. In all his time at sea he had scarcely been able to sleep a wink, because he was forever killing ants and cockroaches and driving away the rats that came prowling around his cabin in search of food.

No sooner had he disembarked in the tiny town of Atuona—a settlement of a few thousand people, surrounded by forested hills and two steep mountains crowned with foliage—than he actually met a prince, on the very dock! This was Ky Dong, an Annamite who went by the nom de guerre he had taken when he decided to give up his career in the French colonial administration of his native Vietnam to dedicate himself to political agitation, the anticolonialist struggle, and even terrorism, it seemed. That, at least, was the verdict of the

Saigon court, which ruled that he was a subversive and sentenced him to life imprisonment on Devil's Island, in remote Guiana. Before baptizing himself Ky Dong, Prince Nguyen Van Cam had studied literature and science in Saigon and Algeria. From Algeria he returned to Vietnam, where he was forging a splendid bureaucratic career for himself before he abandoned it to fight the French occupation. How had he ended up in Atuona? Thanks to the *bête noire* of *Les Guêpes*, ex-governor Gustave Gallet, who met the Annamite in Papeete on a stopover of the ship that was carrying him to serve out his sentence on Devil's Island. Impressed by Ky Dong's sophistication, intelligence, and polished manners, the governor saved his life: he made him an officer at Atuona's medical outpost. That was three years ago. The Annamite had accepted his fate with oriental equanimity. He knew he would never leave here, unless it were to be taken to the hell of Guiana. He had married a Marquesan woman from Hiva Oa, spoke fluent Maori, and was liked by all. Small, discreet, possessed of a rather sinuous natural elegance, he faithfully performed his duties as medical officer and, in this limbo of ignorant folk, did everything he could to preserve his sense of intellectual inquiry and discrimination.

He knew that the new arrival from Papeete was an artist, and he offered to help him settle in and inform him about the place where ("rashly," he said) Monsieur Gauguin had decided to bury himself. And so he did. His friendship and advice were invaluable to Paul. From the port Ky Dong led him to the hut of Matikana, a Chinese Maori friend of his who rented rooms, at the end of Atuona's single little dirt road, which was nearly swallowed up by brush. He kept Koké's chests and bags at his own house until the artist could buy a piece of land and build a place to live. And he introduced him to the people who would henceforth be his friends in Atuona: the American Ben Varney, an ex-whaler who was stranded on Hiva Oa in a fit of drunkenness and now managed the general store, and the Breton Émile Frébault, farmer, businessman, fisherman, and inveterate chess player.

Buying property in this tiny place surrounded by forests was extremely difficult. All the land in the area belonged to the bishopric, and fearsome Bishop Joseph Martin—stubborn, despotic, and locked in a desperate struggle to rescue the native population from the grip of alcohol—would never sell a plot to a foreigner of questionable morals.

Adopting the strategy devised by Ky Dong—whose wide reading, good humor, and grace of spirit made him an excellent companion—Paul attended Mass daily, starting the day after his arrival in Atuona. At church, he could always be spotted in the front row, following the service devotedly, and he frequently confessed and took communion. Some afternoons he went to hear the rosary said, too. His pious, proper behavior in those first days in Atuona convinced Monsignor Joseph Martin that Paul was a respectable person. And the bishop, in a gesture he would bitterly regret, agreed to sell him, for a modest sum, a lovely plot of land on the outskirts of Atuona. At its rear was the Bay of Traitors, a name the Marquesans hated but used nonetheless for the beach and the harbor, and to the front were the two proud peaks of Temetiu and Feani. Along one side ran the Make Make, one of the twenty or so streams into which the island's waterfalls flowed. From the moment he was faced with the magnificent sight, Paul thought of Vincent. My God, this was it, Koké; this was it. The place the mad Dutchman dreamed of in Arles, the primitive, tropical spot he talked of ceaselessly while you were living together in the fall of 1888, the place where he wanted to establish the Studio of the South, the community of artists where you would be master, and everything would belong to everyone, since money and its corrupting influence would be abolished. In this studio artists would live in brotherhood in a setting of matchless freedom and beauty, devoted to the creation of an immortal art: canvases and sculptures whose vitality would endure for centuries. How you would shout with glee, Vincent, if you could see the light here, even whiter than the light in Provence, and the explosion of bougainvillea, ferns, acacias, coconut palms, climbing vines, and breadfruit trees!

As soon as he had signed the contract of sale with the bishop, and was the owner of the land, Paul gave up going to Mass and to hear the rosary. Struggling with an ever-growing number of ailments—pains in his legs and back, difficulty walking, poor vision that grew worse every day, and palpitations that made it hard for him to breathe—he threw himself body and soul into the building of the Maison du Jouir—House of Pleasure—the name he and the mad Dutchman had given the imaginary Studio of the South of their daydreams fifteen years ago in Arles. Working side by side with him were Ky Dong, Émile Frébault, a white-bearded native called Tioka who from now on would be his neighbor, and even the island's gendarme, Désiré Charpillet, with whom Koké got along marvelously.

The House of Pleasure was finished in six weeks. It was built of wood, matting, and woven straw, and like his little houses in Mataiea and Punaauia, it had two floors. The bottom floor, two parallel cubes separated by an open space that would be his dining room, housed the kitchen and the sculpture studio. Above, under a conical straw roof, were the painting studio, the small bedroom, and the bathroom. Paul carved a wooden panel for the entrance with the name of the house, and two big vertical panels flanking the sign, with naked women in voluptuous poses, stylized animals and plants, and invocations that caused an uproar at both the large Catholic and smaller Protestant missions of Hiva Oa: *Soyez mystérieuses* (Be Mysterious, O Women) and *Soyez amoureuses et vous serez heureuses* (Fall in Love, O Women, and You Will Be Happy). From the moment he learned that Paul had had the audacity to decorate his house with these obscenities, Bishop Joseph Martin became his enemy. And when he learned that, besides a harmonium, guitar, and mandolin, forty-five pornographic photographs depicting outrageous sexual poses were displayed on the walls of Paul's studio, he denounced the artist in one of his Sunday sermons as a force for evil, someone the Marquesans should avoid.

Paul laughed at the bishop's rantings, but the Annamite prince warned him that it was dangerous to make an enemy of Monsignor Martin, because he was a man who carried a grudge, and he was powerful and indefatigable. They met every afternoon, at the House of Pleasure, which Koké had stocked well with food and drink bought at the only store in Atuona, owned by Ben Varney. He hired two servants, Kahui, a half-Chinese cook, and a Maori gardener, Matahaba, who was given precise instructions on how to grow sunflowers, as Koké had done himself in Punaauia. In the end, those sunflowers brightened the garden of the House of Pleasure. The memory of the mad Dutchman almost never abandoned you in your first few months in Atuona—why, Koké? You had managed to erase him from your mind for almost fifteen years, and that was probably a good thing, since the thought of Vincent made you uneasy, disturbed you, and might have disrupted your work. But here in the Marquesas, whether because you were painting very little, or because you felt tired and ill, you were no longer able to keep the image of good Vincent, poor Vincent, unbearable Vincent, with his obsequiousness and his fits of madness, from bursting constantly into your consciouness. Nor could you keep from reliving the events, stories, yearnings, and dreams of those eight weeks of difficult cohabitation in Provence fifteen years ago more clearly than you remembered things that had happened just a few days ago, which you often completely forgot. (For example, you made Ben Varney repeat twice in the same week the tale of how, after a spell of hard drinking, he woke up in the Bay of Traitors and discovered that his whaling ship had sailed away and he was stranded without a cent, or even any papers, and without speaking a word of French or Marquesan.)

Now you felt pity for the mad Dutchman, and even remembered him with affection. But in October of 1888, when, after giving in to his pleading and Theo van Gogh's pressure on you to accept his brother's invitation, you went to live with him in Arles, you came to hate him. Poor Vincent! He had placed such hopes in your arrival, believing the two of you would be the pioneering members of the artists' community of his dreams—a true monastery, a miniature Eden—that the failure of his project drove him mad and killed him.

Among the nightmarish trips that Paul had taken in his life, one of the worst was the fifteen-hour journey, with six changes of train, that it took him to get from Pont-Aven in Brittany to Arles in Provence. He was sorry to leave Pont-Aven. Remaining behind were not only several painter friends who considered him their master but also, above all, Émile Bernard and his sister, the gentle Madeleine. Exhausted, he arrived at the station in Arles at five in the morning on October 23, 1888. In order not to wake Vincent so early, he sought refuge in a neighboring café. To his surprise, the owner recognized him as soon as he came in. "Ah, Vincent's artist friend!" The mad Dutchman had showed him Paul's self-portrait, in which he appeared as Jean Valjean, the hero of *Les Misérables*. Helping him to carry his valises and bags, the café's owner led him to the place Lamartine outside the city's walls, very near the Cavalry Gate, which was one of the entrances to the old city, not far from the Roman amphitheater and coliseum. On the corner of the place Lamartine closest to the banks of the Rhône was the Yellow House that the mad Dutchman had rented a few months before, in anticipation of Paul's arrival. He had painted it, furnished it, decorated the rooms, and hung the walls with paintings, working day and night and worrying obsessively over every detail so that Paul would feel at ease in his new home, and in the proper mood to paint.

But you didn't feel comfortable in the Yellow House, Paul. You didn't like the riot of blinding, dizzying colors that leaped out at you wherever you turned your gaze, and Vincent's fawning welcome and flattery discomfited you as he showed you around the house he had arrayed to please you, anxious for your approval. In fact, the house made you feel wary, and somehow oppressed. Vincent was so excessively friendly and agreeable that from the very first day you began to feel that living with such a man would curb your freedom, that you'd have no life of your own, that Vincent would invade your privacy, become a fulsome jailor. The Yellow House could be a prison for a man as free as you.

But now, at a distance, remembered from your House of Pleasure with its majestic views, the mad Dutchman—overexcited, childlike, as solicitous of you as a sick man of the doctor charged with saving his life—seemed to you an essentially good and defenseless person, infinitely generous and free of envy, resentments, and pretentions, devoted body and soul to art, living like a beggar and not caring in the least, hypersensitive, obsessive, inoculated against any sort of happiness. He clung to you like a drowning man to a scrap of wood, believing that you were wise and strong enough to teach him to survive in the wild world. The responsibility he heaped on you, Paul! Vincent, who understood art, colors, and canvases, understood absolutely nothing about life. That was why he was always unhappy, why he went mad, and why he finally shot himself in the stomach at the age of thirty-seven. How unjust it was that those frivolous magpies, those idle Parisians, should blame you now for Vincent's tragic

253

end! Instead it was you who were nearly driven mad by the Dutchman, and even came close to losing your life in the two months you spent with him in Arles.

There was trouble from the start at the Yellow House. The first problem was disorder, which Paul hated but which was Vincent's natural element. They agreed on a strict division of labor: Paul would cook, the Dutchman would shop, and both would clean, on alternate days. In reality, Paul did the cleaning, and Vincent the cluttering. Their first argument arose over the basket of spending money. In a test of the collective property system to be instituted in the Studio of the South, the future artists' colony that they planned to found in some exotic country, they set up a common fund, where they deposited the money sent to them from Paris by Theo van Gogh. A little notebook and a pencil were provided for each to record how much they had taken. In the end, Paul complained: Vincent was taking the lion's share, especially for what he euphemistically noted as "hygienic activities": his dalliances with Rachel, a stick-thin young prostitute, at Madame Virginie's brothel, not far from the Yellow House, on one of the little streets issuing from the place Lamartine.

The bawdy houses of Arles were another source of disagreement. Paul reproached Vincent for making love only with prostitutes; he preferred to seduce women rather than paying for their attentions. And he was having a fairly easy time of it with the women of Arles, who loved his good looks, clever talk, and easy confidence. Vincent assured him that before Paul's arrival he had visited Madame Virginie's only a few times a month; now, however, he was going twice a week. This new sexual ardor distressed Vincent; he was convinced that the energy he expended in "fornicating" (which, as an ex-Lutheran preacher, was what he called it) was subtracted from his work as an artist. Paul mocked the puritanical prejudices of the ex-pastor. In his case, nothing made him more eager to take up his brush than having first satisfied his cock.

"No, no," the mad Dutchman exclaimed in exasperation. "My best work has always been done in periods of total sexual abstinence. My spermatic painting! I did it by spilling all my sexual energy onto the canvas instead of wasting it on women."

"What foolishness, Vincent. Or perhaps I simply have sexual energy to spare, for my paintings and my women."

The two of you disagreed more often than you agreed, and yet sometimes—when you heard your friend speak so candidly and hopefully about his longed-for community of artist-monks in retreat from the world, settled in a distant, primitive country with no links to materialist civilization, dedicated body and soul to painting, and engaged in a brotherhood untouched by shadow—you let yourself be swept away by his dream. It was exciting, of course it was! There was something beautiful, noble, selfless, generous, in the Dutchman's yearning to found that small society of pure-minded artists, creators, dreamers, secular saints, all pledged to art as medieval knights pledged themselves to fight for an ideal or a lady. Perhaps it was not unlike the dreams that spurred on your own grandmother, as, near death, she traveled France trying to recruit disciples for the revolution that would put an end to all society's ills. Grandmother Flora and the mad Dutchman would have understood each other, Koké.

Paul and Vincent even disagreed about the Studio of the South. One night, at a café on the symmetrical place du Forum, where they often sat and drank an absinthe after dinner, Vincent proposed that they invite the painter Seurat to join the artists' community.

"That dot-maker who calls himself a creator?" exclaimed Paul. "Never." He proposed that instead of the pointillist they take Puvis de Chavannes, whom Vincent hated as much as Paul detested Seurat. The argument went on until dawn. You forgot disputes quickly, Paul; not Vincent. For days he would be pale, distraught, turning the matter over in his head. For the mad Dutchman nothing was insignificant or banal; everything touched a central nerve of existence, was linked to larger themes: God, life, death, madness, art.

If the mad Dutchman deserved your gratitude in any way, it was for being the first to whet your appetite for Polynesia, thanks to a little novel that fell into his hands, and which he loved: *The Marriage of Loti* by an officer of the French merchant marine, Pierre Loti. The book was set in Tahiti, and it described an earthly paradise before the Fall, where nature was bounteous and beautiful, and the natives free, healthy, and without prejudice or guile, abandoning themselves to life and pleasure with naturalness and spontaneity, full of primitive vigor and enthusiasm. Life was full of paradoxes, wasn't it, Koké? It was Vincent who dreamed of fleeing decadent, money-mad Europe for an exotic world, seeking the elemental, religious force obliterated in the West by civilization. But he never escaped his European jail. It was you, in the end, who reached Tahiti, and now even the Marquesas, trying to make reality of what the Dutchman dreamed.

"I did what you wanted, I made your dream come true, Vincent," he shouted at the top of his lungs. "Here it is, your House of Pleasure, the House of the Orgasm you tormented me with in Arles. It didn't turn out the way we thought it would. You realize that, don't you, Vincent?"

There was no one nearby, no one who could answer. Only the cat and dog you had just brought to live with you at your new house in Atuona were there, watching you attentively, as if they understood the meaning of your bellows into nothingness, which were surely frightening the chickens, cats, and little horses that ran wild in the forests of Hiva Oa.

They had spent plenty of time in Arles talking and arguing about religion, too. There was such a difference between a Protestant, puritan upbringing like Vincent's and the Catholic education you received in the ten years between 1854 and 1864 that you spent in the small seminary of Chapelle-Saint-Mesmin, near Orleáns, under the spiritual guidance of Bishop Dupanloup. Which was the better preparation for life, Koké? Vincent's was more intense, more austere, stricter, colder, more honest, and also more inhuman. Catholicism was more cynical, more accommodating to man's corrupt nature, richer and more creative from a cultural and artistic point of view, and probably more human, closer to reality, to life as it was truly lived. Did you remember the night it rained and the mistral blew, when the two of you were shut up in the Yellow House and the mad Dutchman began to talk about Christ as an artist? Not once did you interrupt him, Paul. Christ was the greatest of artists, Vincent said. But he scorned marble, clay, and paint, preferring to cast his works in the living flesh of human beings. He didn't make statues, paintings, or poems. He created immortal beings, forging the tools for men and women to make perfect, exquisite works of art of their lives. He spoke for a long time, taking swallows of absinthe, and sometimes saying things you couldn't quite make out. But what you heard him declare at dawn, practically roaring, with tears in his eyes, you did understand, and would never forget.

"I want my paintings to be of spiritual comfort to human beings, Paul, the way the word of Christ was a comfort to them. In classical painting, the halo signified the eternal. It's that halo I'm trying to replace now with the radiation and vibration of color in my paintings."

After that, Paul, though you could never muster much enthusiasm for the spectacles of blinding light and fireworks that were Vincent's paintings, you regarded his violent, extravagant colors with more respect than before. The mad Dutchman seemed drawn to martyrdom in a way that sometimes made a shiver run up your spine.

Although he didn't feel well, his move to Atuona, the construction of the House of Pleasure, and his new friends all cheered Koké. He was happy the first few weeks in his new home, full of plans. Nevertheless, he had gradually if grudgingly come to realize that while the Marquesas might once have been Paradise, they were, like Tahiti, Paradise no longer. Still, the Marquesan women were beautiful, even more beautiful than the women of Tahiti. Or so they seemed to him, though Ky Dong, the gendarme Désiré Charpillet, Émile Frébault, and his neighbor Tioka laughed, telling him that his poor eyesight was fooling him, since many of the lively, friendly Marquesan women who came to the Maison du Jouir to be shown his pornographic photographs—his collection had become famous all over Hiva Oa—and let themselves be photographed and fondled in front of their husbands, weren't the attractive girls he believed them to be, but ugly old women, some with faces and bodies disfigured by elephantiasis, leprosy, or syphilis, diseases ravaging the native population. Bah, you didn't care. What the eye doesn't see, the heart doesn't grieve. It was true that your poor eyes could see less and less. But hadn't you long been saying that the true artist seeks his models in the memory rather than the outside world: in the private, secret sphere of the mind's eye, which in your case was in better shape than your physical eyes? The time had come to test your theory, Koké.

This had been a cause for bitter argument with Vincent in Arles. The mad Dutchman declared himself a realist painter and said that artists must go out into the open, setting up their easels in the middle of nature and seeking inspiration there. To keep the peace, Paul humored him the first few weeks he was in Arles. Morning and afternoon, the two friends went with their easels, palettes, and paints to Les Alyscamps, Arles's big Roman and early Christian necropolis, and each did several paintings of the great avenue of tombs and sarcophagi flanked by rustling poplars that led to the little church of Saint-Honorat. But the mistral rains and gusts soon made it impossible to continue working outside, and they had to shut themselves up in the Yellow House, working from memory or the imagination instead of the natural world, as Paul preferred.

What pained you most was having to accept that in the Marquesas, or on this island at least, not a single trace was left of cannibalism. It was a practice you considered not savage and reprehensible, but virile and natural—hearing you, your new friends looked at you in horror—the sign of a vigorous, creative young culture in a state of constant self-renewal, not yet contaminated by conformism and decadence. In Atuona, no one believed there were any Marquesans who still ate human flesh, on this or any other island; in the remote past, maybe, but not anymore. His neighbor Tioka assured him this was true, and it was corroborated by all the natives he questioned, among them a couple from the island of Tahuata, where there were many redheads. Tohotama, wife of Haapuani—he was called the Witch Doctor—was one of them. Her long hair flowed down her back to her waist, and when the sun was bright, it gave off a rosy glow. Tohotama became his favorite model in Atuona. He even preferred her to Vaeoho, a girl of fourteen—the age you liked your lovers, Koké—who became his wife in his third month in Hiva Oa.

Obtaining Vaeoho required an inland excursion to the valley of Hanaupe, the only trip Koké was able to take on Hiva Oa, with his body so battered. He was accompanied by Ky Dong, an expert on island customs, and Tioka, who was perfectly bilingual. Their hazardous six-mile ride on horseback through dense, damp forests—full of wasps and mosquitoes that raised welts all over his skin—nearly destroyed Paul. The girl was the daughter of the local chieftain of a small native village, Hekeani, and the bargaining with him took several hours. In the end, to get the girl, he agreed to pay for a list of gifts that cost him more than two hundred francs at Ben Varney's store. He didn't regret it. Vaeoho was beautiful, hardworking, and cheerful, and she agreed to give him lessons in Marquesan, since the Maori that was spoken here was different from Tahitian. Although he sometimes asked her to pose for him, Koké preferred the redheaded Tohotama as a model; her ample breasts, broad hips, and heavy thighs aroused him, which was something that didn't happen as often as it once had. With Tohotama, it did. When she came to pose, he always found some way to caress her, which she endured unenthusiastically, with an air of boredom. At last, well fortified with absinthe one afternoon, he maneuvered her to the studio bed. As he made love to her, he heard Vaeoho and the witch doctor Haapuani, Tohotama's husband, laughing and whispering, amused by the spectacle.

The Marquesans were more free and spontaneous than the Tahitians in sexual matters. Married or single, the women mocked the men and brazenly approached them, despite the constant campaigns of the Catholic and Protestant missions to make them obey the norms of Christian decency. The men were still mostly recalcitrant. And some, like Tohotama's husband, didn't hesitate to defy the churches by dressing as *mahus*, men-women, with knots of flowers in their hair, and feminine ornaments on their ankles, wrists, and arms.

Another of Paul's disappointments in his new land was learning that the art of tattooing, for which the Marquesans were renowned throughout Polynesia, was disappearing. The Catholic and Protestant missionaries were fighting fiercely to bring an end to it, as a manifestation of barbarism. Few natives living in Atuona tattooed themselves any longer, for fear of incurring the wrath of priests and pastors. It was still done in the island's interior, in tiny villages lost in the depths of those tangled forests, but the calamitous state of your health unfortunately prevented you from going to see for yourself. The frustration, Koké! To know there were tattooists just a few miles away, and to be unable to go and meet them. He couldn't even visit the ruins of Upeke and its giant *tikis*, or stone idols, in the valley of Taaoa, because the two times he had tried to climb there on horseback, his fatigue and pain had made him lose consciousness. To be here, so close to the hidden places where the stunning art of the tattoo still survived—the secret codified lore of the Maori people, in which each figure was a palimpsest to be deciphered—and to be unable to reach them because of the unspeakable illness, kept him awake at night in frustration; some nights he even wept.

Sadly, decadence had reached the island, too. Bishop Joseph Martin, convinced that the illnesses and plagues rampant among the natives were caused by alcohol, had prohibited it. Ben Varney's store sold wine and spirits only to whites. But the cure was worse than the disease. Since they weren't allowed wine, the Marquesans of Hiva Oa set up clandestine stills to turn oranges and other fruits into liquors that corroded their insides. Indignant, Koké fought the prohibition by filling the House of Pleasure with demijohns of rum, which he gave away to all the native women who came to visit him.

He felt very tired, and for the first time in his life since he had discovered that painting was his calling, when he was still working on the stock exchange in Paris, he had no desire to take up his brushes and sit in front of an easel. It wasn't only his physical ailments—the burning of the sores on his legs, his failing eyesight, and his palpitations—that kept him idle, sipping from a glass of absinthe and water, in which he dissolved a cube of sugar. It was a sense of futility, too. Why work so hard, pouring all the little energy you had left into canvases that, when they were finished and, after a lengthy voyage, had reached France, would languish in Ambroise Vollard's storeroom, or Daniel de Monfreid's attic, waiting for some shopkeeper to spend a few francs on one to adorn his new home?

One day, after a lesson in Marquesan, Vaeoho said something half in French and half in Maori that he didn't understand. Or did you not want to understand, Koké? He made her repeat it several times until he hadn't the slightest doubt what it meant. "Every day you're older. Soon I'll be a widow." He went to the mirror and stared at himself until his eyes hurt.

Then he decided to paint his last self-portrait, as a testament to his decline in this forgotten corner of the world, surrounded by Marquesans who, like him, were sinking into ruin, lethargy, degradation, and despair. He set the mirror next to his easel and worked for more than two weeks, trying to transfer to the canvas the picture that his failing eyes glimpsed with difficulty. It seemed to slip away, evaporate: a man defeated but not yet dead, contemplating the inevitably approaching end with serenity and a kind of wisdom pooled in his gaze, which contained, behind a humiliating pair of spectacles, the summary of an intense life of adventures, folly, searches, failures, struggles. A life that was coming to a close at last, Paul. Your hair was short and white, and you were thin, quiet, waiting with tranquil courage for the final onslaught. You weren't sure, but you sensed that, of the innumerable self-portraits you had done of yourself—as a Breton peasant, a Peruvian Inca on the curve of a pitcher, Jean Valjean, Christ on the Mount of Olives, a bohemian, a romantic—this, your farewell portrait, of the artist at the end of his journey, was the one that captured you best.

Painting the self-portrait reminded you of the portrait of Vincent painting sunflowers you did in the weeks you were confined by the rain and mistral winds to the Yellow House in Arles. The Dutchman had been obsessed with those flowers; he painted them ceaselessly, and often referred to them when he was expounding his theories on painting. They followed the movement of the sun neither by chance nor in blind obedience to physical laws. No, they themselves possessed some of the fire of that heavenly orb, and if one observed them as devotedly and stubbornly as Vincent, one realized that there were halos encircling them. In painting them, while preserving their true nature, he tried to make them torches or candelabras, too. Madness! Upon showing you the Yellow House for the first time, the mad Dutchman proudly pointed out the sunflowers, literally blazing with molten, fiery gold, that he had painted over your bed. You were scarcely able to suppress an expression of distaste. This was why you had painted him surrounded by sunflowers. The portrait was deliberately lacking the vibrant light that Vincent gave his canvases. On the contrary, there was something flat and opaque about it, and in it, the outlines of the flowers as well as the painter were smudged, blurred. Rather than a distinct and coherent human being, Vincent was a shape, a stuffed, rigid mannequin under unbearable strain, at the point of cracking or exploding: a volcano-man. The rigidity of his right arm, especially, which held his brush, revealed the superhuman effort he had to make to keep painting. And all of this was concentrated in his contorted face and dazed expression, which seemed to say, "I'm not painting, I'm immolating myself." Vincent didn't like the portrait at all. When you showed it to him, he spent a long time looking at it, turning very pale and biting his lower lip, which was a tic he had at his worst moments. At last he murmured, "Yes, it is I. But mad."

Weren't you, though, Vincent? Of course he was. Paul gradually became convinced of it; he noted the abrupt mood changes that afflicted his friend, the swiftness with which Vincent could shift from sickening, overwhelming flattery to aggression and absurd arguments, to scolding him for some trifle. After each altercation he fell into a deathly stupor, an immobility that Paul, alarmed, had to shake him from with cajolery, absinthe, or by dragging him to Madame Virginie's to go to bed with Rachel.

Then you made your decision: it was time to leave. This experiment in living together would end badly. Tactfully, you tried to prepare him, dropping hints in your conversations after dinner that, for family reasons, you might have to leave Arles before the year you had agreed to spend together was up. It would have been better if you hadn't, Paul. The Dutchman realized at once that you had already decided to leave, and was plunged into a state of nervous hysteria, of mental collapse. He was like a lover in despair because his beloved is leaving him. With tears in his eyes and his voice breaking, he begged you, implored you, to stay the full year; alternately, he wouldn't speak to you for days but only stared at you with hatred and resentment, as if you had done him irreparable harm. Sometimes you felt infinite pity for him, seeing him as a helpless being who was unfit to face the world and who clung to you because he sensed you were strong, a fighter. But other times you were outraged: didn't you have problems enough without being saddled with the mad Dutchman's?

Things came to a head a few days before Christmas Eve, 1888. Paul awoke suddenly in his room at the Yellow House, with a feeling of dread. In the faint light that came in through the window, he discerned Vincent's silhouette at the foot of the bed, watching him. He sat up, frightened. "What is it, Vincent?" Without a word, his friend slipped out like a shadow. The next day, he swore he didn't remember having gone into Paul's room; he had been sleepwalking, perhaps. Two days later, on the day before Christmas, at the café on the place du Forum, Paul announced that, to his great sorrow, he had to leave.

Family business required his presence in Paris. He would leave in a few days, and if everything could be taken care of, he might come back sometime in the future and stay again for a while. Vincent listened silently, nodding exaggeratedly from time to time. They continued to drink, without speaking. Suddenly, the Dutchman picked up his half-empty glass and hurled it at Paul's face, furiously. Paul managed to duck it. He got up, strode back to the Yellow House, put a few essential things in a bag. As he was leaving, he collided with Vincent, who was just coming in, and he told him he was going to a hotel and would be back the next day to pick up the rest of his things. He spoke without rancor.

"I'm doing it for both of us, Vincent. The next glass you throw might really hit me. And I don't know whether I'd be able to contain myself, as I did tonight. I might leap on you and wring your neck. That would be no way for our friendship to end."

Pale as death, his eyes red, Vincent stared at him, saying nothing. For some time now he had been shaving his head like a recruit or a Buddhist monk, and when he was overcome by sadness or rage, as he was now, his cranium seemed to quiver, like his temples and chin.

Paul left, and outside—you remembered it very clearly—the winter cold chilled him to the bone. On his walk through the walled city he heard families singing carols in some of the houses. He was on his way to the Station, a modest hotel whose owner he knew. As he was crossing the little place Victor Hugo, he heard footsteps very close behind him. A foreboding made him turn, and there, a few feet away, barefoot and with a razor in his hand, was Vincent, glaring at him with terrible eyes.

"What are you doing? What is the meaning of this?" Paul shouted.

The Dutchman turned and ran. Was it wrong of you not to immediately warn the gendarmes about the state your friend was in? Of course it was. But how the devil were you to imagine that poor Vincent, after his frustrated attempt to stab you, would slice off half his left ear and take the piece of bloody flesh, wrapped in newspaper, to Rachel, Madame Virginie's skinny little whore? And then, as if that weren't enough, he had to lie down in his own bed with his head wrapped in towels, which, when you entered the Yellow House the next morning—the place surrounded by policemen and gawkers—

you would see drenched in blood, like the sheets, walls, and paintings. It seemed the mad Dutchman had not only cut off his ear in some barbaric ritual but also baptized the whole scene of his mutilation with blood. And those wretches, those fops in Paris, blamed you for Vincent's tragedy. Because after his terrible act, the Dutchman was scarcely heard from again. First, he was shut up in the Hôtel Dieu of Arles; then, for nearly a year, in a sanatorium at Saint-Rémy, and finally, in the last month of his life, in the little town of Auvers-sur-Oise, where he finally shot himself in the stomach, so clumsily that he lay dying for a whole day, in hideous pain. The Paris idlers who never bought any of Vincent's paintings while he was alive had declared post mortem that he was a genius. And you, because you failed to save him that Christmas Eve, were his executioner and destroyer. Bastards!

Would they discover that you, too, were a genius after your death, Paul? Would your paintings begin to be sold at the same high prices as the mad Dutchman's? You suspected not. And besides, you cared less than you once had about being recognized, famous, one of the immortals. It would never happen. Atuona was too far from Paris, where artistic reputations and fashions were decided, for the triflers there to take an interest in what you had done. And what obsessed you now wasn't painting but the unspeakable illness, which, in the fourth month of your stay in Hiva Oa, attacked again, fiercely.

The sores were eating up his legs, and they soiled his bandages so fast that he finally lost the will to change them. He had to do it himself, because Vaeoho refused, repulsed, threatening to leave him if he made her nurse him. He kept the dirty bandages on for two or three days, until they stank and were covered in flies, which he grew tired of shooing away, too. Dr. Buisson, Hiva Oa's medical officer, whom he had met in Papeete, gave him morphine injections and laudanum. They eased the pain but kept him in a state of mindless somnambulism, a sharp foretaste of the rapid mental deterioration to come. Would you be like the mad Dutchman in the end, Paul? In June of 1902 the pain in his legs made it almost impossible for him to walk. There was hardly any money left from the sale of his house in Punaauia. He invested his last savings in a little pony cart, in which, every afternoon, dressed in a green shirt, blue pareu, and Parisian cap, and with a new wooden staff carved once again with an erect phallus, he drove past the Protestant mission and Pastor Vernier's lovely tamarind trees, toward the Bay of Traitors. At that hour it was always crowded with boys and girls swimming in the sea or riding bareback on the little wild horses, which whinnied and leaped defiantly over the waves. Across the bay, the deserted island of Hanakee seemed a sleeping giant, one of the great whales that were once hunted by the North American ships that so terrified the natives. As they told it, the crews of these ships would ply the native women with drink and then kidnap them, taking them away and making them their slaves. It was an incident involving one of the whaling ships that had given the bay its terrible name. Tired of the kidnappings, the natives of Hiva Oa received the ship's crew with celebration, dances, and feasts of raw fish and wild pig. And in the middle of the feasting, they slit all the sailors' throats. "Admit that they ate them!" Koké bellowed, beside himself, each time he heard this story. "Bravo! Well done! They did right!" Just before the sun set, Koké would return to the House of Pleasure, taking a detour down Atuona's only street. He drove along it very slowly, reining the pony in, from the harbor to the boardinghouse of the Chinese Maori Matikana, waving ceremoniously at everyone, although he could no longer really see who most people were.

Upon his arrival, because they had heard talk of him as the editor of *Les Guêpes*, the island's Catholics welcomed him as one of their own. But his dissipated way of life, his bouts of drunkenness, his intimacies with the natives, and the shocking tales about everything that went on at the House of Pleasure had made them come to see him as a reprobate. The Protestants, whom he had attacked so viciously in *Les Guêpes*, observed him from a distance, resentfully. But the abrupt departure of Dr. Buisson, transferred to Papeete in the middle of June, drove him to approach the Protestant pastor, Paul Vernier, whom he had attacked personally in the magazine. Ky Dong and Tioka took him to see Vernier, saying that he was the only person on Atuona who had any knowledge of medicine and could help him. The pastor, a mild-mannered, generous man, welcomed Paul without a hint of reproach for past insults, and did try to help him, giving him painkillers and salves for his legs. They had some effect, because in July of 1902 he was able to take a few small steps on his own feet.

To celebrate his momentary improvement, and because Paul was an artist, the gendarme Désiré Charpillet had the idea of naming him judge of the traditional July 14 contest between the choirs of the island's two schools, Catholic and Protestant. The rivalry between the missions manifested itself in the most insignificant matters. Trying not to poison the relationship further, Paul made a Solomonic judgment: he declared a tie between the competitors. But the verdict left both churches unsatisfied, and angry at him. He had to retreat to the House of Pleasure in the midst of recriminations and general hostility.

But when the pony cart reached his house, he had a pleasant surprise. There, waiting for him, was his neighbor, Tioka, the white-bearded Maori. With great seriousness, he said that he had known Paul long enough now to consider him a true friend. He had come to propose that they celebrate a friendship ceremony. It was very simple. They would exchange their respective names, without giving up their own. This they did, and from that day on his neighbor was Tioka-Koké, and he was Koké-Tioka. Now you were a full-fledged Marquesan, Paul.

WORDS TO CHANGE THE WORLD

MONTPELLIER, AUGUST 1844

F lora had promised herself that in Montpellier, where she arrived from Nîmes on August 17, 1844, she would do nothing but rest. She needed to recover her strength; she was exhausted. Her dysentery had persisted for two months now, and each night she could feel stabbing pains in her chest where the bullet lay next to her heart. But fate had other plans for her. The Hôtel du Cheval Blanc, where she had a room reserved, shut its door in her face upon discovering that she was traveling alone. "Like any decent establishment, we admit ladies only when they come with their fathers or husbands," the manager admonished her.

She was about to reply, "Well, in Nîmes I was told that the Hôtel du Cheval Blanc was little better than the brothel of Montpellier," when a traveling salesman who had arrived at the same time stepped in, offering to vouch for the lady. The hotelkeeper hesitated. Flora was touched, until she realized that the gallant gentleman insisted on taking a single room for the two of them. "Do you think me a whore?" she cried, turning and dealing him a ringing slap. The wretch was left speechless, rubbing his face. Carrying her bags, she went out into the streets of Montpellier to look for a place to stay. It was noon by the time she found one—the Hôtel du Midi, a small establishment in the midst of reconstruction, at which she was the only guest. In the seven days she spent in the city she lived with the constant bustle and clamor of the builders and laborers who, swinging from the scaffolding, were repairing and enlarging the place. So tired was she that, despite the oppressive noise, she gave up looking for another inn.

In the first four days she held no meetings with workers or any of the local Saint-Simonians or Fourierists for whom she had letters of introduction. But they were not days of rest. She was so tormented by her bloated belly and cramps that she had to see a doctor. Dr. Amador, recommended by the hotel, happened to be Spanish, and Flora was happy to be able to practice with him the language she had scarcely had a chance to speak since her return from Peru ten years ago. Dr. Amador, a fanatic believer in homeopathy—which, raising his eyes to heaven, he called the "new science"—was a gracious, well-educated man in his fifties, dark and long-limbed. He had Saint-Simonian sympathies, and was convinced that Saint-Simon's "theory of fluids," the key to understanding history's progress, also explained the workings of the human body. "The technical and economic sciences will transform society, Doña Flora," he told her, in his baritone voice. It was pleasant talking to him. Faithful to the homeopathic belief that like is cured by like, he prescribed a preparation of arsenic and sulfur, which Flora drank nervously, afraid of being poisoned. But after her second day of taking the strange potion, she noticed a considerable improvement.

This attentive, respectful man, who listened to you deferentially even though the two of you often disagreed, was like the first "modern men" you met, thanks to your boldness and determination, in Paris at the beginning of 1835, upon your return from Peru, after that infernal voyage on which you were nearly raped by a shameless, degenerate passenger, Mad Antonio. Did you remember, Florita? At night he tried to force the door of your cabin, and the ship's captain refused to call him to order; he must have been used to seeing his passengers assault women traveling on their own. You reproached him for it, and Captain Alencar, to excuse himself, responded with this instructive bit of nonsense: "In my thirty years at sea you are the first woman I've seen traveling alone." Quite a horrific little voyage your return trip to France proved to be, thanks to your seasickness and Mad Antonio!

But what did that disagreeable experience matter to you those first few months in Paris, in the little apartment you rented on the rue Chabanais? Your modest income from Uncle Pío Tristán permitted you to live decently. Brimming with enthusiasms and dreams after your year in Peru, which had taught you more than you might have learned in five years at the Sorbonne, you returned to France resolved to be a different person, to cast off your chains, to live fully and freely, to repair the gaps in your understanding, to cultivate your intelligence, and, above all, to do things—many things—to make the lives of women better than yours had been.

It was in this state of mind, soon after returning to France, that you wrote your first book—or rather, your first booklet, a brief pamphlet: *On the Need to Give a Warm Welcome to Foreign Women*. Now you were ashamed by the naïveté of that sentimental, romantic, well-intentioned text, addressing the silent or hostile reception that foreigners received in France. Imagine, to have proposed the founding of a society that would help foreign women settle in Paris, find them lodgings, provide them with introductions, and assist any who were in need! A society whose members would take an oath, write an anthem, and wear an insignia inscribed with the group's three mottos: Virtue, Prudence, and Propaganda Against Vice! Seized by laughter—how silly you were then, Florita—she stretched in her tiny room at the Hôtel du Midi. Even you hadn't been able to resist the mania for forming societies that had taken hold in France.

The booklet was a youthful effort, and revealed your lack of schooling; the manuscript had so many spelling mistakes that the owner of the Delaunay press, near the Palais Royal, had to correct it from beginning to end. Wasn't there anything worth salvaging from it, despite how much you had matured since then? There were a few things, yes. For example, your profession of faith—"The love of humanity is a belief more beautiful and holy than any other, a religion"—and your attacks on nationalism: "The universe should be our nation." The founding of societies was the obsession of the Saint-Simonians and Fourierists. Did that mean you were already in contact with them when the pamphlet was published?

Only through your reading. You read a great deal in your little flat on the rue Chabanais, and then in the one on the rue du Cherche-Midi, in 1835, 1836, and 1837, despite all the headaches André Chazal was causing you. You were trying to absorb the ideas, philosophies, and doctrines of modernity, which you saw as the most effective tools for achieving women's emancipation. From the Saint-Simonian journal *Le Globe* to the Fourierist *La Phalange*, and on through all the pamphlets, books, articles, and lectures you could lay your hands on, you wanted to read everything. You spent hours and hours scribbling in margins, filling notecards, and writing summaries, at home or in the two reading rooms you joined. How enthusiastically you sought to associate yourself with the Saint-Simonians and Fourierists, the two schools that at the time—you had yet to learn of the ideas of Étienne Cabet or the Scotsman Robert Owen—seemed closest to achieving your goal: equal rights for men and women.

The Comte de Saint-Simon, a philosopher and economist who envisioned a "frictionless society in which all are productive," had died in 1825, and his heir, the slim, elegant, refined, and enlightened Prosper Enfantin, was still the leader of the Saint-Simonians. Enfantin was one of the first to whom you sent your little book, with a worshipful inscription. He invited you to a meeting of his followers in Saint-Germain-des-Prés. Did you remember how dazzled you were to clasp the hand of that charismatic lay priest, a ready talker who made the ladies of Paris swoon? He had been imprisoned after the first experiment in Saint-Simonian society in Ménilmontant, where, to foster solidarity among his companions and abolish individualism, he had designed fantastic uniforms: tunics that buttoned in the back and could only be fastened with the help of another person. Enfantin had traveled to Egypt in search of the Woman-Messiah who, according to the movement's doctrine, would be the savior of humankind. He hadn't found her there, and he was still looking for her. The feminist frenzy of the Saint-Simonians now seemed to you lacking in seriousness, an extravagant, frivolous game. But in 1835 it touched your soul, Florita. Reverently, you stared at the empty chair that presided over Saint-Simonian meetings next to Father Prosper Enfantin. How could you fail to be moved upon discovering that you weren't alone, that in Paris there were others like you who found it intolerable that women were considered inferior beings with no rights of their own, second-class citizens? Before the empty chair at the ceremonies of Saint-Simon's disciples, you began to repeat to yourself secretly, like a prayer, "It's you who'll be the savior of humanity, Flora Tristán."

But in order to be the Saint-Simonian Woman-Messiah, it was necessary to become a couple—to go to bed, plainly speaking—with Prosper Enfantin. Many Parisian women were tempted by the prospect. You weren't. Your reformist zeal went only so far.

If the Comte de Saint-Simon had been dead for some time, Charles Fourier was still alive in 1835. He was sixty-three years old when you met him, Andalusa, two years before his death. And nine years later, despite your scorn for his disciples, those theory-obsessed and ineffectual Fourierists, you always remembered him with admiration—and filial affection, though you had few dealings with him. Fourier was the first to receive a copy of *On the Need to Give a Warm Welcome to Foreign Women*, and you offered him your assistance in exalted language. "In me, Master, you will find a strength uncommon among those of my sex, an urgent desire to do good." And, to your great surprise, the noble, immaculate little old man, with his neatly pressed frock coat and kindly blue eyes, appeared in person at number 42, rue du Cherche-Midi, to thank you for the book and congratulate you on your innovative ideas and your passion for justice. It was one of the happiest days of your life, Florita!

You had great difficulty understanding some of his theories (that there existed a social order equivalent to the physical order of the universe discovered by Newton, for example, or that humanity had to pass through eight stages of savagery and barbarism before reaching Harmony, where it would attain happiness); you read *The Theory of the Four Movements*, *The New Industrial World*, and countless articles in *La Phalange* and other Fourierist publications. But it was above all the generous sage himself—the resplendent moral purity that emanated from his person, the frugality of his life (he lived alone, in a modest little flat crammed with books and papers on the rue Saint-Pierre in Montmartre, where one day you brought him an hourglass as a present), his kindness, his horror of all forms of violence, and his staunch confidence in the essential goodness of humankind—who, between 1835 and 1837, made you consider yourself a disciple.

Like you, Fourier was opposed to the unfortunate institution of marriage, believing that it turned women into objects, without dignity or freedom. At first you were enthralled by his theories, and you shared Fourier's assurance that a society's level of civilization was directly proportionate to the degree of independence enjoyed by women. But some of his other assertions puzzled you, like his absolute certainty that the world would last exactly eighty thousand years, and his precise calculations about the transmigration of souls. Didn't these pronouncements seem closer to superstition than to science?

Fourier's disciples, beginning with Victor Considérant, the head of *La Phalange*, didn't think so. Nor did they doubt his faith in the phalanstery as the seed of humanity's future happiness. Even now, in 1844, they managed to believe, as Fourier had, that there were capitalists capable of magnanimous acts. Magnanimous? Suicidal was more like it. Because in the hypothetical case of the triumph of Fourierism, capitalism would vanish from the world. But such a thing would never happen, and you, Florita, despite your meager learning, understood very well why not. Capitalists might be wicked and selfish, but they knew their own interests. They would never finance a gallows on which they themselves would hang. That was why you no longer believed in the Fourierists, why you regarded them with pity. Nevertheless, you had maintained a good relationship with Victor Considérant, who, since 1836, had published letters and articles written by you in *La Phalange* that were often very critical of the journal itself. And despite being aware that you were no longer one of them, he gave you letters and introductions for your tour around France.

When Dr. Amador, the Montpellier homeopath whom Flora saw several times that week, heard her sharply criticize the Fourierists and Saint-Simonians, accusing them of being "weak" and "bourgeois," he laughed at her for her "fiery nature." As he spoke, the Spaniard smoothed the neat gray sideburns that grew down to his chin, and Flora felt certain that he was attracted to her. He was always complimenting you, Andalusa. And yet your cordial relationship came to a rather abrupt end the day you learned, from Dr. Amador himself, that in his classes at the Faculty of Medicine at the University of Montpellier he didn't teach homeopathy, which was not accepted by the academy, but rather the conventional allopathic medicine, which—he had told her in no uncertain terms—he scorned as old and outmoded.

"How can you teach something you don't believe in, and be paid for it, too?" sputtered a shocked Madame-la-Colère. "It makes no sense; it's wrong."

"There now, don't judge me so harshly," he replied, startled by her fierce reaction. "My friend, I have to live. One cannot be absolutely consistent and ethical in life, unless one feels the call of martyrdom."

"I must feel it," said Madame-la-Colère. "Because I always try to behave honorably, in keeping with my convictions. My tongue would fall out of my head if I had to teach things I didn't believe in, just to earn a salary."

It was the last time they saw each other. And yet, although Flora's criticisms had surely stung him, Dr. Amador sent a carpenter to the Hôtel du Midi to see her. André Médard proved to be a keen, agreeable young man. He had formed a workers' mutual aid society, which he invited her to visit.

"Why have you decided not to speak in Montpellier, madame?"

"Because I was told I wouldn't find a single intelligent worker here," said Flora, to provoke him.

"There are four hundred of us, madame," he said, laughing. "I'm one of them."

"With four hundred intelligent workers I could wage revolution all over France, my boy," Flora retorted.

The meeting that André Médard organized for her was a great success. The sixteen men and four women who attended were uninformed, but curious and eager to listen, and they showed interest in the Workers' Union and the Workers' Palaces. They bought some books and agreed to form a committee of five members—one woman among them—to promote the movement in Montpellier. And they told Flora things that surprised her. Beneath the calm semblance of a prosperous bourgeois city, Montpellier, according to them, was a powder keg. There was no work, and many of the unemployed roamed the streets in defiance of the authorities, sometimes stoning the carriages and houses of the rich, of whom there were many in the city.

"If the Workers' Union doesn't hasten to bring about peaceful change, France and maybe even all of Europe will explode," Flora declared, at the end of the meeting. "The carnage will be terrible. To work, my friends!"

Unlike her first leisurely days in Montpellier, the last three were packed with activity, thanks to Dr. Amador's homeopathic remedy, which made her feel euphoric and full of energy. She tried unsuccessfully to visit the prison, and made the rounds of the city's bookshops, leaving copies of *The Workers' Union*. Finally, she met with twenty local Fourierists. As always, they disappointed her. They were professionals and bureaucrats incapable of moving on from theory to action, with an innate distrust of the workers, whom they seemed to see as a threat to their peaceable bourgeois existences. When it came time for questions, a lawyer, Maître Saissac, managed to infuriate her by chiding her for "exceeding the duties of a woman, who should never give up the care of the home for politics." In turn, the lawyer was offended when she called him "a caveman, an uncivilized brute, a social troglodyte."

Maître Saissac bore a certain resemblance to André Chazal as he had looked in 1835, 1836, and 1837, his sallow, crumpled face aged by poverty, bitterness, and rancor. Flora was forced to see him several times and confront him; the souvenir of her war with him was the bullet she carried in her chest, which the good doctors Récamier and Lisfranc hadn't been able to remove. Between 1835 and 1837, Chazal kidnapped poor Aline three times (and Ernest-Camille twice), making the girl the sad, melancholic, shy creature she was now. And each time, the nightmarish judges whom Flora petitioned to demand custody of her two children settled in Chazal's favor, even though he was a derelict, a drunk, a pervert, a degenerate, a miserable creature who lived in a rank hovel where the children could only lead an unhappy life. And why? Because André Chazal was the husband, the one with all the power and rights, although he was a piece of human filth, a man capable of seeking pleasure in his own daughter's body. You, on the other hand, who by dint of your own efforts had managed to educate yourself, publish your writings, and live decorously; you, who could assure your two children a good education and a decent life, were always eyed suspiciously by the judges, who were convinced that all independent women must be sluts. Wretches!

How were you able to write *Peregrinations of a Pariah* at such a frantic time, Florita, while you were fighting André Chazal in court and in the streets? The memoir of your trip to Peru appeared in two volumes in Paris at the beginning of 1838, and in just a few weeks you were famous in French literary and intellectual circles. It was your indomitable energy that made it possible, the energy that only in the last few months had begun to fail you, on this tour.

The book was written in fits and starts, between mad dashes to police stations at the order of examining magistrates, and police summonses to respond to Chazal's wild accusations. As Chazal himself confessed before the judge who tried him for attempted murder, what he really wanted wasn't to wrest custody of his children away from Flora, but to have his revenge, to wreak vengeance upon the woman who, despite being his lawful wife, had dared to abandon him and flaunt her shameless deeds before the whole world in articles and books—telling how she ran away from home, traveled to Peru as an unmarried woman, and allowed herself to be courted by other men—maligning him all the while by presenting him before public opinion as brutal and abusive.

And in the end, André Chazal got his revenge—to begin with, by raping poor Aline, knowing that his crime would hurt the mother as well as the daughter. Once again Flora felt the dizziness that overcame her that April morning in 1837, when Aline's little letter reached her hands. The girl had given it to an obliging water carrier, who in turn personally delivered it to Flora. At her wit's end, she flew to rescue her children, and reported Chazal to the police for rape and incest. Before being taken into custody, he accosted her in the street. The incredible thing was—wasn't it, Florita?—that thanks to the rhetorical skills of Chazal's lawyer, Jules Favre, instead of revolving around her husband's crimes, the trial was made to turn on the deviant character, doubtful virtue, and reprehensible behavior of—Flora Tristán! The judge declared that the rape "was not proved," and ordered that the children be sent to a boarding school where their parents could visit them separately. This was the sort of justice women could expect in France, Florita—and it was the reason you were on this crusade.

The appearance of *Peregrinations of a Pariah* brought her literary renown and some money (two editions quickly sold out) but also problems. The scandal the book caused in Paris—no woman had ever exposed her private life so frankly, or laid claim so proudly to the status of pariah, or declared her rebellion against society, conventions, and marriage as you had—was nothing compared to the scandal it provoked in Peru when the first copies reached Lima and Arequipa. You would have liked to have been there to see and hear what the furious gentlemen who could read French had said upon seeing themselves portrayed so unflatteringly. It amused you to learn that the Lima bourgeoisie had burned you in effigy at the Central Theater, and that your uncle Don Pío Tristán had presided over a ceremony in Arequipa's Plaza de Armas in which a copy of *Peregrinations of a Pariah* was set symbolically ablaze for vilifying Arequipan society. It was less amusing when Don Pío cut off the small allowance you had been living on. Emancipation didn't come cheap, Florita.

The book almost cost you your life. André Chazal never forgave you the merciless portrait you painted of him. For weeks and months he brooded over his revenge. Sketches of tombstones and epitaphs featuring the "Pariah" were later found in his room in Montmartre, dating from the publication of *Peregrinations*. In May of that year he bought two pistols, fifty bullets, powder, lead, and cartridges, without bothering to destroy the receipts. After that, he often boasted at the bar to his engraver friends that he would soon administer justice himself, punishing "that Jezebel" with his own hand. Some Sundays, he took little Ernest-Camille along to watch him practice target-shooting with his pistols. All through August you saw him prowling around the building where you lived on the rue du Bac, and although you alerted the police, they did nothing to protect you. On September 10, André Chazal left his squalid quarters in Montmartre and coolly went to have lunch at a small restaurant a few hundred feet from your house. He ate in leisurely fashion, absorbed in a book of geometry, in which, according to the restaurant's owner, he was making notes. At three-thirty in the afternoon, you spotted Chazal from the distance as you walked home in the stifling summer heat. You watched him approach, and you knew what was about to happen. But dignity or pride kept you from running, and you walked on, your head held high. When he was twenty feet away, Chazal raised one of the two pistols he was carrying and fired. You fell to the ground, the bullet having entered your armpit and lodged in your breast. As Chazal aimed the second pistol, preparing to shoot again, you managed to rise and run to a nearby store, where you fainted. Later you learned that Chazal, the coward, never shot the second pistol, and gave himself up to the police without a struggle. Now he was serving a sentence of twenty years of hard labor. You had freed yourself of him, Florita—forever. The law even allowed you to change Aline and Ernest's last name from Chazal to Tristán. Though belated, it was a true reprieve. But Chazal left you a souvenir, that bullet in your chest which might kill you at any moment if it shifted even slightly toward your heart. Dr. Récamier and Dr. Lisfranc, despite all their efforts and the many instruments with which they probed you, were unable to remove the missile. The assassination attempt made you a heroine, and during your convalescence the little flat on the rue de Bac became a fashionable spot. Many Paris celebrities dropped by to inquire about your health, from George Sand to Eugène Sue, Victor Considérant to Prosper Enfantin. You became more famous than a singer at the Opéra or a lady acrobat at the circus, Florita. But the death of little Ernest-Camille, as sudden and cruel as an earthquake, darkened what had seemed to be the end of your misadventures and the start of a period of peace and success.

Dr. Récamier and Dr. Lisfranc were so kind to you and so devoted that before setting out on your journey to promote the Workers' Union, you drafted a holographic will, donating your body to them in the case of your death, so that they might use it in their clinical research. Your head you bequeathed to the Phrenological Society of Paris, in memory of the sessions you had attended there, which left you with a very favorable impression of the new science of phrenology.

Despite the doctors' recommendations that you lead a quiet life, mindful of the cold metal in your breast, as soon as you were able to get up and go out, your life achieved a hectic pace. Since you were famous now, the salons competed for your presence. Just as you had been in Arequipa, you were drawn into the social whirl of Paris, attending receptions, galas, teas, salons. You even let yourself be dragged to the masked ball at the Opéra, which astonished you with its magnificence. That night you met a thin woman with penetrating eyes, a beauty with classic features who kissed your hand and said, in charmingly accented French, "I admire you and envy you, Madame Tristán. My name is Olympia Maleszewska. May we be friends?" You would indeed be friends—very close friends—a little while later.

If you had been a different sort of person, Florita, you might have become a grande dame, with the popularity you enjoyed for a while thanks to *Peregrinations of a Pariah* and the assassination attempt. By now you'd be like George Sand, an admired and much-praised woman of the world with an intense social life, who also happened to denounce injustice in her writings. A respected salon socialist, in other words. But for good or for ill, you weren't that person. You had understood at once that a siren of the Paris salons would never be capable of changing social reality one jot, or of exercising any sort of influence on political affairs. It was necessary to act. But how?

At the time, you thought writing was the way, that ideas and words would be enough. How wrong you were. Ideas were essential, but if they weren't accompanied by decisive action on the part of the victims—women and workers—those lovely words would vanish like smoke and never be heard outside the drawing rooms of Paris. But eight years, nine years ago, you believed that words in print denouncing the world's wrongs would be enough to set social change in motion. And so you wrote urgently, passionately, on every conceivable subject, straining your eyes in the light of an oil lamp in your little flat on the rue du Bac, from the windows of which you could make out the square towers of Saint-Sulpice and hear the ringing of its bells, which made the windowpanes of your bedroom vibrate. You composed a plea titled *Abolition of the Death Penalty*, which you caused to be printed and then personally delivered to the Chamber of Deputies, without its having the slightest effect on the parliamentarians. And you wrote *Méphis*, a novel about the social oppression of women and the exploitation of workers, which few people read and the critics judged dreadful. (Maybe it was. You didn't care: what mattered was not an aesthetic that lulled people into pleasant slumber, but rather the reform of society.) You wrote articles in *Le Voleur*, *L'Artiste*, *Le Globe*, and *La Phalange*, and you gave talks, condemning marriage as the purchase and sale of women and demanding the right to divorce. Your words were ignored by politicians and provoked the indignation of Catholics.

When the English social reformer Robert Owen visited France in 1837, you went to see him, though you had scarcely heard of his New Lanark, Scotland, experiments in cooperativism and the regulation of industrial and agricultural society by scientific and technical methods. You questioned him at such length about his theories that he was amused—and he returned the visit, knocking at the door of your little flat in the rue du Bac, as Fourier had come to visit you on the rue du Cherche-Midi. Owen, sixty-six, was less of a sage and a dreamer than Fourier, more pragmatic; he had the air of someone who put his plans into action. The two of you argued, then found common ground, and he encouraged you to come to New Lanark to see the workings of his little society with your own eyes. There, by encouraging solidarity instead of greed, promoting free education without corporal punishment for children, and establishing cooperative stores for the workers where products were sold at cost, he was forging a community of healthy, happy people. The idea of returning to England, a country you remembered with aversion ever since your days as a maid with the Spence family, attracted and terrified you. But the possibility kept tugging at your mind. Wouldn't it be wonderful to go, make a study, and find out everything about social issues there, as you had in Peru, and then pour it all into an accusatory volume that would shake the British empire—that society riddled with hypocrisy and lies—to its foundations? Hardly had you conceived the project when you began to seek a way to put it into practice.

Alas, Florita, it was a pity that because of your body, your spirit was no longer as resilient as it was seven years ago, when you could undertake many tasks at once, giving up eating or sleeping if necessary. Now, the labors you imposed on yourself required you to exert immense willpower to overcome your exhaustion, a numbing elixir that seemed to dissolve your bones and muscles, obliging you to lie down in bed or rest in an armchair two or three times a day, feeling that your life was slipping away from you.

She felt that kind of weariness after her second meeting with a group of Fourierists from Montpellier, held at their request. She arrived at the appointed time, intrigued. They had taken up a small collection, and they gave her twenty francs for the Workers' Union. It wasn't much, but something was always better than nothing. She joked and chatted with them until a sudden wave of fatigue made her bid them farewell and return to the Hôtel du Midi.

There were two letters waiting for her. The one she opened first was from Eléonore Blanc. Loyal Eléonore, always so loving and energetic, gave her a detailed account of the activities of the committee in Lyon: new members, meetings, money raised, sales of Flora's book, efforts to attract workers. The other letter was from her friend the artist Jules Laure, with whom she was very close. In the salons of Paris it was said that they were lovers, and that Laure supported her. The first assertion was false, since when Laure, after painting her portrait four years ago, declared his love, Flora rejected him with brusque frankness. She told him categorically that he must not insist: her mission, her struggle, were incompatible with passionate love. In order to devote herself entirely to reforming society, she had renounced affairs of the heart. As incredible as it seemed, Jules Laure understood. Since they couldn't be lovers, he implored her to let them be friends, brother and sister, partners. And that is what they were. In the painter, Flora had found someone who respected and loved her, a confidant and an ally who offered her friendship and support in her moments of need. Laure was financially well-off, too, and sometimes helped her out of material difficulties. He had never spoken to her of love again, or even tried to take her hand.

His letter brought bad news. The owner of her flat at number 100, rue du Bac, had evicted her for not paying her rent for several months in a row. Her bed and all her belongings had been tossed out into the street. By the time Jules Laure was informed and ran to retrieve them and put them into storage, several hours had gone by. He feared that many of her things had been stolen by the neighbors. Flora stood stupefied for a moment. Her heart beat faster, spurred by anger. With her eyes closed, she imagined the shameful scene, the men hired by that pig in a raincoat who always smelled of garlic, taking out furniture, boxes, clothing, papers, dropping them down the stairs, piling them up on the cobblestones. Only after a long while could she sob and vent her rage, insulting aloud the "miserable bastards," "repugnant money-grubbers," "filthy harpies."

"We'll burn all the landlords alive," she shouted, imagining smoking pyres on every corner in Paris, where the wretches smoldered. Finally, when she had plotted enough evil, she began to laugh. Once again, her malevolent fantasies had calmed her: it was a game she had played since her childhood in the rue du Fouarre, and it always proved effective.

But immediately afterward, forgetting that she no longer had a home and had probably lost most of her meager possessions, she began to think how she might give her revolutionaries a minimum of security, providing them with sustenance and a place to sleep as they went about winning followers and preaching social reform. When midnight came she was still working in her little hotel room by the light of a sputtering oil lamp, on a project to establish shelters for revolutionaries that, like the Jesuit monasteries and houses, would always be waiting for them with beds and bowls of hot soup when they went out into the world to preach revolution.

THE LATE-BLOOMING VICE

ATUONA, DECEMBER 1902

~

D id you always want to be a painter, Paul?" the pastor, Paul Vernier, asked suddenly.

They had drunk, eaten the master of the house's delicious runny omelet, and discussed the trouble that Paul would cause himself—in the judgment of Ben Varney and Ky Dong—by challenging the authorities again with his appeal to the Marquesans not to pay taxes. They had laughed and imagined the rage Bishop Martin would fly into upon learning that Koké had just erected two wooden figures in his garden designed to hit the prelate where it would hurt him most: the male figure, horned and praying, had the bishop's face and was called Father Lechery, and the female figure, her big tits and hips thrust out obscenely, was called Teresa, after the servant who was the bishop's lover, according to popular gossip in Atuona. They had discussed whether the mysterious ship they'd seen in the distance, sailing past the island in the rain and the fog, was one of the American whaling ships that were considered bad luck, distressing to the natives of Hiva Oa because they kidnapped people from the island, forcing them to join their crews. But, surrendering to Émile Frébault and Ben Varney's argument that the whaling ships no longer came because there were no whales anymore, they had declared that the ship they spotted didn't exist, that it was a ghost ship.

The Protestant pastor's abrupt question disconcerted Paul. They were talking in the flooded garden of the House of Pleasure. Happily, it had stopped raining. The clouds, upon parting an hour ago, had unveiled a pure blue sky, and the sun was shining brightly. It had rained torrentially all week, and this interlude of good weather was making Paul's five friends—Ky Dong, Ben Varney, Émile Frébault, Paul's neighbor Tioka, and the head of the Protestant mission—very pleased. Only Pastor Vernier didn't drink. The others were cradling glasses of absinthe or rum, and their eyes were merry.

"Did you feel called to be an artist ever since you were a boy?" insisted Vernier. "The subject of vocations, religious or artistic, is very interesting to me. Because I think the two have much in common."

Pastor Vernier was a lean, ageless man, and he spoke softly, savoring each word. He had a passion for souls and flowers; his garden, spreading beneath the mission's two lovely tamarind trees that Koké could see from his studio, was the best tended and most fragrant in Atuona. He blushed every time Paul or the others swore or mentioned sex. Now he was looking at Koké with real interest, as if the question of vocation truly mattered to him.

"Well, this vice of mine attacked me extremely late," Paul reflected. "Until I was thirty I don't think I made a single sketch. I thought artists were bohemians and faggots. I hated them. When I left the navy, at the end of the war, I didn't know what to do with my life. The only thing that didn't occur to me was being a painter."

Your friends laughed, thinking you were making one of your usual jokes. But it was true, Paul, even if no one could understand it, least of all yourself. The great mystery of your life, Koké. You had pondered it a thousand times, without ever coming up with an answer. Had the urge been buried deep inside you since you were born? Was it just waiting for the right moment, the proper circumstances in which to show itself? That was what Ky Dong insinuated, looking narrow-boned in his flowered pareu.

"It's impossible for a grown man to suddenly discover he's a painter, Paul. Tell us the truth."

It was the truth, even if your friends didn't believe you. As far as you could remember, you hadn't shown the slightest interest in painting or any other kind of art while you were sailing the seas in the merchant marine or, later, when you did your military service on board the *Jérôme-Napoléon*. Nor before, at Monsieur Dupanloup's boarding school in Orléans. Your memory had been failing you lately, but of this much you were sure: neither as a schoolboy nor as a sailor did you ever try your hand at painting, visit a museum, or set foot in a gallery. And when you were released from service and went to live in Paris with your guardian, Gustave Arosa, you paid little attention to the paintings hanging on his walls; the only things your guardian owned that roused your curiosity were his fired-clay Inca figurines, but was it for artistic reasons or because they reminded you of the little figures on the pre-Hispanic cloaks that so intrigued you as a child in Lima, in your great-great-uncle Pío Tristán's house?

"So what did you do between the ages of twenty and thirty, then?" asked Ben. The ex-whaler and owner of the general store in Atuona was red in the face and his eyes were bulging a little. But his voice wasn't that of a drunk man yet.

"I was a stock trader, a financier, a banker," said Paul. "And although you may not believe this either, I was good at it. If I'd kept on, I might be a millionaire now. A big cigar-smoking bourgeois, with two or three mistresses. Pardon me, pastor."

They laughed at him. The chortle of the giant Frébault, whom Paul had dubbed Poseidon for his bulk and his love of the sea, was like the rumble of a landslide. Even the inscrutable Tioka, who stroked his big white beard as if mulling philosophically over everything he heard, laughed. You were such a savage that they couldn't imagine you as a businessman, Paul. It was hardly surprising. By now even you couldn't believe it yourself, though you'd lived it. But was it really you, that young man of twenty-three who listened as Gustave Arosa suggested, in an earnest conversation over cognac in his Passy mansion, that you should find work on the stock exchange, where there were fortunes to be made, as he had made his? You accepted the idea willingly, and you were obliged to him—you didn't hate him yet; you still refused to believe that your mother had been his lover—when he got you a job in the offices of his associate, Paul Bertin, a well-known trader. How could that neatly dressed, polite, shy young man possibly have been you, arriving at the office with unhealthy punctuality and throwing himself wholeheartedly for hours on end—without becoming distracted for even an instant—into the difficult endeavor of finding clients willing to entrust the Bertin agency with their income and fortune, to be invested in the Paris stock market? Who among those who had known you in the last ten years could even imagine that in 1872, 1873, and 1874 you were a model employee, sometimes congratulated by Paul Bertin himself, your curt, remote boss, for your hard work and the orderly life you led, shunning the dissipation of the cafés and bars where your colleagues flocked when their offices closed. That wasn't you. You, a responsible man, walked back to your rented room on the rue La Bruyère, and after dining frugally in a little neighborhood restaurant, actually sat down at your creaking, lopsided table to go over papers from the office.

"It seems impossible, Paul," exclaimed Pastor Vernier, raising his voice as it was drowned out by distant thunder. "Was that what you were like as a young man?"

"A disgusting bourgeois in the making, pastor. I can't believe it myself now."

"And how did the change come about?" Frébault's booming voice broke in.

"The miracle, you should say," Ky Dong corrected him. The Annamite prince observed Paul with fascination, a doubtful expression on his face. "How did it happen?"

"I've thought a lot about that, and I believe I have a clear answer now." Paul savored a sharp, sweet mouthful of absinthe, and pulled on his pipe before continuing. "The man who corrupted me, who buggered my career as a bourgeois, was good old Schuff."

Slumped shoulders, hangdog look, weary shuffle, an Alsatian accent that made people smile: Claude-Émile Schuffenecker. Good old Schuff. When that timid, kind, shabby, pudgy man came to work at the Bertin agency—he was better prepared than you; he had studied business and wielded a diploma—how were you to imagine the influence he would have on your life? Your friendly, good-natured colleague, easily frightened and intimidated, looked up to you and admired your strength and determination. Blushing, he told you so.

You became great friends. Only after several weeks would you discover that beneath his timid, reserved exterior, your unprepossessing colleague nourished two passions, which he gradually revealed to you as your friendship was cemented: art and Eastern religions, especially Buddhism, about which Schuff had read reams. Must he still dream of reaching nirvana? But it was the way he talked about painting and painters that surprised you, intrigued you, and, little by little, seduced you. As good old Schuff saw it, artists were another species, half angel and half demon, different in essence from ordinary men. A work of art constituted a reality apart, purer, more perfect, and more orderly than our dismal, vulgar world. To enter the orbit of art was to gain access to another life, in which not only the spirit but also the body was enriched and given pleasure through the senses.

"He was corrupting me and I didn't realize it." Paul raised his glass. "To good old Schuff! He dragged me to galleries, museums, artists' studios. He made me visit the Louvre for the first time, to watch him copy the old masters. And one day, how or when I don't know, in my free time and in secret, I began to draw. That's how it started. My late-blooming vice. I remember the feeling I had that I was doing something bad, the same feeling I used to have as a child in Orléans at my uncle Zizi's when I masturbated or spied on the maid getting undressed. Incredible, isn't it? One day, Schuff made me buy an easel. The next, he showed me how to use oil paints. I had never held a brush in my hand before. He made me prepare the colors, mix them. He corrupted me, I tell you! With his innocent face, with that 'Who me? Who am I?' look of his, good old Schuff turned my life upside down. It's that fat Alsatian's fault I'm here at the ends of the earth."

But rather than good old Schuff, wasn't the decisive factor your visit to the gallery on the rue Vivienne where Édouard Manet's *Olympia* was being shown?

"It was like being struck by lightning, like seeing a vision," Paul explained. "Édouard Manet's *Olympia*. The most impressive painting I had ever seen. I thought, To paint like this is to be a centaur, a god. I thought, I must be a painter, too. I can hardly remember now. But it was something like that."

"A painting can change a man's life?" Ky Dong looked at him skeptically.

Above their heads there was another shuddering blast of lightning and thunder, and a furious wind whipped the trees of Atuona. But the rain didn't start again yet. A thick fog hid the sun, and the forested masses of Temetiu and Feani disappeared. The friends fell silent, until there was a new break in the storm and their voices could be heard.

"It changed me, it confounded me," Paul declared, with sudden anger. "It confused me, it gave me nightmares. Suddenly, I didn't feel sure of anything anymore, not even the ground I was walking on. Haven't you seen the photograph of *Olympia* in my studio? I'll show it to you."

He tramped through the muddy yard and climbed up to the second floor of the House of Pleasure. The wind shook the outside staircase as if to tear it away. The yellowing and rather blurred photograph of *Olympia* presided over the series of plates and postcards from his old collection: Holbein, Dürer, Rembrandt, Puvis de Chavannes, Degas, some Japanese prints, a reproduction of the bas-relief of the Javanese temple of Borobudur. At the start of the downpour seven days ago, he had taken down the pornographic photographs and put them under the mattress to keep them safe from the rain, which came in through the bamboo and got the whole room wet. Many of the soaked pictures would now completely lose their already faded color. *Olympia* was the oldest. You had gone looking for it eagerly after that exhibition on the rue Vivienne, and you had never been without it since.

His friends examined it, passing it around. Upon seeing the luminous naked body of Victorine Meuret (Koké told them that he had met her, and that she wasn't half as beautiful as she was in the painting; Manet had transformed her), challenging the whole world with the defiant, superior gaze of a free woman as her black maid handed her a bouquet of flowers, Pastor Vernier, of course, blushed deeply. Probably fearing that the nude was the beginning of worse things to come, he made his excuses.

"It will pour again any minute now," he said, pointing up at the menacing formations of dark clouds advancing on Atuona. "I don't want to have to swim back to the mission; there's a service this afternoon. Although no one will come in this storm, I'm afraid. There must not be a single plant left standing in my garden. Goodbye, everyone. Delicious omelet, Paul."

He left, slipping and sliding in the mud, and averting his eyes from the grotesque figures of Father Lechery and Teresa as he passed them. Tioka had his gaze fixed on the photograph, and after a long time, still stroking his snowy beard, he asked, in his slow French, "A goddess? A whore? Which is she, Koké?"

"Both, and many other things, too," Paul said, not laughing like his companions. "That's the extraordinary thing about that painting. She's a thousand women at once, a thousand women in one. Something for every taste, every dream. She's the only woman I've never tired of, my friends. Although now I can scarcely see her. But I carry her with me here, and here, and here."

As he said this, he touched his head, his heart, and his cock. His friends greeted this with more laughter.

As Vernier had said it would, the sky rapidly grew darker. The cemetery hill had disappeared now, too, but they could hear the roar of the burgeoning Make Make. When the rain began to fall hard, they ran with their glasses in their hands to take shelter in the sculpture studio, drier than the rest of the House of Pleasure. Wet through, they huddled on the single bench and the sofa that was losing its stuffing. Paul filled their glasses again. As he did, he noticed that the pelting rain had destroyed the sunflowers in the garden, and he felt pity for them and for the mad Dutchman. Ky Dong said he was surprised not to have seen Vaeoho all day: where was she, in a storm like this?

"She's gone to stay with her family, in the village of Hanaupe. She's pregnant, and she wants to give birth there. The truth is, she's using that as an excuse to abandon me. I don't think she'll be back. She's tired of all this, and maybe she has good reason."

His friends looked at one another uncomfortably. Tired of you and your sores, Paul. Your *vahine* couldn't hide her distaste, and you didn't need to be able to see her to realize it. Her face crumpled each time you tried to touch her. Oh well, poor girl. You had become a repulsive mess, a living ruin, Koké. But just now, feeling the warmth of the absinthe in your veins and talking to your friends, you wanted to feel well, despite the fury of the heavens. A few crushed sunflowers weren't going to destroy your life any more thoroughly, Koké.

"In all the years I've lived here, I've never seen it rain like this," said Ky Dong, indicating the sky: cascades of water shook the roof of bamboo and plaited palm leaves, and seemed about to wash it away. Bolts of lightning lit up the horizon for seconds at a time, and then all the mountains of Hiva Oa that surrounded them disappeared, obscured by black and thunderous clouds. Even Ben Varney's store, so close by, couldn't be seen. Behind them, the sea raged. Was it the end of the world, Koké?

"I've never been away from here and I've never seen it rain like this," said Tioka. "Something bad is going to happen."

"Worse than this deluge?" Ben Varney joked, stumbling over his tongue. And turning toward Paul, he resumed the conversation. "So you saw that painting and you gave up everything to devote yourself to art? You're a madman, not a savage, Paul."

The storekeeper was very comical, with his red hair plastered over his forehead in a fringe. He laughed, amused and incredulous.

"If only it had been that easy," Paul said. "I was married, very much so. I had a bourgeois home, a wife who kept giving me more children. How could I give all that up from one day to the next? What about my responsibilities? And the ethics of it? And my reputation? Back then, I believed in those things."

"You, married?" Ky Dong asked, surprised. "In the full legal sense, Koké?"

In the full legal sense, and much more than that. Had you really fallen so deeply in love with Mette Gad, Paul, that willowy, well-educated young Dane, a Viking with long blond hair who had come to spend time in Paris in the winter of 1872? You didn't remember at all. But you must have fallen in love with her, because you took her out, courted her, declared your love, and formally asked for her hand in marriage, something to which Mette's horrible, extremely bourgeois family in Copenhagen finally consented after much hesitation and after conducting a painstaking investigation of her suitor. To satisfy those stuffy Scandinavians, it was a proper wedding, at the mayor's office in the ninth arrondissement and at the Lutheran church of Paris, with champagne, an orchestra, many guests, and generous gifts from your guardian, Gustave Arosa, and your boss, Paul Bertin. And then, after a short honeymoon in Deauville, the two of you moved into the flat on the place Saint-Georges, where you hung the ancient Peruvian cloak that your sister, María Fernanda, and her Colombian fiancé, Juan Uribe, had given you. You did everything that a young stockbroker with a brilliant future should do. That was what you were then, Paul. You worked hard, you made a good living—in 1873 you were awarded a three-thousand-franc bonus, a larger sum than any of your colleagues at the Bertin agency received—and Mette, happy, decorated the flat and burned with impatience to begin having children. In 1874, when your first son was born and baptized Emil (for his godfather, good old Schuff, although without the final *e*, in acknowledgment of the child's Nordic ancestors), you received another bonus of three thousand francs. A small fortune, which Mette Gad gaily set about squandering on purchases and entertainments, never suspecting that the enemy was already within. Her diligent and affectionate husband was secretly sketching, and had begun to take classes in drawing and painting with Schuff at the Colarossi Academy. When she found out, they no longer lived on the place Saint-Georges, but in an even more elegant neighborhood, the sixteenth arrondissement, in a magnificent flat on the rue de Chaillot that Paul had resigned himself to renting to satisfy Mette's delusions of grandeur, though he warned her that it was more than they could afford on his salary.

The Viking discovered your secret vice from another important person in your life at the time: Camille Pissarro. Born on the Caribbean island of Saint Thomas, where he became an outcast after he supported a slave uprising, Pissarro came to Europe and continued imperturbably to pursue his career as an artist of the avant-garde, along with a group of friends known as the impressionists, without troubling himself in the least about the scarcity of buyers for his paintings. He associated with anarchist intellectuals like Kropotkin, who paid him visits, and he called himself a "harmless anarchist, one who doesn't blow things up." Paul met him at the home of Gustave Arosa, who had bought a landscape from Pissarro, and after that, they saw each other often. Paul bought a painting from him, too. Because

Pissarro made very little money, he couldn't live in Paris. He had a small house in the country, near Pontoise, where—a biblical patriarch with the patience of Job—he raised his seven children, who adored him, and endured his wife, Julie, a former maid with a domineering nature. She railed at him before his friends, berating him for his failure to make a good living. "You only paint landscapes, which no one likes," she scolded him in front of Paul and Mette, who were often invited to spend weekends in Pontoise. "Paint portraits instead, or picnics, or nudes, like Renoir or Degas. They're doing better than you, aren't they?"

One Sunday, as they were drinking cups of chocolate, Camille Pissarro mentioned, in a tone of seeming sincerity, that Paul had a "truly artistic temperament." Mette Gad was surprised. What did he mean?

"Is it true what Pissarro said?" she asked her husband, when they were on their way back to Paris. "Are you interested in art? You never told me you were."

The shock and sensation of guilt were like a shiver running straight through you, Paul. No, my dear, it's merely a hobby, something healthier and more stimulating than wasting my nights in bars or cafés, playing dominoes with friends. Wouldn't you agree, Viking? She said yes, of course, with an uneasy scowl. Women's intuition, Paul. Did she guess that dissolution had already crept into her home, and that the intruder would ultimately destroy her marriage and her dreams of becoming a rich and worldly bourgeoise in the City of Light?

After this episode, you felt curiously liberated, with the right to flaunt your new vice before your wife and friends. Why shouldn't a successful trader on the Paris stock exchange have the right to openly dabble in art in his spare time, as others played billiards or rode horses? In 1876, in a daring move, you borrowed *Landscape at Viroflay*, the painting you had given your sister and her new husband as a wedding present, and submitted it to the Salon. Out of thousands of entries, it was accepted. Happiest to hear this was Camille Pissarro, who began to bring you with him as his disciple to the café La Nouvelle Athènes in Clichy, his friends' general headquarters. The impressionists had just held their second group exhibition. While the imposing Degas, bad-tempered Monet, and merry Renoir talked to

Pissarro—a barrel-shaped man with a white beard, unfailingly good humored—you sat in silence, ashamed to be no more than a stockbroker in the company of these artists. When Édouard Manet, the creator of *Olympia*, appeared one night at La Nouvelle Athènes, you turned pale, as if you were about to faint. Overcome by emotion, you scarcely managed to stutter a greeting. How different you were then, Koké! How far you still were from becoming your present self! Mette couldn't complain, because you continued to make good money. In 1876 you received a bonus of thirty-six hundred francs, in addition to your salary, and the next year, when Aline was born, you moved. The sculptor Jules-Ernest Bouillot rented you a flat and a small studio in Vaugirard. There you began to model in clay and chisel marble under the direction of your landlord. The head of Mette that you worked so hard to sculpt—was it an acceptable piece? You couldn't remember.

"Living a double life like that must have been difficult," Ky Dong observed. "Stockbroker for hours every day, and then, in your little bits of free time, painting and sculpture. It reminds me of my years as a conspirator in Annam. By day, a circumspect employee of the colonial administration, and by night, insurrection. How did you do it, Paul?"

"I didn't," said Paul. "But what choice did I have? I was a man of principle. How could I simply say to hell with all my responsibilities—my wife, my children, my security, my good name? Luckily, I had the energy of ten men. Four hours of sleep were enough for me."

"Now that I'm drunk, I have to give you some advice," Ben Varney interrupted, changing the subject abruptly. His voice was unsteady now and his eyes, especially, revealed that he was inebriated. "Stop fighting with the authorities in Atuona, because you won't win. They're powerful, and we aren't. We won't be able to help you, Koké."

Paul shrugged his shoulders and took a sip of absinthe. It cost him an effort to detach himself from the man he had been at thirty-two, thirty-three, thirty-four, back in Paris, torn between his family obligations and the belated passion for art that had taken root inside him with the voracity of a tapeworm. What was Varney talking about? Oh yes, your campaign to stop the Maori from paying the highway tax.

Your friends had been alarmed, too, when you explained to the natives that if they lived a long way from Atuona, they weren't required to send their children to the mission school. And what had happened to you then? Nothing.

The storm had swallowed up the landscape. The neighboring sea, the roofs of Atuona, the cross atop the hillside cemetery, had disappeared behind a gauzy whiteness that was growing thicker by the second. They were already sealed off. The swollen Make Make began to overflow, tumbling the boulders in its path. Paul thought of the thousands of birds, feral cats, and crowing roosters of Hiva Oa that the storm must be killing.

"Since Ben has raised the matter, let me venture to give you some advice, too," said Ky Dong, tactfully. "When you went out to the Bay of Traitors at the beginning of the school year to tell the Maori who were bringing their children to the priests and nuns that they weren't obliged to do so if they lived far away, I warned you, 'This is serious.' Because of you, the number of students in the schools has been reduced by a third, maybe more. The bishop and the priests will never forgive you for it. But this business with taxes is even worse. Don't do anything rash, my friend."

Tioka emerged from his stern immobility and laughed, something he rarely did. "The Maori families who had to come halfway across the island to bring their children to school are grateful to you for telling them about that exemption, Koké," he whispered, as if celebrating some mischievous act. "The bishop and the gendarme lied to us."

"That's what priests and policemen do—lie," Koké said, laughing. "My teacher, Camille Pissarro, who despises me now for living among primitives, would be happy to hear me say so. He was an anarchist. He hated men in robes or uniform."

A long burst of thunder, hoarse and rumbling, prevented the Annamite prince from saying what he intended to say. Ky Dong sat with his mouth open, waiting for the sky to quiet. Since it didn't, he spoke loudly to make himself heard above the storm.

"This tax business is much worse, Paul. Ben is right—you're being unwise," he insisted, in his smooth, feline, purring way. "Counseling the natives not to pay taxes is mutiny, subversion."

"You're against subversion? The man sentenced to Devil's Island for wanting to free Indochina from France?" Paul laughed.

"I'm not the only one who thinks so," replied the ex-terrorist, very seriously. "Many in the village are saying the same thing."

"I've heard the new gendarme say it, in those precise words," Frébault interjected, waving his paw of a hand. "He has his eye on you, Koké."

"Claverie, that son of a bitch? What a shame they've replaced our friend Charpillet with a witless brute like that." Paul pretended to spit. "Do you know when he first started to hate me? When he caught me swimming naked in the river in Mataiea, the first month I lived in Tahiti. The bastard made me pay a fine. The worst thing wasn't the fine, but the way he shattered my dreams—Tahiti, it was clear, wasn't an earthly paradise after all. There were men in uniform there who prevented human beings from living a life of freedom."

"We're serious," cut in Ben Varney. "We aren't saying this to make you angry or to meddle. We're your friends, Paul. You could be in trouble. The school affair was serious enough. But this tax business is worse."

"Much worse," echoed Ky Dong. "If the natives listen to you and stop paying their taxes, you'll go to jail as a subversive. And who's to say you'll be as lucky as I was? You've hardly been here a year and you've already made enemies. You don't want to spend the rest of your life on Devil's Island, do you?"

"Maybe that's where everything is that I've been looking for and haven't been able to find yet—in Guiana," Paul mused, turning solemn. "Let's drink, friends, and not worry about the future. Anyway, all signs up there indicate that this is the beginning of the end of the world for the Marquesas."

The thunder had resumed its deafening concert, and the whole House of Pleasure shook and danced, as if the torrents of water and raging gusts of wind would uproot it and carry it away at any minute. The overflowing waters of the river began to swamp the yard. They were your friends, Paul. They were worried about what might happen to you. They were telling the truth: you were no one, just an apprentice savage without money or reputation, whom priests, judges, and gendarmes could trample whenever they wanted. The gendarme

Claverie, who was also Hiva Oa's judge and chief political authority, had warned you. "If you keep encouraging the natives to mutiny, the full weight of the law will fall on you, and your poor bones won't withstand it; let this be a warning."

Very well; thank you for the warning, Claverie. Why were you embroiling yourself in new messes and predicaments, Koké? Wasn't it stupid? Maybe. But it wasn't fair to collect a highway tax from the miserable inhabitants of a little island where the state hadn't built a foot of roads, paths, or streets, and where leaving Atuona meant being faced on all sides with impenetrable, steeply rising forest. You had confirmed it yourself on that nightmarish trip by mule to Hanaupe to negotiate your marriage with Vaeoho. It was because of the lack of roads that you couldn't leave Atuona, Koké, and you hadn't been able to visit the valley of Taaoa to see the ruins of the tikis of Upeke, something you were so eager to do. A swindle, that tax. Who was pocketing the money that wasn't invested here? One or more than one of those repulsive parasites working for the colonial administration in Polynesia, or back in France. Fuck them. You would keep advising the Maori to refuse to pay it. To set them an example, you had written to the authorities explaining why you wouldn't pay either. Well done, Paul! Your ex-teacher, anarchist Camille Pissarro, would approve of your actions. And far away, in heaven or in hell, Grandmother Flora, that agitator in skirts, would be applauding.

Camille Pissarro had read some of Flora Tristán's books and pamphlets, and spoke of her with such respect that he made you interested for the first time in your grandmother on your mother's side, about whom you knew nothing. Your mother had never said anything to you about her. Did she hold some grudge against her? As well she might have: Grandmother Flora neglected her daughter, leaving her living with wet nurses while she waged revolution. In the end, you read very little of what your grandmother had written. During the day, you had no time for anything but chasing after the agency's clients and informing them of the state of their stocks, and all your free moments—especially those blissful weekends in Pontoise with the Pissarros—were spent painting, painting furiously. In 1878 the Museum of Ethnography opened, in the Trocadero Palace. You remembered it well, because it was seeing the ceramic figurines there crafted by ancient Peruvians—with such mysterious names: Mochica, Chimú—that you had the first hint of what years later would become an article of faith: those exotic, primitive cultures possessed a power, a spiritual vigor, that had vanished in contemporary art. You particularly remembered a mummy that was more than a thousand years old, from the valley of Urumbamba, with long hair, very white teeth, and blackened bones; you called her Juanita. Why did that withered relic so bewitch you, Paul? You went many times to see her, and one afternoon, when the guard wasn't watching, you kissed her.

The funny thing was—wasn't it, Paul?—that just then, when painting had come to matter to you more than anything else, the bosses of the world of the exchange were fighting over you, as if you were a premium stock. In 1879, you accepted an offer to change jobs, and at the new agency you did so well that your bonus that year was a fortune: thirty thousand francs! Mette was ecstatic. She immediately decided to reupholster the furniture and repaper the drawing room and dining room. That year, Camille Pissarro arranged for you to present a marble bust of your son Emil at the Fourth Impressionist Exhibition. The sculpture was nothing spectacular, but after that everyone—public and critics—considered you part of the group. Were you happy with the progress you had made, Paul?

"I didn't have time to be happy, with the frenetic life I was leading," said Koké. "But I was certainly busy. I spent as much of that fabulous bonus as the Viking would let me get my hands on in buying my friends' paintings. My house filled up with Degases, Monets, Pissarros, and Cézannes. The most exciting day that year was the day Degas proposed that we exchange a painting. Imagine, he was treating me as an equal!"

It was that year, too, that Clovis, your third child, was born. In 1880 you contributed eight paintings to the Fifth Impressionist Exhibition. And that same year, Édouard Manet complimented you for the first time, in a roundabout way. "I'm just an amateur, who studies art on nights and holidays," you said, in La Nouvelle Athènes. "No," Manet corrected you, energetically. "Amateurs are those who paint badly." You were stunned and happy. In 1881, good old Schuff, who had invested his inheritance and savings in an obscure business exploiting a new technique for treating gold, began to make lots of money; then, he married the beautiful and penniless Louise Monn, who imagined she was doing well for herself. She wasn't wrong. Good old Schuff gave up the exchange to dedicate himself to art. This frightened Mette: you weren't dreaming of doing anything so foolish, were you, Paul? They began arguing every day.

"Why did you lie to me, and hide your interest in painting?"

"Because I was hiding it from myself, too, Mette."

In the little studio rented from the painter Félix Jobbé-Duval, you stubbornly sculpted, carved, and painted, stealing time away from the exchange. The stories Jobbé-Duval told about his homeland, Brittany, and the Bretons, a primitive, traditional people faithful to their past, who resisted "cosmopolitan industrialization," awakened your interest. Then you began to dream of fleeing the megalopolis of Paris for a land where the past was part of the present, and art hadn't yet become divorced from everyday life. In that same studio you painted works that you were still proud of today: *Interior of the Artist's House, Rue Carcel*; *Nude Study, Suzanne Sewing*, which you exhibited in the impressionist show; and best of all, *The Little Dreamer: Study*. In 1881, when Mette gave birth to your fourth child, Jean-René, the Durand-Ruel gallery bought three paintings from you for fifteen hundred francs, and a famous writer, Joris-Karl Huysmans, wrote a piece praising you. Fortune was smiling on you, Paul.

"Yes, yes, and best of all, the businesses and banks were beginning to collapse," he bellowed, impassioned, trying to make himself heard over the thunder. "France was going bankrupt, my friends. The exchanges, one after the other, were closing down, too. Thanks be to God! My problem was solved!"

His friends looked at him uncomprehendingly. You explained that the economic catastrophe had ruined every Frenchman, except for you. For you it meant emancipation. As a sequel, the crash brought about major political upheaval. Anarchists were hunted down, and Kropotkin was taken prisoner. Camille Pissarro went into hiding, and there was panic in many poor and bourgeois homes. But you, Paul, completely indifferent to these events, continued painting, bursting with impatience. When the Lyon stock exchange closed, Mette had a nervous attack and cried as if someone she loved had died. When the

Paris exchange closed, she stopped eating for several days, growing thin and haggard. You were very happy. That year, you showed eleven oil paintings, one pastel, and a sculpture at the Seventh Impressionist Exhibition. In August 1883, when your boss at the financial office called you in to tell you, his voice shaking and an expression of remorse on his face, that given the dire situation, he had to let you go, you did something that flabbergasted him: you kissed his hands, while crying euphorically, "Thank you. You've just made me a real artist." Wild with joy, you ran to tell Mette that from now on you would never set foot in an office again, and instead would devote yourself exclusively to painting. Speechless and deathly pale, after blinking for a long moment, Mette tumbled senseless to your feet.

"By then, I was much changed," Paul added, cheerfully. "I drank more than I used to. Cognac at home, and absinthe at La Nouvelle Athènes. I spent long stretches of time alone, playing the harmonium, because that inspired me to paint. And I began to dress outlandishly, like a bohemian, to provoke the bourgeoisie. I was thirty-five. My real life was just beginning, friends."

Suddenly, the thunder ceased, and the rain lessened a little. The thirty waterfalls that spouted in Atuona on rainy days from the peaks of Temetiu and Feani had multiplied, and the Make Make spilled over both its banks. Soon a wide ribbon of water crept into the studio and flooded it. Nodding at the fog that surrounded them, Ben Varney sang softly, "It's like being on a whaler." In just a few minutes, they were up to their ankles in muddy water. Soaked, they went to look outside. The whole area was inundated, and a newly fledged river—carrying branches, trunks, greenery, mud, and cans—flowed along toward the main street, taking the garden of the House of Pleasure with it.

"Do you know what that shape there is?" Tioka pointed at some patches that were denser than the clouds settled low over Atuona. "That thing the current is carrying toward the sea? My house. I hope it isn't taking my *vahine* and my children, too."

He spoke coolly, with the calm Marquesan stoicism that had so impressed Koké from his first day in Hiva Oa. Tioka waved goodbye and strode off, in water up to his knees. The curtains of rain and fog swallowed him up almost instantly. Then Ky Dong, Poseidon Frébault, and Ben Varney finally reacted, though very differently from Tioka. In seconds, their fright and surprise had erased the effects of the alcohol. What should they do? They had better run and see if their families were all right, and perhaps take refuge on the cemetery hill. On this flat ground they were much more exposed to the fury of the gale. And if a tsunami struck, farewell Atuona.

"You have to come with us, Paul," insisted Ky Dong. "Your hut won't stand. This isn't an ordinary storm. It's a hurricane, a typhoon. You'll be safer up there with us, in the cemetery."

"Slogging through the mud with my legs in this state?" he said with a laugh. "Why, I can scarcely walk, my friends. You go ahead. I'll stay here, waiting. The end of the world is my element, gentlemen!"

He watched them go, huddled, splashing, the water up to their knees, toward the now-vanished path that became the main street of Atuona once it passed that clump of bushes. Would they make it safely? Yes, they had experience of bad weather like this. And you, Paul? What Ky Dong had said was true; the House of Pleasure was a fragile construction of bamboo, palm leaves, and wooden beams that only by some marvel had managed to withstand the wind and rain so far. If the storm lasted, it would collapse and be swept away, and you with it. Was this an acceptable way of dying? Slightly ridiculous, perhaps. But no more ridiculous than dying of pneumonia. Or slowly rotting away from the unspeakable illness. Since there wasn't a single dry corner in the House of Pleasure, or anywhere to shelter from the buffeting of the wind and rain, he moved slowly—his legs hurt him very much now—to pour another glass of absinthe. He picked up his drenched harmonium and began to play, mechanically. He had learned to master the difficult instrument as a boy, on board ship, when he served in the merchant marine. Music filled the empty places in his soul, soothing him at moments of frustration or discouragement. When he was immersed in a painting or a sculpture— rarely now, since his sight was so bad—it gave him energy, ideas, something of his old will to achieve elusive perfection. Would it come as a surprise, dying like this, Paul? On a remote little island in the middle of the Pacific, in the Marquesas, the most isolated spot on earth? Well, you had decided long ago that you would die among the savages, like just another savage yourself. But then he remembered the old blind woman who had made him feel like a foreigner.

She had appeared out of nowhere a few weeks before, at dusk, leaning on a cane, while Koké was up on the second floor straining his poor eyes to see the deserted island of Hanakee and the Bay of Traitors, which at this time of day were tinted pink by the setting sun. The old woman came into the yard, the dog barking and the two cats yowling, and shouted a few words in Maori that alerted Koké to her presence. She seemed a straggly bundle, a formless being, rather than a woman. She was dressed in rags that she had probably picked out of a rubbish heap, patched and mended with string. Feeling her way with her cane, which she tapped rapidly left and right, she found the path to the house, and—mysteriously—to Paul, who came to meet her. They stood face to face in the sculpture studio, precisely where Koké sat now, frozen to death and staving off his fear with absinthe. Was she blind or was she pretending? When she was very close to him he saw her milky corneas. Yes, she was blind. Before Paul could open his mouth, the woman, sensing he was there, raised her hand and touched his naked chest. Calmly, she felt his arms, shoulders, navel. Then, pushing aside his pareu, she felt his belly and grasped his testicles and penis. She weighed them in her hand, as if testing them. Then her face soured and she exclaimed, disgusted, "Popa'a." It was an expression that Koké knew; it was what the Maori called Europeans. Without another word, and without waiting for the food or gift for which she had come, the old blind woman turned and left, feeling her way out. Being nothing more to them than a foreigner with a hooded cock was just another of your failures, Koké.

He woke up the next morning with his harmonium in his arms. He had fallen asleep on the table full of glasses and bottles, which were now scattered all over the floor. The water was beginning to retreat from his studio, but havoc and desolation lay all around. Nevertheless, the House of Pleasure had resisted the hurricane, although it was damaged in places and part of its roof was gone. And up above, in the pale blue sky, the rising sun was beginning to warm the earth.

19

THE MONSTER-CITY

BÉZIERS AND CARCASSONNE,

AUGUST/SEPTEMBER 1844

$\mathcal{Y}$

At times, Flora compared her travels in the south of France to Virgil and Dante's descent into hell: each city on her itinerary was uglier, dirtier, and more craven than the next. In foul-smelling Béziers, for example, where she spent the night in the unbearable Hôtel des Postes, at which none of the porters or even the manager spoke anything but Provençal, she couldn't get permission to hold a meeting in a single factory or workshop. Bosses and workers barred every door to her for fear of the authorities. And the eight workers who did agree to talk to her took so many precautions—they came to the hotel at night, they entered by the back door—and were so terrified of losing their jobs that Flora didn't even try to suggest that they form a Workers' Union committee.

She was only in Béziers for two days, at the end of August 1844. When she got on the mail boat to Carcassonne, she felt as if she were being freed from jail. So as not to be seasick, she stayed on deck with the passengers who hadn't taken cabins. There, she instigated a quarrel that almost ended in blows, by urging a *spahi*, a colonial soldier recently returned from Algeria, and a young sailor in the merchant marine, to judge which of their jobs was more useful to society. The sailor said that ships carried passengers and goods and facilitated commerce, whereas soldiers were good only for killing. The *spahi*, indignant, showed his scars, and replied that the army had just conquered a colony in the north of Africa that was three times as large as France itself. When he grew incensed and began to hurl abuse, Flora shut him up.

"You're living proof that the French army still turns its conscripts into brutes, as it did in the time of Napoléon."

It would be six more hours until they reached Carcassonne. She sat on a bench in the stern, huddled against some rope, and fell asleep at once. She dreamed of Olympia. It was the first time you had dreamed of her since leaving Paris seven months ago, Florita.

A pleasant dream, sweet, faintly exciting, nostalgic. You had only good memories of your friend, to whom you owed so much. But you didn't regret having broken things off with her so abruptly when you returned from England in the fall of 1839, because that would mean you regretted your crusade to transform the world through intelligence and love. Although you had met her at the Opéra ball you attended dressed as a Gypsy—she was the slender woman with piercing eyes who kissed your hand—you began your friendship with Olympia Maleszewska only months later. She was the granddaughter of a celebrated orientalist, professor at the Sorbonne, and she had worked to liberate Poland from the yoke of imperial Russia. She was a member of the National Polish Committee, which met in exile in France, and she had married one of its leaders, Léonard Chodzko, a historian and patriot who worked at the library of Sainte-Geneviève. But Olympia was primarily a society hostess. She had a well-known salon, which was attended by literary figures, artists, and politicians, and when Flora received an invitation to Olympia's Thursday-evening gatherings, she decided to attend. The house was elegant, the reception gracious, and many famous people were there. Here, the actress of the moment, Marie Dorval, brushed elbows with the novelist George Sand; there, Eugène Sue stood beside the Saint-Simonian Father, Prosper Enfantin. Olympia presided with exquisite tact and hospitality. She welcomed you affectionately, introducing you to her friends with great ceremony. She had read *Peregrinations of a Pariah*, and her admiration of your book seemed sincere.

Since Olympia was so insistent that you visit her salon again, you did, several times, and you always enjoyed yourself. On the third or fourth time, Olympia was helping you take off your coat in the dressing room and smoothing your hair—"I've never seen you look so radiant, Flora"—when suddenly she put her arms around your waist, pulled you to her, and kissed you on the lips. It was so unexpected that you, aflame from head to toe, didn't know what to do. (For the first time in your life, Florita.) Blushing, confused, you stood rooted in place, staring wordlessly at Olympia.

"If you hadn't guessed already, now you know that I love you," Olympia said, laughing. And taking you by the hand, she dragged you out to meet the other guests.

Many times you had asked yourself why you stayed at the salon that afternoon. Had it been a man who had kissed you, you would have slapped him and immediately left the house. You were dazed and disconcerted, but not angry, and you felt no desire to go. Was it simple curiosity, or something else? What did it mean, Andalusa? What would happen next? When, a few hours later, you announced that you were leaving, the mistress of the house took you by the arm and led you to the dressing room. She helped you put on your coat and your little hat with a veil. "You aren't angry with me, are you, Flora?" she whispered warmly in your ear.

"I don't know if I'm angry or not. I'm confused. I've never been kissed on the mouth by a woman before."

"I've loved you ever since I saw you that night at the Opéra," said Olympia, gazing into your eyes. "Can we see each other alone, to get to know each other better? I beg it of you, Flora."

They did see each other, took tea together, and drove in a fiacre around Neuilly, as Flora, telling the story of her marriage to André Chazal, brought tears to her friend's ardent eyes. You confessed that, since your marriage, you had always felt instinctively repelled by the sexual act and that, as a result, you had never had a lover. With infinite delicacy and tenderness, Olympia, kissing your hands, begged you to let her show you how sweet and delightful pleasure could be between two friends who loved each other. After that, whenever they met or parted, they searched for each other's lips.

It wasn't much later that they made love for the first time, in a little country house near Pontoise where the Chodzkos summered and spent weekends. A complicit rustle came from the nearby poplars swaying in the breeze, birds could be heard chirping, and in a room warmed by a fire in the hearth, the enervating, enveloping atmosphere slowly overcame Flora's defenses. Passing swallows of champagne from her own mouth to Flora's, Olympia helped her to undress. Confidently, Olympia undressed, too, and taking Flora in her arms, laid her on the bed, whispering tender words. After contemplating Flora intently and devoutly, she began to caress her. The pleasure she made you feel was great, Florita, truly great, once those first moments of confusion and wariness were past. She made you feel beautiful, desirable, young, womanly. Olympia showed you that there was no need to be frightened of sex or repulsed by it, that abandoning oneself to desire, giving way to the sensuality of touch and the satisfaction of physical desires, was an intense and impassioned way of living, even if it lasted only hours, or minutes. What delicious egotism, Florita. The discovery of physical pleasure, of love without violence, between equals, made you feel freer, more complete—though even on the days you were happiest with Olympia, you couldn't help experiencing a feeling of guilt and wastefulness when you abandoned yourself to bodily delights, a sense that you were squandering your energies.

The relationship lasted somewhat less than two years. Flora couldn't remember a single time it was sullied by argument, coolness, or harsh words. It was true that they didn't see each other often, since both of them had many things to do, and Olympia had a husband and home to look after as well, but when they did meet, everything always went marvelously well. They laughed and cavorted together like two girls in love. Olympia was more frivolous and worldly than Flora, and except for Poland and its tragic subjugation, she wasn't interested in social questions, or the fate of women or workers. And Poland interested her because of her husband, whom she loved very much, in her libertine way. But she was spirited, tireless, and—when she was with you—infinitely loving. Flora enjoyed listening to her relate society intrigue and gossip, because she did it so humorously and ironically. Also, Olympia was an educated woman who had read widely and was well versed in history, art, and politics—subjects she was passionate about—so that intellectually, too,

Flora gained much from her friendship. They made love several times in the little house in Pontoise, but also in Olympia's Paris flat, in Flora's flat on the rue du Bac, and once, with you dressed as a nymph and she as a silenus, at an inn on the edge of the leafy groves of Marly, where squirrels would come to the windows to eat peanuts from your hands. When Flora left for London for four months in 1839, to write a book on the plight of the poor in that citadel of capitalism, they wrote letters two or three times a week, passionate missives telling how much they missed each other, thought of each other, desired each other, and were counting the days, hours, and minutes until they could see each other again.

"I devour you with kisses and caresses in all my dreams, Olympia. I adore the darkness of your hair, of your muff. Since I met you, I despise blond women." Were you thinking these fiery sentences in London as you visited factories, bars, slums, and brothels, disguised as a man, to document your hatred of that paradise for the rich and inferno for the poor? You were, word for word. But then why, as soon as you returned to Paris, on the very afternoon of your arrival, did you inform Olympia that your relationship was over, that you could never see each other again? Olympia, always so sure of herself, such a woman of the world, opened her eyes and mouth very wide and turned pale. But she didn't say anything. She knew you, and she knew that your decision was unappealable. She looked at you, biting her lips, devastated.

"Not because I don't love you, Olympia. I do; you are the only person in the world I've ever loved. I'll always be grateful to you for these two years of happiness. But I have a mission, which can't be fulfilled so long as my mind and feelings are divided between my obligations and you. What I'm about to do requires that I not be distracted by anything or anyone, even you. I must devote myself body and soul to this task. I don't have much time, my love. And as far as I know, there is no one in France who can replace me. This bullet here could end my life at any moment. At the very least, I must leave things well under way. Don't hate me for it; forgive me."

That was the last time they saw each other. Afterward, you wrote your fierce diatribe against England—*Walks in London*—and your little book *The Workers' Union*, and here you were now, on the Pyrenean fringes of France, in Carcassonne, trying to start a worldwide revolution. Didn't you regret abandoning sweet Olympia that way, Florita? No. It was your duty to do what you did. Redeeming the exploited, uniting workers, achieving equality for women, bringing justice to the victims of this imperfect world—these things were more important than the marvelous egotism of love, the supreme indifference to one's fellows that was produced by pleasure. The only feeling you had room for in your life now was love for humanity. There wasn't even space in your crowded heart for your daughter, Florita. Aline was in Amsterdam, working as a seamstress's apprentice, and sometimes weeks would go by before you remembered to write her.

On the very night Flora arrived in Carcassonne, she had an unpleasant encounter with the local Fourierists, who, led by a Monsieur Escudié, had arranged her visit. They had reserved a room for her at the Hôtel Bonnet, beneath the city walls. She was already in bed when a knock at the door of her room awakened her. The hotel manager begged her pardon a thousand times: some gentlemen insisted on seeing her. It was very late; they should return tomorrow. But since they were so adamant, she threw a robe over her shoulders and went out to meet them. The dozen local Fourierists who had come to welcome her were drunk. She felt ill with disgust. Did these bohemians pretend to make revolution on champagne and beer? To one of them, a man with slurred speech and glassy eyes who insisted that she dress so they could show her the churches and medieval walls in the moonlight, she replied, "What do I care about old stones, when there are so many human beings with problems to be solved! Just so you know, I wouldn't hesitate to give the most beautiful church in Christendom for one intelligent worker."

Seeing how irritated she was, they left.

The week she spent in the city, the Fourierists of Carcassonne—lawyers, agriculturalists, doctors, journalists, pharmacists, and officials, who called themselves chevaliers—turned out to be a permanent source of trouble. Hungry for power, they were planning an armed insurrection across the whole French Midi. They said that many officers were with them, and even whole garrisons. From her first meeting, Flora criticized them vehemently. In the best of cases, she told them, their radicalism would lead to the replacement of a few bourgeois members of government with new ones, and in the worst it would provoke a bloody repression that would destroy the emerging workers' movement. The important thing was social revolution, not political power. Their conspiracy plans and violent fantasies only confused the workers, and would distance them from their goals and use up their energies. Such purely political subversion might lead to their decimation by the army, a sacrifice that would be of no use to the cause. The chevaliers had influence in workers' circles, and they attended Flora's meetings at the spinning mills and textile factories. Their presence intimidated the poor, who hardly dared speak before them. Instead of explaining the possibilities of the Workers' Union, you had to spend hours and hours in exhausting political arguments with these schemers, who rallied the workers with their plans for armed uprisings, speaking of the many rifles and barrels of powder they had hidden in strategic places. The seductive idea of seizing power by force inflamed many workers.

"What would the difference be between a Fourierist government and the one that now exists?" shouted Madame-la-Colère, enraged. "What do the workers care who exploits them? It's not a question of seizing power by any means, but of ending exploitation and inequality once and for all."

At night she returned to the Hôtel Bonnet as exhausted as she had been in London in the summer of 1839, at the end of crowded days spent studying everything in that monster city of two million inhabitants, capital of the planet's biggest empire, and headquarters of its most booming factories and largest fortunes. With Olympian disregard for medical advice, she worked from dawn until dusk to show the world that, behind the facade of prosperity, luxury, and power, there lurked the most abject exploitation, the worst evils, and a suffering humanity enduring cruelties and abuse in order to make possible the dizzying wealth of a handful of aristocrats and industrialists.

The difference, Florita, was that in 1839, despite the bullet by then lodged in your chest, you were refreshed after a few hours of sleep and ready for another thrilling day in London, venturing into slums that drew no tourists, that were in fact invisible in travelers' accounts, which delighted in describing the glories of drawing rooms and clubs, the well-kept parks, the gas lamps of the West End, and the charms of the dances, banquets, and dinners at which the parasites of the nobility disported themselves. Now, when you got up you were as tired as you were when you went to bed, and during the day you had to fall back on the blind stubbornness that fortunately you still preserved intact in order to follow the schedule you had set for yourself. It wasn't the bullet that troubled you most; it was the pains in your stomach and your uterus, against which tranquilizers no longer had any effect.

Despite all the hatred you had come to feel for England since you lived there in your youth, working for the Spences, you had to admit that without it and its English, Scottish, and Irish workers, you would probably never have come to realize that the only way to achieve emancipation for women and win them equal rights was by linking their struggle to that of the workers, society's other victims, the downtrodden, the earth's immense majority. The idea came to her in London, inspired by the Chartist movement, which demanded the adoption into law of a People's Charter establishing universal suffrage, voting by ballot, yearly elections for Parliament, and salaries for members so that workers could campaign for seats. Although it had existed since 1836, the Chartist movement was at its height when Flora arrived in London in June of 1839. She followed news of its demonstrations, meetings, and campaigns to collect signatures, and she learned about its excellent system of organization, with committees in villages, cities, and factories. You were impressed. The old excitement kept you awake now, remembering those marches of thousands and thousands of workers through the streets of London. A true civil army. If all the poor and exploited peoples of the world were organized like the Chartists, who could stand against them? Women and workers together would be invincible, a force capable of revolutionizing human existence without firing a single shot.

When she heard that the National Convention of the Chartist movement was then being held in London, she discovered where they met. Boldly, she appeared at Doctor Johnson's Tavern, a seedy-looking bar in a dead-end alleyway off Fleet Street. Into a vast, damp, smoky, ill-lit room smelling of cheap beer and boiled cabbage, some hundred Chartist foremen were packed, among them the main leaders, O'Brien and O'Connor. They were discussing whether it was a good idea to call a general strike in support of the People's Charter. When they asked you who you were and what you were doing there, you explained, in a steady voice, that you brought greetings from the workers and women of France to their British brethren. They looked at you with surprise, but they didn't make you leave. A handful of female workers were there too, and they eyed your bourgeois clothing suspiciously. For several hours, you listened to them argue, exchange proposals, vote on motions. You were rapt. This force, if multiplied all over Europe, would change the world, would bring happiness to the disinherited—you were sure of it. When, at one point in the session, O'Brien and O'Connor asked if the French delegate wanted to address the assembly, you didn't hesitate for a second. You climbed up to the speakers' platform and congratulated them in your wobbly English, encouraging them to continue providing an example of organization and struggle to all the world's poor. You ended your brief speech with a call to arms that left your listeners, believers in peaceful means of action, completely taken aback. "Let's burn the castles, *brothers!*"

Now you laughed remembering your words, Florita. Because you didn't believe in violence. You had made that incendiary appeal in order to express with a dramatic image the overpowering emotion you felt. What a privilege it was to be there, among fellow members of the exploited classes who were beginning to show their strength. You were in favor of love, ideas, and persuasion, and against bullets and the gallows. That was why you were exasperated by the bloodthirsty bourgeois of Carcassonne, who thought everything could be resolved by mobilizing regiments and erecting guillotines in public squares. What could one expect from such fools? There was no hope for the bourgeoisie; their egotism would always prevent them from seeing the larger truth. You, on the other hand, were sure you were on the right path, now more than ever. Bringing women and workers together, organizing the two groups into an alliance that would transcend boundaries and could not be crushed by any police brigade, army, or government. Then, heaven would no longer be an abstraction, and, liberated from the sermons of priests and the credulity of believers, it would become history, the reality of everyday life and all mortals. "I admire you, Florita," she exclaimed, enthused. "O God, if you would only send ten women like me to this world, justice would reign on earth."

Among the Fourierists of Carcassonne, the most flamboyant was Hugues Bernard. A militant in secret societies in France and a member of the Carbonarists in Italy, he wanted civil war at any cost. He was eloquent and seductive, and the workers listened to him spellbound. Flora confronted him; she called him a "snake charmer," a "conjuror," a "corruptor of the workers with your demagogic drivel." Instead of being offended, Hugues Bernard followed her back to her hotel, wearying her with his flattery: she was the most intelligent woman he had ever met, the only one he might have married. If he weren't sure of being rejected, he would try to woo her. In the end, Flora had to laugh. But because he was so flirtatious, she decided to keep her distance from him. Monsieur Escudié, the leader of the chevaliers, tried to win her friendship, too. He was a mysterious, gloomy man, dressed in mourning and gifted with flashes of genius.

"You would make a good revolutionary, Escudié, if you weren't so driven by your appetites, and let love rule you instead."

"You've hit the nail on the head, Flora," agreed the lean, cadaverous Fourierist, in a serious tone, a Mephistophelian expression on his face. "My appetites, the temptations of the flesh, are my greatest trial."

"Forget about the flesh, Escudié. To make revolution all you need is the proper spirit, the idea. Flesh is a hindrance."

"That's easier said than done, Flora," said the Fourierist mournfully, with a look in his eye that alarmed her. "My flesh is a compound of all the legions of hell. You, who seem so pure—if you could see into the world of my desires, you would die of horror. Have you read the Marquis de Sade, by chance?"

Flora felt her legs tremble. She managed to steer the conversation in another direction, afraid that Escudié, once started down that path, would reveal his secret nether world, the lewd depths of his soul where many demons must dwell, to judge by the evil spark in his eye. Yet, on a rare impulse, she suddenly found herself confiding in the lugubrious Fourierist. She was a free woman, and in her forty-one years she had more than proved that she didn't fear anyone or anything. But despite her fleeting adventure with Olympia, sex continued to arouse a vague uneasiness in her, because time and again life had shown her that while carnal desires might lead to passion and pleasure, they were also a slope down which men slid rapidly into bestiality, toward the most savage forms of cruelty and injustice to women. She had been aware of it since her youth, because of André Chazal, who violated his wife and then his own daughter, but she had witnessed it fully on her trip to London in 1839, and the horror would never be erased from her memory. So shameful were some of the scenes she observed that the editors of *Walks in London* made her soften them, and once the book was published, not a single critic dared discuss them. Unlike *Peregrinations of a Pariah*, which was praised everywhere, her denunciations of the blighted London metropolis were silenced by the cowardice of the Paris intelligentsia. But what did you care, Florita? Wasn't that a sign that you were on the right path? "Yes, most definitely," Escudié encouraged her.

It was soon after she arrived in London that she was given the idea of dressing as a man, by an Owenist friend who saw how upset she was to learn that women weren't allowed into the British Parliament. A Turkish diplomat helped her, providing her with her disguise. She had to adjust the baggy trousers and the turban, and stuff the slippers with paper. Although she felt nervous crossing the threshold of the imposing building on the Thames, heart of British imperial power, she completely forget her borrowed identity upon hearing the representatives' speeches. The parliamentarians' vulgarity, and their crude way of sprawling in their seats with their hats on, disgusted her. But when she heard Daniel O'Connell, the leader of the Irish independents, the first Irish Catholic to occupy a seat in the House of Commons and the designer of a strategy of nonviolent struggle against English colonialism, she was moved. He was an ugly man, with the look of a coachman in his Sunday best, but when he spoke—advocating universal suffrage and the abolition of slavery—he became beautiful, radiating decency and idealism. He was such a brilliant orator that everyone listened attentively. Hearing O'Connell, Flora came up with the idea of the People's Defender, which she made part of her proposal for the Workers' Union: the women's and workers' movement would send a spokesman to Congress, paying him a salary to defend the interests of the poor.

In those four months she often dressed as a man. She had set herself the task of giving an account of the life led by the hundred thousand prostitutes who were said to roam the streets of London, as well as observing what happened in the city's brothels, and she could never have explored those low haunts without disguising herself in trousers and a man's frock coat. Even so, it was dangerous to venture into certain neighborhoods. The night she walked Waterloo Road, from its start in the slums to Waterloo Bridge, the two Chartist friends who accompanied her carried staffs to discourage the myriad pickpockets and petty thieves who swarmed among the madams, pimps, and whores. They crowded the pavement, block after block, and in the absence of the police, assaulted lone clients in full view of everyone. The merchandise was shamelessly offered to passersby who came along on foot or horseback or in carriages, inspecting the goods for sale. In theory, the minimum age for human commerce was twelve. But Flora could have sworn that among the dirty, made-up, half-naked little skeletons that the procuresses and pimps touted, there were girls and boys of ten and even eight, tiny creatures with dazed or stupid stares, who seemed not to understand what was happening to them. The brashness and obscenity with which their services were offered ("You can bugger this little doll, sir," "My cherub is willing to be whipped, and she's an expert cock-sucker, master") made waves of hatred rise in her. She was on the verge of fainting. Walking along the interminable street, in shadows that were interrupted every so often by the dangling red lamps of the little bawdy houses, and hearing the disgusting exchanges, the braying voices of drunks, you had the sense of having wandered into a macabre phantasmagoria, a medieval witches' Sabbath. Wasn't this the closest thing on earth to hell? Could there be anything more accursed than the fate of these girls and boys, offered for pennies to sate the appetites of loathsome men?

There could, Florita. Worse than the stretch of whorehouses in the East End, full of girls and boys often kidnapped in villages or the countryside and sold to London brothels and houses of assignation by gangs specializing in the trade, were the West End "finishes," in central London, district of elegant entertainments. There, Florita, you reached the pinnacle of evil. The finishes were tavern-brothels, bar-whorehouses, where the rich and the aristocratic, the privileged members of England's society of masters and slaves, went to "finish" their nights of revelry. You visited them dressed as a fop, with a young man from the French legation who had read your books and who loaned you men's clothing, though he first tried to dissuade you, assuring you that the experience would horrify you. He was absolutely right. You, who thought you had seen human brutality in all its incarnations, had not yet witnessed the extremes to which the humiliation of women could be taken.

The girls at the finishes were not the starving, tubercular prostitutes of Waterloo Road. They were well-dressed courtesans in brightly colored clothing, bejeweled and garishly made up. After midnight, standing in a line like music-hall chorus girls, they greeted the wealthy gentlemen who had been out dining or at the theater or a concert, and had come to end the evening in one of these luxurious hideaways. The men drank and danced, and some went to private rooms on the upper floors with one or two girls to make love, and to beat them or let themselves be beaten, which in France was called *le vice anglais*. But at the finishes, the real entertainment wasn't the bed or the whip, but exhibitionism and cruelty. It began at two or three in the morning, when lords and men of means removed their jackets, ties, vests, and suspenders, and the challenges began. They offered the women—girls, adolescents, children—shining gold guineas to down the drinks they prepared for them. Gleefully, they made them fill up their stomachs, cheering one another on in circles rocked by laughter. At first they gave them gin, cider, beer, whiskey, cognac, and champagne, but soon they began mixing the alcohol with vinegar, mustard, pepper, and worse, to watch the women swallow the contents of the glasses, then fall to the floor grimacing in revulsion, writhing, and vomiting—all to pocket a few guineas. Then, amid applause, the drunkest or most depraved, egged on by their fellows, unbuttoned their flies and pissed on the women, or, if they were particularly audacious, masturbated over them, streaking them with their sperm. At six or seven in the morning, when the revelers, tired of entertainment and sated with drink and cruelty, had fallen into the idiot stupor of the inebriated, their footmen came in and dragged them out to their fiacres and berlins, to take them home to their mansions to sleep off their drunkenness.

Never had you wept so much, Flora Tristán. Not even when you learned that André Chazal had raped Aline did you weep as you did after those two nights in the London finishes. It was then that you decided to end things with Olympia in order to devote all your time to the revolution. Never had you felt such pity, such bitterness, such rage. Awake in Carcassonne, you experienced the same feelings again, thinking about the thirteen-, fourteen-, and fifteen-year-old courtesans—one of whom might have been you had you been kidnapped while you were working for the Spences—gagging down those concoctions for a guinea, letting the liquid poison destroy their insides for a guinea, allowing themselves to be spat upon, pissed upon, and spattered with semen for a guinea, all to provide the rich men of England with a momentary thrill in their empty, meaningless lives. For a guinea! God, God, if you existed, you could not be so unjust as to take Flora Tristán's life from her before she set in motion the worldwide Workers' Union that would put an end to the evils of this vale of tears. "Give me five more years, eight more. That's all I need, God."

Carcassonne was no exception to the rule, of course. In the textile factories, which she was prohibited from entering, the men earned one and a half to two francs a day and the women half as much for the same work. The workday had been lengthened from fourteen to eighteen hours. In the silk factories and wool spinning mills children of seven worked for eight centimes a day, though the law prohibited it. There was fierce hostility to her everywhere. Her tour had become known in the region, and lately her enemies in the cities were sharpening their knives to greet her. Flora discovered that factory managers were circulating flyers in Carcassonne that accused her of being "a bastard, an agitator, and a degenerate who abandoned her husband and children, took lovers, and is now a Saint-Simonian and an Icarian communist." This last bit made her laugh. How could she be both a Saint-Simonian and an Icarian communist? The two groups detested each other. You had sympathized with Saint-Simon some years ago, it was true, but that was ancient history now. Although you had read Cabet's *Travels in Icaria* (and owned a signed copy of the 1840 first edition), which had won him so many followers in France, you had never felt any sympathy for Cabet or his disciples, those traitors to society who called themselves "communists." On the contrary, you had always accused them, in speech and in print, of preparing them-selves—under the guidance of their sage, who was an adventurer, Carbonarist, and attorney in Corsica before he became a prophet—to travel to some remote spot (America, the African jungle, China) to found the perfect republic described in *Travels in Icaria*, free of money, hierarchies, taxes, and rulers. Could there be anything more selfish or cowardly than their escapist fantasy? It was no good fleeing this imperfect world to establish an idyllic retreat for a small group of the chosen, far away, where no one else could come. What was needed was to combat the imperfections of the world as it was, to change and improve it until making it a happy place for all human beings.

On the third day in Carcassonne, an older man who wouldn't give his name appeared at the Hôtel Bonnet. He confessed that he was a policeman, assigned by his superiors to follow her. He was amiable and a little shy, his French imperfect. To her surprise, he had read *Peregrinations of a Pariah*, and declared himself an admirer of hers. He warned her that all the authorities in the region had received instruc-tions to make her life impossible, to set people against her, because they believed her to be an agitator preaching subversion against the monarchy in the working world. But Flora should know she had nothing to fear from him: he would never do anything to harm her. He was so overcome by emotion upon telling her this that Flora planted an impulsive kiss on his forehead. "You don't know what good it does me to hear you, my friend."

The encounter cheered her, at least for a few hours. But reality presented itself again when an influential lawyer abruptly canceled his appointment with her. Maître Trinchant sent a prickly note: "Having learned of your Icarian communist loyalties, I prefer not to see you. Anything we said to each other would fall on deaf ears."

"But my job is to make the deaf hear and the blind see," Madame-la-Colère responded.

She wasn't discouraged, but it did her no good to remember her visits to the bawdy houses and finishes of London. Now she couldn't stop thinking about them. Although she had seen many sad things on her travels in captalism's underworld, nothing incensed her more than the trade in those unfortunate women. Nor did she forget the visits she made with an Anglican church official to the working-class neighborhoods on the outskirts of London, a succession of tumble-down hovels with treadle spinning machines always humming, crowded with naked children rolling in filth. The same complaints were repeated everywhere, like a refrain: "At thirty-eight, at forty, all of us—men and women—are said to be useless and dismissed by the factories. How are we to eat, m'lady? The food and old clothes that the church gives us aren't even enough for the children." In the great gas works on Horseferry Road, Westminster, you almost suffocated trying to see from up close how the workers, wearing only breech-cloths, scraped coke out of ovens that made you think of Vulcan's forges. After just five minutes, you were drenched in sweat and felt that you would die of the heat. They roasted there for hours, and when they poured water on the clean braziers, they breathed in a thick smoke that must have turned their insides as black as their skin. At the end of this ordeal, they were allowed to lie down in pairs on mattresses for a few hours. The plant manager told you that no one lasted more than seven years on the job before coming down with tuberculosis. This was the price paid for the sidewalks lit by gas lamps on Oxford Street, in the heart of the West End—the most elegant street in the world!

The three prisons you visited, Newgate, Coldbath Fields, and Penitentiary House, were less inhumane than the workers' miserable surroundings. It made you shiver to see the instruments of medieval torture greeting inmates in the reception hall at Newgate. But the cells, individual or shared, were clean, and the prisoners—thieves, for the most part—ate better than the workers in the factories. At Newgate, the director let you talk to two murderers, condemned to hang. The first, surly, remained stubbornly mute. But the second, smiling, jovial, and happy to break the rule of silence for a few minutes, seemed incapable of hurting a fly. Yet he had hacked an army officer to pieces. How could he have done such a thing, when he was so obliging and friendly? John Elliotson, a professor of medicine with long sideburns who was a fanatical disciple of Franz Joseph Gall, founder of the science of phrenology, explained it to you: "It is because this young man has two extremely prominent bumps at the base of his skull: the bones of pride and disgrace. Touch them, madame. Here and here. Do you feel them? He was fated to kill."

Flora ventured to criticize only two things about the English penal system: the rule of silence, which required that prisoners never open their mouths—a single word spoken aloud merited extremely severe punishment—and the prohibition that forbade them to work. The cultured governor of Coldbath Fields, an old colonial soldier, assured her that silence encouraged closer communion with God, mystical trances, repentence, and self-reform. And regarding work, the subject had been debated in Parliament. It was decided that it would be unfair to ordinary laborers to allow criminals to work, because the competition would be unjust, since criminals could be hired for lower salaries. In England there was no minimum age for being tried, and at all three prisons Flora saw children of eight or nine serving sentences for robbery and other crimes.

Though it was sad to see such infants behind bars, Flora told herself that perhaps they were better off there; at least they had food to eat and a roof over their heads in their clean cells. In contrast, in the Irish neighborhood of the parish of Saint Gilles, on Bainbridge Street between Oxford Street and Tottenham Court Road, children were literally dying of hunger. They were dressed in rags, and essentially slept out in the open, in flimsy shacks of planks and tin, with no shelter from the rain. Surrounded by puddles of filthy water, putrid waste, mud, flies, and all sorts of vermin—in her boardinghouse on the night after her visit to the neighborhood, Flora discovered that her clothes were full of lice—she had the feeling that she was walking in a nightmare, among skeletons, old men crouched on little piles of straw, and women in tattered clothing. There was garbage everywhere, and rats scurried between people's feet. Not even those who had work made enough money to provide for their families. They all depended on gifts of food from the churches to feed their children. Compared to the misery and degradation of the Irish, the neighborhood of poor Jews in Petticoat Lane seemed less grim. Although the poverty there was extreme, secondhand clothes dealers carried on a lively business in countless hole-in-the-wall shops and basements, where half-naked Jewish whores were also offered, with much fanfare and in broad daylight. The Field Lane market, where all the handkerchiefs stolen on London streets were sold for a pittance—it was necessary to leave behind wallet, watches, and brooches to venture down that narrow street—seemed more human to her, too. It was even agreeable, with its unabashed clamor and the sound of quaint disputes between sellers and buyers seeking a bargain.

At the Hospital of Saint Mary of Bethlehem, known as Bedlam, something happened that made your blood run cold, Florita. Neither your Chartist nor your Owenist friends shared your theory that madness was a social illness resulting from injustice, and a blind, instinctive act of rebellion against established power. And therefore no one accompanied you on your visits to London asylums. Bedlam was old and very clean, with neat, well-tended grounds. As he was showing you the place, the director suddenly remarked that they had a countryman of yours there, a French sailor called Chabrié. Would you like to see him? You stopped breathing for an instant. Was it possible that good Zacharie Chabrié of the *Mexicain*, upon whom you had played such a cruel trick to be rid of his love, had gone mad and ended up here? You endured a few minutes of infinite anguish until they brought the man. It wasn't Zacharie, but a handsome youth who thought he was God. He explained it to you cautiously, in calm French: he was the new Messiah, sent to earth "to end servitude, and save women from men and the poor from the rich."

"We're fighting the same fight, my friend," Flora said, smiling. He winked knowingly in reply.

That trip to England in 1839 was as instructive as it was exhausting. From it there sprang not only your book, *Walks in London*—it was published at the beginning of May 1840, and frightened the bourgeois journalists and critics with its radicalism and frankness, though not the public, which bought out two printings in just a few months—but also your idea for the alliance of society's two greatest victims, women and workers, as well as *The Workers' Union* and this very crusade. Five years now, Andalusa, spent in the superhuman struggle to bring your plans to fruition!

Would you manage it? Yes, if your body didn't fail you. If God only granted you a few more years, you surely would. But you weren't certain you'd live long enough. Maybe God didn't exist, and that was why he couldn't hear you, or maybe he did exist and was too concerned with higher things to bother himself with the material details that mattered to you, like the pains in your abdomen and your uterus. Each day, each night, you felt weaker. For the first time, you were assailed by a foreboding of defeat.

At her last meeting in Carcassonne, the lawyer Théophile Marconi—a chevalier to whom Flora had paid little heed—offered of his own accord to organize a Workers' Union committee for the city. Although doubtful at first, he had finally become convinced that Flora's strategy was sounder than his friends' attempts at conspiracy and civil war. Bringing together women and workers to change society struck him as intelligent and feasible. After her meeting with Marconi, a young worker named Lafitte walked her back to her hotel and made her laugh with a plan that, he confessed with a sly face, he had devised to swindle the bourgeois Fourierists. Posing as one of them, he would offer the chevaliers an investment guaranteed to double their capital, a chance to purchase stolen looms at ridiculously low prices. When he had taken their money, he would mock them. "Your greed was your downfall, gentlemen. This money will go to the coffers of the Workers' Union, for the revolution." He was joking, but there was a mercurial light in his eye that troubled Flora. What if the revolution became a business opportunity for a few rogues? The engaging Lafitte, upon bidding her farewell, asked permission to kiss her hand. She gave it to him, laughing and calling him "a gentleman in training."

On her last night in the walled city, she dreamed of a cast-iron ladle and its eerie clanging. It was a recurring dream, and had come, in a way, to symbolize her trip to England. On many London street corners, ladles were chained to pumps where the poorest of the poor came to slake their thirst. The water those wretches drank was con-taminated—before it reached the pumps it had passed through the city sewers. It was the music of poverty, Florita, and it had been ring-ing in your ears for four years. Sometimes you said to yourself that the clang of those ladles would follow you to the next world.

20

THE SORCERER OF HIVA OA

ATUONA, HIVA OA, MARCH 1903

ॐ

W
hat surprises me most about your whole story," said Ben Varney,
looking at Paul as if trying to puzzle him out, "is that your wife
put up with your madness."

Paul was only half-listening. He was trying to assess the damage
done to Atuona by the hurricane. Before, only the little wooden
steeple of the Protestant mission was visible from the veranda above
Ben Varney's store where they were chatting. But the devastating
winds had blown some trees down and stripped and mutilated many
others, so now it was possible to see the church's whole facade and
Pastor Paul Vernier's immaculate little house, as well as the two
lovely tamarind trees that flanked it, hardly touched by the storm. As
he surveyed it all from the railing, Paul imagined the path to the
beach: it must be completely impassable now, blocked by the mud,
stones, branches, leaves, and trunks the hurricane had left in its
wake. It would be some time before it was cleared and you were able
to resume your evening rides to the Bay of Traitors, Koké. Had the
peaceful Marquesans really set a trap for the crew of that whaling
ship? Had they really killed them and gobbled them up?

"That she stayed with you even though your decision to become a
painter meant the family's financial ruin, I mean," insisted the shop-

keeper. Ever since he had heard the story, he had pestered Paul incessantly for more details. "How could she bear to be with you?"

"She didn't bear it for long, only a few years," you resigned yourself to replying. "What choice did she have? The Viking had nowhere to go. As soon as she did have somewhere, she left me. Or rather, she fixed things so that I would leave her."

Inside Ben's store below, they could hear Varney's wife speaking to some children in Marquesan. In the sky over Hiva Oa the great sunset fireworks display—blues, reds, pinks—was beginning. December's cyclone had claimed few victims in Atuona, but it had wreaked much havoc: huts knocked down, roofs torn from buildings, trees uprooted, and the settlement's only street turned into a pitted and oozing mud slick. But like the House of Pleasure, the American's wooden dwelling had stood firm, sustaining only slight damage, which had already been repaired. Of their friends, the most affected was Tioka, Koké's neighbor, whose hut was swept away by the swollen Make Make, though his family was unharmed. Now the sturdy, white-bearded old man and his relatives were working hard to build another house on a piece of land that Koké had given them within his own property.

"I may not know much about art," the storekeeper admitted. "Well, to tell the truth, I don't know anything about it. But you have to allow it's hard for the average intelligence to understand. You're living a comfortable, prosperous life, and sometime in your thirties you give it all up to become an artist. With a wife and five children! Isn't that what a person would call crazy?"

"Do you know something, Ben? If I had stayed at the stock exchange, in the end I would have killed Mette and my children, even if they sent me to the guillotine for it, like the outlaw Prado."

Ben Varney laughed. But you weren't joking, Koké. When you lost your job in August 1883, you had reached the breaking point. Spending a considerable part of the day doing something you hated, since it prevented you from painting—which by then mattered to you more than anything else—had you on the verge of an outburst that might have ended in suicide or crime. You were sure of it. That was why you were so happy when you lost your job, though you knew that starting a new life would require many sacrifices of you, and especially Mette. And so it did. Tests, Koké. The tests of a cruel and faithless little god to determine whether you were meant to be an artist and, even more difficult, whether you deserved to have talent. Twenty years later, although you had passed every one, the merciless divinity kept sending you new trials. Now had come the most fiendish of all: the fading of your eyesight. As a painter, how could you pass the test of semiblindness? Why this persecution?

A little while after Mette gave birth to their last child, in December 1883—Paul Rollon, who would always be called Pola—the family left Paris to settle in Rouen. You had decided that life would be cheaper there, and that you could make money selling your paintings to the prosperous townspeople, and painting their portraits. The usual pipe dreams, Koké. You sold no canvases, and weren't commissioned a single portrait. And in the eight months you lived in that tiny flat in the medieval heart of the city, Mette daily cursed her fate, cried, and railed at you for having kept secret your determination to be an artist, which had ruined them all. But these domestic quarrels mattered nothing to you, Koké.

"I was free and happy, Ben," Paul laughed. "I painted Norman landscapes, boats, and fishermen in the port. Utter shit, of course. But I was sure that soon I would be a good painter. It was just around the corner. Such enthusiasm coursing through my veins, Ben!"

"If I were Mette, I would have poisoned you," said the ex-whaler. "But then, if you had been a good husband you would never have come to the Marquesas. Do you know what? If someone wrote about all of us who've been stranded here, it would make a great story. Consider it: Ky Dong and you, or even me."

"Your story is the strangest, Ben," said Paul. "Imagine missing your ship because you were drunk. Is it true? Did it happen that way?"

The American nodded, screwing up his red, freckled face.

"The truth is that the other men got me drunk so they could leave me behind," he said without bitterness, as if he were speaking of someone else. "On the whaler they took me for a difficult kind of bastard, I think. The way people see you here. You and I have something in common, Koké. That must be why I like you so much. By the way, what news of your tangle with the authorities?"

"As far as I know, the legal proceedings are stalled." Paul spat toward the nearby palm trees. "Maybe their files were lost or destroyed in the gale. They can't touch me now. Nature, defending art against priests and gendarmes! The cyclone was my salvation, Ben!"

In July of 1884, Mette Gad boarded a ship in the harbor of Rouen and sailed for Denmark with three of the children, leaving Paul in the Norman capital with Clovis and Jean in his care. In Copenhagen, matters improved for the Viking. Her family found her work as a French teacher. And then—dreaming, Koké, always dreaming—you decided to follow her and conquer Denmark for impressionism.

"What is impressionism?" Ben wanted to know.

They were drinking brandy, and the shopkeeper was already tipsy. Paul, however, was perfectly sober, although he had drunk more than his friend. From the hill of the Catholic mission behind them, the wind carried the sound of the choir at the school of the Sisters of Saint Joseph of Cluny. They always practiced at this hour, singing hymns that no longer seemed religious, infused as they were with the joy and sensual rhythms of Marquesan life.

"An artistic movement that no one in Paris remembers anymore, I imagine," said Koké, shrugging his shoulders. "And now, Ben, one last toast. If night comes, I won't be able to find my way home with my eyes the way they are now."

Ben Varney helped him down the stairs, across the fenced-in yard, and into his little trap. As soon as the pony felt him climb in, it started off. It knew the way by heart, and trotted along carefully in the dim evening light, avoiding the obstacles in its path. Happily, you didn't have to guide it, Paul; you wouldn't have been able to. In the dusk, your eyes, weakened by the unspeakable illness, couldn't see the dips or bumps in the road. You felt good. Blind and contented, Koké. The air was warm and soothing, and a soft breeze scented with sandalwood blew. That had been a difficult test of your pride, having to live at 29 Frederiksbergalle, Mette's mother's house, supported and snubbed by your mother-in-law and your wife's uncles, aunts, sisters, brothers, and even cousins. None of them could understand, much less accept, that you had given up a bourgeois life and the world of finance to be a bohemian, which in their minds was synonymous with being an artist. They banished you to the attic, where, because of your shabby and eccentric appearance—which you exaggerated to spite your in-laws, of course, by wearing an Indian feather headdress—you had to stay hidden away while Mette taught French to young men and women of the Danish upper class, since there was the risk that the girls would be upset and the boys offended by your unsuitable appearance, and thus abandon their classes. Things didn't improve when, thanks to the sale of a painting from your collection of impressionist works, you, Mette, and the children left your mother-in-law's to live in a little house at 51 Norregada, in a seedy neighborhood of Copenhagen, which gave Mette new cause to rage at you and lament her fate.

This new test you passed, too. Humiliated and lonely in a country whose language you didn't speak, and where you had no friends or purchasers for your paintings, you worked constantly and furiously. You painted skaters in snowy Frederiksberge Park, the trees of East Park, your first self-portrait; you made ceramic pieces, wood carvings, drawings, countless sketches. One of the few Danish artists who was interested in what you were doing, Theodor Philipsen, came to look at your paintings. For an hour, you talked. Suddenly, you heard yourself telling the Dane that for you, feelings were more important than reason. Where did that theory come from? You were inventing it as you went along. Painting should be the expression of the whole human being: his intelligence, his skill as a craftsman, his culture, but also his beliefs, instincts, desires, hatreds. "Like primitive man." Philipsen didn't attach the slightest importance to what you were saying; he was amiable and dull, like all Scandinavians. But you did. You had spoken without thinking; later, upon reflection, you would discover that those words summed up your artistic credo. And still did today, Koké. Because behind your infinite statements and denials, in speech and in writing, on artistic matters over all these years, the fixed nucleus was still the same: Western art had deteriorated because of its alienation from the totality of existence manifested in primitive cultures. In them, art—inseparable from religion—was part of everyday life, like eating, dressing, singing, and making love. You wanted to recapture that tradition in your paintings.

It was dark when he arrived at the House of Pleasure, which, because of the cyclone, was no longer surrounded by forest but by thin ranks of trees and fallen trunks. This was one of Hiva Oa's traits:

darkness fell in an instant, like a curtain dropping and hiding the scenery. A pleasant surprise—there were Haapuani and his wife, Tohotama, sitting beside the caricatures of Father Lechery and Teresa, which had survived the hurricane. They had just come from Tahuata, the island of redheaded Maori like Tohotama. To what did he owe this happy visit?

Haapuani hesitated and exchanged a long look with his wife, before responding flatly, "I accept your proposal. Necessity has convinced me, Koké."

Ever since he met him, shortly after arriving in Atuona, Paul had wanted to paint Haapuani. The man's character intrigued him. He had been the native priest of a Maori village on Tahuata, before the arrival of the French missionaries. Now no one knew for sure whether he lived on Hiva Oa or his native island, or traveled back and forth between the two. He would disappear for long periods of time and, upon returning, say nothing about where he had been. The natives of Hiva Oa believed he had ancient knowledge and powers because of his former practices, which, according to Ky Dong, he still continued in secret, away from the scrutiny of Bishop Martin, Pastor Vernier, and the gendarme Claverie. Koké admired him for his daring: sometimes, despite his years (he must have been in his fifties), Haapuani appeared at the House of Pleasure dressed and adorned like a *mahu*, a man-woman. Although the other Maori took no notice of this, it would have provoked the wrath of the two churches and the civil authority if they found out. Haapuani had no objections to the beautiful, muscular Tohotama posing—she had done so many times—but he would never agree to let Koké paint him. Each time you proposed it, he got angry. The cyclone had made him change his mind, because if it had caused damage on Hiva Oa, it had brought devastation to Tahuata, destroying homes and farms and leaving dozens dead, among them several relatives of the erstwhile witch doctor. Haapuani confessed: he needed money. Judging by his tone and expression, it must have cost him a great effort to take this step.

Would your miserable eyes allow you to paint him?

Without a second thought, Koké accepted, delighted. They immediately made a formal agreement, after which Paul advanced Haapuani some money. He was so excited by the prospect of painting this new work that he spent much of the night awake, tossing and turning in bed as he listened to the wild cats yowl and watched the moon appear and disappear in a cloudy sky. Haapuani knew much more than he was willing to admit. Koké had tested him when he came with Tohotama, as she posed. He would never reveal anything about his past as a Maori priest, and he always denied that cannibalism was still practiced on some of the far-flung islands of the archipelago. But Koké, obsessed, wasn't convinced by these denials. And sometimes he was able to overcome Haapuani's resistance and make him talk about the art of tattooing. Bishop Martin and Pastor Vernier thought they had abolished it, but it was still alive in lost villages and forests all over the Marquesas, preserving—on the brown skin of Maori men and women—the ancient wisdom, faith, and traditions condemned by the missionaries. On his only trip to the interior of Hiva Oa, to the village of Hanaupe, in the valley of Hekeani, to bargain for the purchase of Vaeoho, Koké confirmed it: the villagers displayed their tattoos freely. And through an interpreter he talked with the village tattooist, a smiling old man who showed him how he imprinted those symmetrical, labyrinthine drawings on human skin, with an artist's finesse and assurance. Haapuani, who grew skittish whenever Koké questioned him about his Marquesan beliefs, was sometimes inspired to reveal the meanings of different tattoos to him. One day, drawing on a sheet of paper with the skill of an expert, he even explained the tangle of references contained in certain designs. The ones he sketched were the most ancient, he said: those serving to protect warriors in battle, to impart strength to resist the wiles of evil spirits, and to guarantee purity of spirit.

The witch doctor appeared the next morning at the House of Pleasure, soon after the sun had risen. Koké was waiting for him in his studio. The sky was clear over Atuona, though out to sea, toward the deserted Sheep's Island, a mass of dark clouds and red flashes of lightning heralded a storm. When he made Haapuani stand where the early-morning light would strike him best, Koké's heart sank. The pity of it! You could see little more than a shape, blurred at the edges, and patches of different shades and depths. That was how your eyes saw colors now: as smudges, fogs. Wasn't it pointless to attempt it, Koké?

"No, damn it, no," he muttered, coming up very close to the witch doctor, as if he were about to kiss him or bite him. "Even if I go completely blind or die of rage, I'll paint you, Haapuani."

"It's best to stay calm, Koké," the Maori advised him. "Since you're always so eager to know what the Marquesans think, that is our principal belief: never be angry, except when your enemy is before you."

Tohotama, who was there somewhere—you hadn't heard her arrive—giggled, as if this were all a game. Mette also had that irritating habit of trivializing important matters by making a joke and laughing. Although they never became friends, the Danish painter Philipsen was very good to you. After he visited the house at 51 Norregada to see your paintings, he prevailed on his acquaintances to convince Denmark's Society of the Friends of Art to sponsor an exhibition of your paintings. It opened on May 1, 1884, with a small but distinguished crowd in attendance. Gentlemen and ladies, attentive and polite, seemed to interest themselves in the paintings, and asked you questions about them in courtly French. Still, no one bought anything; no reviews, favorable or hostile, appeared in the Copenhagen press; and five days later the exhibition closed. You would later boast that the authorities, conservative and traditionalist, had ordered it to be shut down, scandalized by your aesthetic daring. But that wasn't the case. In truth, it was because no one went to see it and it was a commercial failure that your only exhibition while you were living in Copenhagen ended so soon.

The worst thing wasn't your frustration; it was how angry Mette's family was at you for the fiasco. So! The outlandish bohemian gives up his position in society and his respectable job as a stockbroker for art—and this is what he paints! Countess Moltke let it be known that if this grotesquely attired, redskin-imitating, effeminate person stayed in Copenhagen, she would stop paying the tuition of the Gauguins' oldest son, Emil, a charitable duty she had assumed six months before. And the Viking, pale and sniveling, dared to tell you that if you didn't leave, the young diplomats to whom she taught French had threatened to find another teacher. And then she and the children would starve. They kicked you out of Copenhagen like a dog, Koké! You had no alternative but to return to Paris, in a third-class train carriage, taking six-year-old Clovis with you, thus relieving Mette of one mouth to feed as she scraped to support the rest of the family. Your parting, at the beginning of June 1885, was a tour de force of hypocrisy. The two of you pretended to be undergoing a temporary separation demanded by the circumstances, telling each other that you would be reunited as soon as matters improved. Yet deep down you knew very well, and perhaps Mette did too, that you would be apart for a long time, perhaps forever. Were you right, Koké? Well, up to a certain point. Although you'd seen each other only once for a few days in the last eighteen years—and then she wouldn't let you touch her—legally, the Viking was still your wife. How many months had it been since Mette wrote you, Koké?

He arrived in Paris without a cent in his pocket and with a child in tow, and went to stay with good old Schuff, in his apartment on the rue Boulard, from whose windows he could see the tombstones of the Montparnasse cemetery. You were thirty-seven years old, Koké. Had you begun to be a real painter? You were still struggling. Since there was no room in the flat to work, you drew and painted in the streets—next to a chestnut tree in the Luxembourg Gardens, on park benches, on the banks of the Seine—in notebooks and on canvases that your friend Schuff gave you. Without letting his wife, Louise, know, Schuff also sometimes slipped a few francs into your pocket so that at midday you could sit for a while on the terrace of a café. Was it in that summer of 1885 that you sometimes couldn't sleep at night, thinking that everything you were doing might be a huge mistake, an act of madness you would come to regret? No, the period of extreme desperation came later. In July, after selling another piece from your collection of impressionist paintings (there were very few left, and they were all in Mette's possession), you left for Dieppe. Spending the summer there was a colony of painters with whom you were acquainted, among them Degas. They gathered in an extraordinarily gaudy, peculiar house, the Chalet du Bas-Fort-Blanc, owned by the painter Jacques-Émile Blanche. You went to visit them, thinking they would receive you with open arms; but you were told they weren't in, and as the butler sent you away, you spotted Degas and Blanche peeping at you through the curtains. After that, both avoided you as if you were an undesirable. You were, Koké. Lonely, you wandered along the harbor and the cliffs with your easel, paints, and paper, painting bathers, sandy beaches, tall reefs. The paintings were bad. You felt like a mangy dog. It was only natural that Degas, Blanche, and the other Dieppe painters should steer clear of you: you were dressed like a tramp because that was what you were now.

The worst was yet to come, Koké. It arrived with the winter, when you returned to Paris, penniless again. Your sister, María Fernanda, turned over Clovis, whom she had grudgingly cared for while you were in Dieppe. The Schuffeneckers could no longer lodge you. You rented a miserable room on the rue Cail, near the Gare de l'Est, unfurnished. In a junk shop, you found a little bed for Clovis. You slept on the floor, shivering under a single blanket. You had only summer clothing, and Mette never sent you the winter things you had left in Copenhagen. Those last months of 1885 and first months of 1886 were bitterly cold, with frequent snowfalls. Clovis caught chicken pox, and you couldn't even buy him medicine; likely he survived only because he had your strong constitution and rebellious spirit, which made you thrive in adversity. You fed him handfuls of rice, and many days you yourself ate little more than scraps. Then—desperation, Koké—you had to stop painting so that you and the boy wouldn't die of hunger. Just when you thought the solution might be to throw yourself from a bridge into the icy waters of the Seine with the child in your arms, you found work: as a bill poster in the stations of Paris. Congratulations, Koké! It was hard outdoor work and left you smeared all over with paste, but after a few weeks you had saved enough to put Clovis into a very modest boarding school in Antony, just outside of Paris.

Was the winter of 1885–86 the worst moment of your life, the point at which you nearly gave up? No. That was now, although you had a roof over your head and—thanks to Daniel de Monfreid and the dealer Ambroise Vollard—a bit of income which, although minimal, was enough so you were able to eat and drink. Nothing, not even that horrible winter eighteen years ago, could compare to the impotence you felt every day, trying, little better than gropingly, to commit to the canvas the colors and shapes suggested to you by Haapuani's presence—his presence, because almost all you could see of him was a faceless silhouette. That didn't matter so much to you. You still had a clear picture in your head of Haapuani's face, attractive despite his years, and you also had an idea what the painting should be. A handsome witch doctor who is also a *mahu*; a coquettish and distinguished figure with little flowers in his long, silky feminine hair, wrapped in a big red cape flaming at his shoulders, with a leaf in his right hand that stands for his secret knowledge of the world of plants—love philters, healing potions, poisons, magical concoctions—and behind him, as always in your paintings (why, Koké?), two women buried in a leafy glade—real or maybe fantastic, bundled in monkish, medieval hooded robes—watching him, captivated or frightened by his aura of mystery and ambiguity, and his insolent freedom. At the sorcerer's feet would be a dog, of strange bone structure, perhaps hailing from the Maori underworld, and a black rooster. A whitish-blue river and the evening sky would be visible through the trees of the forest in the background. You could see it very well in your mind, but to transfer it to the canvas, you needed to constantly ask the advice of Haapuani himself, or Tohotama, or Tioka, who sometimes came to watch you work, questioning them about the colors, and about the mixes you made essentially by instinct, without being able to check the results. They were more than willing, but they didn't have the words or the understanding to answer properly. It tormented you to think that their inexact information might ruin your work. The painting went extremely slowly. Were you moving forward or backward? There was no way to know. When your helplessness made you groan, or fall to weeping and cursing, Haapuani and Tohotama remained by your side, motionless, respectful, waiting for you to grow calm and take up your brush again.

Then Paul remembered that when he was hanging posters in the railway stations of Paris in that cruel winter eighteen years ago, fate delivered into his hands a little book that he found, forgotten or tossed aside by its owner, on the chair of a café next to the Gare de l'Est, where he went to have an absinthe at the end of the day. Its author was a Turk, the artist, philosopher, and theologian Mani Velibi-Zumbul-Zadi, who united all three disciplines in his essay. Color, according to him, was something deeper and more subjective than could be found in the natural world. It was a manifestation of human sentiments, beliefs, fantasies. All the spirituality of an age, and all its people's angels and demons, were expressed in the values given to different colors, and the way color was used. That was why real artists shouldn't feel themselves bound to literal representation when faced with the natural world: green forest, blue sky, gray sea, white clouds. It was their obligation to use colors in accordance with their innermost compulsions, or simply their private whim: black sun, fiery moon, blue horse, emerald waves, green clouds. Mani Velibi-Zumbul-Zadi also said—how appropriate these teachings were now, Koké—that artists, in order to preserve their authenticity, should give up using models and paint exclusively from memory. If they did, their art would better represent their secret truths. Your eyes had obliged you to do precisely that, Koké. Would *The Sorcerer of Hiva Oa* be your last painting? The question made you retch with sadness and rage.

"After I finish this portrait I'll never pick up a brush again, Haapuani."

"Do you mean that by letting myself be painted I'm sending you to your grave, Koké?"

"In a sense, yes. You'll send me to my grave, and meanwhile I will immortalize you. You'll have the best of it, Haapuani."

"Can I ask you something, Koké?" Tohotama had been so quiet and still all morning that Paul hadn't noticed she was there. "Why have you put that red cape on my husband's shoulders? Haapuani never dresses like that. And I don't know anyone on Hiva Oa or Tahuata who does."

"Well, that's what I see on your husband's shoulders, Tohotama." Koké's spirits rose upon hearing the girl's deep, rich voice, so in keeping with her sturdy body and red hair, her generous breasts, her broad hips, and her heavy, smooth thighs, all those beautiful things that now he could only remember. "I see all the blood that the Maori have spilled throughout their history. Fighting among themselves, destroying one another for food and land, defending themselves against flesh-and-blood invaders or wraiths from the next world. The whole history of your people is in this red cape, Tohotama."

"I only see a red cape that no person from here has ever worn," she insisted. "And those hooded people? Are they two women, Koké? Or are they men? They can't be Marquesans. I've never seen a woman or man on these islands put something like that on their heads."

He felt the urge to caress her, but he didn't try. You would reach out and touch empty air, because she could easily dodge you. Then you would feel ridiculous. But having desired her even for an instant made you happy, because one of the consequences of the advance of the unspeakable disease was the absence of desire. You weren't dead yet, Koké. A little more patience and resolve and you would finish this cursed painting.

Maybe what Bishop Dupanloup liked to repeat when he extolled the heroes of Christianity in his religion classes at your childhood school in Orléans, the seminary of the Chapelle Saint-Mesmin, was true after all: it was when the sinner had fallen lowest that he was compelled to rise highest, like Robert the Devil, the arch-villain who became a saint. It happened to you after that horrendous winter of 1885–86 in Paris. Just when you felt yourself sinking in the mire, you began to rise little by little toward the surface, toward clean air. The miracle had a name: Pont-Aven. Many painters and amateur artists spoke of Brittany, drawn by the wild beauty of its landscape, its isolation, and its romantic storms. For you, Brittany was attractive for two reasons, one abstract and one practical. In Pont-Aven you would find an archaic culture still thriving, people who instead of renouncing their religion, beliefs, and customs, clung to them with supreme disdain for the efforts of the State and Paris to integrate them into modernity. And then, too, you could live very cheaply there. Although nothing went quite as you expected, your departure for Pont-Aven—thirteen hours by train, on the Quimperlé line—in that sunny July of 1886 was the best decision you had made in your life so far.

It was in Pont-Aven that you truly began to be a painter, even if you had already been forgotten by the snobs and dilettantes of flighty Paris. He remembered well his arrival, aching from his long trip, in the triangular little main square of the picture-postcard town in the middle of a fertile valley flanked by wooded hills and crowned by a forest dedicated to Love, to which the salty afternoon air brought a hint of the sea. On the square were the lodgings for the well-to-do, American and English travelers who came there in search of local

color: the Hôtel des Voyageurs and the Lion d'Or. It wasn't these hotels you were looking for, but the modest inn belonging to Madame
Gloanec, who, fool or saint, welcomed needy artists and—magnificent woman—permitted those who didn't have the money for their
room and board to pay with paintings. The best decision you ever
made, Koké! A week after you had moved into the Pension Gloanec,
you were dressing like a Breton fisherman—clogs, cap, embroidered
vest, blue smock—and you had become the leader of the half dozen
young artists who were sheltered there, less because of your painting
than because of your forceful manner, your exuberant talk, your out-
size faith in yourself, and, doubtless, your age. At last you were out
of the abyss, Paul. Now, to paint masterpieces.

Two or three days later, Tohotama interrupted Koké's work again
with some exclamations in Marquesan Maori that he didn't understand, except for the word *mahu*, lost in the flow of sentences. In the
world of shadows and contrasts of light and dark that he now inhabited, he realized that Haapuani had left the spot where he was posing
and, curious, come to look at the painting and see what was so exciting Tohotama. On the canvas, instead of appearing with a pareu
around his waist or naked, the witch doctor, under his red cape, was
wearing a dress as tight as a glove on his slender body, a very short
garment that left his shapely woman's legs bare. Haapuani stood looking at the canvas for a long time without saying anything. Then, he
went back to take up the pose Koké had requested.

"You haven't said anything to me about your portrait," Paul commented, after returning to his painstaking, impossible work. "What
do you think of it?"

"You see *mahus* everywhere," said the witch doctor, evading his
question. "Where they exist, and also where they don't exist. You
don't see the *mahu* as something natural, but as a demon. In that way
you are like the missionaries, Koké."

Was it true? Well, something odd had happened to you a few
months ago, while you were painting *The Sister of Charity*, a painting
for which Tohotama happened to have posed. In the end, you realized
that its subject wasn't the nun, but the man-woman standing before
her, something you were scarcely conscious of while you were painting it. Why this obsession with *mahus*?

"Why don't you tell me what you think of your portrait?" Koké persisted.

"The only thing I'm sure of is that the person in the painting isn't me," responded the Maori.

"He's the Haapuani inside of you," Koké replied. "The one who's had to hide in order to keep from being discovered by the priests and gendarmes. Whether or not you believe me, I assure you that the man on the canvas is you. And not just you. It's the true Marquesan, the one who is disappearing, of whom soon no trace will be left. In the future, people will consult my paintings to see what the Maori were like."

Tohotama laughed, a frank, happy, carefree laugh that brightened the morning, and Haapuani laughed too, but grudgingly. That evening, when the couple was gone and Tioka had come over to talk— he stopped by the House of Pleasure a few times a day to see if Koké needed anything—the white-bearded Maori spent a long time looking at the canvas. To see it better, he brought over one of the pitch torches from the door. Paul asked him no questions. After a while, his neighbor, usually sparing of words, gave his opinion.

"In many paintings, you've painted the island women with muscles and men's bodies," he said, intrigued. "But in this one you've done the opposite: you've painted Haapuani like a woman."

If what Tioka was saying was true, *The Sorcerer of Hiva Oa* looked more or less as you intended it to, although you had painted it almost entirely blind, except in brief intervals when the brightness of the day, your stubborn efforts, or a merciful god had cleared your sight, and for a few minutes you could correct details and brighten or soften the colors. It wasn't just your sight that was failing you. It was your steadiness, too. Sometimes the tremor in your hand was so strong that you had to lie down on the bed for a while, until your body relaxed and the uncontrollable spasms stopped. Only your masterpieces had been painted in states of incandescence like this, Koké. Would *The Sorcerer of Hiva Oa* be a masterpiece? If you could get a full look at the canvas, even just for a few seconds, you would know. But you would always be left with the doubt, Koké.

At the next session, Tohotama talked to him about the painting. Why were you always so interested in *mahus*, in men-women, Koké?

He gave her a silly explanation—"they're picturesque, striking, exotic, Tohotama"—but the question nagged at him for the rest of the day, and he kept turning it over in his head that night, in bed, after he had eaten a bit of fruit, changed the bandages on his legs, and taken a few drops of laudanum dissolved in water for the pain. Why, Koké? Maybe because in the evasive, semi-invisible, persecuted *mahu*, detested as a sinful aberration by priests and pastors, there survived the last untamed vestige of those Maori savages who, thanks to Europe, would soon cease to exist. The primitive people of the Marquesas would be swallowed up and digested by Christian and Western culture—the culture you had defended with so much brio and verbiage, so much exaggeration and slander, back in Tahiti, in *Les Guêpes* and *La Sourire*, Koké. Swallowed up and digested like the Tahitians before them, and corrected in matters of religion, language, ethics, and, of course, sex. In the very near future, things would be as clear-cut for Marquesans as they were for any bourgeois, churchgoing European. There were two sexes and that was enough—who needed more? Man and woman, male and female, penis and vagina: easy to tell apart, and separated by an unbridgeable gap. Ambiguity in matters of love and desire, as in matters of faith, was a sign of barbarism and vice, as degrading in the eyes of civilization as anthropophagy. The man-woman, the woman-man, were abnormalities to be extirpated the way God razed Sodom and Gomorrah. Poor *mahus* still left on these islands! The hypocritical colonists and colonial administrators sought them out to hire them as house servants, because they were known to be good at cooking, washing clothes, caring for children, and keeping house. But in order not to fall afoul of the priests and ministers, they forbade them to dress and array themselves like women. When the *mahus* twined flowers in their hair, wore bracelets on their wrists and bangles on their ankles, and dressed as girls, daring—surely with considerable misgivings and fear of being discovered—to fleetingly display themselves in such attire, they didn't suspect that they were the last gasps of a culture, that primitive man's healthy, spontaneous, uninhibited acceptance of everything inside him—his desires, his fantasies—was soon to be no more. *The Sorcerer of Hiva Oa* was a tombstone, Koké.

Despite what the blind old Maori woman said when she touched your hooded penis, you were closer to the islanders than to people like Monsignor Martin or the gendarme Jean-Pierre Claverie. Or to those colonists, made callous by ignorance and greed, whom you served as a mercenary in Papeete. You understood savages; you respected them; you envied them. Whereas you despised your supposed compatriots.

At least this much you were sure of, Koké. You didn't paint like a modern, civilized European. No one could be fooled into thinking that. Although you had intuited it in a vague way before, it was in Brittany, first in Pont-Aven and then in Le Pouldu, that you understood it with complete certainty. Art had to break free from its narrow mold, from the tiny horizon to which it had been confined by the artists, critics, academics, and collectors of Paris; it had to open up to the world, mix with other cultures, expose itself to other winds, other landscapes, other values, other races, other beliefs, other ways of living and thinking. Only then would it recover the power that the soft, easy, frivolous, materialistic life of the Parisians had leached from it. You had done it, gone out into the world to seek, to learn, to drink deep of everything that was unknown or rejected in Europe. It had cost you, but you didn't regret it, did you, Koké?

You didn't. You were proud of having made it this far, even in the state you were in. Painting had a price, and you had paid it. When you returned to Paris to face the winter after those summer and autumn months spent in Pont-Aven, you were a different person. You had changed inside and out; you were euphoric, sure of yourself, wild with joy at having at last discovered your path. And avid for mischief and scandal. One of the first things you did in Paris was to attack the beautiful Louise, good old Schuff's wife, with whom you had previously only allowed yourself to flirt. Now, in this new rebellious, bold, iconoclastic, anarchic mood, you seized the opportunity the first time you were alone—good old Schuff was giving his drawing classes at the academy—to launch yourself at Louise. Could it be said that you took advantage of her, Paul? That would be an exaggeration. At most, you seduced and corrupted her. Because Louise resisted only at first, more for appearances' sake than out of conviction. And she never seemed to regret her indiscretion afterward.

"You're a savage, Paul. How dare you lay your hands on me?"

"You said it yourself, my lovely. I'm a savage. I don't follow the same rules as the bourgeoisie. My instincts guide my actions now. And this new philosophy will make me a great artist."

A prophetic declaration of principles, Koké. Did good old Schuff ever find out how you betrayed him? If he did, he must have been able to forgive you. A superior being, that Alsatian. Much better than you, certainly, in terms of civilized morality. Which was doubtless why he always painted so badly.

The next day, after some final retouchings, Koké paid Haapuani the agreed sum. The painting was finished. Or was it? You hoped so. In any case, you no longer had the strength or the will to keep working on it.

21

THE LAST BATTLE

BORDEAUX, NOVEMBER 1844

ॐ

When Flora Tristán arrived in Bordeaux on the ill-fated day of September 24, 1844, and accepted an invitation to occupy a box seat at the Grand Théâtre for a concert by the pianist Franz Liszt, she never suspected that that mundane event, where the ladies of Bordeaux came to parade their jewels and finery, would be her last public activity. The weeks remaining to her she would spend in bed, at the house of Elisa and Charles Lemonnier, two Saint-Simonians to whom she had refused to be introduced a year before because she considered them too bourgeois. Paradoxes, Florita, paradoxes, up until the very last day of your life.

She didn't feel ill when she arrived in Bordeaux, just tired, irritated, and disappointed, because ever since leaving Carcassonne, the monarchy's prefects and commissaries had made her life difficult, in Toulouse as well as in Agen, bursting into her meetings with workers, closing them down, and even dispersing the workers with cudgels. Her pessimism was occasioned not by her health but rather by the authorities, who were determined at all costs to prevent her from finishing her tour.

Five years ago, upon your return from London, when, consumed by the idea of forging a great alliance of women and workers for the transformation of humanity, you began the frenetic task of trying to make connections with the workers, how could you have imagined that in the end you would be harassed by a power that considered you subversive—you, a sworn pacifist? Back in Paris, you were not only full of hopes and dreams; you were also bursting with good health. You assiduously read the two main workers' journals, *L'Atelier* and *La Ruche Populaire* (the only publications that praised your *Walks in London*), and you visited and read the writings of all the messiahs, philosophers, doctrinaires, and theorists of social change. This was ultimately more confusing and chaotic than instructive because, among socialist and anarchist reformers, there were many madmen and eccentrics who preached pure nonsense. There was, for example—remembering him made you laugh—the charismatic sculptor Ganneau, who looked like a gravedigger. He was the founder of Evadamism, a doctrine that was based on the idea of equality between the sexes and advocated women's liberation. For a few weeks, you naively took him seriously, but the respect you had for that gloomy personage with fanatical eyes and elongated hands crumbled the day he explained to you that the name of his movement, Evadamism, was derived from the first couple—Eve and Adam—and that he was called Mapah by his disciples in homage to the family, since the word combined the first syllables of Mama and Papa. He was either an idiot or a lunatic.

The police harassment spoiled what might have been a productive visit to Toulouse for Flora, between September 8 and 19. The day after she arrived, she was meeting with twenty workers in the Hôtel des Portes, rue de la Pomme, when Commissioner Boisseneau charged into the room. Big-bellied, with a bushy mustache and a sour look on his face, he didn't even greet her or take off his bowler hat before declaring, "You have no permission to come to Toulouse to preach revolution."

"I haven't come to make a revolution but to prevent one, Mr. Commissary. Read my book first, before you judge me," Flora replied. "Since when does a single woman frighten commissaries and prefects in the most powerful kingdom of Europe?"

The official departed with only a curt "You've been warned."

Her efforts to talk to the prefect in Toulouse were in vain. The ban disheartened her contacts in the city. She managed to hold only one secret meeting, at an inn in the neighborhood of Saint-Michel, with eight tanners. Full of apprehension at the idea the police might discover them, they listened with terrified eyes, glancing constantly toward the door. Her visit to *L'Émancipation*, a newspaper that claimed to be democratic and republican, was another failure: the journalists looked at her as if she were peddling antidotes for nightmares and ill omens, and paid no attention to her detailed presentation of the objectives of the Workers' Union. One asked her if she was a Gypsy. Her indignation reached its height when the most audacious of them, an editor called Riberol, thin as a broomstick and with a lecherous light in his eye, began to wink at her and whisper double entendres.

"Are you trying to seduce me, you poor fool?" asked Madame-la-Colère in a very loud voice, cutting him short. "Have you never looked in a mirror, wretch?"

She got up and left, slamming the door. Your rage subsided as you remembered—the best redress, Florita—how your intemperate reaction left Riberol speechless and openmouthed, his leathery face flushed in shame, amid the laughter of his colleagues.

In Agen, where she spent four days, things went no better than in Toulouse, again because of the police. In the city there were many workers' mutual aid societies, which had been advised of her arrival by the obliging Agricol Perdiguier, the Good Man of Avignon: a magnanimous soul, he disagreed with Flora's ideas yet had helped her more than anyone else. Perdiguier's friends had arranged meetings for her with various guilds, but only the first took place. The meeting brought together some fifteen carpenters and typographers, two of whom were particularly bright and expressed their intentions of forming a committee. They accompanied her to visit the local celebrity, the poet-hairdresser Jazmin, of whom Flora expected great things. But of course the praises of the bourgeoisie had turned the former people's poet into another stuck-up fool. It was a fate no poet escaped, it seemed. He no longer wanted to be reminded of his proletarian origins, and he struck Olympian poses. Round, soft, coquettish, and affected, he bored Flora by telling her how warmly he had been received by eminences like Nodier, Chateaubriand, and Sainte-

Beuve in Paris, and how he had been overcome by emotion as he recited his "Gascogne poems" before Louis Philippe himself. His Majesty, moved, had shed a tear. When Flora explained the reason for her visit and asked for his help with the Workers' Union, the poet-hairdresser grimaced in horror: never!

"I will never support your revolutionary ideas, madame. Too much blood has been shed already in France. For whom do you take me?"

"For a worker faithful to his ideals and loyal to his brethren, Monsieur Jazmin, but I see I was wrong. You are nothing but a prancing little monkey, one more puppet among the buffoons of the bourgeoisie."

"Out, out of my house." The rotund bard showed her the door. "Wicked woman!"

That same afternoon, the commissioner came to Flora's hotel to inform her that she wasn't allowed to hold any meetings in the city. She decided to defy the prohibition, and appeared at an inn on the rue du Temple, where forty workers of different occupations, mostly shoemakers and cutters, were waiting for her. She had scarcely been speaking for ten minutes when the inn was surrounded by twenty sergeants and fifty soldiers. The commissioner, a big, strong man armed with a ridiculous speaking-horn, deafeningly ordered those in attendance to come out one by one and register their names and addresses. Flora asked them to stay where they were. "Brothers, we must make the police come and remove us by force; let there be a scandal so the public learns of this outrage." But almost all of them, afraid of losing their jobs, obeyed the commissioner's order. They left in single file, with their caps in their hands, their heads bowed. Only seven remained, surrounding her. Then the sergeants came in and beat them, shouting abuse and shoving them out. But they didn't touch Flora or respond to her vehement protests. "Hit me, too, you cowards!"

"The next time you disobey the prohibition, you'll be thrown in jail with the thieving women and prostitutes of Agen," the commissioner threatened her in his booming voice; he waved his horn about like the ringmaster in a circus. "Now you know where you stand, madame."

The incident struck fear into Agen's mutual aid societies and guilds, which all canceled their scheduled meetings. No one accepted her suggestion that they organize secret gatherings of just a few people. The ban meant that Flora's last days in Agen were lonely, boring, and frustrating. She was angrier at the workers for their cowardice than at the commissioner and his masters. At the first threat from above, they turned tail and ran!

On the day before she left for Bordeaux, something odd happened. In the writing desk in her room at the Hôtel de France, she found a lovely little gold watch, left behind by some guest. As she was about to take it to the manager, a temptation seized her: "What if I keep it?" The impulse sprang not from covetousness, which at this stage in her life she lacked completely, but from the desire for knowledge: how did thieves feel after committing their misdeeds? Did they experience fear, happiness, remorse? What she felt, in the next few hours, was anxiety, distaste, surges of terror, and a sense of ridiculousness. She decided to turn it in when she left, but she couldn't even wait that long. After seven hours, her distress was so great that she went down to deliver the watch into the hands of the hotel management, lying and saying that she had just found it. You wouldn't have made a good thief, Andalusa.

Upon reflection, Florita, your tour hadn't been such a failure. This rallying of commissioners and prefects in the last few weeks to prevent you from meeting with the workers—didn't it indicate that your ideas were taking root? Maybe you were winning more converts than you suspected. The ripples you had left in your wake would continue to widen until sooner or later they spread into a great movement: French, European, universal. After only a year and a half on this crusade you were already an enemy of power, a threat to the realm. Remarkable success, really, Florita! There was no reason for you to be discouraged; on the contrary. You had made amazing progress since that meeting in Paris on February 4, 1843—organized by Gosset, the magnificent Father of Blacksmiths—where you spoke for the first time to a group of Parisian workers about the Workers' Union. A year and a half wasn't much. But from the weariness in your bones and muscles, it seemed an age.

You had forgotten many of the things that happened during the past eighteen months, so rich in events, enthusiasms, and also failures, but you would never forget the first time you appeared in public to present your ideas before that workers' mutual aid society sponsored by Gosset. Achille François, patron saint of the Paris tanners, presided. You were so nervous that you wet your drawers, though luckily no one noticed. They listened to you, they asked you questions, an argument broke out, and at the end a committee of seven was formed as the organizational nucleus of the movement. How easy everything seemed to you then, Florita! It was an illusion. At the next meetings, your work with the committee was poisoned by the criticisms they made of your still-unpublished text, *The Workers' Union*. Their first objection was to your reference to the "shameful material and moral state" of the workers of France. They thought it was defeatist and demoralizing, even though it was true. When Gosset, Father of Blacksmiths, heard you call your critics "ignorant brutes who don't want to be saved," he taught you a lesson you would never forget.

"Don't let your impatience get the better of you, Flora Tristán. You're new to this fight. Learn from Achille François. He works from six in the morning until eight at night to feed his family, and then from eight at night until two in the morning for his fellow workers. Is it right to call him an ignorant brute simply because he permits himself to disagree with you?"

The Father of Blacksmiths was certainly neither brutish nor ignorant. Rather, he was a font of wisdom who stood behind you like no one else in those first weeks of your ministry in Paris. You came to consider him a teacher, a spiritual guide. But Madame Gosset didn't understand your sublime camaraderie. One night, enraged and in her cups, she appeared at Achille François's house, where a meeting was under way, and flew at you like a Greek fury, bombarding you with insults. Spraying saliva and sweeping her witchlike hair from her face, she threatened to report you to the police—if you persisted in your treacherous schemes to steal her husband! Old lady Gosset thought you were seducing the grizzled workers' leader. Could anything be more comical, Florita? But this episode of proletarian vaudeville showed you that nothing was easy, particularly not the struggle for justice and humanity. And it made you realize, too, that despite being poor and exploited, in certain ways the workers were very like the bourgeoisie.

That concert by Liszt in Bordeaux at the end of September 1844, which you attended more out of curiosity than fondness for music (what would he be like, the pianist whose path you had crossed so many times on the roads of France?) ended like another vaudeville act: you dropped to the floor of your box at the Grand Théâtre in a sudden swoon, drawing the gazes of everyone in the theater, including the furious glare of the interrupted pianist. And your collapse became the stirring finale of a story by a harebrained reporter, who used it to portray you as a worldly sylph. "Admirably lovely, slender and elegant in physique, proud and spirited in bearing, eyes full of the fire of the Orient, long black hair draping about her like a shawl, beautiful olive skin, fine white teeth, Madame Flora Tristán, the writer and social reformer, daughter of turmoil and strife, last night suffered a fainting spell, perhaps as a result of the trance into which she was sent by the superb arpeggios of Maestro Liszt." You blushed to the roots of your hair upon reading that foolish nonsense when you awakened in your soft bed. Where were you, Florita? The elegant room, with its scent of fresh flowers and its fine linen curtains that let in the light, was nothing like your modest little hotel room. You were at the house of Charles and Elisa Lemonnier, who had insisted on bringing you home with them the night before, when you collapsed at the Grand Théâtre. Here you would be better cared for than at the hotel or in the hospital. And so you were. Charles was a lawyer and a professor of philosophy, and Elisa was an advocate for trade schools for children and youths. Fervent Saint-Simonians, friends of Father Prosper Enfantin, idealistic, cultured, generous, they devoted their lives to working for universal brotherhood and the "new Christianity" preached by Saint-Simon. They held no grudge against you for the way you had snubbed them the year before by refusing to meet them. They had read your books, and they admired you.

The couple's treatment of Flora over the next weeks could not have been more solicitous. They gave her the best room in the house, called a distinguished doctor from Bordeaux, Dr. Mabit, Jr., and hired a nurse, Mademoiselle Alphine, to watch over her day and night. They bore the cost of the doctor's visits and medicaments, and wouldn't even let Flora speak of paying them back.

Dr. Mabit said that it might be cholera. The next day, after another examination, he changed his mind, indicating that it was more likely typhoid fever. Despite the patient's state of total prostration, he declared himself optimistic. He prescribed a healthy diet, absolute rest, body rubs and massages, and a restorative tonic to be taken day and night, every half hour. For the first two days, Flora reacted favorably to the treatment. On the third day, however, she suffered a congestion of the brain, with a very high fever. For hours she remained in a state of semiconsciousness, delirious. The Lemonniers called a conference of doctors, headed by a local eminence, Dr. Gintrac. The physicians, after examining her and talking privately, confessed to a certain perplexity. Nevertheless, though her condition was certainly serious, they thought she could be saved. No one should lose hope, or permit the patient to realize the state she was in. They prescribed bleedings and cupping, as well as new drafts, now to be taken every fifteen minutes. To help the exhausted Mademoiselle Alphine, who had been caring for Flora with religious devotion, the Lemonniers hired another nurse. When Flora's hosts, in one of their guest's moments of lucidity, asked whether Flora didn't want a family member to come and be by her side—perhaps her daughter, Aline?—she didn't hesitate. "Eléonore Blanc, from Lyon. She is my daughter, too." The arrival of Eléonore in Bordeaux—that beloved face, so pale, so tremulous, inclining full of love over the bed—restored Flora's confidence, her will to fight, her love of life.

At the beginning of her campaign for the Worker's Union a year and a half ago, *La Ruche Populaire* treated her very well, unlike the other workers' paper, *L'Atelier*, which first ignored her and then ridiculed her, calling her a "would-be O'Connell in skirts." *La Ruche*, in contrast, organized two debates, at the end of which fourteen of the fifteen audience members voted in favor of an appeal to the workingmen and workingwomen of France, written by Flora and printed in the paper, inviting them to join the future Workers' Union. Although she soon overcame her initial fear of speaking in public—she was relaxed and confident, and an excellent debater—she was continually beset by frustration because women rarely participated in the meetings, no matter how often she urged them to attend. When she managed to get some of them to come, they were so cowed and intimidated that instead of being angry, she felt sorry for them. They hardly ever dared open their mouths, and when one did, she glanced first at the men present, as if asking their consent.

The publication of *The Worker's Union* in 1843 was quite a feat. Even now, in the brief moments in which you emerged from the state of suffering and confusion into which your illness had plunged you, you felt proud of your little book. That it had already gone through three printings and reached the hands of hundreds of workers was a triumph of spirit over adversity, wasn't it, Andalusa? All the publishers you knew in Paris refused to print it, making trifling excuses. The reality was that they were afraid of bringing themselves trouble with the authorities.

Then one morning, seeing from your little balcony on the rue du Bac the massive towers of the church of Saint-Sulpice—one of them unfinished—you remembered the history (or legend, Florita?) of the priest Jean-Baptiste Languet de Geray, who one day proposed to build one of the most beautiful churches in Paris, relying solely on charitable donations. And straightaway, he began to beg from door to door. Why shouldn't you do the same in order to publish a book that might become the new gospel for women and workers all over the world? Hardly had you conceived the idea when already you were composing an "Appeal to All People of Intelligence and Resolve." You headed it with your signature, followed by those of your daughter Aline, your friend the painter Jules Laure, your maid Marie-Madeleine, and the water-carrier Noël Taphanel, and without wasting a minute, you set it circulating among all your friends and acquaintances, to persuade them to assist in financing the book. How strong and healthy you still were then, Flora! You could rush all over Paris for twelve, fifteen hours, delivering and retrieving your petition; you brought it to more than two hundred people. In the end, it rallied the support of figures as renowned as Béranger, Victor Considérant, George Sand, Eugène Sue, Pauline Roland, Fréderick Lemaître, Paul de Kock, Louis Blanc, and Louise Collet. But many other important personages shut their doors in your face, like

Delacroix, David d'Angers, Mademoiselle Mars, and of course Étienne Cabet, the Icarian communist, who wanted a monopoly on the struggle for social justice in the universe.

That year, the social range of people who came to visit her at her little flat on the rue du Bac changed radically. Flora was home to visitors on Thursday afternoons. Previously, her guests had been professionals with inquiring minds, journalists, and artists; beginning in 1843, they were mostly the heads of mutual aid associations and workers' societies, and some Fourierists and Saint-Simonians who tended to be very critical of what they considered Flora's excessive radicalism. It wasn't only Frenchmen who made their appearance at the cramped little flat on the rue du Bac, drinking the cups of steaming chocolate that Flora offered her guests, lying and saying that it was from Cuzco. Sometimes there might also be an English Chartist or Owenist visiting Paris, and one afternoon there was a German refugee living in Paris, the socialist Arnold Ruge. He was a serious and intelligent man who listened to her attentively, taking notes. Impressed by Flora's belief in the need to establish a great international movement that would unite all the workers and women of the world in order to end injustice and exploitation, he asked her many questions. He spoke impeccable French, and he requested Flora's permission to return the next week and bring with him a German friend, like himself a refugee, a young philosopher called Karl Marx. They would get along splendidly, he assured her, because Marx's ideas about the working class were similar to hers; he, too, believed that its role was to redeem the whole of society.

Arnold Ruge did return the following week, with six German comrades, all of them living in exile; among them was the socialist Moses Hess, celebrated in Paris. None of them was Karl Marx, who had been detained by the preparation of the next issue of a journal that he published with Ruge: the *Franco-German Annals*. Nevertheless, you met Marx soon afterward, in colorful circumstances, at a small press on the left bank of the Seine, the only place willing to print *The Workers' Union*. You were overseeing the printing of the volume on its old pedal press, when an angry young man with several days' growth of beard, sweaty and red-faced with annoyance, began to complain in atrocious, guttural French, his tirade punctuated by gobs of spit.

Why was the press violating its agreement with him and delaying the printing of his journal to attend to "the literary preenings of this lady who has just come in"?

Naturally, Madame-la-Colère rose from her chair and strode up to him.

"Literary preenings, did you say?" she exclaimed, her voice as loud as the angry young man's. "I'll have you know, sir, that my book is called *The Workers' Union*, and that it may change the course of human history. What right have you to screech like a capon?"

The blustering fellow muttered in German, and then confessed that he didn't understand the expression. What was a "capon"?

"Go look it up in the dictionary and improve your French," Madame-la-Colère advised him, laughing. "And while you're at it, shave off that hedgehog beard, which makes you look like a tramp."

Flushed with linguistic impotence, the man said that he didn't understand "hedgehog" either, and that under the circumstances there was no sense in continuing the conversation, madame. He took his leave, with a surly bow. Later, Flora learned from the owner of the press that the irritable foreigner was Karl Marx, Arnold Ruge's friend. She amused herself by imagining how startled he would be if Ruge brought him along to one of her Thursday gatherings on the rue du Bac, and Flora, holding out her hand before they could be introduced, said, "The gentleman and I are old friends." But Ruge never brought him.

The two weeks that Eléonore Blanc spent in Bordeaux, not moving from Flora's side day or night, made the doctors think that their patient had begun a slow but steady recovery. She seemed to be in good spirits, despite her extreme thinness and her physical complaints. She had very strong pains in her belly and uterus, and sometimes in her head and back. The physicians prescribed small quantities of opium, which relaxed her and kept her in a state of torpor for hours at a time. In her intervals of clarity, she spoke with assurance, and her memory seemed to be in fine shape. ("Have you followed my advice always to ask yourself why things are the way they are, Eléonore?" "Yes, madame, I'm constantly doing it, and I learn so much from it.") In one of these periods she dictated an affectionate letter to her daughter, Aline, who had written her a few heartfelt pages from Amsterdam upon being informed of her illness by the Lemonniers. Flora also requested detailed information from Eléonore about the Workers' Union committee in Lyon, which, she insisted, must lead all the other committees established thus far.

"What are the chances that she'll survive?" Charles Lemonnier asked Dr. Gintrac, in front of Eléonore.

"A few days ago I would have said very few," murmured the doctor, polishing his monocle. "Now I feel more optimistic. Fifty percent, let us say. What troubles me is the bullet in her breast. Given her weakness, a foreign body like that might be displaced, which would be fatal."

After two weeks, Eléonore returned to Lyon, against her will. Her family and work were calling, and she was also needed by her companions in the Workers' Union, of which she was, on Flora's orders—she said so matter-of-factly—the driving force. She kept her composure upon bidding the patient farewell, promising to return in a few weeks. But as soon as she left the room she was taken by a fit of sobbing that all Elisa Lemonnier's reasoning and kindnesses were unable to quiet. "I know I'll never see her again," she kept saying, her lips bloodless from being bitten so much.

And indeed, immediately after Eléonore returned to Lyon, Flora's condition worsened. She began to vomit up bile, which left a lingering stench in the room that only Mademoiselle Alphine, with her infinite patience—she cleaned up the messes and also took charge of freshening the patient morning and night—could bear. From time to time, Flora was seized by violent convulsions that thrust her from her bed, possessed by a strength disproportionate to her body, which every day shriveled a little more, until she was a thing of skin and bones, with sunken eyes and arms like twigs. The two nurses and the Lemonniers were barely able to hold her down during her spasms.

And yet most of the time, under the influence of the opium, she was half-conscious, sometimes with her eyes wide open and lit with horror, as if she were seeing visions. Sometimes she delivered incoherent monologues, in which she spoke of her childhood, Peru, London, Arequipa, her father, and the Workers' Union committees, or embarked on passionate debates with mysterious adversaries. "Don't weep for me," Elisa and Charles heard her say one day, as they were sitting at the foot of her bed, keeping her company. "Rather, follow my example."

After the appearance of *The Workers' Union*, in June of 1843, Flora held daily meetings with workers' societies in neighborhoods in the center of Paris or on the city's outskirts. She no longer had to beg for their attention; she had become known in workers' circles and was invited to speak by many guilds and mutual aid societies, as well as some socialist, Fourierist, and Saint-Simonian groups. A club of Icarian communists even paused in their efforts to collect money to buy land in Texas to listen to her theories. The meeting with the Icarians ended in a shouting match.

What most disturbed Flora at these intense assemblies, which could go on well into the night, was that often, instead of debating the central tenets of her proposal—the Workers' Palaces for the elderly, infirm, and injured; free education for all; the right to work; the People's Defender—the attendees wasted time on trivialities and banalities, not to say stupidities. Almost inevitably, some worker would reproach Flora because her little book criticized workers who "go drinking at taverns instead of devoting the money they spend on liquor to buying bread for their children." At a meeting in an attic on the cul-de-sac of Jean Auber, near the rue Saint-Martin, a carpenter called Roly spat out, "You've betrayed us; you've revealed the workers' vices to the bourgeoisie." Flora replied that the truth should be the main weapon of the working class, just as hypocrisy and lies were generally those of the bourgeoisie. In any case, no matter who was bothered by it, she would continue to call a drunk a drunk and a brute a brute. The twenty workers listening to her were not entirely convinced, but fearing one of the fits of rage that were already legendary in Paris, none of them challenged her, and they even rewarded her with strained applause.

Did you remember, Florita, in the murky, London-like fog in which you were drifting, your mad idea for a Workers' Union anthem to accompany your great crusade, as the Marseillaise had accompanied the great revolution of 1789? Yes, you remembered it vaguely, and also its grotesque, ridiculous outcome. The first person you asked to compose the Workers' Union anthem was Béranger. The celebrated man received you at his house in Passy, where he was lunching with three guests. Half impressed and half mocking, the four listened as you insisted that in order to begin your peaceful social revolution, you urgently needed an anthem that would uplift the workers and move them to solidarity and action. Béranger refused, explaining that it was impossible for him to write on commission, without being inspired. And the great Lamartine also refused, saying that you were preaching what he had already anticipated in his visionary "Marseillaise of Peace."

Then, Florita, you foolishly decided to announce a contest for the best "hymn celebrating human fellowship." The prize would be a medal offered by the always generous Eugène Sue. A grave mistake, Andalusa! At least one hundred proletarian poets and composers entered, determined to win the contest—and with it the medal and fame—by exercising their talent or, if they had none, by any means possible. You could never have imagined that vanity, which you naively believed was a bourgeois vice, could provoke so many intrigues, imbroglios, calumnies, and low blows among the contestants, who were intent on disqualifying one another and taking the prize. Seldom had you been driven into as many rages as you were by those poetasters and musicians, shouting until you were hoarse. On the day that the put-upon jury awarded the prize to M. A. Thys, it was discovered that one of the spurned contestants, a poet called Ferrand—a congenial fool who introduced himself, very earnestly, as "the Great Maestro of the Lyric Order of the Templars"—had stolen the medal and the books intended as the prize, upon discovering that someone else was the winner. Were you laughing, Florita? You couldn't be so ill, then, if you were still strong enough to smile, even if it was in your sleep, and stimulated by those small doses of opium.

You could hear voices faintly, but you weren't able to concentrate or think clearly enough to know what they were saying. As a result, when a presumptuous censer-swinger of Catholicism, a man calling himself Stouvenel, appeared at Charles and Elisa Lemonnier's house on November 11, 1844, accompanied by a priest and assuring the Lemonniers that you were a devout believer who had long ago requested last rites, you couldn't defend yourself—Madame-la-Colère now voiceless, powerless, unconscious—or banish the impostor and priest from your room. Caught off guard and deceived, Elisa and

Charles Lemonnier, tolerant of all beliefs, swallowed the falsehood and let them come in and do what they liked with your inert body. Later, when Eléonore Blanc, indignant, informed them that Madame Tristán would never have permitted an obscurantist bit of pantomime like that if she had been able to protest, the Lemonniers were filled with regret and outrage. But the false Stouvenel and the crowlike priest had already done as they pleased, and caused a rumor to run in the streets and squares of Bordeaux that Flora Tristán, champion of women and workers, had solicited the help of the Holy Church on her deathbed to enter eternal life at peace with God. Poor Florita!

As soon as she had the first samples of *The Workers' Union* in her hands, Flora sent copies to all the guilds and mutual aid societies whose addresses she could find, and distributed a leaflet about the book in three thousand workshops and factories all over France. Did you remember how many letters you received from readers of your manifesto? Forty-three. All offered words of encouragement and hope, but some asked fearfully whether being a woman wouldn't present a great obstacle. Had it, Florita? Not really. Somehow or other, you had been able to do a great deal to promote an alliance of workers and women in the past eight months, and you had established many committees. There was little more you could have done if you had been wearing trousers instead of a skirt. One of the letters you received came from an Icarian laborer in Geneva, who ordered twenty-five copies for his fellow workers. Another was from Pierre Moreau, a locksmith in Auxerre and an organizer of mutual aid societies, who was the first to urge you to leave Paris and begin a great circuit of France and all of Europe, propagating your ideas and setting in motion the Workers' Union.

You were convinced, and began your preparations immediately. It was a marvelous idea. As you explained to the excellent Moreau, to anyone else within earshot, and to yourself in those frenetic months of preparation, "There's been plenty of talk in parliaments, pulpits, and meetings *about* workers, but no one has ever tried to talk *to* them. I'll do it. I'll go in search of them in their workshops, at their homes, in the taverns if necessary. And when I'm there, where I can see their suffering, I'll awaken them to their fate, and make them escape despite themselves from the hideous poverty that degrades them and kills them. And I'll convince them to unite with us, the women, and fight."

You had done it, Florita. Despite the bullet next to your heart, your ill health, your exhaustion, and the ominous, anonymous malady eroding your strength, for eight months you had done it. If you hadn't had more success, it wasn't for lack of effort, conviction, heroism, or idealism. It was because things never succeed as well in this life as they do in dreams. A pity, Florita.

Because the pain, despite the opium, was making her toss and cry out, on November 12, 1844, the doctors ordered that poultices be applied to her abdomen and cupping glasses to her back. Nothing helped. Two days later, they announced that she was dying. After moaning and shrieking for half an hour in a state of feverish exaltation—the last battle, Madame-la-Colère—she fell into a coma. By ten o'clock that night, November 14, she was dead. She was forty-one years old, and she looked like an old woman. The Lemonniers cut two locks of her hair, one for Eléonore Blanc and the other for Aline.

A brief dispute arose between the Lemonniers and Eléonore about Flora's instructions for her burial, which all three had heard. In keeping with Madame Tristán's last wishes, Eléonore believed that her head should be presented to the president of the Phrenological Society of Paris, and her body to Dr. Lisfranc so that he could perform an autopsy on it at the Hôpital de la Pitié before his students. Then what was left of her remains should be tossed into a common grave, with no ceremony whatsoever.

But Charles and Elisa Lemonnier declared that Flora's desires should not be heeded, for the sake of the cause that she had championed with such courage and generosity. Women and workers, today and in the future, should be able to kneel at her tomb to pay their respects. In the end, Eléonore gave in to their arguments. Aline was not consulted.

The Lemonniers commissioned an artist from Bordeaux to make a death mask of Flora's face, and they bought a plot in the old Carthusian cemetery to receive her remains. A vigil was kept over her for two days, but there was no religious ceremony and no priest was allowed entrance to the wake.

The burial took place on November 16, just before noon. The funeral procession left the Lemonniers' house on the rue Saint-Pierre, and wound its way slowly on foot along the streets of Bordeaux to the cemetery, under a gray and rainy sky. Among the mourners were writers, journalists, lawyers, a number of townswomen, and nearly one hundred workers. The latter took turns carrying the casket, which weighed almost nothing. The coffin cords were held by a carpenter, a stonecutter, a blacksmith, and a locksmith.

During the funeral at the cemetery, the Lemonniers noticed the presence, on the fringes of the crowd, of Stouvenel, as he called himself, the person who had brought the priest into their house. He was a thin man, dressed all in black. Despite his visible efforts, he was unable to contain his tears. He seemed distraught, racked with grief. As those in attendance began to disperse, the Lemonniers went to confront him. They were struck by how haggard and drawn he seemed.

"You lied to us, Monsieur Stouvenel," Charles said, sternly.

"That's not my name," he replied tremulously, breaking into a sob. "I lied to you to do her a good deed. The person I loved most in this world."

"Who are you?" asked Elisa Lemonnier.

"My name isn't important," said the man, in a voice impregnated with suffering and bitterness. "She knew me by an ugly nickname, with which the people of this city used to mock me: the Holy Eunuch. You can laugh once my back is turned."

PINK HORSES

ATUONA, HIVA OA, MAY 1903

He knew that his life had entered its final stretch when he realized, at the beginning of 1903, that he no longer needed tricks or flattery to coax the girls of the school of Saint Anne—run by six nuns from the order of the Sisters of Saint Joseph of Cluny, who crossed themselves in alarm whenever they encountered him in Atuona—to the House of Pleasure. Ever more frequently, and in ever greater numbers, they were escaping from school to pay him clandestine visits. They didn't come to see you, of course, although they knew very well that if they entered the house and put themselves within arm's reach, you—more for tradition's sake than pleasure, now that you were an invalid and half blind—would stroke their breasts, buttocks, and sex, and urge them to undress. All of which made them run and squeal in gleeful excitement, as if this were a sport even riskier than plying the waters of the Bay of Traitors in a Maori canoe. What they really came for was to see the pornographic photographs. These must have become mythical objects, the very emblems of sin, in the eyes of the teachers and students at the Catholic mission schools and the little Protestant school, and all the other residents of Atuona. They also came, of course, to howl with laughter at the caricatures in the garden of Bishop Joseph Martin—Father Lechery—and his housekeeper and presumed lover, Teresa.

Why would these girls come to the House of Pleasure so freely if they still considered you a threat, as they had in the first months—the first year—of your stay in Hiva Oa, Koké? In the pitiful state you were in now, you were no longer a danger: you weren't about to deflower them or make them pregnant. You couldn't have made love to them even if they had let you, because for some time now you hadn't had an erection, or felt even a flutter of sexual desire. There was only the excruciating burning and itching of your legs, the stabbing pains, and the palpitations that made you gasp for breath.

Pastor Vernier had persuaded him to stop injecting himself with morphine, at least for a while, because his body had grown so accustomed to the shots that they no longer had any effect against the pain. Obediently, he turned the syringe over to the shopkeeper Ben Varney so that he wouldn't be tempted. But the plasters and rubbings with a mustard ointment he ordered from Papeete didn't soothe the stinging of the sores on his legs, the stink of which also attracted flies. Only the little drops of laudanum calmed him, sending him into a vegetative state from which he barely emerged when one or another of his friends came to see him—his neighbor Tioka, who by now had rebuilt his house, the Annamite Ky Dong, Pastor Vernier, Frébault, Ben Varney—or when the girls from the school of the Sisters of Saint Joseph of Cluny burst in like a flock of birds to stare at the couplings of the erotic postcards from Port Said, bright-eyed and buzzing noisily.

The presence of those impish, mischievous girls at the House of Pleasure was like a breath of youth, something that distracted you for a while from your ailments and made you feel good. You let the girls wander into every room and poke through all your things, and ordered the servants to offer them food and drink. The nuns were educating them properly; as far as you could tell, none of your clandestine visitors had taken an object or a drawing as a souvenir of the House of Pleasure.

One day, cheered by the good weather and a lessening of the burning of his legs, he made his two servants help him into his pony cart and went for a drive down to the beach. The sight of the setting sun glinting on the small neighboring island of Hanakee—that motionless and eternal whale—moved him to tears. And he longed for his lost health more keenly than ever. How you would have liked to be able to scale the steep, wooded slopes of the mountains of Temetiu and Feani, Koké, and explore their deep valleys, in search of lost villages where you could watch the secret tattooists at work and be invited to join them in some feast of rejuvenating anthropophagy. You were convinced: in the hidden depths of the forest, where the authority of Monsignor Martin, Pastor Vernier, and the gendarme Claverie didn't reach, all those things still existed. As he returned along Atuona's main street, his weak eyes glimpsed, in the field next to the buildings of the Catholic mission—the boys' school, the girls' school, the church, and Bishop Martin's house—something that made him rein in the pony and move nearer. Ranged in a circle and watched over by one of the nuns, a group of the smallest girls were playing a game, amid happy shouts. It wasn't the glare of the sun that blurred the students' faces and the outline of their bodies, clad in missionary gowns, as the girl in the center of the circle approached one of her playmates to ask something and all the rest ran to change places; it was his failing sight that obscured his view of the game. What was the girl in the middle asking the other children in the circle as she went up to them, and what did they reply when they sent her on her way? It was clear that the exchange was a formula that all repeated in rote fashion. They weren't playing in French, but in the Marquesan Maori that Koké found difficult to understand, especially in the mouths of children. But he immediately guessed what game it was, and what the girl in the middle asked as she skipped from one child to another in the circle, and was always rebuffed with the same refrain.

"Is this the way to Paradise?"

"No, miss, go and ask on the next corner."

A warm feeling invaded him. For the second time that day, his eyes filled with tears.

"They're playing Paradise, aren't they, Sister?" he asked the nun, a small, thin woman half swallowed up in the great folds of her habit.

"A place you'll never see," the nun replied, making a sort of exorcism with her small fist. "Go, stay away from these children, I beg of you."

"I used to play the same game when I was small, Sister."

Koké spurred on his pony and turned it toward the murmur of the Make Make River, alongside which stood the House of Pleasure. Why did it move you to discover that these Marquesan girls played the game called Paradise, too? Because seeing them, a picture had formed in your memory, clearer than anything your eyes would ever see again in the world, of yourself as a curly-headed boy in short pants and smock, also running back and forth in the center of a circle of cousins and children from the neighborhood of San Marcelo, asking in your Limeñan Spanish, "Is this the way to Paradise?" "No, try the next corner, sir; ask there," while, behind your back, girls and boys traded places around the circle. The house of the Echeniques and Tristáns, one of the colonial mansions in the center of Lima, was full of Indian, black, and mixed-blood servants and footmen. Locked up in the third courtyard, where your mother had forbidden you and your little sister, María Fernanda, to go, was a lunatic relative whose sudden cries terrified the children of the house. You were frightened, but you were fascinated, too. The game of Paradise! You had yet to find that slippery place, Koké. Did it exist? Was it an illusion, a mirage? As the nun had just predicted, you wouldn't find it in the next life, either, since it was most likely that there a spot was reserved for you in hell. When, hot and tired from playing Paradise, you and María Fernanda retreated to the drawing room full of oval mirrors, oil paintings, and soft, comfortable rugs, your great-great-uncle Pío Tristán was always sitting beside the enormous latticed window, from which he could look out into the street without being seen, having his inevitable cup of steaming chocolate, in which he sopped the Limeñan cakes called *biscotelas*. He always offered you one, with a good-natured smile. "Come here, Paul, naughty boy."

It wasn't only the unspeakable illness that began rapidly to worsen at the start of the year 1903. Your clash with the authorities, in the person of the gendarme Jean-Pierre Claverie, also turned bitter, tangling you in a legal snarl. One day, you realized that Ben Varney and Ky Dong hadn't been exaggerating: at the rate things were going, you would end up in jail, with all your meager belongings confiscated.

In January 1903, one of the traveling judges sent every so often by the colonial administration to make the rounds of the islands to settle pending legal cases came to Atuona. Maître Horville, a bored magistrate who relied on Claverie's advice and judgment, concerned himself primarily with the case of twenty-nine natives from a small settlement in the valley of Hanaiapa, on the north coast of the island. Supported by the testimony of a witness, Claverie and Bishop Martin accused them of illegally producing alcohol and getting drunk, in violation of the rule that prohibited the natives from consuming alcoholic beverages. Koké assumed the defense of the accused, and announced that he would represent them before the judge. But he wasn't able to play his role as their defender. The day of the hearing, he appeared dressed like a Marquesan, barefoot and wearing only a pareu, his chest naked and tattooed. With a defiant air, he sat on the ground among the accused, cross-legged like the natives. After a long silence, Judge Horville, whose eyes were shooting sparks, expelled him from the hall, charging him with disrespect for the court. If he wanted to assume the defense of the accused, he would have to dress like a European. But when Paul returned three-quarters of an hour later, in trousers, shirt, tie, jacket, shoes, and hat, the judge had already presented his verdict, sentencing the twenty-nine Maori to five days in prison and a fine of one hundred francs. Koké was so upset that at the entrance to the building where the trial had been held—the post office—he vomited blood and lost consciousness for several minutes.

A few days later, his friend Ky Dong came to see him late at night, when all of Atuona was sleeping, with some alarming news. He hadn't heard it directly, but from their common friend, the merchant Émile Frébault, who in turn was a friend of the gendarme Claverie, with whom he shared a passion for *tamara'a*, the feasts of food cooked underground with hot stones. The last time they went out fishing together, the gendarme, overjoyed, showed Frébault a communication from the authorities in Tahiti authorizing him to "take steps at once against that man Gauguin, until he is ruined or destroyed, because by attacking obligatory schooling and the payment of taxes, he is undermining the work of the Catholic missions and subverting the natives whom France has promised to protect." Ky Dong had noted down this sentence, which he read in a calm voice, by the light of an oil lamp. Everything about the Annamite prince was smooth and feline; he made Koké think of cats, panthers, and leopards. Had his good friend really been a terrorist? It was hard to believe that a man of such suave ways and gracious speech would set off bombs.

"What can they do to me?" he asked at last, shrugging his shoulders.

"Many things, and all of them serious," Ky Dong replied slowly, in a voice so low that Paul had to lean forward to hear him. "Claverie hates you with all his heart. He is pleased to have received this order, which he must have requested himself. Frébault thinks so too. Be careful, Koké."

How could you be careful, sick, with no influence or resources? In the state of mindless somnambulism into which he was sunk deeper each day by the laudanum and his illness, he waited for the unfolding of events, as if the person against whom such intrigue was about to be unleashed was not him but his double. For some time, he had been feeling gradually more insubstantial, more disembodied and ghostly. Two days later, a summons arrived. Jean-Paul Claverie had brought a suit against him for slandering the authorities—in other words, the gendarme himself—in the letter Paul had written announcing that he wouldn't pay the highway tax in order to set an example for the natives. With a speed unprecedented in the history of French justice, Judge Horville ordered him to attend a hearing on March 31, again at the post office, where the charge would be presented. Koké dictated a quick letter to Pastor Vernier requesting additional time to prepare his defense. Maître Horville rejected his plea. The hearing on March 31, 1903, took place in private and lasted less than an hour. Paul had to acknowledge the authenticity of the letter, and the harsh terms in which he had referred to the gendarme. His statement—disorganized, confused, and with little legal grounding—ended abruptly when a stomach spasm made him double over and prevented him from speaking. That same afternoon Judge Horville read his sentence: a five-hundred-franc fine and a mandatory three months in prison. When Paul expressed his decision to appeal the verdict,

Horville, in a contemptuous and menacing fashion, assured him that he would personally see to it that the court in Papeete resolved the appeal in record time, and increased the fine and prison time.

"Your days are numbered, filthy swine," he heard the gendarme Claverie whisper behind him, when, with difficulty and stumbling over the seat, he got into his pony cart to return to the House of Pleasure.

"The worst of it is that Claverie is right," he thought. He shivered, imagining what was to come. Since you weren't in a position to pay the fine, the authorities, which meant the gendarme himself, would take possession of all your belongings. The paintings and sculptures that were still at the House of Pleasure would be seized and auctioned off by the colonial authorities, probably in Papeete, and sold for a pittance to horrible people. With the little energy he had left, Koké determined to save what could still be saved. But he didn't have the strength to do up the parcels, and he sent Tioka to ask the help of Pastor Vernier. As always, the head of the Protestant mission of Atuona was a model of understanding and friendship. He brought string, cardboard, and brown paper and helped Paul wrap a batch of fourteen paintings and eleven drawings to be sent to Daniel de Monfreid in Paris on the next boat, which was scheduled to sail from Hiva Oa in just a few weeks, on May 1, 1903. Vernier himself, helped by Tioka and two of Tioka's nephews, carried the packages to the Protestant mission by night, when no one could see them. The pastor promised Paul that he would take charge of getting them to the port, making the shipping arrangements, and ensuring that they were stowed properly in the ship's hold. You hadn't the slightest doubt that the good man would keep his promise.

Why didn't you send Daniel de Monfreid all the paintings, drawings, and sculptures from the House of Pleasure, Koké? This was something he asked himself many times in the following days. Perhaps it was so you wouldn't be more alone than you already were on this final leg of your journey. But it was stupid to think that the pictures piled up in your studio would keep you company, when all that your eyes could distinguish were colors, lines, certain forms, amorphous shapes. It was absurd for a painter to lose his sight, when it was the essential instrument of his vocation and work. What a cruel way of unleashing your anger on a poor dying savage, God, you shit. Had you, Paul, really been so bad in your fifty-five years that you deserved to be punished like this? Well, maybe you had. Mette believed it, and told you so in the last letter she wrote you—a year ago? Two years ago? A bad husband, a bad father, a bad friend. Was it true, Koké? Most of these paintings had been painted months ago, when your eyes, though weakened, weren't as useless as they were now. They were quite vivid in your memory—their contours, their nuances, their colors. Which was your favorite, Koké? *The Sister of Charity*, without question. Swathed in wimple, habit, and veil, and symbolizing terror of the body, freedom, nudity, and nature, a nun from the Catholic mission stood in contrast to a half-naked *mahu*, who, with perfect ease and assurance, faced the world as a free, artificial man-woman, his sex invented, his imagination unfettered. It was a painting that showed the total incompatibility of two cultures, their customs and religions; the aesthetic and moral superiority of the weaker, subjugated people and the decadent, repressive inferiority of the stronger, dominant people. If instead of Vaeoho you had set up house with a *mahu*, he would probably still be here caring for you, since it was well known that the wives most faithful and loyal to their husbands were *mahus*. You weren't a full-fledged savage, Koké. That was what you lacked: pairing up with a *mahu*. He remembered Jotefa, the Mataiea woodcutter. But you were also fond of your paintings and drawings of the little wild horses that proliferated on the island of Hiva Oa, sometimes suddenly approaching Atuona and crossing the town in a pack, at full gallop, frightened and beautiful, their eyes wide, trampling everything in their path. You especially remembered one particular work, in which you had painted little pink horses, like clouds in the sky, gamboling happily in the Bay of Traitors among naked Marquesans, one of whom, mounted on a horse, was riding bareback along the edge of the sea. What would the fancy folk in Paris say? That it was a demented bit of nonsense to paint a horse pink. They couldn't know that in the Marquesas, before the sun sank like a ball of fire into the sea, it lent a rosy glow to animate and inanimate beings, turning the whole face of the earth iridescent for a few miraculous minutes.

After May 1, he was almost unable to get out of bed. He remained in his studio on the upper floor, sunken in a lassitude in which time seemed to stand still, scarcely noticing that the flies weren't just flocking to the bandages on his legs now; they crawled all over his body and face, and he didn't even bother to brush them away. Since the burning and the pain in his legs had redoubled, he asked Ben Varney to return his syringe. And he convinced Pastor Vernier to supply him with morphine, reasoning in such a way that Vernier couldn't argue with him.

"My good friend, what is the sense of suffering like a dog, like a man flayed alive, if in a matter of days or weeks I'll be dead?"

He injected the morphine himself, fumblingly, without bothering to disinfect the needle. The drowsiness relaxed his muscles and muted the pain and the burning, but not his fantasies. On the contrary, it roused his imagination, made it crackle. He relived in images what he had written in his fanciful, highly colored unfinished memoirs, about the ideal life of the artist, the savage in his jungle, surrounded by fierce, amorous beasts, like the regal tiger of the forests of Malaysia and the cobra of India. The artist and his mate, two sensual beasts, too, enveloped in deliciously foul and intoxicating feline scents, would spend their proud, lonely lives making art and seeking pleasure, far from the stupid, cowardly city masses, of no interest to them. It was a pity that the forests of Polynesia had no wild beasts or rattlesnakes; only mosquitoes proliferated here. Sometimes he saw himself in Japan instead of the Marquesas. That was where you should have gone in search of Paradise, Koké, rather than coming to mediocre Polynesia. In the cultured country of the Rising Sun, all families were peasants nine months of the year, and artists for the remaining three. An exceptional people, the Japanese. They hadn't experienced the tragic separation of artist from everyone else that precipitated the decline of Western art. In Japan, everyone was everything, peasant and artist all at once. Making art didn't mean imitating Nature, but mastering a technique and creating worlds different from the real world: no one had done that better than the Japanese printmakers.

"Dear friends: take up a collection, buy me a kimono, and send me to Japan," he shouted with all his might into the emptiness that surrounded him. "Let my ashes rest among the yellow men. It is my dying wish, gentlemen! Send me to the country where I was always meant to be. My heart is Japanese!"

You laughed, but you firmly believed everything you said. In one of the few moments in which he emerged from his morphine-induced semiconsciousness, he recognized Pastor Vernier and Tioka, his name-brother, at the foot of the bed. In an imperious voice, he insisted that the head of the Protestant mission accept, as a keepsake, his first edition of *L'après-midi d'un faune*, which had been a personal gift from the poet Mallarmé. Paul Vernier thanked him for it, but a different matter was troubling him.

"The wild cats, Koké. They come into your house and eat everything. In the state of inertia you're left in by the morphine, we're afraid they might bite you. Tioka has offered to let you stay with him, where he and his family can care for you."

He refused. The wild cats of Hiva Oa had long been his good friends, like the wild roosters and wild horses. They didn't only come looking for food when they were hungry; they also came to keep him company and to take an interest in his health. Anyway, the cats were too intelligent to eat a festering creature whose flesh might poison them. You were pleased when your words made Pastor Vernier and Tioka laugh.

But, hours or days later—or perhaps sooner?—he saw Ben Varney (when exactly had the shopkeeper arrived at the House of Pleasure?), sitting by the foot of the bed. Varney looked at him with sorrow and compassion, saying to the others gathered there, "He doesn't recognize me. He's confusing me with someone else; he called me Mette Gad."

"That's his wife, who lives in some Scandinavian country—Sweden, maybe," he heard Ky Dong purr.

Ky Dong was wrong, of course, because Mette Gad—who was, in fact, his wife—wasn't Swedish but Danish, and if she were still alive, would live not in Stockholm but in Copenhagen, translating and giving French classes. Paul wanted to explain this to the ex-whaler, but his voice must not have been working, or else he spoke so quietly that they couldn't hear him. They continued talking among themselves about you, as if you were insensible or dead. You were neither, since you could hear and see them—but in a strange fashion, as if a curtain of water separated you from your Atuona friends. Why had you remembered Mette Gad? It had been a long time since you received news of her, and you hadn't written to her, either. There she was now: her tall silhouette, her masculine profile, her fear and frustration upon discovering that the young man she had married would never be a new Gustave Arosa, a champion in the wilds of business, an affluent bourgeois, but an artist of uncertain fate who, after reducing her to a working-class existence, sent her off with her children to Copenhagen so her family could support her while he set out to live as a bohemian. Would she still be the same? Or would she have become old, fat, embittered? He wanted to ask his friends if the Mette Gad of today was still anything like the Mette of ten or fifteen years ago. But he discovered that he was alone. Your friends had gone, Koké. Soon you would hear the yowling of the cats and detect the light step of the roosters, their cockadoodledoos ringing in your ears like the whinnies of the little Marquesan horses. They all returned to the House of Pleasure as soon as they realized you had been left alone. You would see the cats' gray forms stalking around you, see them sniff with their long whiskers at the edges of your bed. But despite what your friend Vernier feared, they wouldn't leap on you, whether out of indifference or pity, or because they were frightened away by the stench of your legs.

The image of Mette merged for a few moments with that of Teha'amana, your first Maori wife. Your most persistent memory of her, curiously enough, was not her long blue-black hair, her lovely firm breasts, or her thighs glistening with sweat, but the seven toes on her deformed left foot—five normal and two tiny growths— which you recalled obsessively, and which you had faithfully portrayed in *Te nave nave fenua* (The Beautiful Earth). In whose hands must that painting be now? It was only a good painting, not a masterpiece. A pity. You were still alive, Koké, much as your friends, when they appeared beside your bed, seemed to doubt it. Your mind was a seething cauldron, a vortex incapable of retaining an idea, image, or memory long enough for you to understand or savor it. Everything that cropped up disappeared in an instant, replaced by a new cascade of faces, thoughts, and figures, which in turn were replaced before your consciousness had had time to identify them. You weren't hungry or thirsty; you felt no pain in your legs or pounding in your chest. You were overcome by the curious feeling that your body had disappeared, had been eaten away, rotted by the unspeakable illness, like a chunk of wood devoured by the Panamanian termites that could make whole forests disappear. Now you were pure spirit. An immaterial being, Koké. Beyond the reach of suffering and decay, immaculate as an archangel.

This serenity was suddenly disturbed (when, Koké? sooner? later?) when you tried to remember if it was in Pont-Aven, Le Pouldu, Arles, Paris, or Martinique where you began ironing your paintings to make them smoother and flatter, and washing them to fade their color and dull their shine. The technique elicited smiles from your friends and disciples (which ones, Paul? Charles Laval? Émile Bernard?) and at last you had to acknowledge that they were right: it didn't work. The memory of this failure plunged you into a deep depression. Was it morphine that rescued you from that cloud of gloom? Had you managed to pick up the syringe, insert the needle into the little bottle, draw up a few drops of liquid, jab the needle into your leg, arm, stomach, or wherever your hand fell, and inject yourself? You didn't know. But you had the feeling of having slept for a long time, in a night without sound or stars, in utter peace. Now it seemed to be daytime. You felt rested, calm. "Your faith is invincible, Koké," he shouted, exultant. But no one must have heard, because your words had no echo. "I am a wolf in the forest, a wolf without a collar," he shouted. But you didn't hear your voice this time either, whether because your throat no longer emitted sounds, or because you had been struck deaf.

Some time later, he became convinced that one of his friends, surely the loyal Tioka Timote, his name-brother, was there sitting beside him. He wanted to tell him many things. He wanted to tell him that, centuries ago, after fleeing Arles and the mad Dutchman, on the very day he returned to Paris, he had gone to see the public execution of the murderer Prado, and that the image of that head, severed by the guillotine in the pale light of dawn, amid the laughter of the crowd, had appeared to him many times in his nightmares. He wanted to tell him that twelve years ago, in June 1891, upon arriving in Tahiti for the first time, he had seen the last of the Maori kings die,

King Pomare V, that immense, elephantine monarch whose liver had burst at last, after months and years spent drinking, day and night, a deadly cocktail of his own invention, made of rum, brandy, whisky, and calvados, that would have killed any normal human being in a matter of hours. And that his burial, witnessed and wept over by thousands of Tahitians who had come to Papeete from all over the island and the neighboring islands, had been at once splendid and ridiculous. But he had the impression that the indistinct person he was addressing couldn't hear him, or couldn't understand him, because he was leaning very close, almost touching him, as if trying to catch some part of what he was saying or see whether he was still breathing. There was no point in struggling to talk, in wasting so much effort on words, if no one could understand you, Paul. Tioka Timote, who was a Protestant and didn't drink, would have severely condemned the dissolute habits of King Pomare V. Did he silently condemn yours, too, Koké?

Later, an infinite time seemed to pass in which he didn't know who he was, or what place this was. But it tormented him even more to be unable to tell whether it was day or night. Then, with perfect clarity, he heard Tioka's voice.

"Koké! Koké! Can you hear me? Are you there? I'm going to get Pastor Vernier, right away."

His neighbor, usually impassive, spoke in an unrecognizable voice.

"I think I fainted, Tioka," Paul said, and this time his voice issued from his throat, and his neighbor heard him.

A little while later, he heard Tioka and Vernier bounding up the stairs, and saw them enter the studio, alarm on their faces.

"How do you feel, Paul?" asked the pastor, sitting beside him and patting him on the shoulder.

"I think I fainted once or twice," he said, shifting. He saw his friends nod. Their smiles were forced. They helped him sit up in bed, and made him drink a little water. Was it day or night, friends? Just past noon. But the sun wasn't shining. Dark clouds covered the sky, and at any moment it would begin to rain. The trees and bushes and flowers of Hiva Oa would give off an intoxicating fragrance, the green of the leaves and branches would be intense and liquid, and the red of the bougainvilleas would flame brightly. You felt enormously relieved that your friends could hear what you were saying, and that you could hear them. After an eternity, you were talking, and conscious once again of the world's beauty, Koké.

Pointing, he asked them to bring close the little painting that had accompanied him for so long: the landscape of Brittany covered in snow. He heard them moving about the studio; they were dragging an easel, then making it squeak, doubtless adjusting the screws so that the snowy landscape would face his bed and he could see it. But he couldn't see it. He could only make out some vague shapes, one of which must have been Brittany as it appeared in the painting, surprised under an onslaught of white flakes. Even though he couldn't see it, it comforted him to know it was nearby. He shivered, as if it were snowing inside the House of Pleasure.

"Have you read *Salammbô*, the novel by Flaubert, Pastor?" he asked.

Vernier said he had, but added that he didn't remember it very well. A pagan tale about Carthaginians and barbarian mercenaries, wasn't it? Koké assured him that it was lovely. Flaubert had described in blazing color the great strength, vigor, and creative force of a barbarian people. And he recited the first sentence, whose musicality he loved. *"C'était à Mégara, faubourg de Carthage, dans les jardins d'Hamilcar."* "Exoticism is life, isn't it, Pastor?"

"I'm so pleased to see that you're better, Paul," he heard Vernier say, tenderly. "I have to give a class at school, to the children. You don't mind if I leave for just a few hours, do you? I'll be back this afternoon, in any case."

"Go on, Pastor, and don't worry. I feel fine now."

He wanted to make a joke ("By dying I'll beat Claverie, Pastor, because I won't pay his fine and he won't be able to put me in prison"), but he was alone again. A little while later, the wild cats had returned and were prowling the studio. But there were wild roosters there too. Why didn't the cats eat the roosters? Had they really returned or was it a hallucination, Koké? For some time now the sharp dividing line between life and dreams had vanished. What you were living now was what you had always wanted to paint, Paul.

In this time outside of time, he kept repeating, like one of the Buddhist chants dear to good old Schuff:

Fuck you

Claverie

I died

Fuck you

Yes, fuck Claverie: you wouldn't pay the fine and you wouldn't go to jail. You won, Koké. He had the confused impression that one of the lazy servants who almost never appeared at the House of Pleasure anymore—maybe Kahui—had come up to sniff him and touch him. And he heard him exclaim, "The *popa'a* is dead," before disappearing. But you must not have been dead yet, because you were still thinking. He was calm, though sorry not to be able to tell whether it was day or night.

At last, he heard voices outside. "Koké! Koké! Are you all right?" It must be Tioka. He didn't even try to reply, because he was sure no sound would come from his throat. He heard Tioka climbing the stairs to the studio, and then the sound of his bare feet on the wooden floor. Very close to his face, he saw his neighbor's face, so grieved and distraught that he felt infinite sorrow for the pain he was causing him. He tried to say, "Don't be sad, I'm not dead, Tioka." But of course, not a word came out. He tried to move his head, a hand, a foot, and of course, he couldn't. In a very hazy way, through half-closed eyes, he saw that his name-brother had begun to hit him on the head, hard, bellowing each time he dealt a blow. "Thank you, my friend." Was he trying to beat death out of you according to some dark Marquesan rite? "It's hopeless, Tioka." You wanted to weep you were so moved, but of course not a single tear fell from your dry eyes. Always in the same dim, slow, shadowy way in which he was still conscious of the world, he saw that Tioka, after hitting him and pulling his hair to bring him back to life, had given up his efforts. Now he began to sing beside the bed, wailing with bitter sweetness and rocking in place on both feet, performing the dance with which the Marquesans bade farewell to their dead. Weren't you a Protestant, Tioka? It pleased you that beneath your neighbor's apparent evangelism, the religion of his ancestors had always been lurking. Since you could see Tioka mourning you and saying his goodbyes, you couldn't be dead yet, could you, Koké?

In the time outside of time in which Paul existed now, Monsignor Joseph Martin and his entourage, two of the members of the Breton order of the Brothers of Ploërmel who ran the boys' school at the Catholic mission, came into the studio led by Koké's servant Kahui. He had the sense that the two brothers crossed themselves when they saw him, but that the bishop didn't. Monsignor Martin bent over him, looking at him for a long time, the sour expression on his face not altered in the slightest by what he saw.

"What a sty this is," he heard him say. "And what a stench. He must have been dead for hours. The corpse reeks. He'll have to be buried as soon as possible, or the putrefaction could breed disease."

He wasn't dead yet. But he could no longer see, whether because someone in the room had lowered his eyelids, or because death had already begun its march, starting at his painter's eyes. And yet he could hear quite clearly everything that was said around him. He heard Tioka explain to the bishop that the stench wasn't the smell of death, but came from Koké's diseased legs, and that he must just have died, because less than two hours ago he had been conversing with Tioka and Pastor Vernier. A short or a long time later, the head of the Protestant mission came into the studio too. You were aware (or was it a final fantasy, Koké?) of the coldness with which the enemies, locked in a permanent fight for the souls of Atuona, greeted each other. And although he could feel nothing, he knew that the pastor was trying to give him artificial respiration. Bishop Martin scolded Vernier sarcastically.

"What are you doing, man? Can't you see he's dead? Do you think you can bring him back to life?"

"It is my duty to try everything possible to keep him alive," Vernier replied.

Almost immediately, the tense, pent-up hostility between the bishop and the pastor erupted into an open war of words. And although you were growing steadily weaker and more distant (your consciousness was beginning to fade, too, Koké), you managed to hear everything they said, even though you were scarcely interested in their argument. And yet it was a fight that in other circumstances you would have enjoyed enormously. Angrily, the bishop ordered the Brothers of Ploërmel to pull down the painter's filthy, obscene pictures, to be burned. Pastor Vernier said that no matter how offensive they were to decency and morality, the pornographic photographs were part of the estate of the deceased, and the law was the law: no one, not even the religious authorities, could dispose of them before a legal decision had been reached. Unexpectedly, the disagreeable voice of Jean-Pierre Claverie—when had that odious individual entered the House of Pleasure?—spoke up in the pastor's defense.

"I'm afraid that's right, Your Grace. It is my duty to take an inventory of all the possessions of the deceased, including those repulsive things on the wall. I can't allow you to burn them or take them away. I'm sorry, Your Grace."

The bishop said nothing, but the noises you heard must have been the growl and rumble of his insides protesting at this unforeseen obstacle. Almost without pause, a new dispute broke out. When the bishop began to dictate instructions for the burial, Pastor Vernier, usually so retiring and conciliatory, objected with unusual energy to the dead man's being buried in Hiva Oa's Catholic cemetery. He said that Paul Gauguin's ties to the Catholic Church had been cut; that for some time his relationship with it had been nonexistent, even hostile. The bishop, raising his voice to a shout, responded that the deceased, it was true, had been a notorious sinner and a scourge of society, but he was born a Catholic—which meant that he would be buried in consecrated ground, and not in the pagan cemetery, no matter who objected. The shouting match continued until Claverie intervened, saying that as political and civil authority on the island, it was up to him to decide. But he wouldn't do so immediately. He preferred to wait until tempers had cooled so that he could weigh the pros and cons of the situation in peace. He would make his ruling by the next morning.

And then you didn't see or hear or know anything, because you were finally altogether dead, Koké. He didn't see or know it when

Bishop Joseph Martin triumphed in the two battles pitting him against Vernier over the still-warm body of Paul Gauguin, resorting to methods that were not the most appropriate by either the prevailing legal or moral standards. That night, when Koké's body lay alone in the House of Pleasure—except perhaps for some marauding wild roosters and cats—Bishop Martin had the forty-five pornographic photographs stolen from where they were pinned up in the studio. Perhaps he intended to burn them on an inquisitorial pyre, or perhaps he meant to keep them for himself, to occasionally test his strength of will and power to resist temptation.

Nor did Paul see or hear or know it when, at dawn on May 9, 1903, before the gendarme could come to a decision about his burial place, Bishop Martin sent four native bearers, under the orders of a little priest from the Catholic mission, to place the body in a coffin of rough planks supplied by the mission itself, and carry it quickly, while the inhabitants of Atuona were just beginning to stir in their huts and rub the sleep from their eyes, to the hill beside the Make Make. They buried it there hastily, in the Catholic cemetery, thus winning the bishop a point—a body or a soul—in his feud with his Protestant adversary. When Pastor Vernier, accompanied by Ky Dong, Ben Varney, and Tioka Timote, appeared at seven in the morning at the House of Pleasure to bury Koké in the lay cemetery, he was confronted with the empty studio and the news that Koké's remains had already been laid to rest in the place determined by Monsignor Martin.

Nor did Paul see or hear or know that his only epitaph would be a letter from the bishop of Hiva Oa to his superiors, which, with the passage of the years—Koké now famous, acclaimed, and much studied, his paintings fought over by collectors and museums around the world—would be cited by all of the artist's biographers as a symbol of the injustice that is sometimes the lot of those who dream of reaching Paradise in this earthly vale of tears: "The only noteworthy event here has been the sudden death of an individual named Paul Gauguin, a reputed artist but an enemy of God and everything that is decent in this world."